The Queen

The Queen Series Book One

Christina L. Barr

Table of Contents

Chapter One

When I was a young girl, I learned the price of being born into a world of privilege and prestige. My earliest memory is of someone taking care of me. As a toddler, my feet rarely touched the ground. I was always passed along to another pair of helping hands. While I appreciated the attentiveness of familiar strangers, I still possessed a deep longing for the loving arms of my mother.

When I was five, I was allowed to drink and eat whatever I wanted, so I wasn't watched with so much intensity, but it was still extreme. My room was big enough to house my imagination, but I often looked outside my window and wondered what it would be like to play with the other children. There were plenty around my age and several who shared my features. I didn't understand why they weren't like me and why we always had to be separated by such grand walls.

When I was six, all my innocent dreams of playing outside came to an end, and I found myself wishing for the days when I had nothing to do. I was taught constantly about the humans and their world around me, but not much about what I truly was and what was expected of me.

When I was eight, I was finally allowed to leave the shelter of my room. I was still under strict supervision, with two guards on each side of me, but at least I was allowed to leave. I was excited to see other faces and other rooms. I remember nearly stumbling down the winding staircase, and one of the guards caught my hand and saved me. I looked up at his stoic face and smiled. I read about parents and the roles they played in human culture. The father was supposed to protect their daughters from harm and teach them about strength. I wondered where my father was and why I had never seen him before. But for that brief moment, I pretended the guard was my father and that he gave me a kind smile.

For the first time in my life, I was able to go outside and see the faces of the field servants, who were not allowed in my mansion. They all bowed their heads in quick acknowledgment, but I didn't feel like they worshiped me or possessed a great deal of admiration. They all spoke to each other while they stared, and their gossip buzzed about like the melody of bees.

One elder accompanied me to the place he wanted to show me. We took a path up a grassy hill and to a white dome. Inside, there were boys smaller than me and grown men training with black curved knives. I read about violence and studied the cruelties of humans and their wars, but I had never been around such visceral beings. But as soon as they noticed I was in the room, their battles ceased, and they bowed to me.

I was flattered and began to blush. In my books, valiant knights would fight to protect their princess. What more would they do for a queen?

"Do you see any that you like?" he asked.

"That I like?" I looked around the room closely. Mostly everyone had similar features. Our hair was the color of honey. All of them either had hazel eyes—like me—light, or dark chocolate brown. I was too young to be concerned with intricate features like shoulders and cheekbones. How was I supposed to decide such a thing based on looks alone? "I don't think so. May I speak to any of them?"

The elder sneered at me. "You don't need to worry about their personalities, my virgin queen. Men—as far as you're concerned—are only for mating and protection."

I looked out at all the men again. Even the young boys seemed to be fierce protectors. I still couldn't decide. "I'm not sure, elder."

I could tell in his eyes he wasn't pleased with me, but I didn't understand why I was being forced to make such a decision while so young. "That is alright, my virgin queen. You haven't reached maturity yet. None of these warriors would be of any use to you now."

As we were about to leave, my eyes spotted a woman watching me from a high balcony. I had never seen another woman who wasn't working before. She was allowed to stand by herself and oversee the men. There were even small boys who held onto her legs as if she were the only thing in the world they trusted.

"Who is she?" I asked, mesmerized. She didn't look much different than me, and I could sense something between the two of us. She was trying to tell me something in her hazel eyes.

"That's the queen."

"The queen?" My eyes bucked at the sudden revelation. "Is she my mother?" I didn't wait for any confirmation. I wanted to speak to her and touch her. I wanted her to hold me like I saw a mother do in one of those human books. That was a mother's job, and every child was supposed to have a mother and a father. "Mother!"

Before I could break a couple of feet free, I was captured by my guards. "Release me!" I ordered, but none of them heeded my word. They called me their queen, but I did not rule with the authority of Queen Elizabeth or Catherine the Great. I was only a little girl being told what to do. "Mother!"

I hoped she had some sort of power over the people, but if she did, I never saw it. She watched expressionlessly as they carried me away from the woman who gave me life.

I was spellbound. I could not think of anything else other than my mother and her eyes. Though she did not smile, I sensed she was happy to see me. I think she might have been sad for me, though. Was it pity? Everyone appeased all of my needs. What reason would she have to want something different for me? The only longing I had in my life was for her and my father.

But I did often wonder about the children who held onto her. They must have been my brothers. Why did they get to know her and feel her comfort? I read that parents are supposed to instill morals and values in their children. I had no direction other than my thousands of books. What lessons were supposed to be absorbed into my heart, and what was supposed to be a cautionary tale? I wasn't always sure.

When I was a little older, some of the women made me a special garden. I loved flowers so much that they exported them from all over the planet. I spent so much time with them, their various scents were infused into my skin. I would sit under my cherry blossom tree until I fell asleep on a bed of petals. I often wore lilies in my hair, but I switched up the flowers to match my wardrobe. I really liked to wear jasmine, but the elders hated it. The pollen got everywhere.

One day, when I had fallen asleep outside, I felt the gentle arms of someone holding me. I thought I was only dreaming of my mother and father—like I often did—but then I felt her stroking my hair. I woke and saw the queen's hazel eyes staring straight into mine. I still wasn't sure if I was dreaming, but I didn't care. I made myself more comfortable, and I rested my head on her bosom while she hummed a beautiful melody to me.

I was so peaceful that I was about to be lulled back to sleep, but I fought myself, so I could hear her finish the lovely—but sad— song. When she finished, she kissed me on my forehead.

"Is this a dream?" I whispered.

"No, my young virgin queen."

I smiled and held her soft hands. She, too, had the scent of flowers embedded in her skin. I think she smelled of camellias. "How come we've never met before?"

"Because it's improper."

"Improper?" I sat up in her lap. "But you're my mother. My place is at your side."

She stroked my chubby cheeks and smiled. "I know they make you read a lot of books about humans. It's filled your head with many ideas about family, but that's not us. You are a virgin queen, and I am the queen of the colony. We have certain duties. You have been chosen."

"For what?"

"To replace me."

I gulped. It was a lot of responsibility, but one I had been trying to convince myself I would be ready for. "But I can't replace you until you die. You won't die until you're old and I've had many children of my own to love you as I do."

She laughed, and I didn't have the slightest idea why. "I love your optimism, my daughter. I wonder if you got it from your father."

"What was he like?" I asked, amazed. I thought I would never get the chance to know.

"I'm not sure," she admitted. "I didn't find any mates based on personality. I was sent a few warriors."

"Sent?"

She laughed again. "You were chosen, but I'm not sure you have the heart of a queen. This is a terrible burden, my daughter. You have to sacrifice everything you are for this colony. Can you do that?"

"I think I can…" I wasn't aware of what other sacrifices I'd have to make, but how could I complain about my life? I was grateful for my many luxuries.

"I think you are too kind," my mother said. "Don't you want to experience love?"

"Love?" I read many stories of old traditions. Men would do crazy things to have the women they wanted, whether they had to fight to the death in a jousting match or pay a large dowry. I even read a tale about a man who worked seven years for the love of his life, but then his father-in-law tricked him and gave him the older daughter. He didn't try anything dishonest, and he didn't give up on his one true love. He worked another seven years to have her, and he was so in love that the years only seemed like days. It was impossible not to think about boys when there were such fantastic knights in history. I was a queen. I should have been able to find someone so valiant for myself.

"You think of it. I know you do." Mother hugged me tighter and kissed my forehead again. "I used to be as naïve as you. Dreams are beautiful. They keep you young and innocent, but I have learned hard lessons, and I am not a child."

"I won't be a child forever." I looked forward to growing up. I could do what I wanted and be a real queen. "Maybe I'll stand up to the elders and pick a king for myself. You can be at my wedding."

I looked up, so my mother could see my nice and wide grin, but she refused to smile with me, and I could no longer smile either. "You cannot find love, my daughter. It would be fruitless as long as you have this curse."

"Curse?" I asked, confused and even offended. "My life isn't a curse!"

"You cannot be queen unless I am dead," she said sternly. "You will never rule this colony. The elders rule. They give you what you need to survive, but they'll never give you what you want. You'll never be able to fall in love, and if you do, you will shatter your heart. Then the light in your brilliant eyes will die, and you will become a cold shell until you have a daughter that you're forced to abandon. Does that sound like a gift?"

My shoulders slumped, and I hung my head down low. "No." I didn't expect her to scold me so, but I told myself it had to be out of love. I read that proper parenting requires being tough. "But you haven't abandoned me. You're here."

"I'm only here to give you a gift." Her finger found its way under my chin, and she raised my head to see her eyes. "If you accept it, then you can live a normal life. You won't have all of this attention, but you might have a chance to find love, and start a family—if you can learn to control yourself."

At the time, I had no idea there was a power, deep inside me, that needed to be controlled. I only knew that I was a little girl looking for love. "Is this the best choice for me?"

"I promise this is your best chance, my daughter."

I took a deep breath and held my mother's hand. "Then please, save me, my queen."

"Be calm and be still." She wrapped her arms around me and pressed me close. I closed my eyes as I felt weak and cold. Once I realized she was forcing the coldness on me, I tried to push away on instinct, but she held me tighter. "Your mother knows best."

I was afraid, but I trusted my mother. Why would she want to cause me harm? She must have had my best interests in her heart, but I was beginning to hurt. "Mother—"

"It's almost over."

"Stop her!"

I looked up and saw many guards running toward us. It startled me, but she clung on tighter. "What's going on?"

I thought my arms might break as I was ripped from my mother. I screamed from the pain, but then I screamed to have her in my arms again. The guards pulled her out of my garden. I ordered them to stop, but they did no such thing. My mother didn't give such commands. She walked with them peacefully, but her eyes begged to have me again.

"Why won't you let me be with her?"

"Your mother is a selfish woman. She doesn't want you to rise as you should. She was trying to take your power away. Then you would be just like every other mundane member of the colony."

"What? Why would she…?" My lip quivered, and I was soon going to cry. I had never done so in front of the elders. I wiped my eyes quickly, but I moaned silently to myself.

"Stop crying," he ordered. He took care of me ever since I could remember, yet he sneered his nose in disgust. "You do not even know the queen. Displaying emotion for her is sickening."

I didn't mean to, but I whimpered louder. I wiped my eyes until they hurt, but I couldn't stop myself from looking foolish to him. "She said she wanted to help."

"Her only purpose was to make you like the rest of the children in the colony. Never believe her lies of compassion. It isn't taught to creatures like us."

I nodded my head and finished off my last few tears. I didn't know if I should believe the elders or if my mother did truly want to help me, but that didn't matter. My mother was kept far away from me, and I was put under constant surveillance to make sure she would never touch me again.

Years passed, and I spent my time studying how to become a proper and poised lady. Many young men in our colonies were taught how to be respectable humans, so those who were ready could infiltrate their society and become desirable partners. We looked just like humans. They wouldn't be able to tell the difference between our two species until it was too late. The elders were not concerned about any of us straying away. They said they had methods to call us all back home if we were ever to lose our way.

When I was eleven years old, I was taken to see the soldiers every day, and I watched them train. I wondered if any of them watched me intently every day and fantasized about me being their wife. I didn't need to cook them meals and nurse children, but I kind of liked the idea of taking care of someone. I think I had so much more to give than what I was allowed.

One day, a boy kept staring at me. I remembered he stood by my mother. He could have been my brother, but I wasn't sure. He looked enough like me. He continued training and tried not to give his interest away to the elders, but I felt his eyes on me quite often.

"I want to talk to some of the boys."

The elders smiled, pleased. "That is good news, my queen. Please, take your time."

I made eye contact with my supposed brother, but I shied my eyes away from him, so the elders would not become suspicious. I walked through the room and watched the warriors spar with each other, but they weren't dueling so viciously. Their eyes kept following me, and it was difficult to be inconspicuous. I circled the room twice; the elders and all the boys were still watching me. I couldn't wait any longer, and I stopped at the boy and his training partner.

They both nervously bowed before me. I hoped the others standing would block the elder's vision of me, but the rest of the boys followed suit and landed on their knees.

A small and nervous laugh escaped my mouth, but I quickly composed myself. "Rise."

The entire room did as I instructed in one swift motion. There was no way to be discreet, so I took the hand of the boy I believed to be my brother. "Is there something you would like to say to me, young warrior?"

He nodded, but he looked around cautiously. It was clear he didn't want the elders to hear. "Soon you'll be mature. I hope when you become of age, you will be patient and meditate on your maturity. Be cautious. I believe our queen would want it that way."

"How well do you know the queen?"

"My queen," one of the elders said, "I believe it is time to continue your studies."

It was clear the elders knew I was onto something, but I still had no idea what the warrior was trying to tell me. I took a moment to find the answer within his eyes, but I was not the clever detective I thought I was.

"Virgin Queen."

I sighed heavily, yet quietly. "Excuse me. I'm afraid I have to leave."

"Of course, my queen."

I felt his desperation reaching out to me as I tore myself from his presence. It created a hole inside my heart that could only be filled with the truth of my mother's intentions. I watched and waited for a way to escape the watchful eyes of my guards and the elders, but they were even more vigilant than usual. I was only alone when I slept, but I could still feel the guards standing outside my door. It seemed like I would never be able to decipher my mother's message, nor would I be able to ever feel her embrace again.

A little more than a year later, I received my answer when I woke up early in the morning to a pain in my lower abdomen. It was something I had never experienced, and I whimpered while I wished for someone to make it better. All it would take was a word, and a medical team would have been doting on me, but I didn't feel like being bothered with anyone.

Even if I skipped out on breakfast, my instructors would come to begin their lessons. I couldn't send them away without explaining why I felt so sick. When I started to get out of bed and noticed the sheets, I realized what was happening and my mother's warning.

I had read about coming of age and the process of puberty. I knew the elders would have liked to hear about my maturity. The start of menstruation meant I could produce children, and they made it very clear that they desired for me to start right away.

As much as I wanted to hold a baby in my arms and to know that it was mine, it still scared me to be a mother. I didn't possess any womanly features, including the necessary hips. But if they knew I was menstruating, they would expect me to pick a boy right away, and I had no favorites.

I covered the sheets with my blanket and rushed into the bathroom. I felt the colony's obligations surrounding me until I physically felt like I was suffocating. Each breath I took was a struggle for survival. I sat in the shower and hoped the steam would soothe my lungs. It did, but it didn't take any of the pressure off.

It dawned on me what my mother meant. "But why does she want me to hide it?" Maybe it was because she wanted me to have a normal life and start a family on my own terms. When I met my mother before, I was too young to notice we really weren't far apart in age. She couldn't have been much older than thirteen when she gave birth to me.

But could that have been the only reason? I had an aching feeling in my heart that she was concerned about something else. Should I have heeded the warning from the woman who tried to steal my destiny, simply because I was born from her flesh?

I was not sure what I was supposed to do, but my body commanded me to sit in that shower. The servants would come to bring me breakfast and tutor me, but I could not force myself to do anything that would pull me away from the comfort of the scalding shower on my abdomen.

The water soothed me so much that I accidentally drifted back into a peaceful sleep, and I awakened to the sound of the shower curtain being pulled back. I covered my tiny body in shock from seeing one of the elders, especially since he looked so overjoyed. "What is the meaning of this?"

"You have reached maturity, my queen." He handed me a towel to wrap my body and waited impatiently while I covered myself. "This is a glorious day indeed."

I was trembling. I knew not what would become of my mother and me, but there must have been a good reason why she wanted me to keep my womanhood a secret. I walked out of the bathroom and saw all the elders were in the room smiling, while one of my servants changed the sheets. She was older than my mother, and she was crying silently to herself. "Is everything alright?" I asked everyone.

"All is in proper order," one of the elders said. "Pay no mind to her. We can have her whipped if her mood is upsetting you."

"Please don't," I begged. "That isn't necessary."

But she was upsetting me. Whatever horror I was about to endure, I knew she was painfully aware of it. "I wish to get dressed. I want to be alone."

"Of course!" one of them said. "Please, put on one of your finest dresses, my queen."

I gave a nod. I wore nice things every day. I could hardly understand why my pain was a reason to wear something magnificent, but who was I to question them? As soon as they left, I looked through my closet, but there was nothing I felt like putting on.

My servant finished changing the sheets and came into my closet. She observed me unnervingly until I touched a white dress. "You don't want to wear something like that," she said. "You should wear something darker."

I drew my hand back and walked over to a beautiful black dress that shimmered in the light. "Something like this?" I usually didn't wear black, but I didn't want to be inappropriate.

"That would be perfect," she said sadly. "You're about to go to a funeral anyway."

"What do you mean?" I never attended one myself, though I had observed the servants performing some far from my window.

"Nothing," she corrected quickly. "I'm sure the elders don't want me to say."

"But I am your queen!"

She laughed with an uncomfortable bitterness. "In this world, that is only a title. You are a slave, just like the rest of us." No one had ever been so bold as to speak to me in that manner. If I willed it, she could be killed. Was that not real power?

But I didn't possess that sort of cruelty or finality. "Please, leave me."

She bowed and did as I asked, just as I suspected she would. I was a queen! But then, I was still upset. I did as the elders instructed and put on that fine black dress. Other servants came in and curled my hair. My skin was perfect, so makeup wasn't required, but they put a little bit of blush on my cheeks, a bit of gloss on my lips, and just a dash of eye shadow. I looked at the woman in the mirror, and I began to feel a terrible knot in my stomach. I looked beautiful, but I didn't feel glamorous. Honestly, I felt as if someone were stabbing me in my lower abdomen, but I couldn't let that hinder me while the elders waited for me.

I was escorted down into a chamber made of stone and painted with ancient symbols of my people. I had only been in there when I was very small, and of course, when I was born. There was a pit with green and thick liquid inside it. I nearly licked my lips from remembering the taste of the sweet nectar. It was surreal being in there again and seeing the giant bed that I was born on, sitting on a platform like a throne. That was soon to be my legacy.

"My daughter," my mother said as she came down the stairs, accompanied by several guards.

A smile came to my face. I didn't realize I had completely forgiven her until I saw her once more. "How are you, Mother?"

She hesitated as if something were wrong. "I've been doing as well as expected." I didn't realize she was aware of the danger she was in, and I was completely oblivious.

"It's good to see you again."

She smiled wearily and reached out her arms for me. I was surprised she wanted to display such an improper form of affection in front of the elders, but I craved it myself. I looked at the elders to see if it was permissible. They clearly did not trust my mother, yet they nodded and let me walk into her arms. She was slightly trembling, and I didn't understand why. "I love you," she said.

I blushed furiously. Emotionally, I felt like I was going to melt inside of myself. "But you don't know me."

"Of course, I do, my daughter." As she parted from me, her lips made contact with my cheek. I still remember the scent of her skin to this day, like a rose dying in the cold air of a chilling fall. "I know you very well."

I felt like a silly little girl, and I swayed from side-to-side to watch my dress swish back and forth. I don't know why I was so embarrassed. Perhaps it was too much joy for me to know what to do with it. "I am a woman now. What motherly advice do you have to give?"

She took a deep breath as an elder came up from behind. "The only advice I can give is to remember that you are a queen."

"How can I forget?"

"No." She bent down and whispered. "You are a real queen with authority. They need you a lot more than you need them. Find your voice."

I nodded as she endowed me with a great power that I would keep deep inside of me for years. "I will try to remember that."

Mother tried to smile, but then I noticed a glimmer in her eye that shimmered. It was a tear that sparkled as the light hit it. I didn't understand until she fell forward and grasped onto my tiny shoulders with her strong hands. I gasped and looked down at her bloodied stomach. I had never seen so much blood, and I instinctively screamed so hard that I lost my voice after a few seconds.

It was as if the ground had reached up and swallowed my feet. I mumbled out words that meant nothing, but they translated my severe pain as my eyes saw an elder holding a bloodied knife. It was then that I felt a rage inside of me that I never knew existed. I had read about it, but I never understood such a thing until I laid eyes on the man who murdered my mother.

I tried to make a run toward him to avenge her, but a heavy hand fell on my shoulders and planted me further into the ground. I struggled to break free, but then my mother's eyes began to go dark, and her mouth opened wide.

Without meaning to, my mouth opened wide as well, and a wispy light poured into me. It was warm, vibrant, and it filled me with a satisfaction that was even greater than my royal nectar. I didn't realize I was hungry until I feasted on her life-force that flooded my body, and filled me with a new strength I had never felt before. But even though I was revitalized, I could feel my mother growing colder. I grabbed her wrists because I didn't want to let her go. But I could feel no pulse resonating through my fingertips, and the warm stream of light was gone.

Her body fell on top of me, and my tears fell on top of what used to be the queen of the colony. I tried to scream, to unleash my horror, but nothing came out besides raspy and silent cries of a little girl, who had no choice but to become a woman.

"All hail the queen," an elder said as he wiped away my mother's precious blood on a crisp, white handkerchief.

"All hail the Queen," the rest of them yelled.

I hugged my mother's head and buried my own into her, so they didn't have to see my tears. They would have seen me as weak, and I knew I could not afford to be naïve and childish anymore. I was the only queen remaining. The colony would live or die on my account.

That was my first great price of being born into a world of privilege and prestige, and it wouldn't be my last. But if I had any say in the matter, I wouldn't be the only one who had to suffer.

Chapter Two

My life drastically changed when I became the only queen. I thought I was protected and doted on before, but I noticed there was special attention on me. My servants helped me to look more like a woman, and I was taken to the warriors' training grounds at least twice a day. I was looked at with a different fondness and curious eye, but it disturbed me. I wasn't ready to be desirable, but that's what they tried to make me. It was painfully clear that the elders were not willing to be patient about reproducing. I felt them breathing down my neck as I walked up and down the rows and watched the warriors.

I would usually find a warrior, not too much older than me, and stop long enough to make eye contact. The elders would get excited and whisper to each other. Then the closest one would lean down and speak softly in my ear. "Have you found one that you enjoy?"

I would smirk to myself. "No." They looked ridiculous when their shoulders slightly slumped. It was only a minor satisfaction, but one I put them through, over and over again, every day. It was the most we spoke to each other, and while I found it amusing, it slowly wore on my nerves after we went through the process for about two years.

Though the elders were very frustrated with me, they slowly gave me some much-needed space. When I wasn't circling my many potential suitors, I was in my garden reading. The elders believed I was studying—sometimes I was—but I was usually reading a story about a dashing young man capturing the heart of a princess. They were silly stories of valiant heroes and pure maidens that filled my head with nonsense. It was the nonsense my mother wanted me to have for myself, so I refused to let my dreams die.

I was captivated by the tale of a son of a knight. His father served and loved the queen, but he could not marry her due to his commoner status. On a chilling winter's night, a wicked witch led an army into the kingdom and destroyed everyone who stood in her path. The witch was unstoppable, and the queen and king were slain, but the knight made an oath as they were dying to protect the princess until she reclaimed her throne. He was able to flee and raise his son and the princess safely. They were poor, but capable people of the enchanted forest. The princess was even a more capable hunter than the knight's son.

They built a happy home, and though the knight still felt the wound in his heart from the death of his beloved queen; he took comfort in the green eyes of the princess, who inherited them from her mother.

Their peace did not last forever, and one of the witch's scouts was able to find the knight. A small army returned, and the brave knight took on as many as he could, so his son and the princess could escape together.

The son became her knight—though she did not need protection—and they traveled far to seek aid from another kingdom that the witch was going to conquer. There was a celebration thrown in honor of the princess, and she honored her new knight with a dance. It was then that the two discovered, through their suffering, that they created an unbreakable bond. The princess granted her knight a kiss, and the two fell in love.

They wished to wed before they entered the final battle to reclaim her kingdom, but the princess stumbled upon the secret that the king's soul had been taken and replaced by darkness from the witch. Before the princess could warn her knight, she was captured and brought before the witch.

I read my book all day, and I was losing the sunlight. I was forced to return to my room with the book pressed against my chest, with absolutely no shame.

When I entered my room to finish the tale, I noticed there was a shadow waiting for me under the door. I paused and turned around to my guards, but they were not alarmed. "Are the elders waiting for me?"

"I don't believe so," he said.

"Then who is in my room?"

"They said there was a gift waiting for you."

I swallowed the vast lump in my throat, and then it manifested into a large rock in the bottom of my stomach. "I am not accepting gifts right now. It's late, and I don't wish to be disturbed."

"We only do as we are told."

"And I am the queen, and I am giving you orders!" I had never been so forceful before, but I was desperate to remain the "Virgin Queen." I was not ready to give life if it meant my death. I had barely lived any sort of life for myself. "Remove this man from my chambers immediately!"

They were conflicted. Everyone took orders from the elders. We never questioned. We never disobeyed, but the will of the queen was never at odds with the will of the elders. It was a new predicament. A part of me suspected they would dismiss me immediately, but there was a bigger part of me that decided that was unacceptable!

The guards looked around at each other and didn't speak their troubles aloud, but their eyes conveyed their concerns greater than anything audible. Then, one of them spoke up. "May I go get the elders for you, my queen?"

I crossed my arms and looked displeased, though I was quite satisfied with their conflict. "Hurry."

He scurried off, and I faced my door, so I could giggle to myself. I used the first bit of my power, and it paid off drastically. Perhaps I could be a real queen instead of a child bearer. Perhaps none of my predecessors tried before. All I had to do was be assertive!

When the elders arrived, I nearly laughed when I saw how upset they were. I contained my satisfaction and repressed it to a smug grin. "Who gave you permission to let someone into my room?"

They were absolutely appalled. "There are usually women in your room. They clean it for you every day."

"But that's not a woman in there, is it?"

"It's a young warrior—"

"Who I did not choose! You cannot make this decision for me. I will not allow you."

Again, they were completely upset. One of them was practically fuming, but my mother's killer was calm. He was always calm with me. I suppose his age taught him how to be patient. "He wants to have dinner with you."

I lost my composure and my breath for a moment. "Dinner?"

"Yes, my virgin queen." My smug grin transferred to his face, but it was much more malevolent than mine. "I know you have many silly notions in your head like a human, so we've arranged for a warrior who is part human. He was more than thrilled to be chosen."

My heart began to beat faster the more I thought about him waiting for me with a perfect meal. It was just like any basic date I had read about. Was it possible that the boy waiting in my room was destined to be my first and only love?

"I will go to him." I hated that I made the elders happy, but I could not deny myself that opportunity. There was a chance they would never indulge my fantasies ever again.

"Have a nice night, my queen." Their happy smiles did nothing but send chills down my spine. Though they were conspirators plotting my eventual demise, I opened the door and met the warrior face-to-face.

"My queen!" He was handsome. I remember he had teeth so perfect; they seemed to shine in the light. Every time he grinned, I felt as if he were robbing the world of his beauty.

"Don't bother bowing," I said fast enough before he could. "If you do that, then it will make this date awkward."

"Alright..." Unfortunately, I made him feel very awkward, and he subconsciously hunched forward with his head aimed down toward my feet. It wasn't a proper bow, but still a bow. "Your cooks have prepared a wonderful meal for us."

I inhaled the aroma that captivated my room. I knew one particular scent from anywhere, and I followed it to my dining room, where the large spread was waiting for us. Before I could reach my seat, the young warrior rushed to pull the chair out for me. I usually had servants who did that, but I was impressed that someone who trained nonstop every day knew how to be a gentleman. "Thank you, young warrior."

"You are welcome, my queen." When I think back, I can still remember the slight quiver in his voice. He looked to be about seventeen. If he were outside of the colony and lived in a city, he probably would have been very sly and charming with a woman. "I'm nervous," he admitted.

"That's fine. I am as well." I was intrigued by my book, but I set it down on the table and decided to pursue my own romance.

There was no need for living vicariously through a book when I could write my own story.

His eyes spotted my book as he sat down. "You like to read?"

"I love to read!" I'm sure I started glowing as I spoke about it. Books gave me wings to escape my island of torment.

"My mother also loved books," he said with a small, admirable smile.

I was very intrigued. I never heard about anyone else's mother. "You weren't born in this colony?"

"No. My grandfather was commissioned with the task of studying humans. He was able to conceive a child with a woman who fell in love with him."

I leaned across the table in excitement—something the elders hated. "What about your parents?"

"My father fit well into human society. He didn't realize he was different until he was called to return. I was only a baby."

"Called?"

He nodded. "He heard the voice of the queen telling him to return, and he remembered who he was. He couldn't leave me with a human, so he brought me back home to the colony as well."

I never heard of such a power before. If other queens possessed it then, surely, I did as well. Though I had no idea how to access such an ability, it was more proof that the elders required my assistance. I only needed them for convenience. "And what about your mother?"

"I don't remember her."

"And do you miss her?"

"Not when I have you." He smiled. "I do miss your mother, but I'm certain you shall be an even greater queen."

I, suddenly, wasn't feeling very romantic and tried to hide my face in the golden chalice filled with green elixir. It immediately tingled my tongue and warmed my skin. Nothing quite satisfied me like the ambrosia. Once I got a taste of it, I couldn't stop until every drop rested inside of my belly.

"Are you thirsty?"

I politely wiped my mouth with a napkin. I did not want to hinder my appearance as a young lady. "Ever since I received my mother's life-force, I've had a hunger I can't quite explain. This elixir, which I drank when I was a baby, is the only way to free myself from it. I drink some every morning and night."

"And what happens when you don't?"

"I'm not sure." I couldn't stand the thought of being without it, and no one ever allowed me to find out.

"Are you ever curious about life outside of the colony?" I asked.

"No," he said, rather bored. "My father tells me many stories. He had a mundane life and a boring job that he was not fond of. He wasn't as good as others when it came to infiltrating, and his life had no real merit. He was glad to return home."

My heart—along with all my expectations—began to fall. "I'm sure your mother found merit in it." If he could justify his father leaving his mother so easily, then how was I to believe he was genuinely interested in exploring a relationship with me? "Do you want to be here with me?"

"Yes!" He expressed nervous excitement and gripped the table. "There is something about you that is hard to describe. The other warriors also feel it. When you come in our presence, there is an aura around you—a scent even—that drives us to want you."

My cheeks began to redden deeply. "I was unaware that I possessed all of you so."

"I didn't notice it until after the queen died. It was faint at first, but it's steadily becoming stronger. After you leave our training facility, it's like the floorboards are soaked in your grace."

Though I was still skeptical, my heart began to beat as if it were fluttering. "Do you believe in love?"

"Love?" he asked with a slight chuckle, but it was condescending and hurtful.

"Yes. Love. I'm sure your father must have explained it to you."

"I love you," he spouted quickly.

I laughed at his unexpected response. It didn't feel sincere. There was no way it could have been. "You know little about me." Was it because I was beautiful? I looked no different than the other women of the colony. It couldn't have been my thirst for knowledge or my passion for books. He did not share those passions and didn't seem to respect them. He merely related it to his mother, and he cared very little for her. I doubted he truly knew what it meant to love someone, and if he were only claiming to love me to appease my tender heart. "Do you love your father?"

He looked puzzled. "I have not seen my father since I was a boy."

"Why?"

"Because my duty is to train, and he is to protect the borders of the colony. There is no reason for us to see each other. It would not serve you."

"I'm telling you now that it will." I realized how brainwashed he was. Had I truly ruined this boy? He had his own will, but his mind was incapable of serving it. I deprived him of perhaps the only relationship in his life with value, with my title alone. He wasn't even a thought before I saw his shadow in my room. How could I have such power over him without having any at all? "Find your father and tell him that you love him."

And even with my orders, he still seemed so confused. "If it is your will, then so shall it be."

He could not be my husband. He didn't understand love, and he never would. He didn't even understand that, somewhere in the world, his mother was hoping she would receive a phone call from the police saying they found her baby boy. How could he give me what he had never been taught?

"I wish to read my book in peace. Perhaps we can plan another date." I was being rude by excusing myself, but I grabbed my book and started heading for my bedroom.

"I'm not supposed to leave yet."

I turned around and saw that he began to follow me. I was indignant and even a little startled. "You leave when I command it!"

"The elders said I was to be the first of your mates." He took a few steps closer. His voice still quivered, but perhaps it was excitement. "They said I could not leave the room until you carried my seed in your womb."

"There's been a terrible misunderstanding." I wanted to run, but I did not want to lead him any further to my bedroom. I could not show him how terrified I was of him. I had to still be the queen! "Leave immediately."

I was firm and commanding, but he was unmoved. "They also said if you try to resist, then I should be forceful."

I gasped when he grabbed my arms, and I was unprepared for his lips on my own. It was a kiss that made me breathless and even weak in the knees, but I thought those symptoms were only supposed to be caused by endearing passion, not wild lust.

I pushed against his chest and became dizzy. I had no air, and in a panic, I forgot to inhale through my nose. He was stronger than I, and I could not force him off until I dug my nails into his skin. He drew away and yelled in pain long enough for me to rush into my bathroom and lock the door. "Help!"

The door bounced, and I feared it would fly right off its hinges. I threw my body up against it in an attempt to stop him, but I did not stand a chance. Our warriors were born powerful, and he was a trained killer. "Guards!"

"Your guards have retired for the night. The elders are watching the doors. They will not stop me, nor will they allow me to leave."

I was nearly thrown off my heels from the banging on the door, but I remained and pushed as hard as I could. I knew it wasn't enough, so my eyes quickly searched the bathroom for anything sharp to protect myself. There was a white vase with a beautiful magnolia sculpted into it. I was very fond of it, but I pressed my luck and made a run for it.

The door flew open, and his arm grabbed the back of my dress just as my fingertips touched the vase. I nicked it into my hands and crashed the vase into his head. Unfortunately, it didn't even faze him.

"You cannot take my purity from me!" I screamed. "It's something I have to give away." He stopped for one second, and our eyes made contact. He did not know he was committing a wrong. I hated him for what he was about to do to me, and yet I took pity on him. His father taught him to abandon love and freedom for the betterment of the colony. What could my tears possibly mean for someone who did not possess a soul?

"I'm sorry, my queen, but your mission has been compromised by your emotions. Your duty is to breed. The fate of this colony rests on your shoulders."

I knew there would be no escape once he collided with my lips again. It didn't matter where it happened. It didn't matter if either of us found it pleasurable. As long as he had breath in his body, he would do exactly what the elders instructed.

"No!" I blinked and opened my eyes to release my last few tears, and then they evaporated right off of my face, from the warmth of his life leaving his body and entering mine, in the same manner my mother's did. It was just as unexpected, but I must admit, I wasn't as horrified as I used to be. I tried to resist my mother's life force from entering my body, but I welcomed every piece of him. Finally, I had a meal that was even more appetizing than my ambrosia.

When I witnessed the last bit of light in his eyes dimming, I pulled myself away and let him fall on the broken pieces of the vase. Even though it was over, I was still unsettled. I didn't notice my tears returned until I felt them slide down my neck. From that point on, all manner of composure faded, and I trembled as I walked to my bed and climbed on top of it.

The elders were suspicious when the screaming stopped and came in to spy like perverts. I would not speak to them at first. I didn't exactly impede their investigation. After one look at the warrior's body, they pieced together what happened.

One of the elders charged and pulled me off the bed by my arm. "What have you done?"

What had I done? They sure had some nerve! "What did you do to me?" I went into a mad craze and hit his chest. Every ounce of hatred that I had for him, I released. I thought my attacks would be completely futile, but he winced every time I made an impact, and the sound of my fist pounding into his chest was too deep to have no effect at all. "Why am I like this? Why?"

My assault ended when his backhand swiftly impacted my face and knocked me back into bed. I had never been struck before. The pain was foreign to me, and I huddled into a ball while I sobbed.

"You were supposed to mate with this boy. He was perfect!" I had upset the elders before, but I had never seen them enraged.

"You're wretched," I mumbled. "You're evil—"

"It's your books." He sneered and shook his head at me. "We try to educate you, and then you betray us by becoming a romantic nut! We have to destroy them."

"No!" I leaped from my bed and onto the back of the one who struck me—my mother's murderer—and tried to choke him with my skinny arms. With very little effort, he flipped me over his back and dragged me to the fireplace, so I could bear witness to his cruelty.

It didn't matter if my books were filled with the dullest history or the most exciting fiction. They took each book from my shelves and fed the roaring fire. I struggled to break free, but the strength of the elders was even greater than that of the warriors. "Leave them alone. It's all I have. Please!"

The last book to be burned was my current read. I wanted to learn if the princess and the knight would overcome the witch, but I was too powerless to save their world, and I had to watch it burn.

After every single word was wiped from existence, I was released. I didn't have the strength to fight, and I fell to my knees. I wished the cruelest death upon them because there was nothing else I could do.

"We will send more men," they warned. "You will mate, and you will replenish our colony."

"And maybe your warriors will end up dead like this one!" I could not let them have every constant victory over me. It was true that I was the queen, and the colony was depending on me. Those were just the facts. I needed to have children, but they would not bully me into ruining the only thing in life that I ever wanted for myself. "I deserve to find love. You will not stop me."

They were furious. I didn't think I could be as strong as my mother, but I think my rebellion was foreign to them. Maybe her will was inside of me—making me stronger—so I could be strong for the both of us. But just because they were unprepared for my challenge didn't mean they wouldn't accept it.

"We shall see."

They did not want to bother with my presence any longer, and I was left alone with a dead body in my bathroom. Ten minutes before, that would have frightened me, but everything changed. I stood over his corpse and made a declaration to myself: I would fight with everything I had.

But within my newfound strength, I had a crushing revelation. My entire life, I saw myself as the beautiful damsel or the graceful maiden. I was the princess searching for her knight. But with my newfound abilities, I finally discovered that, after all this time, I was the powerful witch.

Chapter Three

There was a polite and cautious knock at my door. No one barged in on me anymore. Everyone was afraid of my power, with good reason. Though no one's presence pleased me, I had nothing better to do than to bother myself. "Come in."

My least favorite elder entered. "Virgin Queen."

I smirked at his disgust with that phrase. "I bet you never thought you'd be calling me that for this long."

"It is a problem."

"Perhaps I shall remain a virgin forever," I teased evilly, just to see him squirm.

"And destroy our colony?" he chuckled and shook his head. "I don't believe you'd want that."

I never could convince the elders I was quite that selfish, but I took pleasure in how annoyed they were with my hesitancy. "Well, I can decide how long I choose to remain celibate."

"I'm afraid you're running out of time. If you remain celibate past the age of twenty-one, you will lose your ability to conceive. Can you honestly say you don't have a maternal bone in your body?"

I tried to remain poised and in charge, but I was rattled. I did very much want children. The elders, unfortunately, knew that about me. I had no choice but to reach some kind of agreement. "We have a problem. All of your men are afraid of me now."

"I'm aware," he said curiously. "Why haven't you escaped? You're strong enough now."

"And how would I get off this island? Where would I go?" I wasn't too naïve to know that reading knowledge and having the experience to solidify it were two different things. "Besides, these are my people. It doesn't matter how much they fear me. I'm still their queen."

He smirked, receiving the answer he hoped for. "I believe we've reached a compromise."

"I'm listening."

He circled around me. The elders knew of my power, yet they were not afraid. I would have made an example out of one of them, but I didn't quite have the strength. Perhaps there was too much evil to suck out. "We're going to free you, so you can find love on your own terms."

I cocked my brow at him. "There's no catch?"

"No catch. We simply want our colony to live."

I had to be suspicious. They never had my best interests at heart. "But you're telling me to find a human. If I love him, I can't bring him back."

"You're the queen. You can do as you please." He couldn't even manage to say that without chuckling. "Choose a location, and we will bring you there."

There had to be something more I didn't understand. The elders were proud, and they might have been desperate, but a compromise seemed far beyond their capabilities. I had to assume they were trying to trick me, but I was so enticed by the idea of actually finding love. Leaving my world to find a human mate…it was so romantic! If I were lucky, he could be my king and not just a pawn. "I'll be ready to leave tonight."

He smiled happily and slightly bowed his head. I didn't sense even the slightest bit of mischievousness from him. It was strange, but he truly seemed to have no ulterior motive and left me alone with my thoughts.

"A human…" I spoke softly to myself. I had no idea what the world was really like. The elders were serious about cutting me off to punish me. All I could think about were silly stories about princesses and knights fighting to keep them safe and win their hearts. I wasn't as innocent as those women, but I blamed that on my environment. The elders turned me into a killer, but it wasn't in my heart to be that cruel. I could be better. It was time to start believing in fairytales again.

A couple of my maids came in and gathered clothes for me to wear, but I didn't have much to blend in with. I only wore the finest dresses. I saw they packed some more practical clothing, but none of it was mine. I was becoming quite nervous, but it was a chance I had to take.

In the evening, my least favorite elder joined me for dinner. Though he despised me, he loved giving me orders. I suppose that's why he volunteered to be the one who conversed with me. He spoke about how frightened he was that I would reveal the nature of the colony to the humans. I had to assure him many times, until the point of annoyance, that I would not be any trouble.

"Have you decided where you want to go, Virgin Queen?"

That was one thing I couldn't quite decide on, but if I didn't have an answer, I wouldn't be able to leave. I got out of my seat and walked over to a small table in my living room that had a globe on it. I gave it one good spin and closed my eyes. When I felt good and ready, I placed my finger on the globe, and it came to an abrupt stop. When I opened my eyes, I smiled. "Sunny California."

"You don't care about anything important. Do you know the crime rate? Political views? What about the neighborhood you are going to choose?"

"I will be fine," I told him. "I want a house near the beach, so I can feel the sand between my toes, the wind in my hair, and I only want to be a breath away from the ocean."

"And what will happen if there is an earthquake?"

"I will survive." I smiled happily. Living anywhere in the world would have made me excited. I would choose the tundra of Alaska if it would give me freedom and a chance for love.

He sighed heavily. "I refuse to fight about this with you, Virgin Queen. If you want to live there, that is fine. As long as we begin on a path to keeping our colony alive, I will choose to be satisfied."

I hated how he pretended his only goal was protecting the colony. I wouldn't allow him to justify his cruelty for such a noble cause. "Leave me."

"So soon?" he chuckled. "We will not see each other for a long while. You will be alone."

"Alone?" I was intrigued about living by myself with the freedom to do whatever I wanted, but the notion did frighten me just a little bit. "No servants will accompany me?"

"I would hate to have any influence over your decision, my virgin queen, but we will have guards watching from afar to make sure you are safe."

I knew they'd be watching for more than my safety. As soon as they were the least bit suspicious of pregnancy, they would probably whisk me away and leave the father of my child wondering where I had gone. Well, I wouldn't let that happen. If I could manage a traditional wedding, I would.

"It will be odd surviving on my own, but I assure you, I will not miss you, any of my guards, or the elders."

"You truly hate me?" he asked, fascinated. "I have only done what was necessary to make you strong. I only wish to make this colony strong."

"Well, you have made me miserable." I would not allow his lies to poison my mind. He meant nothing to me, and he would always be nothing.

I thought he would have been satisfied hearing about my frustrations, but he seemed displeased that I despised him so. "Before I retire, I need to know what name you have chosen for yourself."

"A name?" I had never thought of needing one before. Everyone knew who I was. Having a title seemed just fine enough.

"Yes. Humans address themselves by name. It wouldn't be proper if you didn't have a name, and you need one to have proper documentation."

For some reason, I thought of my mother and the scent of her skin as she died. "Rose."

"You need a first and last name."

I had no idea what would be proper. "I permit you to choose. Now, leave my sight."

He slightly nodded his head and excused himself from my presence. No, I certainly would not miss him breathing down my neck and giving me orders. He was lucky I was unable to take his life force from him. If I could, I truly would be a queen with absolutely no opposition.

But the time for concentrating on my royal status was coming to a close. In less than twenty-four hours, I was going to live as a normal human looking for love, like they all did, every day of their lives.

As I waited for the night to end and for morning to rise, I watched the world from a balcony in my bedroom. Somewhere, outside of my colony, there were real people allowed to do what they wanted without rhyme or reason. They could dance because they loved music, and it compelled them to let the rhythm interpret itself through their bodies. The laughter of children echoed through the streets like the heartbeat of the earth. I never danced, and no one would dance with me if I asked. No one ever sang, besides my mother. I could still hear her song in my head. It haunted me, and I was grateful to at least have that sad song to remember her by. It was better than recalling how she was stolen from me.

I swore to myself that I would have a husband, and we would raise our daughters and sons the way I wanted to be raised. I didn't want to have children who suffered as I did. I could make things in the colony change. I had to.

In the morning, there was a great hush in my home, except for the whispers of the servants. No queen had ever left, and that frightened them more than the awful things I had done to my warriors.

They still performed their tasks, and an unusual garment was ironed and waiting for me on my bed after I washed and had eaten. I had read about the garments in magazines. They were jeans and a pink blouse. I had to grow accustomed to wearing pants if humans liked to wear them every day.

The elders escorted me out of my home and rode in the carriage to the shore. I never explored our island, but there wasn't much exploring to do. Farms were stretching across the land, and I had a lot more followers than I realized.

When I saw the shore, I became more excited than I had ever been in my life, but I was also terrified. I didn't know how to survive on my own, and though I was eager to try, there was a part of me that didn't think I had what it took.

There was a huge ship waiting at the docks that sailed all around the world to get supplies for the colony. There was also a beautiful yacht that would help me arrive in style. I would be leaving with only the captain and a servant.

"This is your chance," my mother's murderer said. "If you wish to stay here in the colony, you may. There are plenty of soldiers who—"

"They are all completely terrified of me." None of them would make suitable partners, and the elders didn't want them to be. They were pounds of flesh.

"I understand. Just be safe, my queen." He smiled at me as if he cared.

"I believe I'll be a lot safer away from you." I didn't waste any more time hesitating. I boarded the yacht that would take me away from the only home I had ever known, and the prison that destroyed every hope I ever had. The only way to make my dreams come true was to leave.

The captain and my servant bowed before me, but they were too afraid to look me in the eye. I ignored their fear and decided to rest in my cabin. It would take about a week to get to California from our island, and I was used to being alone.

I wished I had a book with me. The first place I planned to visit was a bookstore or a library. I would carry home a thousand books if I could. I would try to find the one I never finished. Oh, that notion excited me the most!

Love didn't have to be my only objective. I could discover life. I could experience the adventures in my stories. I was strong enough to protect myself, and I wasn't afraid to try new things. My arms would welcome the world.

I looked out the window and watched the water. It was my source of entertainment, and the hours went by slowly. My only company brought me meals three times a day. At night, I stretched my legs and walked along the deck. The servant girl made sure she was in her cabin by the time I came outside, to avoid me, which was fine. I didn't want to make her feel uncomfortable.

This cycle continued for several days, until I saw birds flying during one of my strolls. I had read in a book once that it meant we were close to land, and I was ecstatic! As soon as I saw the coastline, I yelled and jumped. "Land!"

My servant came running to see the commotion. "Are you alright, Virgin Queen?"

"I am. I'm sorry to have alarmed you." I turned around and finally looked into her eyes. We both seemed to be the same age. At a glance, we could have been twins. "Did you know the former queen?"

"I did." She trembled and was anxious to leave, but her feet were planted firmly on the floorboards until I released her. "I grew up in her home, and I served her as well as I could. I was only thirteen when she passed."

"Thirteen?" I asked with a cautious curiosity.

"Yes."

I was also thirteen when I lost her. It was fair to assume she was my sister, especially if my mother kept her. "What was she like?"

She suddenly craved my attention so she could speak of my mother. "She listened, and she watched the world. She understood more than the rest of us."

She was right. There was still so much I didn't understand and couldn't comprehend. There was information the elders withheld, just so they could make themselves superior to me. I assumed they tried to do the same to my mother, but she was too wise for those snakes.

"She spoke of you."

"She did?"

The servant girl nodded and beamed a smile. "She cared about you. She thought you would be stronger than her because of your heart."

I noticed her eyes glistened. I was unaware that any of my people felt love. They had respect and honor for the former queen and me, but nothing compared to what I felt in my heart for her. "She was your mother?"

"She was."

"Then you are my sister?"

I grabbed her hands, but she trembled at the touch. "We have many sisters. It doesn't mean anything."

"It means more to me than you know!" I felt her trying to gently pull away, but I held on tight. "I know I am your queen, but I am coming here to have a normal life. I want to find love. It would be nice to have a friend to confide in. Who can fulfill this role better than my own sister?"

She shook her head and spoke quickly out of nervousness. "I was not told to accompany you. I was to wait on the yacht until you were ready to return home. I have no name. I have nothing to offer you other than my service. I—"

"Camellia!" She was just as bright and radiant as the lovely flowers I adored. "I am fond of them, so that will be your name. You will join me and be my sister." I laughed. "You can show me how to cook!"

"If that is your wish—"

"It is." I released her from my grip, but she was still uneasy. I understood, but for the first time in some years, I was truly ashamed of my reputation. "Please, do not fear me."

She attempted to calm herself, but it was hard to stay still, and she kept looking back toward the door that led to the deck below. "Is it true you killed warriors that came to mate you?"

Was that all people knew about me? The elders were the villains. If only they saw them as I did. "Yes, but do not judge me. You don't know what they tried to do to me."

She swallowed hard and nodded. "Camellia will be my name."

"And perhaps we can find you a husband as well!" I said excitedly.

"That is not my duty. I am not allowed to—"

"I am the queen," I squealed. "You are supposed to do as I say."

Camellia uneasily agreed. I would have to convince her that love was worth discovering and that there was more to life than fulfilling my needs. If I could open Camellia's mind, then I could change things for my people as well.

"Prepare my things. I wish to be ready to leave as soon as we arrive."

"Yes, my queen."

"Rose," I said. "Only address me as your sister, Rose."

"Yes, my Rose." She awkwardly bowed and went down below to my cabin to pack. She neatly gathered my things in suitcases. She even packed a bag and took what few possessions she had with her.

The outside world certainly was strange. It was well after midnight, yet many people were walking around the docks, some of them stumbling. There was loud music, and several people congregated near a stand.

"They're drunkards," Camellia said. "I'm sure you won't find a mate over there, my queen."

"Call me Rose."

"I apologize." She struggled with carrying two large suitcases down the dock to a black limousine. The captain came and grabbed two, but I knew there were still several others.

"Would you like me to help?"

"Don't be ridiculous," the captain said. "Our duty is to take care of you."

"I don't want to be a burden."

"You're not," said an older man from behind. He was dressed in a black suit and hat. "You are the reason for our survival." He was polite enough to help Camellia with my luggage and aid the captain in carrying the rest. "Why are there two passengers?"

"I want her to come with me," I said. "I believe she will aid me in my primary objective."

My driver did not speak another word on the matter and opened the door for us. I read about cars and had seen pictures, but neither of us had ever been in one before. It was a lot nicer than being in a carriage. The leather seats were even warm. I could have fallen asleep right there and then.

Camellia and I waited silently while men loaded barrels from the yacht and loaded them in the back of a red pickup truck. I assumed it was my royal elixir. I needed it to survive.

When all my things were loaded, the driver got inside, and the car began to move. I was a little startled and grabbed the seat. My sister resisted the urge to laugh, but she ended up snickering. When I caught her, she cleared her throat. "I'm sorry, my queen."

"Rose."

"Sorry, Rose." I could hardly blame her for laughing at my expense over such a silly thing.

My driver listened in on our conversation, but we didn't have much of one. Camellia was still uneasy around me. On top of being afraid, I was still the greatest figure in her life. Of course, I was a bit intimidating. My driver was more impressed, though, and he kept looking at me through his mirror.

I was curious about him as well. I estimated he was somewhere in his fifties. He had a full set of frosted grey hair, and his wrinkles were only noticeable when he smiled. He seemed kind. "How long have you lived with humans?"

"Thirty-six years," he smirked. "Rose Queen."

"Is 'Queen' my last name?" I asked with a chuckle.

"It's fitting, don't you think?"

"I suppose." My people were hopelessly loyal, so I had no choice but to concede. "You serve me without question, despite having so many ties to the humans, Mr...?"

"Jones. I may not be in the colony, but I am always serving you."

"And how do you serve your queen by being a driver?" I asked with a smug smirk.

I was only picking with him, and he offered a smile to show that I hadn't offended him. "I do what I must to provide for my three boys. The eldest is on the fast track to politics. The second is a high-profile lawyer, and my youngest is an excellent doctor. One day, the Call will be made, and they will know whose side they are on."

I recalled my very first date and the young warrior who told me about the Call. It made his father abandon his mother. It was my power, yet I was clueless, and I wasn't sure if I would ever want to use it. "And what about their mother?"

"She has no idea what we are." He didn't seem very torn up about lying to the mother of his children.

"And if and when I make the Call, for all of my followers to return, you and your boys will come?" I was out looking for love, and yet I was born with the ability to take it away from everyone who wanted to help me.

"If that is what the Call is, then we will all return to the island."

"And what else might it be?" I asked curiously.

He looked up into the mirror, and we both saw each other's eyes. "A call to action."

I was not completely naïve. There was a reason why we grew our numbers and learned about human culture. Scouts left to observe, and some left to plant more of us in their society. One drop of blood from a queen was enough to always be one of us. We could take over simply by continuing to grow, but there was no guarantee that we could breed with the entire human race. One day, the elders would advise a full-scale invasion. Everyone who wasn't one of us would be killed. It might have happened in my lifetime, or it might have happened hundreds of years into the future, but humans would be wiped out, sooner or later. "And do you think humans deserve to be invaded?"

"I do, and you will see soon enough."

I looked at Camellia, but she didn't offer any opinion on the matter. She wouldn't know any better, regardless.

I would see soon enough with my own eyes, and I would make my own judgments. I wouldn't make the Call unless I absolutely needed to. I didn't plan on destroying humanity, and I couldn't imagine they would do anything to give me the impression they needed to be, but I would keep my eyes open.

Chapter Four

We pulled up at a white, beautiful home near the beach. It wasn't as large or grand as my mansion on the island, but it was more than adequate.

"I will get your things," Jones said. "The front door should already be open."

"Come on!" I grabbed Camellia's hand and ran for the front door. Camellia nearly tripped on the stairs, but I was too excited to slow down. The house was fully furnished. It wasn't glamorous, but rather comfortable. I noticed there was a bookcase in the living room, but there weren't any books.

"Is there something not to your liking?" Camellia asked.

"There are no books." I rushed into the kitchen and checked every cabinet and drawer. There were forks, spoons, plates, napkins, and even plastic containers for leftovers. They thought of those things, but they couldn't put the things I wanted on a bookcase. "They did this on purpose."

"Don't worry, my—"

"Rose."

"Rose. Sorry!"

I grabbed her hand once again. "Let's find you a room." I dragged her up the stairs and to the biggest room with the biggest bed. It wasn't as much space as I was used to, but it was more than enough for the time being. There were two other rooms. One of them had a white bedspread that was incredibly soft. I took advantage and jumped on it. "You can stay here!"

I found it amazing how incredibly incapable she was of having fun. I never jumped on my bed either, but I had the desire built deep inside of me. She wouldn't even join me for a good plop!

"The elders wanted you to be alone. They thought you wouldn't be able to handle it, and you would beg to return home."

I knew they were up to something. They always assumed I was a child, even though I was stronger than all of them, and proved I could protect myself from their beloved warriors. I wouldn't return home without being married unless I was kicking and screaming. "I'm determined to find my own way. I'm not asking you to stay to take care of me. I'm asking you to stay because you're my sister."

She carefully sat on the bed next to me and pleaded. "You literally have dozens of other sisters. I do not wish to pick a fight with the elders, and I don't want to disobey you, but—"

"Don't worry about the elders." I sat up and held her shoulders. Then, I shook her to get my message through. "Enjoy yourself, Camellia! I order you to have a life."

"I'm not sure what you expect me to—"

"Smile!"

Camellia slowly, and awkwardly, grinned until she felt comfortable enough to show her dazzling white teeth, and they shone like pearls. "Like this?"

I laughed at her silly expression. "Perfect!" We were going to be the best of friends.

Mr. Jones and the rest of the men moved in our things. They put the barrels of elixir in the basement and locked them up for safekeeping. I trusted that Camellia wouldn't sneak into my supply, but you never could be too safe.

When we were settled in, the other men left, but Mr. Jones waited to speak to me. He gave me a cellphone. He walked me through it, and it seemed simple enough. "If you need me, I'm on speed dial. Here's a debit card. There is plenty of money on it, but please do not buy anything suspicious or anything you can't take care of. The yacht will be here in three months, to take you back home, unless you instruct otherwise."

"Three months? That wasn't a part of my deal with the elders."

"Those are our instructions. You have three months to find yourself a mate, and then you will be retrieved. Warriors will be around the entire time to make sure you are safe. If you're in trouble or if you need me to drive you somewhere, tell me immediately. Everything is within walking distance from your home."

"Is there a bookstore?"

He smiled, but it was to cover up how unsatisfied he was. "There is a place where you can buy books, yes."

"Good." I didn't care if the elders thought they were a bad influence on me. Frankly, I rather enjoyed annoying them.

"Would you like me to drive you anywhere now?"

"No. I am fine. Thank you." I had a little bit of anxiety about being left alone, but I really did want him to go. If I could help it, I wouldn't be calling Mr. Jones at all.

He was hesitant and practically crept out of the house. He was waiting for me to change my mind and beg him to take me back home to my prison. Well, my mind was made up, and there was no going back.

As soon as the door shut, I felt free. "Camellia!" I outstretched my arms and spun around. "I'm so happy!"

She ran from her room and leaned over the balcony. "What is it, my...Rose?"

"We need food for a feast. We need to go to the bookstore. We need to find handsome boys to love!"

"That's all good and well, but don't you think we should wait until the morning?"

I stopped and looked out of the window. "I suppose so." I didn't see how I could possibly sleep, but I calmed myself and headed to my bathroom to prepare for bed.

Nothing was like when I first arrived. All my toiletries were set out, nice and neat, in proper spots to maintain functionality. There was even a pair of pajamas folded by a clean towel. "I've already unpacked your things," Camellia said.

"You didn't have to do that."

Camellia lowered her head and breathed heavily. She shook from frustration and, eventually, teared up. "I really don't know what else to do. What purpose do I have other than to serve?"

"Hey!" I grabbed her face and pulled her into my eyes. "You have to find that out for yourself, just as I wanted to be more than a baby carrier."

"That is your duty."

"Our mother wanted more for me. She didn't want me to sacrifice my heart, and I swear that I won't. I need you to find your heart as well, Camellia." If my mother wanted that for me, she would want the same for all her children. I could feel my mother with me, and I did my best to transfer some of my will to Camellia as we stared at each other intensely.

"May I be excused?" she asked while trying to mask her fear.

I let her go. I suddenly feared what would happen if I accidentally triggered my power to absorb her life-force. I became an expert at it over time, but I certainly didn't mean to absorb my mother. I didn't want to take any chances with my sister. "Rest up. We will have a busy day tomorrow."

She nodded and transitioned into a bow. I let it slide. She would get used to seeing me as family eventually, but I couldn't expect to reprogram her in a day.

I took a long shower to relax my muscles, but it didn't prepare my body for sleep. My mind was still working too much. I fully expected to meet the love of my life. It might have taken a few days, weeks, or months. If I were lucky, I would meet him tomorrow. I only hoped he would learn to accept me for who and what I was, or else I would have to abandon him, and he would never know his children.

I slipped into bed and covered myself with a blanket. It was warm outside, but there was a chill in the house. The air conditioner was the culprit, but I did not know how to adjust it, and I didn't want to disturb Camellia until the morning. It was a minor price of freedom, and it could hardly compare to everything else I had suffered in my life thus far.

In the morning, I did not wake up early to begin my studies. The servants didn't wake me for breakfast. The elders didn't barge in to bother me with some trivial task. Instead, I slept until I was incapable of falling back asleep.

I snuck downstairs and into the kitchen. There were several different paninis and homemade hash browns prepared. Camellia was stuffing her face when I came in. "Is it good?"

She blushed and ripped the cheese from her mouth. "I apologize!"

"For what? Lunch looks delicious." There were plates set out on the table, and we both reached for one at the same time. "I can serve myself, Camellia."

"Right." She drew her hands away and waited to see if I would actually pull through.

"I am capable." I killed dozens of men with my bare hands. I could handle reaching across the table and placing a sandwich on my plate. "I do need your help, but I want you to show me how to do things."

"Like what?"

"Well, I would like to go grocery shopping with you the next time you decide to go."

"I'm sorry," she panicked. "I thought you would enjoy sleeping in, and—"

"I did, Camellia. Thank you for thinking of me. I can tell you're going to be a great sister. After lunch, we will find a bookstore to fill these empty shelves."

I got dressed and decided to bravely hit the streets with Camellia. She was a little bit familiar since she had traveled earlier. It was strange walking through the streets of a human city. They were busy and incredibly loud, but they seemed to be enjoying themselves.

Children were riding on shoes with wheels, taking up the sidewalk. They were trying to avoid people while they shoved by everyone. One of them would have run me down if Camellia hadn't pulled me out of the way. "They're quite impatient."

"Barbaric is more like it!" If I hadn't pulled on my sister's arm, she would have probably run after those children and made them suffer. I was more curious about their behavior. My people never went out of line, but they weren't free to make their own choices.

"They seem like they're having fun, Camellia. We will have to find a way to entertain ourselves."

"Isn't that why we're going to a bookstore? That's safe and proper entertainment."

"It's not an adventure, though." There was more to my life than sitting in a room and studying. The elders feared books were giving me ideas, so what fun would I be if I didn't act out on them? "I want to read all of the books the elders deprived me of, but I want more. I'm not going to meet a real boy while my nose is in a book."

"I would suggest going to the beach, but neither of us owns a swimsuit."

"I'm sure there are plenty of swimsuits to buy at the clothing store." I recalled seeing some humans dressed in swimsuits late last night. I thought it was odd and inappropriate, but I would have to blend into their society. Even though we weren't on the beach, there were still plenty of women dressed in bikini tops and shorts. I personally thought you should look like a lady on every occasion, but I suppose they could justify their scandalous dress because of the heat.

Camellia stopped at an old, small shop that had a neon sign with an owl holding a picture of a book. "This is the bookstore, Rose."

I felt like I was about to burst wide open and squealed from excitement. I ran inside and was starstruck. I ran to the first book I could reach and inhaled the scent of the pages. "It's beautiful!"

Camellia had quite a satisfied grin. "Is there something, in particular, you're looking for?"

"Yes, but feel free to grab just about anything that seems interesting. I don't care what it is. I just want to be surrounded by books." I grabbed a green basket by the door and filled it to the brim.

"Are you going to be able to carry all of that?"

I raised my head and peeked over the top shelf. There was a boy there—a real-life, human boy. He had short hair, dark like the night sky, and darling green eyes. I read about emerald eyes, but I thought my books were exaggerating about how beautiful they could be.

"Is there something wrong?" His smile was charming, and the cutest looking dimples appeared in his cheeks.

"Why do you ask if there's something wrong?"

"Because you're looking at me weird." I suppose that was true. It was odd seeing someone who looked so different. His face was rounder, and though he might have been about my age, he had more of a boyish quality to him that made him look fifteen. I'm not sure if that's what made him look so innocent. "I don't have something on my face, do I?"

"No, I'm sorry." I felt like such an improper fool. "I didn't mean to stare."

He began walking, and when I realized he was rounding the corner so he could come closer to me, I began to panic a little bit. "I can help you with those."

I pulled my basket away as his hand came toward me. "I'm strong enough to carry these. I think I'll pick up a few more and be on my way."

He laughed. "I think it'll take you long enough to read what you've already got."

I swung the basket behind me where he couldn't reach. "I'm a fast reader. Besides, I don't know if I'll read them all. I just like having the option."

He crossed his arms and nodded. "Is there a book I can help you find?"

"Why? Is this your place of employment?"

"No. I used to work here, but unfortunate circumstances have led to my termination."

"Does that mean you were fired?"

He attempted to keep a straight face, but he exploded into a short laugh. "Kind of. But there were no hard feelings, so I still come here and get a couple of books when I'm looking for something new to read."

I liked him. He was humorous, and his eyes were very endearing. "What's your name?"

"Noah." He outstretched his hand. "And what's your name?"

I heard about handshakes, but I had literally never performed one. It was a common human gesture to signify partnership, but I never had an equal. Despite all my preaching to Camellia about thinking of me as a sister, I discovered that I was uncomfortable with seeing myself as a commoner. But I had to get over my pride if I were going to blend in with the humans and find a man to love. So, I shook the young boy's hand. "My name is Rose."

"Rose?" he spoke with the sweetest romance. "It means purity, zeal, unity, friendship." He smirked and stroked his chin. "Passionate love! Which does your name mean?"

He was not the smooth seducer he pretended to be, and I had a good laugh at his expense. "I'm impressed you know so much about flowers."

"My mother was a florist. I used to think knowing all about plants was lame, but sometimes I go hiking and camping with my cousin, and I always keep him from falling into poison ivy or whatever."

"I suppose that makes you a very good cousin."

"Indeed, I am." He tried once more to reach for my basket. "Let me help you."

I took a step back, and he got the hint. "I don't need help, but thank you for being polite. It's nice to meet a true gentleman."

"Maybe I'm not a gentleman." He shrugged his shoulders and dug his foot into the floor. He could barely even look at me, and his voice became very faint. "Maybe I'm only being polite because I think you're beautiful."

His eyes slowly found mine, and I gasped in awe. He wasn't the knight or the prince I read about. His face wasn't the only boyish quality to him. He was much smaller compared to my warriors. Even without my super strength, I could have probably overtaken him. He wasn't much bigger than I, in muscles or in height. But he was sweet and adorable. "I'm not quite sure what to say."

"Well," Camellia poked her head over the shelves and glared at Noah, "she hardly knows you, so you can't come to our house. If you would like to see her again, it needs to be somewhere out in public, where you can't chop her up into little pieces."

"Look at him!" I said playfully. "He's hardly a threat."

"Hey, I'm threatening!" His offended tone lowered to a small whisper. "Sometimes…"

He truly was adorable, and it didn't matter that he was trying to be a charming snake; he was more like a kitten. "My sister, Camellia, is correct. We were planning on going to the beach."

"That's awesome because I will be at the beach later today. My cousin is in a surfing competition."

"That sounds fascinating!" I didn't know if I had enough balance to keep myself on the board, and I admired those who could do something so incredible.

"Yeah, it's pretty cool," he said quietly and seemed a little uninterested. "So, is it a date?"

I blinked a couple of times quickly. "Sure." I didn't mean to agree to a technical date, but he was a good boy. What did I have to be afraid of? "It's a date."

I didn't regret my decision because he looked so incredibly happy. I was flattered that being in my presence would illuminate his life so. I grabbed a few more books, paid for them, and headed back home with Camellia by my side. I didn't want our book bags to bust before we made it home, so we had to hurry.

I noticed Camellia had a strange expression on her face all day. She clearly wanted permission to speak, but she blurted out her feelings once we returned home. "I know you want someone different, but I didn't think you meant someone like him."

I laughed because I could not believe how judgmental she was. "Just because he's not a warrior?"

"I think he's a cute human, but men are for mating and protection. He can't protect you, and he might produce heirs that are also unable to protect you."

"You sound like the elders, Camellia. I can protect myself, and all the men in our colony were trained, just like my future children shall be. I'm not worried about anything besides the matters of my heart."

I knew by the look on her face that she could have spent the rest of the day complaining about her two reasons to dislike my new friend, but I gave her a stern look, and she silenced herself. She was still afraid of her queen, and that would have to do until she trusted me.

"And what shall we wear to the beach, my queen?"

"I think it's time we engage in the timeless human ritual." I grinned from ear to ear. "Shopping!" I definitely appreciated my hundreds of dresses, and I wore a new dress every day. It would be interesting to completely select something off a rack without a servant's opinion.

Camellia was even more intrigued because she had never had such privileges. "Then what are we waiting for?"

The two of us ran, with our arms locked together, from our beach house to the streets where the shops were. There was a little shop that looked like a hut. It was decorated with sticks and Christmas lights. It was kind of appalling, but it had its own special charm.

Camellia leaned over close to me and spoke quietly in my ear. "How are we going to find anything up to your standards in a place like this?"

"Don't be so negative, sister. We have to at least look."

"Can I help you ladies out?" asked a sales associate. She was dressed in a pair of very tiny blue jean shorts and a pink belly shirt. She had bright, beautiful, yellow hair, and her skin was golden brown, but it clearly wasn't her true skin color.

"We would like to see your bathing suits."

She pointed to a couple of wooden racks. "That's what we have left. We had a sale, so there was a mad rush. It was totally insane!"

Camellia and I thought it was a bit rude that she didn't lead us over, but we were big girls. Unfortunately, there wasn't much fabric to look through. Everything we picked up was two different pieces that were more revealing than our underwear. "Is there anything less…inappropriate?" Camellia asked the sales associate.

The girl laughed, but she seemed a little offended. "It's totally appropriate for a beach."

I found a yellow bikini top that had a matching bottom. I held it up against my body to gauge how covered my breasts would be. "I think my sister means we would like something less revealing. Do you have anything that will cover the midsection?"

"We only have bikinis." I'm not sure why she looked at us as if we were so odd. "Sorry, but I think you girls would look totally fab!"

"Fab?" I asked, confused.

"Fabulous. I just shortened it…" She laughed. "You two aren't from around here, are you?"

"We're from Iowa." I read over the details of my cover so many times during the journey to California that it came out as easily as the truth. "We lived on a farm our whole lives until we decided to see the world. Perhaps we'll become actresses."

"Well, good luck. It's hard in a place like this. I know." The bell attached to the door sounded off, and the sales associate looked to her new customer. "Let me know if you need anything."

I was going to try my bikini on, but I had to search high and low for Camellia. Every time I pulled out one piece, she shook her head stubbornly. I was finally able to find black bikini shorts and a white strapless top. It was the only time her head didn't automatically shake, so I pressed the outfit into her chest and shoved her into the changing room (which was really just three walls and a curtain).

I felt uncomfortable trying on my bikini, but we had to blend in, and it would be strange if we went to the beach without the proper attire. I never really thought much about my body before. I admired myself while in pretty clothes, and all I had to ask myself was if I was pleased enough to present my body to the world to be judged. I took a deep breath and pulled back the curtain.

"I don't know about this, Rose!" Camellia said in frustration.

I felt pretty good about my body, but I kept my arms crossed to cover myself. I needed Camellia to share my embarrassment, so we could both feel better. "Let me see you."

She took a deep breath and pulled back the curtain. Before I could say anything, Camellia gasped and pulled my arms away, so she could clearly see me and be appalled. "You cannot let men see you like this. They will go mad!"

"And what about you?" I might have been much stronger than her, but she worked constantly, sometimes doing hard labor in the fields. Her entire body was toned, and on top of that, her breasts were a little bigger than mine. She was also taller than me. "Your body is beautiful."

"I am nothing!"

I held her still and smiled after having a good look. "You will also make men go mad. We could find you a husband."

She shook her head and covered her breasts. "We cannot go out like this!"

"OMG!" yelled the girl who hardly assisted us. "You two look pretty D."

I looked to Camellia, but she was just as clueless as I was. "What does that mean?"

"Decent."

"That's not much of a compliment," Camellia said, irritated.

She laughed and shooed her hand at us. "No, it's totally a good thing. You two should get those."

I did notice Camellia glance at a mirror and finally smile. She must have known she was an attractive woman. "Okay." But before we left, she grabbed us some Pareos—a wraparound skirt— so we wouldn't have to be completely inappropriate all day if we didn't want to be. "This is pretty expensive for barely any fabric."

"Don't worry about it," I told her while at the register. "I have a lot of money."

The sales associate had a small smile that she was trying to hide. "I thought you girls were farmers."

"My father sold his land for an offer he couldn't refuse."

She nodded her head a couple of times before handing us our bags. "Come back any time, ladies."

Camellia tried to take the bag, but I hurried to do it myself. "I've got it. Let's go home and prepare."

I rushed out of the store, and I wasn't really looking. I wasn't even out of the door for two seconds before I was rammed and knocked to the ground. The bag left my hand, and the clothes went flying across the sidewalk. I didn't have time to realize what had knocked me down before Camellia started hitting and screaming at the boy.

"How dare you?" She pushed him off and helped me up in pure panic. "Are you hurt, my—?"

"I'm fine, sister." Maybe anyone else would have been hurt, but I was already back on my feet, and his arm was scraped up. "Are you alright, sir?"

"I'm okay." He shrugged. "This is nothing." I noticed he had a skateboard and deduced that it was the cause of his fall. He was no different from those reckless kids rollerblading earlier.

Camellia was still angrily glaring at him, but I was fine and reserved my grudges for the elders. "Take my hand."

He hesitated but accepted my strength. When I pulled him up, he hovered a few inches above me in height, but I got a good look into his eyes. They were just as pure and radiant as Noah's, but he was much different. His skin was kissed by the sun, and his features were much more masculine, even though he was also a boy. He was probably only a year or two older than me. His hair was longer than Noah's, and it wasn't very neat, but I assumed that was because he was riding like the devil. All in all, he was very…something. I had yet to figure out what I wanted.

"You owe her an apology!" Camellia demanded.

"Of course!" he said. "I'm sorry. I was just running late to a thing at the beach."

"A surfing competition?"

"Yeah." He looked surprised. "You goin'?"

"I plan on it. Yes." When he smiled, I felt extremely strange. He didn't have adorable dimples, but it was bright and perfect. He had a lightness to him that no one in the colony possessed. He was clearly…happy.

"Cool." His eyes shied away before looking into my eyes once more, and smirking. He was naturally charismatic, and he unwillingly enchanted me with his spell. "It'll be nice to see you there."

He decided to demonstrate how much of a gentleman he was and began to pick up our things, but Camellia violently snatched my bikini out of his hands and stuffed them back into the bag. His eyes widened, and he stepped away from her. I was glad he demonstrated some wisdom.

I wanted a few more seconds to admire his face, but Camellia continued to glare, and she made him feel uncomfortable on purpose. He tried to ignore her, but it only got worse, and then he stepped away and grabbed his skateboard.

"I didn't get your name."

"I didn't give it." He smiled and stepped on his skateboard. "If you're so curious, make sure you find me. I'll tell ya."

Camellia scoffed in disgust as he rode away, but she didn't need to be so offended for me. I knew about human traditions and courting. He was keeping me interested, and I certainly was. "I like him."

"He's rude! He's completely rude, and you don't need rude children."

"Camellia—"

"You are producing the future of our colony," she fumed quietly. "Every male you consummate with has to be acceptable."

"I only plan on mating with one person." Many queens before me had several different men to aid in the process, but I planned on being a traditional human. I was intrigued by old-fashioned love. "I'm searching for a husband, and I'll probably never find someone up to your standards, Camellia. Let me be free!"

"Fine!" She threw her hands up in the air. "You can find your rude human tonight, but let's not forget you already made plans with Noah."

I pouted. "It's not as if he proposed to me." They were both cute boys, but they obviously weren't the only boys in the country. True love was out there waiting for me, and I knew that I could find it—if I hadn't already. "I'm exploring my options."

Chapter Five

Camellia and I went home to prepare for the event at the beach. She decided to help me get dressed first. She still wanted to take care of me, and I didn't know if it was because Camellia thought I was incapable or because she didn't know what else to do with herself. I didn't protest because I liked that we spent time together. Camellia, obsessing about how my curls fell, felt sisterly.

Camellia was going to do her own hair, but I insisted. My sister claimed she didn't want to burden me, but I had the suspicion Camellia was afraid I would burn her with the curling iron. I eventually ordered her to let me do it, and she kept her mouth shut and remained perfectly still, while she moaned in terror. I was offended, but I made sure to be extremely careful. It took me twice as long, and I probably didn't get close enough to her roots, but I didn't want her to burn.

"You did a pretty good job," Camellia said while running her fingers through her hair.

"You didn't believe in me?"

She was afraid to answer.

"I don't exactly blame you, Camellia. Don't fear my wrath. I have none to give to you."

She slowly looked toward me, but not quite in the eye. "Thank you, my queen."

I smiled and grabbed my sister's hand. "Let's go have some fun."

We looked just like the humans, but Camellia and I felt so out of place. There were humans of all shapes and sizes, proudly boasting their forms, while I felt incredibly indecent. We both walked with our arms covering our bare stomachs. Were they incredibly indecent, or was I acting like a complete prude?

I placed my arms at my side and continued to walk down the beach. I smiled and held my head up in confidence. Noah thought I was beautiful, and there was a chance he was going to be my husband.

"Do you see your date?"

There were many men there, many who were bigger than Noah. They were built more like my warriors, except they were glistening from the water shining in the sun. It was strange that I didn't immediately capture their gazes. At home, all the men stopped and waited for me and my decisions. Now, I had to compete against other women to be the center of attention. Perhaps it was the humbling experience I needed, but I didn't exactly enjoy it.

"Hey." I heard a husky and masculine voice and quickly turned around. He had dark brown hair and eyes, as crystal blue as the water. He was still wet from coming out of the water, and my eyes accidentally followed a stream that slid down his chest, then through the crevices of his perfectly sculpted abdomen.

"Hello." My voice quivered from nervousness. He was so handsome; I didn't know what to do with myself.

"Are you ladies here for the competition?"

I waited to see if my sister was going to speak. Instead, she stared at our beautiful friend with wide and mystified eyes.

"We are. My name is Rose. This is my sister, Camellia."

"Camellia." He spoke her name with a smirk. "Would you mind if I took your sister? Maybe I can buy you a soda or something."

I instantly blushed. His grin was adorable, but he was clearly very manly. He must have also been a little older than me. I was flattered, and a big part of me wanted to accept his offer, but I already had too many obligations. "I would very much enjoy that, but I have to decline for now. I'm meeting a date here."

"That's great," he laughed, "because I was actually asking for your permission to take Camellia."

I wasn't used to being made into a fool, but I needed to get knocked down a peg or two. "Great. Please do." I nudged Camellia toward the gorgeous boy.

"Excuse me!" She grabbed my arm and pulled me away in quite the panic. "I don't know what to do."

It amused me that she thought I would know any better. "Just be your wonderful self."

"I don't know what that means," she moaned.

"Then go figure that out." I suppose neither of us knew who we truly were. I spent so long fighting to protect my innocence that I became a monster. Camellia spent so long meeting my needs that she didn't know the desires of her own heart. I wanted better for both of us. I needed there to be something more.

She reluctantly unclasped her fingers from my arm and shuffled over to her admirer. Camellia giggled when she took his muscular arm, but he must have thought it was adorable because he laughed.

I did envy her, but I had other commitments. I combed the beach for Noah. He was down near the water, scurrying about on his knees, while he set up a picnic on some large beach blankets. I thought it was sweet of him, and just about anything was better than my first date. "Hello, Noah."

"Oh, hi!" He stood and laughed nervously once he got a good look at me. "I'm not finished setting up. I was gonna go grab some burgers off the grill, and—"

"Take your time, Noah. There's no need to rush or to try to impress me so. Be casual."

"Casual? Right." He took a deep breath and shook himself. "I'll be back. Just enjoy a beverage and snacks." He ran away and nearly lost his footing, but he regained his balance before falling face-first in the sand. I chuckled a tiny bit at his bumble, but I still thought he was adorable.

"Sorry about my cousin," said the familiar voice of a stranger from behind. He was the boy who ran me down earlier. "He can kind of be like a little puppy sometimes."

"He's your cousin?" I suddenly felt very inappropriate. I was at the beach because of Noah, but a part of me did want to run into the attractive stranger again. "That's quite a coincidence."

"Not really."

"Why do you say that?"

"My father was his father's brother, so it's not exactly so mind-blowing." He took a seat next to me and raided Noah's picnic basket. "So, are you two serious?"

"No. We just met." I was appalled that he showed no restraint and began eating a bag of chips. "Don't you think it's rude to steal from your cousin?"

He snickered. "He took all this stuff from my house. It's more mine than his. If you should be sharing this meal with anyone, it should be me."

He must have thought he was adorable when he offered me the bag, but I snatched it out of his hands, irritated. "Do you completely lack charm, or am I unworthy to see the real you?"

"Maybe I like you, and that's why I feel like I don't have to play you, and be some perfect guy that we both know I'm not."

"Oh, how did I ever become so lucky?"

"You were born that way, beautiful." He smirked, and it broke every bit of revulsion I might have ever had about him.

But there was something that I couldn't quite shake. "You said that Noah's father was your father's brother, and he takes your food, so I'm assuming—"

"His parents died." He shrugged like it wasn't supposed to be a big deal. I knew better than anyone why it was important to appear strong, even though your entire world might be breaking. "We took him in. He's like my little brother."

"Austin," said Noah nervously, "shouldn't you be preparing for your big race?"

"I'll be fine, little cousin. I'm just spending some quality time with the girl you said was 'so beautiful you thought she was an angel.'"

"You honestly said such a wonderful thing about me?"

"Maybe, I did." Noah sat down with a plate of grilled burgers and hot dogs. "I was…excited."

"He was ecstatic!" Austin patted me on the shoulder. "Don't break his heart."

I made quick eye contact with Noah and was instantly wracked with guilt. He had no right to claim me, but he was obviously smitten. "Like I said, this is our first date. No one's heart is compromised yet."

"You should really get going," Noah insisted. "You need to be focused."

"Yeah, yeah." Austin stood, but he made sure to leave us with a parting gift and removed his shirt. I'm not sure if he was trying to undermine his cousin and seduce me, but I'm certain the way he raised his brows up and down was meant as a flirtation, born from complete arrogance. "Wish me luck!"

Austin left us, but I still felt like a piece of him was with me. "He's quite daring."

"That's one way to look at it." Noah rolled his eyes. "Are you hungry?"

"Yes. Thank you."

Noah was a gentleman and prepared a plate of food for me. I heard humans lacked manners, so I was glad to know that he was respectful. "Where's your sister?"

I smiled widely. "She found an attractive boy who was interested in her, and I encouraged her to get to know him."

"What are you and your sister up to?" Noah's eyes shied away as he handed me my plate. He was fully blushing. "You're so beautiful; you could be models or actresses."

"We just want to enjoy the city and go from there. We're exploring."

"That's how my cousin is. If it weren't for his mother, I think he'd be a beach bum for the rest of his life."

"What do you mean? Is he lazy?" I asked, alarmed.

"No," he quickly corrected. "He's actually the exact opposite. He loves extreme sports. He's always looking for a thrill. I think something stable—like a relationship—would drive him crazy."

"I see…" I'm not sure why that disappointed me, but I got the feeling Noah wanted me to feel that way.

"So, you don't have any dreams or goals for yourself?"

"I do, but none of them involve a career. I'd like to find true love, settle down, and have ten children—perhaps twenty." I noticed his eyes bucked, and I quieted down. I had to remind myself that most humans only like to have one or two children. "What about you, Noah?"

"Uh…" He shrugged. "I don't know."

"You seem like you know." I could sense he was upset, not indecisive.

"I wanted to become an engineer. I wanted to make things and leave an impression on this world before I fade away." He seemed frustrated and maybe a little tired.

"I'm sure you could do that. Why do you doubt yourself?"

He shook his head. "That's not important." He gave me a small smile and held my hand. "I'm just glad we're here together."

I looked at his hand on top of mine. It was a common gesture, and yet it was meant as something very important. I was expecting sparks to fly or butterflies, but I didn't feel anything other than his warmth. For the moment, that was acceptable. "I am too."

The competition began, and my curiosity pulled me away from Noah's grip. I followed a crowd of people to the shore. Noah trailed behind. He was supportive of his cousin but not nearly as excited as I.

Austin and a large group of fit and cute boys waited on the edge of the beach, but I noticed Austin was different from all the other boys. They all had a certain fire in their eyes, but he was incredibly special. If I could judge the competition on a pure gaze of determination, then I would have pegged him from the start. He never had any doubt that he would succeed.

I wished I had that much assurance. I was stubborn and determined, but I was also afraid that no matter what I did, I would suffer the same fate as my mother. There was a chance I wouldn't truly know love and would, one day, have a daughter who would kill me. If only I could share his confidence. Then, I would never have to be afraid of anything.

I jumped at the gunfire, but never took my eyes off Austin as he paddled against the rough rising waters. It was a fantastic day for such a competition. The waves in the distance were ferocious, and I had no idea how anyone could tame such a thing, but they all faced the challenge. Those who tackled the waves were overpowered quickly. I thought Austin would be one of the few who barged in headstrong and clumsy, but he was graceful and calm. He respected the power of the water, and instead of barreling through the storm, he rode the wave as if they were one.

I'm not sure why I found him so enchanting at that moment. Other boys knew the secret to riding the wave. There were more impressive tricks. But whatever the reason, I couldn't keep my eyes off him.

"Don't do it," Noah mumbled under his breath.

I looked on anxiously and saw that Austin was riding further out in the water. The waves were dangerously high. I shielded my eyes, but I peeled my fingers away. I had to see if his daring act would pay off.

The waves rose until the water became a hollow tube for Austin to ride through. I was so nervous he would fall; my heart felt like it was pounding in the bottom of my stomach. As he came out of the tube, he turned his body hard, and his board turned vertical and shot him up into the air. My mouth dropped from pure amazement, but Noah was not impressed.

"Bad move."

"What?" I turned my head to see Noah shaking his, and by the time I looked back, Austin was lost to my eyes. "Where is he?"

"He got ahead of the wave and wiped out."

I could not believe he was so calm. Austin could have hit his head and drowned. "Will he be alright?"

"He does this all the time. He thinks he's a professional."

I waited breathlessly for him to rise to the surface. I assumed he would be disappointed in his defeat, but I saw his smiling face reemerge, and it was quite refreshing. "He's alright!"

I weaved my way through bodies until my toes were wet and squishy. I didn't bother waiting for Noah, but he followed me to greet his smiling cousin. "That was amazing!"

He brushed off my compliment with a casual smile. "I totally wiped out."

"Even that looked thrilling!" The elders would never allow me to do such a dangerous thing, but I was powerful enough to handle myself. What was the point in setting off on an adventure if I didn't do anything...adventurous! "Do you think you could teach me how to surf?"

Austin's eyes instantly flew to his cousin. "Do you mind, Noah?"

Noah glanced at me and then nervously stared at his feet. "Well..."

My nostrils flared up. "I've had enough people try to run my life, and they have also failed. No one speaks for me." I was offended that Noah considered he could control me, but I was even more offended that Austin bothered to ask. What did he think I was? A child? A dog? A toy? They might not have known it, but I was a queen, and neither of them was my king. "I want you to teach me how to surf."

Austin still looked to his cousin, but Noah awkwardly smiled. "I like a woman who knows what she wants. Have fun."

Austin slightly shrugged. "How about tomorrow at noon?"

"We can't start any earlier?"

He laughed. "I'll barely be out of bed any earlier than that!"

"Alright. I'm looking forward to it." I could hardly wait. I wanted to be daring and confident like him. I wanted to be fearless, bold, and…happy. I knew he could get me to where I needed to be. I could just see it in his eyes.

Noah cleared his throat.

Austin took a step away from me, and I faced Noah. For a moment, I had forgotten about him. "Noah, I had a very nice time."

He smiled. "Maybe we could do it again sometime."

"Yeah. Sure. Maybe sometime…" My eyes accidentally found Austin again. I didn't mean to see him and make Noah uncomfortable, but Austin was quite magnetic. "I have to go find my sister. Goodnight, boys."

"Night," they both said.

I was quite pleased. The humans did have much to offer me, and I was sure I could find someone handsome and strong enough to be my husband. In the meantime, I would observe my two prospects and decide whether either of them was worthy. Honestly? I had high hopes.

Chapter Six

When I reunited with my sister, she was waiting by a surfboard shop, blushing immensely, and holding her hot cheeks. I envied her. I had a wonderful night, but she was having a much less complicated time finding love. "How did you enjoy yourself?"

"I can't believe he would want me! Out of all the girls here, he chose me. He wants to hang out tomorrow." She grabbed my arms and shook me. "Will you come?"

"I can't. I have surfing lessons."

She cocked her brow. "With Noah?"

"No, with his rude cousin, Austin."

Her excitement died down, and she crossed her arms. "Which one of these boys do you like?"

"My heart has made no commitments." I didn't think there was anything wrong with taking the time to decide. Yes, Noah was a very sweet boy, but I wasn't sure about him. Perhaps I read one too many fairytales about sweet boys who also enjoyed daring adventures, and looked perfect as well. There might have been no such man, but I was curious to find out for myself.

When I woke up in the morning, Camellia had already made breakfast for me. I briefly scolded her for not waking and teaching me how to make the meal myself. But even after her meal, I wasn't satisfied. There were no human means that could satisfy me.

I went down into the basement and poured myself a glass of royal nectar. I wasn't aware of any of the other queens that were addicted to it so far beyond adolescence, like I was. I didn't know too much about the other queens at all. I figured it had something to do with the number of lives I consumed. As long as I had the nectar, I didn't have to hurt anyone ever again. The cold, green liquid sliding down my throat and filling my stomach was all the pleasure I needed.

After I got dressed in a cute bikini, I was ready to start my afternoon with Austin. Camellia had to leave for her date a little bit before I did. I wished I could have had her final look of approval before I left, but I did ask for some independence. I should have very well been able to do my hair without Camellia babying me.

I arrived on the beach exactly at noon, but my instructor was nowhere to be seen. I walked along the shore, but I still didn't spot him. I sat on the beach until my skin started browning.

I was beginning to enrage. I never had to wait for anyone in my life. It was improper to show up late, especially without any warning. Camellia was right about Austin. He was completely rude, and I shouldn't have wasted any time on him.

It was forty minutes after the hour when I finally saw him treading down the beach with a surfboard in hand. He had a pair of sunglasses on like he was the coolest thing in the entire world. I had no intention of letting his swagger and unusual charm sway me in the least bit. Not even his dazzling smile or his rippling abs, was going to make me forgive him. "Are you ready to start your surfing lessons?"

"I am," I said coldly.

His mouth tensed. "Then where's your board?" he asked, irritated.

I shrugged. "I don't have one."

"Did you think you were going to use mine?" he asked rather rudely.

"I suppose I wasn't thinking." I spent all that time being angry at him when I should have been properly preparing myself. "I'm sorry. I'm being a poor student."

"It's fine." Austin sighed heavily. "We'll find you a nice, big board to start with."

We went to the surf shop right off the beach. There were a lot of nice boards that caught my eye, with different flower designs on them, but Austin often shot me down. He picked out a couple, but they were either too plain or very boyish. I eventually found another floral beauty near the back of the store, and it was huge compared to the others. If I weren't abnormally strong, I'm not sure if I would have been able to handle it. "Is this fine?"

Austin took a glance at it and spoke like he was bored. "It's perfect."

I paid for the board and returned to the beach with Austin walking a safe distance from my side. "You seem to be acting oddly toward me."

He cocked his brow. "How would you know if my behavior is odd?"

"Are you usually short and cold with everyone? Yesterday you were annoyingly close and embarrassing."

That made him chuckle. "I know my cousin likes you. He's like my brother, so I'm not screwing things up with him for you."

I gasped, completely appalled by his pure arrogance. "I asked you to teach me how to surf, not to be my boyfriend! And for your information, Noah and I went on one date. It's not up to either of you who I choose."

"There is no choice. You and I aren't gonna happen if it's gonna hurt Noah."

The nerve of him! I came closer to Austin, so I could properly tell him how insignificant he was. "I admire and respect that, but you presume too much. My sister finds you to be rude, and now I agree. You're no good for me."

"Good." He smiled maliciously. "Then I'm not gonna treat you like a princess."

"Good, because I'm not a princess," I smirked and held my head up proudly. "I'm a queen."

He threw his head back and laughed hard, but quietly. "Well then, your highness, let's start with the basics. Drop and give me twenty."

"Twenty what?"

He rolled his eyes in an overdramatic manner. "Pushups. Situps. You've gotta be strong if you're gonna paddle out to those waves."

"Are you trying to scare me?"

He tilted his head up, and his smug smile was quite adorable. "You just don't seem that tough to me."

But I wouldn't let his good looks or intimidation tactics hinder me. I had never performed a pushup myself, but it didn't require much intellect, and though I hadn't worked my arms to be in pristine condition, my abnormal strength made them as easy as walking.

I glanced up at Austin for a split second to see his eyes widen. I smiled victoriously, but I was a good student and turned over on my back, so I could quickly complete twenty situps as well. And once I was finished, I sprang right in his face and reveled in my glory. "Anything you can do, I will learn how to do it better. I am strong, I am powerful, and whether you want to or not, you will show me some respect."

He peered into my eyes for what seemed to be a long while. I think he was waiting to see if the fire in my eyes would extinguish, but I was quite determined to burn all the way through his soul, and deep into his heart. Whether or not I decided to love him, he certainly would not forget me. He would forever carry the mark of my flames on his scarred heart.

"Alright, your highness." His eyes brightened. He couldn't hide how absolutely impressed he was with me. "Let's surf."

We started small. I got on my board and paddled around a little while. I tried not to show Austin that I was nervous. I had never been able to swim anywhere besides my own personal swimming pool, and it wasn't more than six feet deep. The elders couldn't take the risk of my drowning. They wouldn't have liked the fact that I was risking my life in an entire ocean.

I had to get used to the board, and once I proved to be competent enough to lie on my stomach and wave my arms, Austin decided to demonstrate exactly what he expected me to do. He got on his board and picked a small wave to ride on. It was a completely swift motion. The ocean had its own rhythm to it, and he was completely in tune with every beat. Their song was graceful and gorgeous. I just wanted my chance to sing as well.

After his simple trick, he glided back toward me. "Your turn, princess."

"I'm a queen," I grunted.

"Then make the waves obey!" he dared to mock.

It didn't honestly seem that difficult, so I took a deep breath and paddled my way to my very first wave. I was determined to conquer it with ease and prove to Austin how superior I was to him. I could power through my fear, just like I had to do every time the elders sent their warriors to rob me of my purity. I barreled right through, and when I got to my wave, the song I longed to sing came to a screeching finish as the waves overtook me.

In an instant, I was powerless. There was no one to command and no one to fight against. I struggled to get to the surface, but I was tossed so violently that I wasn't sure which way was up and down. I thought of Austin's smart remark and became furious. I could not make nature obey my whims. I was nothing but common.

I finally discovered which way was up and clawed to the surface. My board was connected to my foot, but it took me a moment to find it, so I could rest and regain my breath.

And just when I thought I couldn't get any lower, my dear teacher floated right over to me with a grin. "I thought you could do everything I could do better."

"In time!" I was so angry. How could he not even show the slightest bit of concern for me? I could have drowned!

For his inconsiderate behavior, I became even more determined to conquer the water. I got back on my board and waited for another wave. But it made no difference. Every time I attacked the wave, my ferociousness proved to be worthless.

"You seem a little frustrated," Austin laughed. "Do you want to quit?"

"Never!"

He was going to burst out in laughter until he saw how furious I was, and he compressed it into a brief chuckle. "Your board is broken. That's it. You're done."

I looked behind me at half of my board. I hadn't realized I had been taken through that rough an ordeal. But if simple humans could handle it, I certainly would. "Let me borrow yours."

"Has anyone ever told you that you're stubborn?"

"Many times."

He grinned hard and paused. "We'll try again soon. I promise."

He got off his board and offered it to me, so I could lie on it while I swam back to shore. I considered rejecting his offer. I was strong enough to survive on my own, but I didn't want to discourage Austin when he was finally demonstrating decency and charm. "Thank you."

It was nice that he was being a gentleman, but I didn't want him to think I had given up. I was a little worn out from the unexpected level of difficulty, but I could quickly try again. "How about tomorrow?" I asked as soon as our feet hit the sand.

He chuckled and shrugged his shoulders. "I don't know. I've got other things to do."

"Why can't I get another board and try again?"

He shook his head. "I've ruined you."

"No, you haven't."

"I've created a beach bum."

"No!" I pulled on his arm in desperation. "I can restrain myself. I just want to surf again."

"Knock yourself out." He started to walk away.

"Stay!" I pulled on him again. "It's no fun alone."

He stared at me for mere seconds, but in that brief moment, I didn't think he was rude or confrontational. He was...well, I'm not sure. He was no prince—that, I was certain about—but I think I felt something connecting the two of us.

Then he pulled his hand away and opted to awkwardly scratch his head. "I promised I would help with dinner tonight." His eyes darted into mine, but then stayed steady. He almost seemed guilt-ridden that he was trying to run away from me. He had nothing to apologize for. We had no commitments. "You and your sister should come."

I blinked hard and opened my eyes wide. Austin made it very clear that he had no intention of courting me. I was pleasantly surprised that he changed his tune. "We would enjoy that."

"Noah would like that too," he quickly said while nodding.

I did appreciate what he was doing for his cousin, and I admired his loyalty. I wished there was a way to appease them both, but I didn't feel the connection to Noah that I should have. "Don't push me into liking Noah. If we're meant to be, it'll just happen."

"You'll click?"

"What does that mean?"

He briefly laughed in disbelief at my ignorance until he saw I was genuinely confused. "It means you'll just get each other. You'll...connect."

My entire body perked up. "Without meaning to?"

"Yeah..." And once again, he was incredibly awkward instead of his confident and collected self. Was it me who made him so uncomfortable? I found myself wishing that it was. "I'll text you my address. Be there at five."

"I will!" I yelled out to him because he rushed away from me. I would go to that dinner because I wanted to figure out our connection. I wanted to know if Austin and I "clicked."

Chapter Seven

Camellia was not home before me, and I had forgotten my key. It was irresponsible of me, so I sat patiently on my front porch for my sister. I did not want to call and disrupt her date with the handsome human. I had about forty minutes to be alone with my thoughts about Austin and Noah. Noah was incredibly kind and sweet. He was a gentleman, but he lacked a natural charm and tried too hard to be what women thought of as attractive. Was he justified in pushing since I didn't have a natural connection? Austin was trying not to attract me, and yet I was, for some reason. And then they were both cousins who considered themselves to be like brothers. Was it right for me to even consider them both, or should I have just done what they both wanted and given Noah a chance?

When Camellia was dropped off on the street, I was relieved. I was hoping she could weigh in on my dilemma. "Did you have a nice time?"

"It was wonderful." I smiled and blushed uncontrollably. I hadn't realized how much I enjoyed myself until I confessed. "I think Austin could show me a lot of fun things. You know, our driver said the humans were terrible, but I think they're amazing."

She narrowed her eyes at me. "You've only met two."

I could sense her frustration. "Do you not like yours?"

"I do, but he made me uncomfortable today." She tried to brush by me and opened the door to our house quickly, but not before I spotted a dark mark on her neck that was reddish–purple.

"What is that?"

"It's a hickey." She must have been very upset about it to snap at me. Then she covered it up with her hand. "Don't look at it."

"Did he hurt you?" My anger rose inside of me. I was suddenly flooded with memories of young warriors testing my will.

I destroyed their lives, and I would destroy anyone who hurt my sister!

"No." Camellia seemed alarmed by my reaction. "I liked it at first…But I stopped things before they went too far. I should never see him again."

"I don't understand." She was protecting him from my wrath, so he couldn't have been completely despicable. She seemed upset about the possibility of cutting things off, but she was ashamed of her mark. Nothing I had ever read was that complicated. "Is he terrible?"

"No. He was actually wonderful." She shrugged and smiled. I dare say there was a gleam of magic in her eye. "He made me laugh, and we went bowling. I had a nice day, but I know he wants more out of me than what I can give."

"What are you talking about, Camellia?" I felt the pang of anger again. If he took advantage of her in any way, he certainly wouldn't get the opportunity to do it again.

"I saw him help a little girl pick out a bowling ball. He was so kind and patient with her. I commented on his technique, and he said he had a big family and wanted one as well." Her voice began to break up as she struggled through her hysterical tears. "I can't bear children! None of us can except for you."

"That's not true," I insisted. I never saw any other pregnant women, but I was certain that was because the elders made them live in fear. "I permit you to have children. I don't care if it's forbidden."

"It's more than forbidden. It's impossible. You make it so." She hid her bitterness well from her face, but it came through her voice. "You emit pheromones to stop everyone else from producing."

I wasn't sure what to say. Clearly, I was the queen for a reason. If the elders didn't need me, they would get rid of me. They were probably anxious for my daughter to be born, so they could slaughter me as they slaughtered my mother. It made perfect sense, and Camellia spent more time with my mother than I ever did. She was probably privy to more secrets than I. "If I do, I assure you, it's unintentional."

"I know, but I still can't have a family with him." She tried to shrug it off like it didn't matter, but her tears were stronger than her façade of bravery and fell like rain down her cheeks. "Even if this weren't temporary, and if Thomas truly fell in love with me, I could never accept his love. It would be selfish. I can't give him what he needs."

I had no idea that I could hurt so many people without touching or knowing them. She couldn't have been the only subject to feel such a way. And if she were, then it was because she was the only woman who traveled outside of our colony. I exposed her to the potential of love. I broke her heart. "I'm so sorry."

"It's not your fault, sister." She wrapped her arms around me and squeezed. I ruined her chance at motherhood, and yet she felt compelled to comfort me. "You were born to be my queen, and I was born to serve you."

I held her for a little while, but I felt sick. I thought it was the guilt rising inside of me, but then it became a pain gnawing from the inside of my stomach. "I'm famished. Excuse me." I let her go and headed for the door in the kitchen that led down into the basement.

"I will cook you something."

"No. This is a different hunger…" I poured myself a glass of my royal nectar and sat on a countertop for a little while. I was different from all the other girls in my colony because I drank the royal nectar as a child. How could such a thing set us apart? And was there a way to change all of them or to change me? Was it too late to make a difference?

Or was it me who was ruining everything? Camellia was reluctant to find love. She was reluctant to join me at all. I exposed her to boys and opened her heart up to possibilities. Perhaps she would have been happier living at home on the island. She would have never known she wasn't happy.

Or would she?

"This is terrible."

"Rose?" Camellia hesitantly came down the stairs. I was glad she was always respectful toward me, but I didn't like that she was still afraid. "I can show you how to fix dinner if you'd like."

I smiled. She was wonderful not to hold a grudge, or at least hide it so well. "I would, but we were invited to dinner tonight. Austin wants us to go to his house."

"Will Noah be there?" she asked. cautiously.

I rolled my eyes. "Yes. We're just going as visitors, Camellia."

She was uneasy, but she wouldn't dare protest it. I would have never listened anyway. "It would be rude not to bring anything. We'll make something quick, like a salad or a fruit tray."

Camellia didn't really have to teach me how to make a fruit tray, but she did show me a couple of different cutting techniques. We had grapes, strawberries, apples, pineapples, raspberries, blueberries, cantaloupe, and watermelon. It was quite a glorious platter, especially the way Camellia arranged everything in a circular pattern. I was quite proud of it.

We wore beautiful sundresses. Camellia tried to cover her hickey with makeup, but she still felt embarrassed and wrapped a scarf around her neck. It was probably for the best. I called Mr. Jones to give us a ride, and I didn't want him to know that a man had touched Camellia. The elders were probably furious that she joined me. They would probably melt the flesh right off their bones if they found out I encouraged her to find love.

Mr. Jones seemed happy to see us when he came to our door, but when he saw Camellia's scarf, he glared slightly. "How have you two ladies been?"

"I doubt you don't already know," I snipped. The elders had warriors constantly watching. They were supposedly my protection, but I knew they would scoop me up and take me back home if they reported that I did anything too extreme. Going out with two boys was right on track for their agenda. They probably would have liked for me to consummate with twenty and be on my way.

"Why do you dislike humans?" I asked while riding in the limousine.

"They're violent, untrustworthy, selfish, and they hate anything that's not like them."

"That's not true." Noah and Austin weren't that way at all. Noah was kind and thoughtful. Austin might have been rude and arrogant, but he was loyal toward his cousin.

"You'll find out eventually," Jones said. "If those boys found out what you were, what you could do, and some of the things you've done, they'd never forgive you. They might report you to human scientists, and have you strung up in a lab somewhere until they can destroy the rest of us."

"They would never!" I imagined Austin would be impressed and amazed by what I was. Someone so adventurous had to be open to strange possibilities. Noah would be understanding and amazed. He thought I was an angel when he first saw me. He could easily accept and appreciate that I was something else.

"It's their way," he strongly insisted. "Your job is to replenish our society. Camellia's job is to serve—only to serve—your needs. The humans' job is to destroy. It's our nature, and we cannot fight our destiny when it's embedded in our DNA."

Jones had indeed said some alarming things. Camellia was probably terrified that she would be shipped back to the elders and punished. He hinted at knowing of her indiscretions, and she didn't make it better by rubbing her scarf. But he must have thought my journey to find true love was also a farce.

But if he truly thought there was nothing more to our lives, other than living, what was the point of our grand rise to power? "You think we deserve to destroy the humans?"

"I think if the humans had the same abilities and opportunities as us, we'd already be dead."

"If we destroy them, then we are no better."

"We're cleansing humanity because we are better. If the humans discovered us, they would purge us. They would pour fire from the sky until we were nothing but ash. At least our infiltration will join us all together. We will be united under your rule."

"My rule?" I almost laughed. My people were fed the elder's lies, and they loved fattening themselves on every fictitious word. I didn't rule them.

But that was something to consider much later. My priority was finding love and starting my own family. Everyone—especially the elders—agreed upon that.

"I'll call when we're ready," I told Jones after he parked in front of Austin's house. He was polite and got out of the car to open my door. "If I run into any problems, I'm sure some spy will inform you."

He smiled. "Have a good night, my queen."

I was incredibly nervous about coming to dinner. I wanted to see the boys, but since I wanted to especially see Austin, I thought it was best to avoid Noah and spare his feelings. But the only true way to spare them was to stay away from Austin. It sounded simple enough, but I would never know because I surely didn't want to try.

We knocked on the door, and Noah's beaming face was there to greet us in a manner of seconds. "Good evening, my dear ladies."

"Good evening." Camellia glanced at me with a small smile. I knew she would have preferred for me to be with a man of greater physical stature, but she obviously thought he had much better manners and, therefore, deserved me more than Austin.

"Good evening, Noah. I hope all is well." I would be kind and gracious to all my hosts, but I certainly had no intention of giving him any falsehood.

"I'm great. I'm glad you came over tonight." He stepped out of the way so Camellia and I could enter the deliciously smelling house. "Austin and I cooked dinner tonight."

Camellia seemed very excited, but I felt even more awkward. I considered whether I should have simply told Noah I didn't like him in that way, but it would have made our evening even more difficult to get through. It could wait until we were in private.

"Ladies," Austin came from around the corner with a cute smirk, "it's nice to see you both again."

I tried to avoid his eyes. I didn't want Noah or Austin to know how infatuated I had become, but I'm sure they could both sense it. If the radiant glow I emitted wasn't enough of a hint, my giddy smile certainly gave it away.

"Austin," Noah said, "why don't you show the girls where they can put their fruit tray?"

"Certainly." Austin motioned his head toward the dining room, and Camellia followed him. I didn't go after them. I didn't want Austin to think he had power over me.

"Allow me to escort you to the dining room." Noah reached out his hand for me to take.

I paused for a moment, but I decided following him couldn't have been too bad. "Lead the way."

Austin had a very lovely home. It was warm with many bright colors, and the walls were covered with pictures of Austin and Noah as children. As I looked at each one, their stories became clearer. Camellia and I might have been actual sisters, but they had a life together. They had a bond. I regretted I couldn't fill my own walls with pictures of skinned knees and camping trips, but it wasn't too late to live and make our lives together.

We walked in on Camellia laughing at something Austin said. When she noticed that I saw her enjoying the company of my rude potential, she silenced her mouth with a strawberry.

"Camellia," I beamed, "would you mind aiding Noah in the kitchen?"

"Certainly." She grabbed Noah's arm and allowed him to lead her away.

I leaned against the table as I watched Austin. He picked a few grapes from the tray and popped them into his mouth. I reached out to grab a slice of pineapple, but he decided to change it up, and our fingers collided. We both drew our hands away, and I giggled. I didn't know why I was so infatuated. It was intriguing how my mind and body reacted when he licked his finger to get the stickiness off. Why did I think something so foul and disgusting was attractive? "Do you like my fruit tray?"

"I do." He began to chuckle. "You don't cook a lot, do you?"

I became incredibly indignant and tensed up. "Why do you assume that?"

"You seem a little high-maintenance."

"I assure you that I'm not!" I had been through too much for him to make such an assumption about me.

"I bet you wouldn't last five minutes in the wilderness."

I walked around the table and faced him. He might have been able to surf better than me—for the moment—but I was stronger than him. I was faster than him. He was not, and never would be, tougher than me. "Put me to the test."

He grinned so smugly; I wanted to beat that right off of him. I could show him what I had done to the warriors who tried to show their superiority. It wouldn't be so easy for him to establish dominance, but displaying my real powers might have frightened him. I would allow him to live in his fictitious world. I found it adorable.

"I'm going camping next weekend. You and Camellia should come rough it out with my friends and me."

But just because I chose to let him be delusional didn't mean I lacked the desire for some measurable degree of satisfaction. "Challenge accepted."

"Cool. I'm going too." Noah and Camellia returned with a pot and a big bowl of Caesar salad. I really felt for Noah. He was so eager to be helpful, even desperate to please me.

"Noah," Austin pleaded, "in your condition—"

"I'll be fine," he seethed. Noah's eyes darted at me, and his frustration with his cousin doubled. "Don't embarrass me."

I certainly felt their tension. I almost wanted to grab Camellia and give the boys their privacy. But really, it only seemed like Noah was willing to fight. Austin seemed a bit dumbfounded.

Camellia cleared her throat. "You should try the meatballs. Noah made them himself."

"I'm impressed." I placed my hand on his shoulder, and that seemed to calm him down enough to begin dinner.

The boys were wonderful hosts. They lacked a certain finesse with plating, but if they were being honest about making everything from scratch, then they indeed had promise.

In the midst of my second helping of spaghetti, Camellia decided to make small talk. "So, where are your parents?"

"They took a vacation."

"Without the two of you?" It seemed absolutely appalling! I wanted Camellia to travel with me, and she exceeded my expectations as a companion. How could their parents expect to gain happiness without their loved ones?

Austin's eyes tried to make contact with his cousin, but Noah's were pointed down. "I insisted they went without us," Austin said.

"Why?"

Noah's eyes sank further until they were pointed at his twiddling thumbs in his lap. They were hiding something, but Noah couldn't even utter any excuses, other than mumbles.

"I had some things I needed to take care of." Austin nodded and smiled at his cousin. "Noah stayed with me."

Noah didn't speak a word of agreement, so I chose not to believe his lie. "That's noble of you." I thought I could guilt him into telling the truth, but all I did was make him more miserable.

"It's a shame that your parents aren't here," Camellia said to Austin. "It would be nice to see where you two come from." She looked dead at me. "I think you should know genetics before making any rash decisions."

"Decisions?" Austin asked with a cocked brow and chuckled. "Do you plan on breeding with us?"

I was in the middle of gulping water and began to choke violently. They all rushed to my side in a panic while I struggled for air. Austin patted me on the back hard, but Noah was too impatient. He wrapped his arms around me and squeezed. Neither of them was doing any good. I needed a moment—not a massive panic from my would-be heroes.

"I'm fine!" I pushed Noah away, but I felt the lingering touch of his arms around me. I assumed his intentions were noble, but by the way his face reddened, he certainly noticed touching my breasts. He even hid his hands behind his back to conceal his weapons of choice. He was so bashful, it was contagious.

Camellia hadn't noticed the encounter, but she was already angry anyway. "If either of you had any hopes of pursuing a medical degree, I suggest rethinking your life's ambitions."

"They were only trying to help." I cleared my throat and took my seat once again, as did everyone else. Everything was incredibly uneasy, though. "Camellia and I moved here to enjoy life. We want to explore, try new things, and meet new and interesting people."

"I can help with that," Austin said. "I know a lot of people and travel to a lot of interesting places. I'd love to be your guide."

"He doesn't know that much about culture," Noah said quickly. "Art, history, science—"

"They wanna have an adventure, not a nerdfest."

"These ladies wanna know about nature—"

"You barely like to go outside. You don't understand people or how the world works. How are they gonna have adventures with someone who only fantasizes about them from reading too many books?"

"I don't know. How are they supposed to have adventures with someone who's barely competent enough to read a map book?"

"Boys!" I was appalled. I suspected Austin was capable of being vicious—even though it seemed like he adored his cousin—but Noah was too sweet to say such things. "Perhaps Camellia and I should go until you both work out your issues."

"No, I'm sorry." Austin moaned and ran his fingers through his beautiful hair. "I don't know what got into me. I'm sorry."

"I am too." Noah couldn't even look at his cousin. "I swear, we're not this way. There's no dysfunction at all. Austin is my best friend."

Then, it all became clear. One of the warriors told me I produced a scent that made them all desire me. They could feel me when I came into a room. They were all polite in my presence, but I noticed as we all matured, there was a proper fire in their eyes. Even the frightened ones competed for my affections.

"I still think we should leave—"

"Not before I give you something!" Noah got up and rushed away. From the pounding, he probably ran up to his bedroom.

Austin impatiently tapped his finger on the table. He tried to fight off his combative nature, but it gnawed at his insides that Noah fetched something to impress me. He only seemed mildly irritated, and I made a silent wish that it wouldn't evolve into anything greater.

Noah returned to the living room with one hand behind his back. He meant it to be a total surprise, but I knew the scent of roses, and I caught a glimpse of the bouquet when he rounded the corner. However, I was baffled by the colors. "I made these for you."

He placed the bouquet in my hands, and I stared at it for a while. The roses had various shades of colors that blended from red to blue to green, and everything in between. It was odd but extremely beautiful. "How'd you do this?"

"It was a simple experiment I learned in school. You put white roses in multiple colored dyes, and it changes to match." He showed me the bottom of some stems split in two. "If you put them in two different colors, they mix. I figured since you liked flowers, you might enjoy this. I know it's simple, but—"

"It's wonderful."

He sheepishly smiled. "A rose for my Rose."

My heart leaped, and my face lit up like a bashful fool. "But you've given me at least a dozen."

"It's not much." He shrugged. "I'd give you the entire world if I could."

I didn't mean to be captivated by his simple gesture, but it was so thoughtful, it was impressive. Austin and I did possess natural chemistry that moved me, but if I only cared about that, I would have mated with one of my warriors. I was looking for a man to love, and it became clear that Noah was prematurely falling in love with me.

"That's sweet," Austin grinned, but his voice was bitter. "Did you want to surf tomorrow, Rose?"

"No," I said quickly. I had to give them space to clear their minds. I didn't want to rule their hearts with my unnatural advantage. "We'll reschedule."

"But you're not getting out of that camping trip." He crossed his arms stubbornly. "You're roughing it out with us."

I did want to experience camping, but not at the expense of Noah's feelings. "I might have to break our deal."

"But you promised—"

"Don't pressure her," Noah said.

Camellia glared at Austin as if she were ready to strike him. "Rose can decide to do whatever she wants to."

Austin was as arrogant and bold as usual, and true to form, he only addressed me with a cocky smirk. "I'll let you out of our deal if you play me in a game of basketball and win."

"What?" I was vaguely familiar with the sport, but I was confused as to why he thought such a proposition would be of any interest to me.

"How could she possibly beat you?" Noah whined.

"Challenge accepted!" I didn't mean to blurt out, but I was so outraged by Noah's doubt. I suppose Austin knew that about me, and I couldn't help but play right into his hands.

"Then follow me, princess."

Camellia tried to hit Austin as soon as his back turned, but I grabbed her hands and forced her to calm down. We followed Austin and Noah outside from a safe distance. "Do you know how to play basketball?" she asked quietly.

"I read a book on it once. You dribble and shoot. It's not more complicated than that." That's what I believed, and yet I was deeply impressed with Austin's skill as he dribbled the ball effortlessly through his legs. I hadn't played any sports. I hardly even walked long distances. Was it really wise of me to engage in such a battle?

"What is this going to accomplish?" Poor Noah. He lacked the common nature that I shared with Austin. He might not have been able to honestly compete.

"She's competitive." Austin threw the ball and laughed when I barely caught it in my chest. "She can't stand to lose."

I gripped the ball tight. "And I won't." I would not be made into a fool. If I could beat the elders my entire life, I could certainly win a physical game as a superior being.

"First to five wins. I'll even give you a free shot."

I looked at the rim in front of me. Austin was probably magnificent at every single physical activity, but he was a fool to underestimate me. If I could work quickly, then I could defeat him. I pushed the ball to the ground, and it bounced up too high, and I took a step back before it slammed me in my face. Austin laughed, but I ignored him. I caught the ball and was careful about using my strength. It felt incredibly unnatural dribbling, and Austin didn't make it any better by the way he laughed, but I stayed focused.

"Come on, princess."

I grunted and made a run for the basket. I nearly lost the ball, but I kept going. I had to keep pushing if I expected to dazzle Austin. I might not have had the impressive height of a basketball player, but I had great strength in my legs. Jumping up to the rim for a legendary slam dunk was child's play.

Camellia and Noah roared in praise and applauded. Even Austin was blown away and clapped in amazement at me. "Were you an Olympic jumper in another life?"

"It was nothing, really." I found a better rhythm with the ball. I figured I couldn't aim and shoot very well. I'd have to dunk it every time to win.

"Try it again," he warned.

I bounced the ball a few times and caught my breath. I had nothing to worry about. I just had to remain focused. I hurried for the basket again, but he removed the ball easily from my fingers. I turned around just in time to see Austin effortlessly score a point.

He gloated by swaying his face directly in front of mine. "Wasn't that pretty?"

I rolled my eyes and went after the ball. "You're not as impressive as me, but that was good." I had to rethink my strategy. If he could steal the ball so easily, then I would never get the chance to dunk. I dribbled with one hand and tried pushing him back with my other shoulder. He kept laughing out of amusement. I kept waiting for him to go after the ball, and I was so antsy about it! When I thought he was going in for the kill, I panicked and pushed him back, with too much of my strength, and sent him flying across the asphalt and right under the rim.

Noah and Camellia burst out into laughter. I wanted to, but I had to keep my head in the game long enough to jump right over my cocky friend to score another point.

"She's amazing!" Noah said in pure awe.

"She's magnificent." Camellia turned to Noah and smiled. "She's a leader—a warrior in her own right. She's used to strong men. If you can't prove you're strong, you don't stand a chance."

He gulped. I wasn't sure if it was right for Camellia to give him hope and a strategy.

As Austin got up, he hissed in pain. His arms were scratched and burned from skidding. I didn't mean to hurt him, but he didn't look like he minded all that much. "How are you so strong?"

"Maybe you're just not as tough as you thought."

Noah snickered quietly, but Camellia laughed loudly and obnoxiously. I chuckled at first, but I saw the pain he so nobly tried to mask.

"I think I've humiliated you enough."

"No, we'll finish our game. Despite fouling me badly, I will struggle through this unfair injury and completely dust you."

"But you'd win anyway…" I saw it in his eyes. He wasn't willing to lose, and he was going easy on me. I'd have to hurt him to win, and I didn't want to do that. "I concede to you."

I tried to touch his arm, but he pulled away. He didn't have to be tough. It was unfair that I pushed him, regardless of my superior strength. But despite what his bleeding arm told me, he was quite manly. "Please, go camping with me."

I smirked. "I figured by that display of skills, I won the right to back out of our deal."

A small grin threaded across his lips. "That's why I'm asking for your company." My heart grew still as he took my hands and gently kissed them. "Princess, please honor me with your presence."

My cheeks burned; I thought my entire head was bright red. My eyes darted to Noah, who looked more hurt than insane with rage. I wanted to spare his feelings, but I was having too many of my own. I almost felt nauseous and dizzy. How would I feel if his lips actually touched mine?

But I couldn't think about such things. "I told you already, I'm a queen." I pulled my hands from Austin. I couldn't allow him to hold such a power over me—not yet. "I'll think about it."

I did my best not to make eye contact with Noah. I grabbed Camellia's arm, and we both went inside the house to gather our things. I was so flustered that I splurged on what was left of the fruit tray while Camellia called our driver. I felt the boys watching me from the doorway, but I wouldn't turn around. I couldn't let Austin make things worse.

"Rose—"

"Goodnight, Austin." I couldn't let him take me. I wasn't ready. Camellia was right. We knew too little about him. What if I fell in love and didn't find out how awful he was until it was too late? I had to slow things down and stop my heart from singing; its vibrato was practically aching against my chest. "Noah, please walk me to the door."

We waited outside in silence for Mr. Jones. I never looked behind us to see if Austin was spying from a window or a cracked door. He was jealous that he couldn't give me a goodbye kiss. He didn't have a reason to be. Noah wasn't getting one either.

Mr. Jones appeared within ten minutes of being called. Camellia immediately entered the limo, but Noah shuffled in front of me to stall. "It was a weird night," he said.

I nodded and looked to the limo. I could either have that terribly awkward conversation with Noah, or I could make a run for it and leave him practically crying from worry about where we all stood.

But I was a queen, and Noah was not more intimidating than the elders. "I know that camping isn't your thing, but if I decide to go, I don't want you to think you're excluded. Austin and I are just friends. We're all just friends right now. Do you understand that?"

"I do, and I'm hoping I can change your mind about that very soon." With nothing left to lose, Noah took a deep breath of courage and quickly kissed my cheek. "Goodnight."

Noah rushed inside the house, hunched over. I think he was terrified to know how I genuinely felt about him. My answer might have broken his heart when I first walked into the house, but he left me feeling surprisingly confused. The touch of his lips was still on my cheek, and it made me strange—even happy. So many of my warriors desired me, so his affection wasn't anything new. However, I found his adoration flattering.

"Are you coming?" Camellia asked through the open window.

"Of course." I rubbed my cheek. I didn't want to remember what his radical hope and optimism felt like. I already knew what it was. If I didn't, I wouldn't have journeyed so far from home to find the love of my life. I didn't want to ponder how Noah and I might have been more similar than I imagined.

Chapter Eight

"Three days." Camellia and I walked down the street, enjoying frozen yogurt on a blazing hot day. We tried not to talk about my complications with boys, but we hadn't developed many hobbies yet besides shopping, and we were on our way to take care of that current obsession. But she couldn't exactly stay silent.

"Three days is not a long time, Camellia. Let's not think about it."

"You have to consider which boy you want. You have to return to the colony sometime, and hopefully, you'll have enough seeds to replenish the colony until the next queen."

I adored my sister, but I hated it when Camellia reminded me that she was another product of our environment and bound to the ways of tradition. I didn't like tradition at all. "I'm returning to the colony with a husband, Camellia. Everything about the colony is going to change."

"What will the elders think?"

"I don't care." I laughed and became so excited. "Maybe I'll fire them, and my king and I will have supreme rule." I looked to my sister to share my happiness, but she was offended. "Why are you looking at me so strangely?"

She didn't want to speak. I noticed Camellia had a lot more bite to her personality than when we first met, but her eyes told me she was still frightened. But she liked to speak, so she spoke anyway. "I would say that sounds like treason, except you're the queen." She shrugged and threw her hands up. "I'm not sure what to make of all this."

To say I felt a sting from her betrayal was an understatement. If I lashed out at her, I would stunt her process of becoming an individual, and she'd remain exactly who the elders wanted her to be, but how could I not respond? "I'm your queen and your sister. You should be faithful toward me. If you only knew what the elders have tried to do to me—"

"What have they done?"

There was fury in my face. It was difficult living, every day of my life, with the burden of what they made me do to my mother. They made me a monster among my people, and the elders were believed to be righteous in all they did. If I could have destroyed them the same way I did my mother, their corpses would already be nourishment for the soil. But she wouldn't understand what I went through. It was my burden. "It's nothing I wish to discuss on the sidewalk, on the way to buy more bikinis, Camellia."

I tried to walk away from her, but she grabbed my arm. She let me go as soon as our eyes made contact. She swallowed hard and pressed through. "You mentioned it. I want to know."

I looked around. I didn't want the humans to know about what we were. I thought the whole world would stop so they could listen, but they didn't miss a beat and continued bustling about in their own private worlds. I was going to use their eavesdropping as an excuse to hold off, but I was in charge anyway. I didn't need an excuse. "Not now, Camellia."

She held her tongue and followed me inside the bikini shop. The same sales associate lit up as we entered. "Hi, ladies! What can I do for you today?"

I noticed there was a boy behind her, leaning up against the wall and reading a magazine. His eyes darted up toward us, and a small smirk came to his face. He dove his eyes back into the magazine.

"We can handle ourselves, thank you."

They had a greater variety than last time. There still weren't any one-pieces, but I did find a blue and white set that had thicker straps. "I'll get this for when I surf. I was afraid that my top would come off in the water right in front of Austin."

There was a laugh in my voice, and it irritated my dear sister. "Well, if you plan on having any more surfing lessons, you should probably go camping with him."

"Do you want me to go camping with Austin?" I was baffled. I don't think Camellia hated him, but she was giving it some effort.

"I think it'll be an interesting experience, to say the least. I think if you do, it's a bigger step than you want to admit. I think you're going to end up with him." She seemed less than impressed with that outcome. "If you want anything different, you'll have to make an effort to stay away from him. I see his heart in your eyes."

I tried to resist the oncoming smile. It was no fun if she didn't share my enthusiasm, but it still came on full force. I could practically feel Austin in every pore. I felt his energy when we surfed together in the water. He had such passion for life, and yet he was so careless and free. I fought for everything I had, yet I truly had nothing to show for it. I needed his freedom. "Do you think Austin would make a good king?"

She took a moment and answered carefully. "I think he and Noah would both rise to any occasion for you." I wondered if Camellia spoke so carefully to spare my feelings, or if it was to avoid my wrath.

Our cheerful fashionista disappeared into the back room when we were ready to check out, so the young man enjoying his magazine decided to take a go at it. "Can we get your address?"

"For what purpose?" Camellia asked.

"We keep track of our customers. We mail coupons, promotions, and rewards out all the time. It looks like we didn't get your address last time, so—"

"Certainly." I had Camellia fill out a form, so we could hurry along. We talked about going out to dinner, so we visited other stores and picked out some dazzling dresses and shoes. When we couldn't decide between two, we bought them both. We left the hard decisions for later at home.

When we returned, we laid out all the dress options on my bed. There were six in total that I considered. None of them was down to my knees. I ruled out a red dress that was too short. I ruled out a purple dress because it was long-sleeved, and I thought it would be too hot. I ruled out the white one because I was afraid of getting it dirty, and then the gold because I thought it was too flashy. Then I was down to a black and blue dress. The blue dress had one shoulder, and the black one didn't have any. I thought it might have been too scandalous, but I held it against my body and stared in the mirror anyway.

"I think you'll look amazing in that," Camellia said from the doorway.

"Thank you." I swayed my hips happily as I stared at my reflection. I was suddenly so excited about going out. I made a secret wish to myself that Austin would join us, but I didn't need him to have an amazing night. I think I just wanted him to see me.

Camellia stayed in the doorway silently until I noticed she was uncomfortable. "I still want to know what you stopped yourself from saying earlier."

I hoped she would forget. Oh, well. I tossed the dress back on the bed and focused my eyes on a spot on the ceiling. "You were afraid of me. Terrified. You would tremble in my presence, and I knew good and well that you had more than enough reason to." I smiled sadly and decided I was too brave not to face her. "What were the rumors you heard?"

The fear in her eyes seemed just as strong as on our first day. I thought she had grown bold, but Camellia barely gathered enough courage to speak. "That you killed everyone who displeased you. Many fear you, and they fear their deaths."

I needed her to understand it wasn't my fault. I may have been a monster, but I was not the villain! "The elders wanted me to produce heirs as soon as I was old enough. They sent me warriors and told them not to leave my room until I was impregnated. I wasn't ready, but they were determined to use force and go against my will."

I took a step forward, and I think it took everything within her not to run away screaming. All she did was flinch and draw her hand back when I reached out for her, but I was quick to grab on. "And then what?"

"I discovered I could suck the life-force from their bodies."

Her eyes widened, and in a quick gasp, all her breath was gone. I let her hand go, so she wouldn't be afraid.

"It made me stronger than them all, so now the elders leave me be. They agreed to let me leave the colony because they want me to mate, not because they care about me. I—"

"What happened to our mother?"

I shouldn't have hesitated. I thought about it every day. I knew sooner or later, I would have to confess. I only hoped that when I exposed myself, I would also be able to expose the elders as well.

"Tell me what happened!" she screamed with tears in her eyes. I loved my mother, but I forgot that Camellia truly knew her.

"When I became of age..." My hands felt warm and wet. I could smell her scent in my nose. I could feel her life on my tongue. "They stabbed her right in front of me, and then I accidentally took what was left of her life-force."

"No…" She grabbed her head and dropped to her knees.

"From that day, I've been trying to live my life on her terms like she wanted me to! I'm trying to honor her memory."

"You killed her…?"

I dropped to my knees and grabbed her shoulders. She sobbed in such pain. "Camellia, it was an accident. I think all queens do this when they come of age. Mother tried to spare me from it. She tried to make me normal, but she didn't have enough time." I hugged her in my chest. I didn't want to see her eyes, in case they imprisoned me with shame.

"Rose…" She pulled away, and our eyes slowly met. "One day, you'll have a daughter, and she'll kill her mother just as you killed ours, and so on?"

I had an odd sense of relief and lightly laughed, but it became a burst of pain. I held Camellia's face, and our heads touched as we sobbed together. After I ruined her so, she was still scared to lose me. I don't think I had ever been afraid to die, but I never had anyone to leave behind. "I want to change everything, Camellia. That won't happen to me." I was determined to survive. I was going to have a family, and Camellia was a part of it!

"I need space and time to think." Camellia pushed until I let her go. She rushed out of the room, and I did my best to respect her wishes. I could give her an hour. I could give her the night. If canceling our dinner would mend our relationship, then how could I deny that? But when I heard loud thumping down the stairs, I rushed out of my room to catch her just before she walked out the door.

"Camellia?" I ran down to her. She had a stuffed duffel bag hanging from her neck. Either she packed remarkably fast, or she always planned to leave me when she was too afraid. "Are you returning to the colony?"

"I don't know." She gripped onto her strap and looked down at her feet. "I'm going to stay with Thomas tonight and see how I feel."

I glanced at the scarf wrapped around her neck. "Are you sure that's wise? What about temptation?" She was so upset about a hickey. How was she going to handle something more?

She shrugged her shoulders and then glared at me. "I've lived through your temptation of sucking my life. I think I can avoid his temptation of me as well."

My chest ached. I couldn't even breathe for a few agonizing seconds. Our time together had been brief, but we had a connection. I thought my sister knew me. "I was never going to hurt you."

"Not as long as you have your royal nectar. If it ran out, could you trust yourself around me? Could you trust yourself around anyone?"

I wanted to tell her she didn't have to be scared. I wanted to tell her I would never hurt anyone I loved, but then I remembered my mother. "Take care of yourself, Camellia."

She nodded slowly, awkwardly, and with great hesitation. She turned the knob on the front door handle, but she had to stop herself before she left. "Do you think you can handle yourself?"

I was greatly disappointed. I was hoping she had seen the error of her ways. "I wanted to be alone in the beginning. I'll be fine."

Her lip quivered, and her face instantly reddened. Wasn't that what she wanted to hear? She was the one leaving me. I was a queen! Was she expecting me to beg? Never! "Goodbye."

And then, she left me. I backed away slowly until I reached the couch. I forced myself not to cry. I was strong. I might have been surrounded by servants my entire life, but I was truly alone anyway. I could survive a few days without Camellia.

I sat in my garden for a while and concentrated on the scent of the flowers, the fresh air, and the warmth of the sun. Everything in nature required a balance. When it rained, the world was replenished. When it was warm enough, the water would return to the sky and wait to replenish the earth again. Too much water could kill everything. A storm would leave destruction in its wake, but when it was over, new life would replace the old. That's how it was with people. Humans died, and more humans were born. All life was a cycle. I only hoped that when it was my time to come to an end, I had produced something to keep my legacy going.

I couldn't get distracted. I might have hated the elders, but we all agreed that I had a mission to perform. I couldn't waste time when it came to love, so I dialed my cellphone to Austin's house.

"Hello?"

My heart trembled. "Hi, Noah. Is Austin there?" I tried not to be too obvious, but I obviously was.

"No. He's out with Laura."

"Laura?" Even without all the details, my heart was torn out and replaced with inexplicable rage. I didn't know how to take such angry hurt. I tried to catch my breath and compose myself, but it was difficult.

"Yeah..." He paused for a long while. "He didn't tell you about—?"

"I don't need to know!" I couldn't hear about Austin's betrayal. It was far too great. I had to move on from him. "I was supposed to go out with Camellia, but she opted to eat dinner with her boyfriend. I'd like some company tonight. Do you mind? I'll take care of all the expenses myself."

"Are you asking me to be your date then?" There was fear and uncertainty in his voice.

We both had that in common. "Noah—"

"I'd love to!" He laughed nervously. "You won't regret this."

Again, I found his admiration of me charming, and I felt more relaxed with the whole scenario. "I'll pick you up at eight."

I hung up the phone and went upstairs to get dressed. Camellia took the flatiron, so I tried to wear my hair in a bun, but I couldn't get it to form in any way that I liked. A ponytail wasn't proper with my dress, so I just decided to brush it well and wear it down and flat. I recalled how Camellia would do my makeup. My skin was smooth and without any blemishes, so I didn't use foundation. My only real trouble was that my mascara got on my eyelids, and I put on a little too much blush, but it was nothing tissue couldn't fix. I already missed Camellia's final approval to boost my confidence. I looked good, but I could have done something better.

Mr. Jones was waiting for me when I got outside. When he noticed I was without Camellia, his brow raised, and a tiny smirk curved on his face. I was instantly irritated with him, but I did need him.

"Is Camellia coming out?" he asked as if it weren't a question at all.

"No." I slammed the door and looked through the window. I wasn't in the mood for his gloating.

"Is she not feeling well—?"

"She's spending some time with her boyfriend," I snapped.

Through the rearview mirror, I saw the anger fume up in his face. He did speak calmly, though. "She's not going to engage in intercourse, is she?"

I rolled my eyes. "You're all biting your nails in anxiousness to see if I will whore around California, and she's not allowed to find a commitment with someone she genuinely cares for?"

"That's not Camellia's purpose—"

"Our purpose in life is to find our own purpose. No one can tell you who you are. I am her queen. I can tell her what to do, but not even I have the authority to control her heart and will." I had to somehow protect Camellia from the colony spies. I seethed my next words as threateningly as possible. "Let her be."

Mr. Jones didn't say another peep, and that's exactly how I preferred it. He might have been my loyal servant, but he might as well have been my enemy. He couldn't respect my choices.

But Mr. Jones was pleased to take me to a boy's house. I think he was displeased when he saw the small stature of Noah, but he still knew better than to speak a word when Noah got inside the car.

"This is really nice..." His voice quivered, and he sat as far away as possible in the car. The poor boy was terrified of me. I knew by the way he was with me that he was a virgin. I thought if he knew he wasn't alone, he'd be less nervous.

"I'm a virgin as well."

He did a triple take, each time looking more confused and embarrassed. "Excuse me?"

"I'm a virgin." Even with poor human etiquette, I realized how absolutely awkward the situation became. "It's because I choose to be."

"I figured that. You're so beautiful..." Noah turned bright red before looking out the window. "I imagine you have guys beating down your door."

I looked out the window miserably as I reflected on my past and the many men I had to kill. "You have no idea..." I turned to Noah, who slowly nodded uncomfortably. "I don't mean to sound like I'm full of myself—"

"You don't!" He threw his head back and sighed in frustration at how socially ridiculous he was. "Why'd you even tell me that? Do you not want to be a virgin...?"

I instinctively pressed my legs together and pulled my dress down a little further. "For the meantime, I will remain. I want to be celibate until I'm married. I want to fall in love first. I want to be committed."

"That's wonderful." Noah's eyes widened when he realized how insincere he sounded. "I mean, I used to kind of think like that—"

"Used to?"

"Well...I'm not a man-whore!" He laughed hysterically. "Obviously, I'm not a man-whore if you know I'm a virgin." He narrowed his eyes at me and looked puzzled. "Wait, how do you know I'm a virgin?"

"Lucky guess." I chuckled. He was so odd, and I felt like I could relate in some way. "Don't change the subject, though."

He tapped his fingers on the window. I didn't like that he found such difficulty forming his thoughts, but I suppose I did put him in a terrible position. "I could wait if a girl wanted to wait, but if she didn't want to wait, I'd be okay with..." He caught himself and cleared his throat to stop smirking. "...going all the way..."

Noah was so red in his face, and after reading my facial expression, that didn't make him feel any less complicated. I don't know how he read me, but I wasn't upset. I understood males needed to breed. I'd feel it too, eventually.

Then, he finally exploded. "This is such an awkward conversation, especially since I know you like my cousin more than me!"

"Noah—"

"But he's slept with just about every girlfriend he's ever had," he mumbled.

I felt a sting in my heart. We were supposed to have a connection, and yet he was out with some human floozy. "Including Laura?"

Noah was silent for a couple of seconds, but then eventually rubbed the temples of his head and sighed again. "No. You misunderstood. Laura is his agent. Austin has a lot of professional athletic dreams, and she believes in him."

My mouth dropped. "You misled me."

"Not really." He bobbed his head from side-to-side. "I mean, I thought you might have taken it the wrong way, but...I didn't lie to you, Rose."

I crossed my arms and leaned back into my seat. "I didn't think you could be devious."

"Well, I can surprise you in more ways than one." He gave me a little, cute smirk.

I cocked my brow. "Is this the part where you tell me you're a serial killer?"

"I meant that I'd like to surprise you in a positive way!" He laughed nervously again. "I know I'm a horrible flirt—"

"You are."

"But I like you." Noah was surprised by his bravery. I was surprised as well, but I did enjoy his confidence. "I know you like Austin—and he's into you too—but I want a fair shake in this. All I'm asking for is a shot."

I could tell he and Austin were related before. They had the same shapes in their noses and eyes, but I realized they had the same look when they knew something completely. "Something tells me you're not usually so bold."

Noah shrugged, and all that confidence sank into his shoulders. "All I have is today. Not everyone is fortunate enough to have a future. If I can't ever have one, then when I'm in my final moments, with my life flashing before my eyes, I'd like to stay in the ones spent with you." Noah's eyes fell into his lap as his voice trailed off. "Maybe God would let me stay there. Maybe that could be my heaven…"

I couldn't respond. My mind was a swirling motion that all seemed to circulate back to his eyes.

"I'm sorry." He slapped his hands against his face. "That sounded like a really bad line, didn't it?"

"No." My heartbeat traded for a faster tempo. "Maybe, but it was quite swoon-worthy."

Our eyes locked, and I gave him an opportune moment to change everything between us. I did love how strong Austin was, and it did bother me how weak Noah seemed, but it wasn't terrible to be vulnerable. I used to believe in the silly things he said. I loved them. I even relied on them. My harsh reality forced me to live as a wicked witch in the eyes of my people. I had to be fearless, strong, and even frightening. But Noah made me realize that I wanted someone to treat me like a princess.

"I didn't even think about what just came out of my mouth," he spoke amazed. "I guess it's all the books I read. I'm a horrible, cheesy, creep."

"You're not." I knew Noah was too socially awkward to take his chance, so I reached across the seat and touched his warm hand. Then, he genuinely looked confused as to what he should do next. But that was fine. We needed to go one step at a time. "I think you deserve a fair shot."

From the smile on his face, you'd think he just found a treasure chest as big as Japan. I didn't know how to break his moment of ecstasy, but I didn't want to either. Maybe he desperately needed his moment. I think we all do sometimes.

Mr. Jones drove us to a restaurant with quite an intimate setting. There was a long line of people standing just to get in, and half of the restaurant was outside on a giant terrace. But it was decorated beautifully with small lights that made it seem like the stars were dwelling with us on earth, and there was a wonderful view of the beach from afar.

"Wow. This is a really nice place." Noah tugged on his tie. I thought he was dressed appropriately. He had on a pair of black slacks, a baby blue long-sleeved shirt, and a black vest to match his pants. "I don't want to sound rude, but can you afford it?"

"I can." I bypassed everyone and went right to the male greeter.

He smiled and bowed as soon as he recognized me. "Follow me, Ms. Queen."

Noah was stunned, but he didn't question and followed me inside. When I told Mr. Jones about my dinner plans, he assured me arrangements would be made to make me feel like a queen. One of the hosts led us out to the terrace and gave us a table right on the edge of the balcony.

Noah picked up a menu and glanced at a couple of items, but I noticed that something was bothering him. "I don't feel comfortable with you paying. I'm the man on this date. I'm supposed to be the provider."

"Or perhaps you're my trophy boyfriend."

He jerked his neck back. "What place in what contest did you get to deserve me?"

"I can't tell if you think highly or poorly of yourself."

"I'm undecided," he mumbled.

I didn't like that he was so unsure of himself. Why would he fight so hard to convince me he was my best choice if he thought so low of himself? Did he think I was also low and deserved less? "What do you think of me, Noah?"

"I think the world of you!" he said quickly and perhaps a little too loudly. Then, he calmed down. "You're gorgeous—obviously. I love the way you carry yourself. You're so regal, like real royalty. You have a certain glow and aura about you that makes me feel unlike anything I've ever experienced."

So, I was right after all. My powers could affect humans. I was making Noah and Austin fall in love with me. It would only get worse over time. One was bound to be hurt.

Noah rubbed his chest and knitted his brows together. He also broke out into a sweat. I wondered if I was somehow making him sick. "Are you alright?"

"Yeah," he lied. "I'm alright."

"Really?" If I were making him sick with desire, then I needed to get as far away as possible. "Are you sure you don't need to go home?"

"No. I'm okay. I just need to go to the bathroom." He got up and rushed away. I saw him pace one way and then turn around. Then, he finally asked a waiter and found the bathroom. He was such a special creature, and I wasn't sure if that was a compliment or not.

At that point in time, I was sure I still preferred Austin. I was doing my best to be open to Noah, but it didn't make any sense as to why I was complicating my life. I could only marry one boy. I could only try to have one king. Noah was sweet and loving, and my people needed to experience that. However, I needed someone who could stand up to the elders. Austin would do that.

But Austin wasn't exactly perfect. He might not have been dating Laura, but I didn't doubt that he had commitment issues. With my powers, that might not have been a problem, but I wanted real dedication. He was very competitive and passionate, but maybe too relaxed about important things. If he weren't assertive in leading, then he was going to be passed over.

I wanted a revolution for my people. I was learning so much while living with Camellia. If there were a way I could help my people live their own lives, and if I could give them the chance to find love and create their own families, I would feel like I truly accomplished something. The elders believed we were better than humans, and yet I craved their lives. At least they were free. It was too bad they had no idea we planned on wiping them out one day. If it weren't in my rule, it was likely to be my descendants.

Noah was missing for a few minutes. I took the liberty of ordering Noah water with lemon, and when he returned, he certainly looked like he could have used it. He was completely flushed of color and exhausted. He guzzled down the drink and took a moment to catch his breath.

"Noah, what's wrong?"

"Nothing." As much as he wanted to dismiss it, he recognized my slight glare would not allow him to drop it. "I'm not feeling well tonight."

I felt as if I were a burden. "Then why did you agree to this date?"

"Because I never thought I'd get another chance to date you. I had to seize the moment." He clenched his fist as a demonstration of his seriousness, but he lacked conviction.

"You're not used to this whole 'seize the moment' and 'live for today' thing, are you?"

"I have a different perspective now." He tapped his glass and stared at the slowly melting ice.

"And why is that? What exactly changed your life?"

His eyes collided with mine. "The fact that mine is ending."

My chest suddenly ached. "What do you mean?"

"I'm very sick, Rose." He smiled sadly and continued to tap on the glass. We both stared at each small ripple he created with the slightest effort. "That's why Austin and I didn't go on vacation with his parents. I didn't feel up to going, but they spent so much money on it already. Austin begged them to go, and he agreed to stay and watch over me."

"That's very admirable of him." I knew Austin had a kind heart. It was strange when the two of them bickered in front of me at dinner, but I couldn't hold them accountable for something I influenced them to do.

I knew that it was tough for Noah to see me spending time with Austin. That's why when he talked about Austin positively, it made me care about both of them more. "He's always taken care of me. After I was diagnosed, he sacrificed a lot for me.

"He lives life to the fullest, and I always lived so carefully." His eyes had a special gleam of pride in them, and his smile was infectious. "I've been a coward with no voice. Now, I want to be a part of the world. I want people to remember that I lived in it. The end of my life became my beginning."

"Then let's make it memorable."

We ordered everything that interested us. We had a taste of a fancy chicken and dumpling soup, Caesar salad, the juiciest steak I ever had, the most succulent lobster, crab cakes, and chocolate cheesecake that made me moan inappropriately. We ate until we couldn't possibly stuff any more food in our mouths.

After dinner, we went down to the beach and walked barefoot along the shore. I thought about trying to convince him to surf with me. I knew he would have given it his best effort, but it seemed wrong. It was something special I shared with Austin, and I was scared to overexert him. Besides, it was nice. Dare I say, it was even romantic! The moon was full, his hand was soft, and he did look quite handsome.

"You've got a little food baby going on there." He reached over and patted my stomach.

"I can't believe you just said that! A girl does not want to hear such things."

"I think it's cute." He pointed to his tiny gut that used to be nonexistent. "We made these food babies together!"

I laughed, but I felt so uneasy. I could sense his fear. "Are you afraid of never having children?"

"I guess."

"I think about children all of the time."

He smirked. "You've got baby fever?"

"Bad." I noticed his nose scrunched up. "I'm too young, aren't I?"

"Well, you're on a biological clock. I guess I am too."

He didn't know the half of it. My window of opportunity to mate was only until I was twenty-one. I could have had babies until I was dust, but that was only if I had already consummated by then. After I mated, I could decide when I was going to have a baby. I bet a lot of humans wished they had such an ability, but I was at a disadvantage. How many young men wanted to settle down at the age of eighteen or around that?

I knew I could get Austin to have sex with me, but he probably didn't expect repercussions, and popping out around six kids was definitely a big one. Noah wanted something to leave behind. What was a greater legacy than that of his blood? I could give him an heir if I really wanted to.

But then I wouldn't have a king.

"Uh-oh."

"Uh-oh?" I asked. "What's wrong?"

"We've gotta get out of here." Noah pulled on my hand and led me away from the beach. We briskly walked away, and then we ran.

"Shouldn't I know what we're running from?"

"Austin was surfing and…"

I stopped and pulled my hand away. "Did he see us?"

"I don't know." He was really out of breath and pale. Maybe he was even a little hurt by how fast I withdrew from him. "I think I should get home."

I nodded. We had eaten and talked. We had a late-night stroll on the beach. That was enough for a proper date. Since I met the requirements of a fair shot, we could go home. If I wanted to dump Noah right there and then, I was allowed to do that. He couldn't complain.

"Take me home first," I commanded Mr. Jones.

"Yes, ma'am."

Noah dug his fingers into his thighs and tried not to look at me, but he stared like a stalker. I hoped it would be a short and quiet journey, but he couldn't contain himself. "Will we have another date?"

"I don't know." He made me feel wonderful, but I still liked Austin. I had to figure some things out before I strung Noah along. Noah's illness complicated everything. He couldn't be my king, but I wanted to be there for him. I wanted to make him happy until the end. My judgment was compromised.

"I freaked you out, didn't I?" He threw his head back and collapsed into the seat. "What girl wants to live her life with a dead man?"

"You're not a dead man, and I'm not freaked out, Noah. I need to figure some things out. You know that I have feelings for Austin—"

"But do you have feelings for me?"

"I don't know what I feel." My stomach was all in knots. Noah made me feel half of the right way, I guess. Things felt pure and honest with him. I didn't feel safe like he was my protector, but I suppose I didn't need one. I was still missing fire. Not everything had to be about passion, but I needed some excitement in my life.

When we pulled up to my house, Noah stared at it for a while in awe. I don't know why. It wasn't that much grander than his home. Perhaps it was the fact that it was mine. "Can I walk you to the door?"

"Sure." Mr. Jones got out of the car so he could open up my door, but Noah made sure to rush out, so he could run to the other side and help me to my feet. I took his hand and smiled uncomfortably, and I'm sure he knew how uneasy I suddenly was.

I had the revelation that Noah was being more than a gentleman when he offered to walk me to the door. He showed classic signs of being a pig when he waited for something else to happen. Why would I invite him in for something to drink or eat? We stuffed ourselves past the point of gluttony. He would have just mentioned if he had to pee. "I guess this is goodnight."

"Yes," I assured. He was not getting inside my house and bumbling through a seduction plan. It was never going to happen.

But he wasn't budging. Then, I noticed his eyes never fell on the door. His eyes were glued directly to my lips.

I blushed. I had never kissed anyone willingly before. Noah was in no way smooth. I didn't have anything to be nervous about. If it were absolutely horrid, I'm sure he wouldn't tell anyone about it. Wouldn't it be both of our faults if it were bad? Could it be just me? Could it be no one's fault?

I realized how deeply I was thinking about it. Was it because I admired his deep optimism? We were connected in that sense. I wanted to find love, and he wanted to experience it before he passed on. What if I couldn't fulfill my dream? What if he never got the chance either?

The next thing I knew, our lips were touching. I committed as much as I knew how to, but it lacked a certain spark. His lips felt nice, but nothing evolved on my part. It wasn't terrible, but it also wasn't anything else.

When I backed away from Noah, not even he looked happy about it. "Was that a pity kiss?"

No wonder why he didn't indulge himself. He must have felt like such a victim, and I had no right to do that. But one way or another, we needed to know if we could continue. "Does it matter?"

A slow smirk formed on his lips. "Not right now." Then, the shy and quiet boy, who was afraid to sit next to me in the car, grabbed the back of my neck and pulled me in for a kiss. Our lips were parted, and after a few seconds, I could taste Noah's lips and his tongue. It was strange. But when it was over, I felt good. It was all very…special?

Noah was no good after that and became a smiling mess. "That was my first kiss."

"It was mine too." I touched my mouth. I couldn't believe what I had just done, and I certainly couldn't believe I had just done it with Noah. When our lips touched, that was pity. When he crashed into me, it was pure desperation. It was wrong, and I didn't know if my heart was pounding because it should have never happened or because it did.

"I hope that's not our only first," he muttered.

"Noah!" I lightly punched his chest. He tried too hard to sound like one of those Playboys. I understood Noah had urges like any other man, but he was not a pig. "We have to take things one step at a time. I still like Austin—"

"I'm not pressuring you to be exclusive—"

"Are you seriously encouraging a love triangle? No point of the triangle is supposed to encourage the triangle!" I didn't want to do that to the two of them. They were blood-related, and they deeply loved each other. What decent person would voluntarily get in the way of that? I didn't think I was that self-centered.

Noah shook his head. He looked like a sad puppy, and I thought it was adorable. "I wish you didn't like him, but if you need time for me to woo you, then I'll just have to improvise."

I crossed my arms. "And what if Austin demands I never see you again? Or what if I tear you two apart?"

"You're just a girl," Noah said. "We can survive you."

I took a deep breath and tried not to be offended. "And what if Austin wants us to be exclusive?"

Noah snickered and had the confidence to walk with a little bounce in his step back to the car. "Mention that word to Austin and see if he doesn't turn blue in the face."

Noah was willing to commit to me immediately, but he wasn't long-term because he was dying. Would Austin be unable to promise himself to me, even though he had a full life to live?

My fairytale was certainly a lot more complicated than I imagined. But if Noah was giving me permission to figure things out, then I planned to do exactly that. I was going on that camping trip with Austin, and by the time I came back to the real world, I was going to know exactly who I would choose.

Chapter Nine

My hunger woke me up early in the morning by gnawing on my stomach like a starving and vicious bear. Any normal human would have had a tummy hangover from all the food I consumed the night prior, but mine felt empty. I guess that's what happens when you consume the life-force of twenty-plus warriors and your mother.

I grabbed a glass of my royal nectar and headed up the basement steps. I was going to drink my nectar while I enjoyed reading the newspaper. I took a seat on the couch, but someone rang my doorbell before I could take a sip. I rushed to the door, thinking that Camellia was returning home. I didn't even think to look through the peephole or question the person's identity.

When the door opened, Austin barged right through. "You're coming camping with me."

I blinked in shock a few times before closing the door. I faced him with the full wrath of my irritation. "You are not allowed to just barge in here! How dare you—"

"I know. It was rude of me. I'm rude, right? I know. Camellia hates me; you don't know why you like me, yadda, yadda. I need you to come with me."

I crossed my arms and smirked deviously. I was tormenting him, and instead of ending his suffering, I decided to fester his wounds. "Why?"

He looked at me with a tight and determined jaw. I waited anxiously for his grand speech, but then he threw his hands up in the air and whined like a child. "I don't know!"

I laughed as I sympathetically patted his shoulder. "Sure, you do." Feeling confident that Austin was a slave to my whims, I strutted around the room. "You're afraid that if I don't go, Noah won't go, and the two of us will get closer."

"I'm not intimidated by my cousin." He spoke as if he thought what I said was a joke, but he marched in front of me as if he were angry. "I just don't get why you're dating him if you've got feelings for me."

I wondered if Noah told him everything or if Austin just knew because…well, it was obvious. Even with him standing over me, we could feel each other pulling. He even began to smirk adorably, and I couldn't help but blush. "If we were going to date, would we be exclusive?"

He took a step back and looked amazed. "What sort of person did Noah paint me to be?"

"I'm not stupid!" I was offended that he was trying to be coy. He seemed like the type to bounce around. "You must have enjoyed the company of a couple of different women."

"Oh!" he said loudly, "and am I to believe that…" His tone quickly changed from seeing the brightness in my cheeks. "Oh, my! You never have, have you?"

Why did he and his cousin have to make things so incredibly awkward? I couldn't even look at him while he gazed at me like some sort of outcast! "I'm not embarrassed, so don't try to embarrass me."

"I'm not trying to make you feel embarrassed. It's cool that you're a virgin. I wouldn't pressure you. I'm not one of those guys. I'm just…" He shrugged. "Casual."

"Casual?" I understood he wasn't a pig or wouldn't overstep my boundaries, but he was still unsettling. "It's not casual to me. It's life and love. I couldn't give my virginity to someone who failed to realize how precious my purity is to me."

"I get it." He was still uncomfortable, but I saw his heart through his eyes. He was opening his mind up to the idea, or I at least tricked myself into the idea that he was. "I'm not ready to settle down or anything, but we could be exclusive. I can't even think about other girls when I'm around you. It's like you confuse me or something."

I cocked my brow. "Is that supposed to be a compliment?"

"It's reality." It was my ability playing tricks on his mind, wasn't it? Was it wrong of me to take advantage of him, knowing good and well that I didn't want him to take advantage of me? I could keep him from tempting himself with other women—and perhaps even myself—but there I was, willing to at least indulge myself, just a little bit.

"Excuse me!" I realized I was nowhere near ready for my first kiss with Austin. I hurried upstairs to my bedroom and changed into a pair of blue jean shorts and a white tank top with a giant butterfly on it. I wished I could have picked out something sexier or more elegant, but I didn't want to keep him waiting. Then, I rushed to the bathroom and brushed my teeth. I couldn't kiss his lips with morning breath! He'd never want to kiss me again. I scrubbed my tongue and teeth until I felt squeaky clean. I brushed my hair, swiped some deodorant under my arms, and rushed to the stairs.

I took a deep breath to gather myself and walked down the steps in a slinky and sexy manner. "So, about this camping trip...?"

My legs felt as if they were trapped in a pit of tar, and they slowed until I was stuck on the middle step. The glass of royal nectar that I left on the coffee table was in Austin's hands. It was in the process of being set back down where it once was, but the contents of the glass were gone, and only a green stain remained. "What did you do?"

"Sorry." He set the glass down and wiped the residue from his lips. He appeared to be a bit dazed. "I was just curious about your protein shake. I took a little sip, but then it was so good—"

"You shouldn't have done that!" I ran down the stairs and picked up the glass in disbelief. I was desperate for myself to be delusional. A human drinking my royal elixir would have repercussions I couldn't even imagine. It made me different than all of my people. What if I somehow changed him? What would he change into?

"Sorry." I recognized the look in his eyes. He didn't understand how deep he was in, but he was addicted. "You should bottle that and sell it. It's really good."

I set the glass down and held my face in my hands for a while. I didn't know what I should do. He would crave the elixir. I didn't know to what lengths he would go to get it. Maybe it would be a taste that he'd never forget but could manage to live without. There was no way for me to tell. I just couldn't let him have any more ever again. "Do you feel strange?"

"Not in particular." He laughed nervously. "Why are you freaking out?"

"Because you're rude, disgusting, and a thief!" I punched him in the chest, and he rubbed the sore spot.

"But you'll come on this trip with me?" he asked.

He didn't deserve to be in my presence, but I was afraid of what would happen if I left him alone. What if he changed into a mindless follower like Mr. Jones, or what if he became an obsessive control monster like the elders? What if his body couldn't take any change, and he just died? "Fine."

"What about Camellia?"

If she had never left, Austin wouldn't have been in such a mess. "We got into a fight, and she left to live with her new boyfriend for a while."

He blinked hard in shock. "What happened? You two seem inseparable."

"Truth be told, we don't know each other that well." I took such a liking to Camellia that it was almost difficult to think of how my life was without her. I had nothing but my fading dreams and making the elders miserable. That was no life. "We came here to bond, but there are some things in my past that she had a hard time accepting."

"Whoa!" He touched the sides of his head. "My head is spinning. What kind of past does someone like you have?"

"It's none of your business." I very well couldn't tell him I sucked the life-force from my mother and had a taste for it ever since. That might have left him with some reservations regarding me and the future of our relationship. "Please, leave."

"Sorry about your shake. I'll buy you some more vegetables—"

"Go." I needed him to leave. I was already hungry, and I couldn't allow him to find out where I hid my elixir. The stash could only be mine, and mine alone.

Austin still seemed to be waiting for me to change my mind. I don't know if it was more elixir or my lips he wanted to taste, but he was unworthy of both. Another ten painfully-dragging seconds passed by, and then he walked to the front door and opened it. "I'll pick you up tomorrow at seven in the morning."

I nodded. I intensely watched Austin; I was surprised he could stand to leave without getting another glass. But my elixir satisfied me for a meal. Maybe a human like him would be quenched for days or even months. By the time he remembered the taste, maybe he would have forgotten where it came from.

Austin walked out of the house, but then he started to turn around to tell me something. I didn't care and slammed the door in his face. I didn't want to give him the opportunity to ask for another glass, and I was mad at him. He should have known better than to drink it in the first place!

My day alone in the house was uneventful, and it dragged on, kicking and screaming. I waited by my phone, thinking Noah was going to call me at any moment to inform me that something strange was happening to Austin, but that call never came.

I also waited by the phone in case I got a call from my sister. I didn't need her. I was certain that I didn't. I managed to make my own food. I got a lot of reading done. I took a long bath that I drew myself. I could survive without her.

However, I wanted her by my side. I liked sharing my hopes with my sister, and I wanted to experience the world with someone who cared about how it made me feel. I never had that until Camellia came into my life.

Before I went to sleep, I went to her room and sat in her bed for a while. She didn't have many possessions besides the clothes we bought together. I still couldn't believe she would choose to be in the presence of a stranger rather than be in mine. Did she truly fear her death, or was she simply angry at me for what I had done to our mother?

If Camellia couldn't understand, then how was Noah or Austin supposed to accept how and what I was? If they found out we were slowly infecting the entire human population, so a queen could one day rule them, wouldn't they feel betrayed? Wouldn't they want to stop me? They deserved to know the truth, but that would endanger all my people, and it was my job to protect them first and foremost. Love was a privilege I could only afford if it proved it wasn't a major inconvenience.

The day fell slowly, and the night didn't help either. I might have had four hours of straight sleep, and the rest of it came in short bursts. I wanted to hurry my camping trip with Austin along. If we could survive each other for a few days in the woods, with his cousin eyeing us with guilt-beaming eyes, I would believe we could make it through anything.

Bright and early, I got up and packed everything I thought I would need, including a cooler filled with bottles of my elixir. I had a lock on it, so Austin couldn't steal any from me again. I wouldn't have brought any with me at all, but I was afraid of what I was capable of without it.

Austin was true to his word and knocked on the door at seven. I wondered why he was on time for a camping trip but so late with other obligations in his life. It didn't matter. I was well-prepared when I let him in to grab my bags.

"Whoa, are you bringing all of this stuff?"

"What?" I only had the cooler and four bags. It didn't seem like a whole lot to me. What if I didn't like what I had on and needed to change?

He laughed to himself and shook his head. "Okay. We are going into the wilderness. It's not total and complete wilderness, but it's probably more than what your delicate heinie is used to. You do not need a bunch of clothes. You need shorts, T-shirts, underwear, a swimsuit, and supplies to keep you smelling nice. Everything else is nonessential, and you don't need it. Decide what you want to keep and what you want to leave behind."

"But how can I decide?"

I don't know why he laughed again. It was a serious question! "If we were running for our lives through a forest with an angry grizzly bear after us, what do you picture yourself running in that will keep you alive?"

I eliminated two bags instantly. I only had my casual clothes and another small bag that had my shampoo, soap, and other toiletries remaining.

"Thank you." He reached to grab my bag, but I pulled it away. "I know the self-proclaimed 'queen' is used to having people do things for her. I can carry your bag. It's not a big deal."

He certainly pegged me correctly, but I didn't want him to carry them, because he thought I was weak. "I can manage the weight. I got them down the stairs."

"I'm trying to be a gentleman."

I slightly glared but decided to trust in his word. He grabbed my bags, but I kept the cooler in my hands. Even when we packed everything up in the back seat, I put it in myself. He slightly glared at me with a ton of suspicion.

"We share food on this trip."

I had to just tell him, or he would have freaked out. "It's the drink you gulped down. It's not a shake. It's a medicine that I need to live."

"What do you mean?" he panicked. "Are you sick?"

"Not like Noah," I said quickly. "I'm healthy as long as I drink it. The ingredients are rare—priceless even—and it has side effects."

He tried not to look concerned. "What kind of side effects?"

I had no idea what to look for. My side effects made me able to procreate, keep other women in the colony from having children, and gave me the ability to control them whenever I decided to "call" them. But since he was a man, my only real concern was that he would start sucking the life out of people. "Have you noticed anything out of the ordinary?"

"No, but—"

"Then don't worry about it." I poked him hard in the chest. "And stay out of my stuff!"

Austin decided to leave it at that. He was probably very concerned and hoped nothing important fell off or shriveled up. Good. I needed him to stay away from my elixir. One glass might not have made a difference.

He opened the door to his van and introduced me to the group of boys who were all staring and studying me. "These are my buddies. That's Dylan, Skylar, and Pete. Of course, you know Noah." Austin's friends were all about his age. Dylan and Skylar both had shaggy hair and a sluggish wardrobe. Pete was dark-skinned and a little neater with his dress and hair, and he was buff while the other two were leaner. They all had attractive qualities, but Noah and Austin still looked the best.

I got inside and sat next to Noah in the middle seats since Austin was driving, and Pete was in the front passenger seat. Skylar and Dylan sat in the back. "I'm glad you decided to come along."

Noah struggled to hide his blush.

Skylar stroked his chin and smirked while he observed me closely. "Austin wasn't kidding when he said you were smoking hot!"

Austin's eyes bucked through the rearview mirror, so I knew it was true and giggled. "What else has he said about me?"

"Don't listen to another word these idiots tell you," he said. "You know that I know you're hot, so let's leave it at that."

I was very amused. If they were anything like Austin, I expected to have a lot of fun. "Are you all extreme surfer types?"

"We like to surf," said Dylan, "but we're not as extreme as Austin."

Pete turned around, excited to announce his passion. "We like to skateboard and free run."

"Free run?" I was unfamiliar with the term, even though I studied most human sports.

"It's when you just...go!" Skylar had a lazy speech to his words, but he spoke like he truly believed in every single one. "You flow through your surroundings in a fluid and continuous motion. The mind calculates what you need to do to make it to where you need to go, in the fastest way possible, and your body just listens. It's awesome."

It sounded very intriguing. "Do you free run?" I asked Austin. I was quite excited for him to show me something new, and I was certain I could best him with my superior strength.

"Sometimes," he said. "The more committed you are to the art, the better you are at it."

"Art?" Noah mocked quietly.

"Yes," Pete was incredibly irritated. "It's an art. It's a sport."

"I'm sorry if we have a difference of opinion," he mumbled.

"Cool it," Austin warned. "We have a couple of hours before we get to where we need to be."

Noah didn't really say anything. Austin and his friends did most of the talking, and they certainly were enthused about their sports. They talked about movies and some other things, but I didn't know any of the references. I listened and enjoyed their conversations, though. Noah was very quiet. He interjected a few things, but Austin's friends would get defensive or vice versa. He eventually stopped talking altogether until all of the conversations died down, and he wouldn't have to fight for my attention.

"Rose..." Noah pulled his backpack from underneath the seat, and he took out a thick book with a bouquet of roses on the cover. "I got you this book. I hope you like it."

My eyes instinctively darted upward into the rearview mirror, and Austin's eyes were there to greet me. Noah was incredibly quiet, the road was very loud, and the radio was playing rock music, but Austin knew that Noah was trying to show him up again.

I felt the engravings of the flowers on the hardcover before turning a couple of pages. There were pictures of flowers from all over the world and information on each one. The book even told the meaning of each flower and its significant history. There was a solid purple bookmark with a golden string sticking out from the pages, near the front of the book. I looked to Noah, and he urged me on with a small nod, so I turned to his page. There were quite a few pages on roses, but the one he had saved told the meaning behind their different colors and on what sort of occasions you would give one. I recalled the first day we met, and how precious Noah was when he stroked his chin and asked if my name meant "passionate love."

"What's so funny?"

I shook my head. I didn't want the other boys to hear my thoughts and tease us. "This is very nice, Noah. I just don't understand the occasion."

"You're always an occasion."

A rough hand came from behind and violently roughed up Noah's hair. "Isn't the little baby so sweet?"

"Lay off him." Austin seemed so restless. He probably wished he had sat next to me, but it was good that I was near Noah. I seemed to be his only ally. Perhaps Austin thought about that and allowed us to keep each other's company.

"So, what's your story?" Dylan asked.

I knew the cover story backward and forward, but it was strange telling it without Camellia. That only opened up the door for more questions, but I couldn't remake my world without her. "My sister and I are from a farming family that recently got rich by selling our land. We moved out here to discover ourselves and the world."

Pete nearly turned all the way around in his chair, amazed. "Really?"

"Rose is ready to settle down, get married, and have babies," Noah said with a smile. He was devious and tried to strike fear into their hearts. "She wants all of this now."

I can't say they lost interest, but I certainly noticed the apprehension. Dylan was even so bold as to ask: "Where's your sister?" He might have been curious about her whereabouts, merely because he was curious, but there was a particular smirk on his lips and a gleam in his eye that told me he anticipated she was also attractive.

"She didn't want to come along." I was trying not to think of her. I was afraid Camellia hated me. Who else did she have to blame for taking our mother? She didn't understand the elders and how awful they were. Only I knew the full extent of their cruelty.

"Why didn't she—?"

"That's enough questions about my personal life. I'm not in the mood to speak anymore." I shut my eyes and leaned on Noah. I figured if they believed I was trying to sleep, they would leave me be. I wasn't the least bit tired, though. Even if I were exhausted, I wouldn't have been able to sleep with Noah's heart pounding so loudly and quickly against his chest. Eventually, his beating heart returned to a normal pace, until his arm slowly landed around me. His heart truly became a rocket then. But eventually, he regained his control. I loved how shy he was. Was it possible that my powers made him fall in love with me so deeply? I couldn't believe that. There was too much sincerity within the rhythm of his heart.

We drove to a campsite in the mountains. There were other families parked in the area when we arrived, but they had big campers like little homes on wheels. When we parked, we grabbed our things and prepared to move. "Are we not camping in one of those things?"

Austin laughed. "No. We brought tents. We're gonna sleep in the mountains."

He pointed up the trail, and my eyes followed. I was intimidated by the climb, but I noticed Noah attempted to mask his concern. I wanted to enjoy my trip and prove myself to Austin, and I didn't know how well I could do that while worrying about Noah.

Dylan wrapped his arms around mine and Austin's neck. "Five boys and one seriously hot hottie. What shall we do with ourselves?"

Austin smiled in excitement. "I can think of a couple of things."

I was the only one who packed a duffel bag instead of a backpack. Austin and every other boy offered to carry it for me, but I held it firmly in my hands. I would not let them treat me like a little damsel. I wanted the same respect they showed each other, so I had to properly earn my keep.

We hiked up the trail. I stayed by Noah's side. I didn't want him to be left behind. He was the least physically fit out of all of us, and he always wanted to stop and take pictures at every little thing he saw. I couldn't blame him. The land was decorated in vivid greens, and the sky was bright to bless our journey. I had seen a lot of trees from where I lived, but I never explored the land. I never left my palace much.

The higher we went up, the thinner the air became. I tried not to think of Noah being inferior, but Austin kept looking back and slowing down. Eventually, he just stopped and turned around. "Are you alright, Noah?"

"I can keep up." He lightly panted, and he was flushed with color.

"We can slow down."

"I can keep up!" He stubbornly continued to walk and purposely brushed by Austin with his shoulder. But before he got ahead, he seethed to his cousin, "Don't embarrass me."

Austin's friends snickered and marveled at Noah's behavior, and how he "dissed" Austin. I couldn't properly judge the situation. I didn't know what it was like to die.

Austin caught up with Noah and pleaded with him. "I'm not trying to embarrass you. I just want to help."

Noah wouldn't listen and pushed his legs until he was a good distance ahead of all of us, but that didn't last too long, and once again, we two were lagging behind the rest of the group. I knew he hated it, but he didn't have to be so angry.

"You should be nicer to your cousin."

Noah was firm and held onto his anger. "He only asked for me to come along because he wanted you to see how physically inferior I am."

"Or perhaps he didn't want you to be alone in the house." Perhaps, subconsciously, Austin might have wanted to prove something, but I don't think he seriously plotted against his cousin. He was terribly arrogant. He might have been annoyed that I was also interested in Noah, but he didn't think he was serious competition.

"I'm not a child!" he snapped. "I can take care of myself. I told you that I've been camping before."

"But you're ill and—"

He stepped in front of me and looked me dead in the eye. "I don't need you babying me either, Rose."

I felt his desperate need to be treated like a real person. In a way, it wasn't fair. He didn't want us to treat him with pity because he was dying, but he wanted us to act like it was all right for him to do anything, to live his life to the fullest until his end. How was I supposed to find balance with such extremes?

"Okay." I was at least going to try to respect his wishes. I suppose I was no different from him. I wanted freedom from the burden of my title, and yet I wanted the respect that my title offered. Perhaps people were incapable of equality because no one truly wanted to be treated totally fair.

Austin led us to a small clearing in the forest and threw down his backpack. "Let's camp here."

I looked around. There wasn't even a bathroom around for miles. I was quickly beginning to regret my decision, but I kept my mouth shut. I was going to endure and prove that I was capable.

"Are you going to cook us anything, sweetheart?" Pete asked with a smile that he mistook for charming.

"Excuse me—?"

"We'll cook our own food," Austin interjected quickly. "I've got some hot dogs for lunch. You guys can start setting up camp. I'll take Noah and Rose to look for firewood."

I did give Pete a good glare, but that was the end of the confrontation. We listened to our leader and performed our tasks. Noah, Austin, and I weren't that far from each other while we picked up our sticks and logs, but Noah tried to be separate from us. He needed time.

"Did you like your book?" Austin finally asked after several minutes of silence.

"I did." I was amused by his jealousy, even though he was so nonchalant about it. "There's an easy way to get over the fact that your cousin is buying me presents to impress me."

"Which is?"

I perked my head up. "You could also buy me presents!"

He narrowed his eyes. "Are you encouraging us to get into a bidding war for you, because that sounds a little bit like prostitution to me."

I scoffed in utter and complete disgust before punching him. "Why, I've never heard such a degrading thing in all my life!"

I didn't mean to hit him so hard, but I knocked all the wood right out of his arms. "Ouch!" He rubbed the sore spot. "Jeez, princess, you've got a mean jab there."

I rolled my eyes to cover up my super strength by demeaning his pride. "Don't be such a baby. Real men wouldn't complain."

"I didn't technically complain. That was a compliment."

I didn't want to fall all over myself when it came to him, but he was so cute when he grinned like he already knew I was falling for him. I couldn't let him be in control! "And stop calling me 'princess.' I find it demeaning."

He threw his hands up and looked to the sky for answers. "Who would find that 'demeaning'?"

"A queen."

He gazed at me, and I knew I had managed to impress him again. "You are truly full of yourself."

"Who else should I be full of?"

Austin broke out into a full smile, and it felt like the whole entire world made a sudden stop. I didn't understand why everything changed, but the entire universe shattered underneath our feet, and we were the only ones left standing, and I had absolutely no idea why.

"What?"

He turned his head away and laughed quietly to himself.

"Why are you laughing?"

"Nothing." Austin's eyes darted at me, but I searched out his gaze until he caved. "Sometimes, I wonder why I like you, and if you're worth all of this trouble. Then, you say things like that and…" He shrugged. "I'm just into you. I like that passion."

I smiled. "Passionate love…" I spoke quietly to myself.

He smirked like a scoundrel and began closing in for a kiss. "If you wanna call it that—"

"No." I pushed on his chest. I was not going to kiss him with his cousin near, or if the moment wasn't absolutely perfect. It definitely felt like a nice moment, but it wasn't the right time. "Noah asked me what my name meant when we first met, and that was one of the options. I didn't answer his question."

"That's because you hadn't met me yet."

I tried to brush him off, but I blushed very hard. I wished Noah had made me feel the way Austin did. Austin made me want him with very little effort at all. It was just another example of how life wasn't fair.

"Is this enough?" Noah came and stood close enough to make us uncomfortable, so Austin and I stepped away from each other.

"No need to be coy." Noah was visibly jealous, but he was trying his best to be casual about it. "We're competing for you. It's out in the open, so don't get quiet on my account."

I looked to Austin, and he didn't know what to do. "I don't want to be rude."

"It was rude to go surfing with Austin after our first date."

"You had no claim over me, Noah. You didn't then, and you certainly don't now. Neither of you do!" I didn't want to be so dramatic, but my feelings flared up so fast that I threw the wood down and rushed off. Noah acknowledged that I had feelings for Austin and invited the competition, so I wouldn't brush him off. They could have made a pact and refused me, but neither of them wanted that. Whatever decision I made, they had to respect it. I hated that I didn't know what I wanted. I hated that they were related. I hated everything about the situation. It was not fun having my heart pulled in two different directions, and I didn't appreciate Noah treating me like I was a cruel puppeteer orchestrating their suffering.

I went back to our campsite, and the boys tried to say something to me, but I rushed by them until I found a proper tree to climb. I had never climbed one before, but I certainly had the strength to accomplish such a thing. I lost my footing once or twice, but I was able to make it up a nice, sturdy branch.

I sat up there for a while and wondered about my dear sister, Camellia. She didn't want me to date both of them. She just wanted me to make a decision. If I had to make a quick one, I would probably choose Austin. I didn't want it to be that simple, though. Noah begged me not to make it so. He had so much to persevere through, and I guess I didn't want to add heartbreak to the list. Was it right to string him along? Noah didn't want me to treat him differently for being sick, and yet he was depending on it.

It was all so very confusing!

"Hey!" Noah called from below. "We've got hot dogs if you're hungry."

I never had one before, but I was hungry for something. I would have to hold off on my elixir until I could get some time alone in my tent. "I'm coming down." I would have jumped, but I knew Noah would have made it into such a big deal. Even after I finished climbing, he looked at me in awe. "What?"

"It's just really cool you can climb like that."

I hadn't realized I did anything that spectacular. "Squirrels can climb trees. If you're so impressed with that, I'd hate to see how you overreact to a bird in flight."

"Well, if you start flying, I'll make sure to really overreact." Noah smiled and hoped he would infect me, but I still wasn't in the mood. Then, he pouted like a pup. "I'm sorry for acting like a jerk."

"You're not acting like a jerk. You're acting like a spoiled child. You can't have everything both ways, Noah. Do you want me to figure out my heart, or do you want me to jump to conclusions?"

"I don't wanna rush you." He scratched his head and looked down at our feet. He was such a child. "In some ways, this is the hardest thing I've ever had to do."

But I was entertaining a child. I was closer to his age than Austin's, but I stopped being a child the day I killed my mother and took her place as queen. I could be patient with him, but only if he could learn to be patient with me. "You two can fight for me. I'm flattered—honored even. But the day you two start fighting over me, that's when neither of you can have me."

He gulped, and that didn't inspire confidence. "I understand."

"Good." I didn't believe a word of it, though. They might have been the best of friends and like brothers, before I showed up, but I was working on their nerves. I had a genuine fear that sooner or later, I was going to break them, and it would be an all-out war.

Chapter Ten

Pete and Dylan might have pressed on my nerves, but with the help of Skylar, they set up quite a nice place for me to sleep. My tent was pretty spacious. I could even stand up in it, and there was enough space for a queen-sized blow-up mattress. I didn't think to bring any of those things. It was a good thing Austin considered my needs.

Skylar, Dylan, and Pete were sharing a tent while Austin and Noah shared one. I hoped the two of them would be alright at the end of the night. I didn't want them to suffocate each other with their pillows. But I was grateful I didn't have to share any space with the boys. They'd never leave me to my thoughts. Besides, I needed my privacy, so I could drink my elixir in peace. It fueled me with enough strength to face the group and handle whatever afternoon plans the boys had.

Pete was putting out the fire that we used to cook hot dogs. Austin and Skylar were missing. Noah was sitting on a rock and enjoying a good book. Dylan decided to be annoying and snatched it out of his hands like a pestering child. Noah went on the attack and tried to get it back, but Dylan was very quick for a human, and Noah tired easily. I came up from behind and snatched the book from Dylan. "Seriously?"

Dylan leaned in close to my ear. "You're no fun."

"That's because you're not amusing." I handed the book back to Noah.

"Thank you." He seemed too unsatisfied to be grateful.

"I love books as well, but we should be enjoying our surroundings."

"That's what I was trying to get the little runt to do!" Dylan placed his hand on Noah's shoulder and squeezed. "Ain't that right?"

Noah brushed his hand away. "Do people pay you to be this obnoxious?"

"I've gotta make a living somehow." He winked at me, and I instantly felt nauseated.

Thankfully, Austin and Skylar emerged from the woods carrying more firewood. We quickly found out that we didn't collect enough. "We should catch some fish for dinner."

"That sounds fascinating!" I had read many stories about fishing, and many settlers and ancient civilizations wouldn't have been able to survive without knowing such a prominent skill. "I'd like to see that transpire."

"I'll show you," Austin said. "But are you ready for your first thrill?"

That's exactly what I was looking for. "Certainly."

"Then change into your swimsuit, and we'll be off!"

I was still shy about wearing a swimsuit, and I felt odd knowing that my pheromones would be working on all the boys. But if any of Austin's friends overstepped their boundaries, they were going to end up as my breakfast!

With that assurance in my mind, I changed into the new bikini that I was saving for surfing with Austin. I emerged from my tent shy, but I received a grin of approval from Pete that was enough of a confidence boost. I would have liked to be indignant about their glances, but the reality of the situation was that I was gazing myself. Pete's body was impressive. He was fit like some of my strongest warriors. Austin's body was the next nicest. Skylar and Dylan had abs showing, but they were small. Noah came out of his tent with a T-shirt and shorts. I knew he couldn't have had anything to be embarrassed about. He didn't need to be ashamed of his body.

We went to a lake that was against a high cliff with several giant rocks bulging out. As soon as I saw the crystal blue water and the look on Austin's face, I knew what they were going to ask of me. Dylan, Skylar, and Pete didn't even wait to announce their plans. They just started climbing the rocks and fearlessly dove in.

"That looks fun!" The elders would never let me do such a thing. I wished they could have been there to complain just before I dove in.

"It also looks dangerous," Noah nagged. I suppose I could have hit my head against a rock, but all of Austin's friends came back up perfectly fine, and they prepped themselves to do it once more.

"Live on the edge a little bit!" Austin was practically begging me to join in on the fun.

I really wanted to, but I looked at Noah. I figured he wasn't going to jump in. I didn't want him to be the only one left out of the fun. "I'm okay."

Austin moaned in frustration but then ran off to join his friends. It was like they didn't require any thought when they moved. They were like little monkeys, and then they jumped and flipped like professional acrobats. It was so graceful and raw, and I so badly wanted to be like them. Instead, I sat on the ground and watched like a coward with Noah.

"You don't have to sit this out on my account," he said.

I couldn't believe he would get up the nerve to fight so hard for me, but he couldn't overcome a little bit of height. "Why doesn't this fit into your 'live your life to the fullest' tour?"

"I guess, besides when I push past the pain in my joints and climb up the rocks, I wonder if I'll be able to jump far enough from all of the rocks piled up near the bottom of the cliff, and land into a part deep enough to be safe."

I understood all of that, and it made perfect sense, but I was still itching to try it for myself. How hard could it be if Austin and all of his friends could do it continuously? I was very tempted to just leave Noah alone to his fear, but I didn't want to be talking about how great the experience was near the campfire, and for him not to have anything to say.

I wished Camellia were there. I felt like a part of me would always be losing out on something if she weren't near, and I didn't want him to be left out either. "Try it with me. Please. I promise we'll be safe."

"And if we're not?"

"We'll die together."

I don't know why he suddenly perked up, and his chest got a little bigger, but I had given him some sort of boost. He stood up and dusted the dirt off his trunks. "Okay."

He offered me his hand, and I held on tight, so he wouldn't let any doubt enter his mind. Even when Skylar, Dylan, and Pete saw me holding onto Noah's hand and began to snicker, I wouldn't let go. Even when I saw the disheartened look on Austin's face, I still wouldn't let go. I didn't set Noah's hand free until we climbed up the rocks together.

The other boys were climbing up about twenty-five feet above the water. I thought ten was enough to get us started. There was a rock big enough to be a ledge for both of us. I waited patiently while Noah struggled to make it over to our diving ledge. I reached out to help him when I felt like he wasn't going to quite make it. That little bit of exercise was strenuous for him. I hoped I wasn't pushing him too hard. He was terrified, and so was Austin. He could put his life on the line, but he clearly couldn't watch anyone else do it.

"Are you ready?" I latched onto his sweaty palm. "We can do this together."

He gulped and gave me a very slow and extremely hesitant nod.

"On three." I shook myself. I didn't know why I was suddenly nervous. I had superior strength! I would be fine.

"You can do it!" Skylar yelled. "Come on, Noah!"

"Yeah, Noah!" Even Dylan chimed along, which caused a cheer from the rest of them. Austin was still deathly afraid, but he did show his support and yelled for his cousin.

"One...two..." I looked at Noah. I think he was begging me to never get to that number. His lips were quivering. I wanted to hug him and be motherly, but I wouldn't let him be a baby. Camellia told him once that I needed a warrior, and I needed him to be strong if he wanted to truly be on my radar. There was no going back. "Three!"

We jumped together, and I screamed in excitement, and Noah screamed like a little girl. In the midst of the fall, I began to laugh at him, and before I knew it, I had a mouth full of water. I never lost Noah, because his hand was gripping so tightly onto mine. But there was a moment when we were both under that we saw each other, and Noah had such a wide and infectious smile on his face. He let out a cheerful scream underneath, and I laughed, but we both had to quickly rise to the surface after that. Noah coughed for a while, and Austin nearly jumped in to save us.

"I'm okay," Noah said. "I'm okay..." I really hoped I hadn't ruined him the way Austin ruined me, but I could once again see the resemblance between Noah and Austin, and that wasn't necessarily a good sign. "I think I wanna do that again."

Austin let out a big sigh of relief before becoming his usual self. "Rose, I bet I'll go higher than you!"

All our eyes were drawn to Austin as he dared to climb a little bit further up than the rest of us. He must have been up forty feet, and then he waved like the cocky jerk we all knew him to be.

"That's so dangerous..." Skylar seemed to be proud and terrified for him at the same time.

Was it really that dangerous? If his daredevil friends doubted their fearless leader, then perhaps I should have been terrified for him and gone up to stop him. "Austin!"

"Don't worry about me!" There was barely anything for him to hold onto as he climbed. He didn't have enough footing at that level for a proper dive. Was he really trying to impress me, or once again outdo me? He was going to die, and that fool was going to do it with a cute smile on his face. "I hope you're watching, Rose!"

"Austin, don't!" Noah screamed, but his idiot cousin paid no heed to any of our warnings, and he let go of the rocks and pushed himself as far away as possible. He didn't have any technique to his dive like all the other times. He was simply falling with his legs dangling and aiming toward the bottom. I wanted to cover my eyes from the horror, but it would be dishonorable not to witness his death after he had especially requested it.

We all rushed to the edge of the lake and waited for Austin to come back up. It seemed like an eternity, but he really came right back up, whooping and hollering with pure ecstasy. He was such a thrill-seeking junky! Then, he had the nerve to smirk at me. "Challenge!"

"Don't!" Noah latched onto my arm and was determined to tackle me if need be.

Austin was challenging me with his eyes, but he must have expected I had enough sense not to go any higher than he did. There wasn't even that much footing where he had gone. He must have been incredibly strong and had an impressive grip to even get that high without any climbing gear. I didn't know so much about my grip, but I knew I was strong.

"I can't say no to a challenge..."

"You can't!" Noah grabbed my arms and stared into my eyes. "You will hurt yourself, Rose. This isn't a joke. You could die."

I bit my lip and thought about it. If Austin could do it, surely I could as well. Maybe I could go a little bit higher than him. I would survive, of course. Noah didn't know he was overreacting. But I couldn't let them know how powerful I was. "I won't jump."

"Too scared, princess?" Dylan mocked, and it sounded like Styrofoam pieces rubbing against each other, and pins prickling my skin.

"Don't screw with her." Austin pointed his finger angrily before breaking into laughter. "She's a 'queen.'"

"That's it!" I shook myself free, and Noah's arms fell away like limp pasta noodles. "I'm jumping."

Austin looked alarmed and chased after me as I walked to the rocks. "You don't have to prove anything."

I couldn't believe he would dare say such a thing. "When you challenge me, I have to prove my superiority. You know that I do." We were the same type of creature, two sides of the very same coin, a light to one's shadow, and everything else that would connect the two of us together. If I had provoked him, he would have done the same thing.

But since he provoked me, I had to take it further to a point where he wouldn't be able to compete with me. Getting up to about twenty-five feet wasn't that hard. Pushing myself to get to about forty feet, as he had done, was proving to be difficult. I was very cautious as to where I placed my feet. I didn't climb like a spider. I just didn't possess the skill. I might have been very strong, but I didn't know if I was invulnerable. Nothing ever got the chance to hurt me, but I knew I was not immortal.

"That's too high!" Noah screamed. "Rose, stop!"

Austin was terrified and rushed up the rocks as if he could stop me from doing what I needed to do to defeat him. That's when I decided to pick up the pace. "Don't do it!" he warned.

I was up about as high as he was, but that wasn't the end of his bet. I had to go up a little bit higher. I reached a rock that stuck out a little bit further than all the others. I thought I could use it as my ledge, but when I tried to step up higher, the rocks underneath my foot fell, and I slipped. I heard everyone yell in intense fear. I gasped, but I still held on tight to my new ledge.

"Stay there, Rose. I'm coming!"

"Don't bother." I pulled myself up. There wasn't enough of a ledge for me to sit, but once I climbed a little bit higher, I was able to rest my heels on the rocks.

"Please, don't," Austin begged. "I shouldn't have screwed with your emotions. I'm a rude jerk, and you don't have to take it for anything more than that."

I looked down at him for a few seconds. He wasn't that far, but he certainly couldn't stop me. He never expected that I'd do it. He didn't think anyone was as crazy as he was. Well, he was wrong. "See you down below."

"No!" I heard their screams as I jumped. My heart was racing a little bit faster than usual, but I was having the time of my life.

I crashed into the water, and it was different from before. It didn't hurt, but I really felt it. And then I came in so much harder and faster than before. My eyes were wide open, and I knew as soon as I was submerged that my feet were going to touch the bottom. By the time I moved my arms to try to swim out of the way, my feet had already pressed into the dirt. I was forced into a crouch, and I pushed myself up and flipped a few times. I was reminded of when I was submerged in the ocean. I was at the mercy of the water's depths, and now I was at the mercy of the fact that it was too shallow. I was able to stop myself, and I swam to the top. I gasped for air and feared that I had dislodged my spine, but I seemed to be okay.

The boys all cheered for me, but it was too soon to be celebrating. I shook out my legs to make sure nothing was broken. I felt completely fine. If I didn't have my increased strength, I would have probably broken myself. I was very shaken, but I didn't want the boys to know that.

"That was exhilarating!" I threw my hands up into the air, and they all cheered louder for me.

"Bow to the queen!" Skylar yelled.

"That was awesome!" Dylan roared and clapped so hard that his hands looked like they would explode.

Even the very cool Pete was clapping and whistling my praises.

My two love interests were silent, though. Noah was holding onto his chest, and the color hadn't returned to his face. I hoped he wasn't having a heart attack. And as far as Austin…

"I can do it too!" he proclaimed from the very top of the cliff that might have been higher than sixty feet above the water.

"Don't!" I screamed. If he stopped and thought about it, he should have figured out it wasn't deep enough to land safely. I couldn't tell them I hit the bottom of the lake in full force. They never would have believed me, and if they did, they would have rushed me to a hospital. "It's not deep enough. I was too close to the bottom. You'll hurt yourself, Austin!"

"No." He stubbornly shook his head. "I've gotta do it too."

Once again, there was screaming, and another stupid soul who couldn't stand for others to tell them what to do. He was going to kill himself because I couldn't bite my tongue and let him be on top. I couldn't bear to watch, so I covered my eyes and whimpered for his end.

Noah's arms wrapped around me, and I screamed for Austin's life. I just knew there was no way he was going to make it. But in a few seconds, there was a giant splash. I prepped myself to cry and completely mourn him. There was silence for a few more seconds, and then there was another splash and screams of glee.

I opened my eyes when Noah practically threw me to the side to chase after his cousin with the rest of Austin's friends. Even he was impressed enough to tackle him in manly congratulations. I couldn't encourage his behavior. It was dangerous, and I was baffled how he even survived without an injury.

After they finished roughhousing, Austin was practically strutting toward me with a proud smirk on his face. "How did you do that?"

"You basically did it, too. I just did it higher—like I said I would."

In a flash, my hand slapped right across his face. I would like to say that it was just a reflex born from my rage, but I had to think about it, so I didn't snap his neck. All the other boys gasped, but then there was silence from them as I breathed loudly, in through my nose and out of my mouth. That awful jerk worried me so much, and all he could do was smile about it as if his life were a big joke!

He didn't say a word to protest what I had done, though I had hurt him, and by the way he tensed up his face, I knew he was angry. He seemed to want to fight back, but he resisted with every ounce of restraint he had.

"You're impossible!" That was all I could think to say before rushing back to the camp, so I could be away from those fools.

They must not have all jumped from the top of the cliff since they came back alive later. Noah came to get me when they all decided to go fishing. I did want to learn how to catch a fish, but it turned out to be far more disgusting than I imagined. Of course, I had seen worms in my garden, but I certainly never picked one up!

The boys had a good laugh at my expense when I tried to put the worm on the hook. It was slimy, and I couldn't stop screaming about how it squirmed. Noah bonded with Austin's friends after proving he was willing to risk his life doing something idiotic, so I became the subject of their subjectivity. After I powered through their laughter, Pete showed me how to throw a cast, and then I waited. All the boys were much better at fishing than me. Noah caught two fish, but I had yet to get one when an hour passed by. I was stubborn and determined at first, but then my stomach started growling, and my mind was focused on other things.

The boys started a healthy competition to see who could catch the most. Austin caught two, but Noah had just gotten his third. Austin congratulated his cousin with a hardy pat on the back, and Noah relished the moment. It got me thinking about how I was stepping in between both of them. Noah said they would survive me, and I hoped it was true. If it weren't, then perhaps I should have just packed my bags and left to find another suitable mate.

But what would happen if I found someone else up to my standards? What would happen to Noah and Austin? One way or another, I was trying to take over their world. I didn't plan on being a conqueror, but that wasn't up to me either. My daughter had a destiny, and so would hers.

Was it possible for my people to live with humans in peace? I enjoyed all of them so far. They seemed very capable of controlling their own destinies, and I couldn't even decide who I wanted to date. But I was leaving an effect on humans, and I didn't necessarily know if it was a positive one. Austin could have died because of my antics.

Why didn't he, though? Was it because of my elixir? Did I somehow change him? If I did, then what was he changing into?

"You seem a little distracted," Noah said.

"Do I?"

"Yeah." He pointed to my tugging fishing line.

I was ecstatic and reeled in the line as quickly as possible. It was bad enough that all those boys were showing me up. I couldn't let myself be thrown into total and complete defeat! When I finally pulled it above the lake, I caught a minuscule being that only rewarded me with resounding laughter from my so-called friends.

I threw the line down and stomped away back to the campsite. Noah chased after me, but he was of no help. He was snickering! "What's got you all gloomy?"

I rolled my eyes. No one else would share my concerns. "I was worried about Austin when he jumped off that cliff. He's so reckless."

"He'll do anything to impress you."

"And you think he'll lie to me about being exclusive?" I asked with a cocked brow. I got the sense that Noah didn't one hundred percent trust that Austin would be kind with my heart. Perhaps somewhere among the pure selfishness of wanting me, there was also a desire to protect me.

"I don't know." He looked at a few rocks that he kicked along our path. "He always said lying took too much effort because then you'd have to remember all of the lies to protect your first lie. It's just not his style. He may make promises he can't keep, though."

Austin was quick to speak and to act. It was like his mind was already made up by the time he thought to ask anything. He would probably make many promises he couldn't keep, just like most men anyway.

"What do Austin's friends think of me?"

Noah chuckled. "I think they're ready to fight Austin for you."

I certainly didn't need any more fighting over me. I had enough complications with the cousins. "Did you tell Austin that we kissed?"

"I may have mentioned it when I got home from our date." Noah grinned very hard, but it faded once he realized I wasn't amused. "Are you embarrassed or something?"

"No..." Kissing Noah certainly wasn't like every book I had ever read, but it still felt nice. I enjoyed his company thoroughly, and once passion faded, it was important to like the person who remained. Emotionally, Noah made me feel perfectly adored, and his admiration was honest and pure. If I wanted a husband to undoubtedly love my children, I would have chosen him.

But I did have passion with Austin, and it was becoming too difficult to ignore the way he made me feel. My mind had many reservations, but my instincts were telling me just to go. We had a physical pull. The elders would have rooted for us to be together, so I could start creating children. "I think you should know that I may kiss him. I almost did."

I admired Noah for his effort in trying not to display how upset that made him. "I understand we're competing for you. I'll be happy with what you decide."

"Are you sure?" he looked like he was going to explode from panic. "You seem so angry sometimes with Austin, and I don't want to be the reason why you two are at odds."

"There are other reasons. Austin doesn't agree with my 'last hoorah' way of life. He thinks I should take care of myself and live longer, instead of giving up and making the most of what I have left." Noah looked at me. "Which do you think is better?"

"I wish I knew…" I wanted my freedom, and I was willing to do just about anything for it. I had a window of opportunity to find a mate, but Noah didn't have time. "I have some older relatives who believe I should behave a certain way. I disagree with them. That's really why I came out here."

"What do they want you to do?" he laughed. "It's not like you're prostituting yourself out or something. You're a good girl. They can trust you."

Being a "good girl" by human standards is exactly what they didn't want me to be, but I don't think it would have made sense to Noah if I explained my people expected me to whore around the planet. "They want me to marry someone I don't love."

Noah's eyes widened. "And you're trying to fall in love quickly with someone else to make them stop talking about it?"

"I guess you could say that." Everything was happening so quickly with Noah and Austin. Really, they were the first two boys I got to know. There must have been hundreds of suitable partners.

"Maybe you should take your time. You actually have some."

"It's more complicated than you understand." I did have a few years to mate, but the elders didn't want to give me that. They had their spies lurking around now. They'd try to take me back home kicking and screaming if I took a second longer than they expected. Of course, I'd kill every single one of them before that happened.

When we all returned to the campsite, we discovered Skylar had managed to catch four fish. He was so calm and still, and then the fish just came to him. I wished I had mastered his technique. Austin hated that he lost, but Noah didn't seem to mind so much.

I was still a little steamed at Austin, so I observed Noah as he skinned the fish. His technique was very precise, and he was quick. I didn't need a husband who could cook, but I did enjoy the thought of a loving husband bringing me breakfast in bed.

It was going to be such a shame for the world when he died. "What kind of disease do you have?"

"Lupus." He didn't miss a beat. He didn't stop performing his task to tell me with sad eyes. It was just plain, simple, and inevitable.

"Lupus?" I asked strangely. I remembered some reading on the subject. "Isn't that a girl's disease?"

Noah stabbed the tip of his knife into the cutting board and then looked at me, completely annoyed. "Yes. Nine out of ten people who have it are women, and most of them are women of color. I'm a white guy with lupus. It's strange, but statistics don't mean anything when you have the same symptoms."

"I'm sorry!" I was being completely inconsiderate. "Isn't it manageable?"

"Mine is serious." He took his knife and continued cutting through the fish. "I'm always sick. I've got heart problems. Everyone is always paranoid I'll get Pneumonia, or an infection, or something I can't shake. They want me to take medication, but they're not the ones with hair falling out! They should respect that I'd rather die happy than live with my body as a prison."

Noah finished his final piece and just sat and stared at the skinned fish for a while. I didn't know how to even describe the look in his eye. It gave me chills, but in a very haunting way.

"I can't imagine what you're going through, Noah." I lived in the most glorious prison possible, and it upset me every day. My only freedom was what I decided to do with my body. It was the only thing that was mine, and that's why it was so important that I gave it willingly to someone who would love and appreciate me. I suppose—in a way—it was my prison, but it was also my salvation and all I really had to fight for.

Noah and I were alike in that way as well. It was his body and his life. He should have been free to make his own decisions like I wanted to. But I didn't want to lose Noah prematurely. I cared far too much for him. "I can't tell you what the right call is, but all I can tell you is that I want you to fight because I'm selfish. That's why everyone wants you to fight. We don't want to lose you."

"And I don't wanna lose myself, so I'd rather let go." He rubbed his chest and leaned forward a bit. I had never noticed his gestures before, but Noah was always in pain or discomfort. Could I really fault him for making the best of his life and deciding to let go when it was his time? He had the right to take control of his life, didn't he?

"I'm kind of tired." He set the cutting board in my hands and then stood up. "I'm not gonna eat. I'll see you in the morning."

I wanted to stop him, so we could talk a little bit more, but to be truthful, I had absolutely no idea what I would say to such a boy in such a situation. "Goodnight."

Austin might have been enjoying the company of his friends around the campfire, but his eyes often wandered in my direction while I talked to Noah. He managed to catch Noah's departure to their tent, and he was puzzled and worried. I decided to walk over to Austin, so he could cook Noah's fish along with the others. "Here you are."

"Thanks."

I grabbed my folding chair and set it in an open space between Dylan and Skylar. I didn't want to squeeze next to Austin and make myself look desperate. "So, have you ever considered a career in extreme sports?" Dylan asked.

"I haven't considered any sort of sport, to be honest."

"Do you work out a lot?" Skylar asked. "You're fast, you're strong, you've got great endurance, you're competitive and fearless. You could probably do anything."

"Austin is teaching me how to surf." I couldn't even mention it without smiling. I couldn't wait to get back in the water.

Dylan smiled. "Well, I'm a better surfer than Austin so—"

"You are not!" Austin snapped.

"Hey, she's not married, so she's free rein!"

"You're so charming," I teased sarcastically. I'm not sure what Dylan could have possibly been thinking. He was certainly an entertaining person, but how could I choose him over Noah or Austin after acting so horridly? I wasn't a beach volleyball to be passed around. If he genuinely liked me, then he had to fight for my affection.

"We have a skateboarding competition in a few days." Pete was different. He had manners. "You should come and check out our skills. You'll also get the chance to see how incredibly lame Austin actually is."

"I can hold my own," Austin said.

I cocked my brow. "You did crash into me on a skateboard when we first met, correct?"

"Dude," Pete laughed, "that's a bad omen."

Dylan pointed his finger in Austin's face and laughed. "You're doomed to fail!"

"We're not doomed!" he insisted. He didn't like that I laughed along, but I didn't believe that either. I thought we had a pretty good chance of making it, despite the complications.

The food we had was very tasty and rustic. We had a hardy potato stew to go along with our fish, and since Noah didn't eat, there was plenty to go around. The boys were impressed with how much I could eat, and they thought it was a positive.

I wondered what my life would have been like if I had friends growing up. Austin and his friends were so close. They told me funny stories about their past, and they could finish each other's sentences as if their thoughts were connected. I only had Camellia, and she didn't know anything about me. The real me frightened her.

Things began to get strange when Dylan opened a cooler and grabbed a couple of beers. I read about alcohol. I knew about it in a common social venue, but I didn't understand, given the effects.

"Do you want one?" Dylan held a can up to my face. I took a good whiff of the beverage and was revolted by the smell.

"No, but thank you for asking." I didn't know what I would be like if I lost my inhibitions. Perhaps I would have been more fun. Maybe I would have started spitting out the secrets of my heritage and my people. That would endanger everything. Then there was my worst fear: that I would suck them dry accidentally. I couldn't afford to lose myself in such a way.

Things accelerated to a whole new level when my sweet Skylar pulled some sort of drug out of his pocket and lit it up. I knew it wasn't a cigarette, and I certainly wasn't comfortable with how the smoke felt in my lungs or the terrible smell. "Thanks for dinner, but I think I'm gonna retire for the night."

The boys looked disappointed, but I didn't care. I hurried off to my tent. It was best I separated from them anyway. I needed another glass of elixir, and I didn't need Austin foaming at the mouth as I devoured it.

I had a few minutes alone before I sensed Austin outside of my tent. He creepily paced around for another minute, like a stalker, before poking his head through the slit. "Hey."

I was reading a book, but I took my focus off it long enough to give him a good glare. "What's up?"

He shrugged sheepishly. He looked so much like Noah, but I didn't think he was so adorable. "Why did you leave?"

I shut my book and set it down. "Drugs and alcohol aren't really my scene."

He laughed, but he didn't look too amused. "I'm not gonna do drugs."

"But all of your friends do?" I could smell the smoke on his clothes, and I didn't like it at all. Noah said he didn't like lying, but he also said his cousin would tell me things to please me. "I don't buy it, Austin."

"You're overreacting. Just listen to me—"

"I need my space!" I saw him getting closer, so I snapped. I didn't know if I could trust him. I didn't need some drug addict ruling my people. "Leave me."

He crossed his arms and smirked. "I'm twenty-one. I'm allowed to drink."

I couldn't believe that he dared to burden me with his presence after I rejected him. "I don't want to be with someone who has impaired judgment."

Then he laughed and dared to take a seat next to me on my air mattress! "I didn't drink a single sip. I didn't smoke any joints. I'm clean."

I got close enough to smell his breath. Maybe he was telling the truth, but I didn't know if I could trust him. "Yeah, but you smell like weed. This whole entire mountain reeks of it now, so thanks for that."

He laughed again! Was he mocking my feelings? "It's not really my scene either."

"Oh, really?"

Austin nodded slowly, and he wasn't so smug anymore. "Noah tried something harder once because he was following my example and his 'last hooray' mentality. I was so pissed at him, but then I was pissed at myself." Clearly, Austin didn't exactly approve of Noah living for the moment, but I certainly couldn't tell if he would resort to such foolish tactics.

"And what about the other boys?"

"I don't judge my friends. They're good people. I just don't do it anymore. I can't..." He took a deep breath as his abundant shame overtook him. "I want Noah to look up to me. I know he does for certain reasons, but I want him to be proud because I'm a good man, not because I can ride a wave and get cute girls to talk to me."

"That's admirable of you." Obviously, he was a natural flirt, but Austin was trying to resist me for the sake of his cousin. I wondered if I didn't pursue them both (and if I were a normal girl), would he have left me alone? It certainly seemed like he loved Noah enough.

"I love how much you love him, but he feels like you're smothering him."

"He's dying. I don't know how close I'm supposed to be, or how far. No one knows how to deal with this. I'm doing the best I can." I hadn't noticed how emotionally affected Austin was by Noah's condition. I could see how terrified he was of losing him. I had never loved anyone like that in my life. I missed my mother and what she could have been to me, but I didn't know her. It must have been torture.

"I understand." I felt terrible. I didn't want Noah's last days to be filled with hatred toward Austin because of me. "Ever since I found out Noah was sick, I've been questioning things..."

"About us?"

"About everything." I pouted. I didn't want him to know how much he weighed on my mind. "Are you afraid that if we became romantic with one another, it would really hurt him? I want him to be happy. His idea of heaven is the time he spends with me. How am I supposed to deny a person like that?"

His eyes widened, and he turned away with a small smile. I thought he was going to laugh, but he seemed a little bit prideful. "It's hard to compete with that."

Then he shook his head. "No. I don't want to compete. I just…I wish I didn't like you this much!"

It surprised me how frustrated he was about it. The only resistance he demonstrated was the day he taught me how to surf, and I wouldn't even say his effort was that valiant. But maybe I was wrong. Perhaps he was fighting with everything he had.

"We've talked about you. We said we'd be happy for one another, no matter who you choose, but I think we're both full of crap." He laughed again, but he seemed so disappointed in himself and in the fact that he couldn't just do the right thing by his cousin.

I was being cruel. I had to try to give him some clarity. I had to help Austin realize he was under a spell of my pheromones. "Why do you like me so much? I'm just like any other girl—"

"You're really not," he insisted quickly with a dashing smile. He was gentle as his hands cupped my face and pulled me into his eyes. "Your spirit—that fire—it's the brightest thing I've ever seen. There's a lot about you that reminds me of myself, except you're the most perfect version. I think having you in my life would make me better."

I blushed radically and tried to hide my face. I had been praised before, but this was different. I felt unworthy of it all. Was I truly so spirited? I annoyed the elders, but it's not as if I started some sort of revolution. My people were trapped, and they didn't even know it. The only difference between us was that I could see my prison bars. "You think I'm perfect, but I feel like a songbird trapped in a cage."

A smirk curved on his face, and he leaned in closer to my lips. "Then allow me to free you."

I absolutely couldn't do what he was asking of me. Noah was a tent away, and my lips had touched his a few days ago. I tried to push up against Austin's chest to make him stop, but his hand landed on top of mine, and his heartbeat pulsed through my fingers and electrified my body. Somewhere amongst our electricity, my good sense was lost in his will to have me. His lips encountered my own, and it wasn't the awkward and inexperienced kiss that I had before. When I kissed Noah, I felt his innocence, sincerity, and also his desperation. In Austin's lips, I felt uncontrollable sparks that tingled my entire body, and it involuntarily made my hands feel on his muscular chest. Austin desired me, and it thrilled me how much I desired to have him.

Was that what love was supposed to feel like? My fairy tales praised good deeds from knights and princes, and their damsels loved them out of gratitude and attraction. But I hadn't read much about pleasure and the physical reaction I received. Once I had a taste of him, I didn't ever want it to stop. That frightened me. I could kill him in an instant, and he thought I was merely a simple girl. How could we love each other with such lies in between us?

"Stop." I pulled my head back, but he dove right back in.

"Why?"

That seemed like a very difficult question for me to answer. I did very much like Austin, but it wasn't enough to persist. If I wanted a whim of intimacy, there wouldn't be so many dead warriors fueling my unnatural strength. "I want to wait."

"But don't you need to breed?"

"What?" I quickly pulled away from Austin and looked into his glossed eyes.

"What?" he asked, puzzled.

I knew what I heard. I did not imagine it. I grabbed his face and made him focus on my eyes. "Austin, what did you just say to me?"

He furrowed his brows as he thought back as hard as he could. "I don't know." He chuckled nervously. "Was it weird or something?"

"You asked me about breeding!" I cleared my throat and calmed down. "Yes, it was weird."

"I'm sorry!" Austin backed off from me. If I didn't know any better, I'd think he had been missing for the last minute or two of his life. He was so confused, and that made me terribly uneasy. If I weren't making out with him, then who was I kissing just then?

"I'm gonna go..."

I didn't protest his leaving. I felt dirty and embarrassed that the two of us got so heated. I needed some proper distance to think, and he certainly needed some distance from me.

I poured myself a glass of elixir to calm my nerves, but as the liquid oozed down my throat and rested inside my stomach, I came to a sudden revelation. Every time I drank my elixir, I could feel it. I really felt it, and not in a way that water makes you feel clean, or soda fizzes your tongue, or the way chocolate milk is rich and creamy. It had its own special energy. What if it were something more than a chemical composition to make me different? Austin's wording was very specific. It couldn't have been a run-on joke from our dinner party. It wasn't a conscious decision. I'm not even certain if he was in charge of his own actions. What if there were something inside of it bound to duty like the elders, warriors, and everyone else who lived in my colony?

Austin had one glass of my elixir. What was it doing to him? And if one glass could affect him so, then what was it still doing to me?

Chapter Eleven

I managed to fall asleep, even though I was worried sick about Austin. I concluded that I had to be away from him. I didn't know if that meant I would permanently choose Noah, or find another man altogether, but it was for his own good. I needed to breed, but not with whatever was happening inside his head. We were supposed to be camping for another two days. If I couldn't convince everyone to drop the rest of the trip, I would just have to hold off Austin the best I could.

I hated to say it, but I needed to talk to the elders. They would know what kind of damage the elixir would have on mere humans, and whether or not I was insane for thinking there might have been something alive inside of it. I needed to know the truth, and they were the only ones with the answers.

My worry woke me up in the middle of the night. All the boys were still in their tents. I peeked inside at Skylar, Dylan, and Pete. They were all in a very deep sleep and would probably wake up with incredible hangovers. I tried to spy on Noah and Austin, but I heard their voices when I walked by. I couldn't afford for any of them to hear my call, so I snuck a few miles away.

"I know you're out there watching me. Your queen commands your presence right here and now!" I waited for a few seconds. All seemed silent, but I was no fool. The elders would not give me a true opportunity to be free. "If I have to find you myself, I will destroy you! You must know my reputation."

Within a few seconds, a man in black jumped down from the trees and landed in front of me on his hands and knees, practically groveling. "I'm sorry, my queen. It is my mission to watch you in the shadows. I am your protector."

"Do you honestly believe I need any protection from the likes of you? I've killed many of your kind. You're a spy for the elders. Don't insult my intelligence."

He wouldn't admit to it. He valued his meaningless life too much. "What do you require, my queen?"

"I need to get in contact with the elders immediately. I assume you have a line of communication."

I couldn't see much of his face under his mask, but I saw sweat around his brow. "I am only to report if there is an emergency."

I grew impatient and raised him by his neck. How quickly they could forget their fear of me! "Does the end of your miserable life constitute a proper emergency?"

He must have been an elite warrior for the elders to trust him so much. A little pain was beyond him. But when I began to squeeze his neck just a little bit, he grunted and pulled a silver phone out of his pocket. "Here you are, my queen."

I threw him to the ground. I think I abhorred violence as a child. A part of me still did, but fear was universal, and if it were the only way to keep me superior to the elders in the eyes of my people, then so be it.

The phone only had one number programmed in, so I dialed it and waited for the sound of my most hated foe. "Hello?"

I paused for a moment to swallow my hatred like a golf ball lodged in my throat. "Elder."

"Virgin Queen." My mother's murderer was always smug and self-righteous. "This is quite a surprise."

"I'm sure you're pleased to hear from me," I said sarcastically. "But I don't have time for small talk."

"Are you ready to come home?" He was all too pleased with my admittance of defeat. Even if I wanted to go home, I would have changed my mind right on the spot.

"No, but you'll be pleased to hear that I have found two men of interest."

"Will you mate them both?"

"That's not my purpose. I wish to find a husband. One will be sufficient."

"I understand." He wasn't pleased, but he also didn't sound like he believed me either. "What can I do for you, Virgin Queen?"

I despised the fact that he had the information I desperately needed. If it weren't for the fact that I deeply cared for Austin, I would have continued stubbornly stumbling through the dark. "I need to know what my elixir is. I feel unique energy when I drink it, and I know it made me the way I am. How is that possible? What is it made of?"

"That sort of information is beyond you."

"Beyond me? I am the queen! Nothing is above me, especially you. If you have that sort of knowledge, I deserve to be privy to it as well."

I heard his heavy and furious breathing. He was probably biting his nails in anticipation of the day when he could ram his blade through my stomach. When he spoke, he seethed his words through his teeth. "It's certainly not anything created from fruits, vegetables, or any mortal means. Consider it to be Fate."

"Fate?" I laughed. "You expect me to accept such a thing?" It wasn't Fate who decided my mother should die, so I could take her place. It wasn't Fate who burned my books and forced me to be a killer. The elders did that. That's what they decided, and I couldn't blame my hatred on some silly notion.

"Believe what you want to believe, Virgin Queen, but every time you nourish yourself with that royal nectar, you are connected with your divine purpose. You are fulfilling yourself with Fate's will."

I could feel something when I drank it. There was a deep satisfaction that soothed me, but there was something else. There was an energy. It didn't feel good or dark. It just was what it was. I didn't know if I'd call it "Fate," but it was real. "Is there more to it than that?"

"Perhaps," his smugness quickly returned, "but that's a conversation we can have when you return home as a true and mature queen."

"What would happen if a human tasted my nectar?"

"That would depend on what Fate had planned for him." He became very stern with me. "You must not let humans have your royal nectar, Virgin Queen. There will be dire consequences."

Something was certainly wrong with Austin, but I couldn't let him know of it. My spies could have quickly turned into assassins. "Don't worry about it. I was merely curious."

There was silence on his end for a little while. He must have been suspicious of me doing the unthinkable and was probably preparing for it. "I'll see you home soon."

"Don't count on it." I scoffed and hung up the phone before throwing it down into the warrior's chest. "I'm done. You may go."

"Yes, my queen." He disappeared far up into the trees and leaped branch to branch until he was safe from my sight. He performed with such grace and strength that it was almost difficult to imagine how inferior he was to me.

I walked back to the campsite. It was only right that I gave the boys some distance, but it was important that I kept my eye on Austin. What if Fate wanted him to become a soul-sucking creature? Or what if Fate wanted him dead? Was Austin at risk of becoming a monster or a cripple? Either one would be my fault.

The closer I got, the more I heard yells. I soon realized it was unmistakably Noah doing most of the yelling, and Austin's voice rose every so often. I figured they could only be arguing about one of two things: Noah's condition or their relationship with me. I couldn't let them say cruel things to each other over either. I didn't want them to lose each other as I lost Camellia.

I ran to the boys as fast as I could. But when I arrived, I was curious to hear what they would say while not in my presence, so I hid behind a tree while they bickered.

"What are you even doing with her?" Noah yelled. "You can't possibly care about her as much as I do."

Austin slapped his forehead in frustration and then exploded on his young cousin. "We like each other, Noah. I'm sorry she's more interested in me than you, but—"

"She's just another thrill for you. She means more to me than that!"

"She means a lot more to me, too." Austin seemed embarrassed to even admit it, but I could tell in his mumbles that there was a clear moment of honesty.

"Besides, how does she coincide with your glorious plans of death, Noah?" he asked, terribly sarcastically. "You won't take your medicine. You won't half fight to live longer. Do you plan on getting close to her and then just going out in a blaze of glory? How is that fair to her?"

Noah was stumped for a second and pouted until he muttered, "It makes it more special."

"You're being selfish! If you want her so bad, fight to stick around! Stop throwing guilt on her face to get inside her panties!"

Noah slightly blushed, but he was furious at the accusation, and his entire face turned beet red. "There are a lot of girls you've only been with to get inside of their panties. Rose means the world to me. You don't deserve her!"

Austin was stung for a second but recovered quickly with a vicious smirk. "Then why were the two of us just making out in her tent, Noah?"

Noah's face looked physically pained. I felt awful. What would happen if I decided to marry Austin?

But Noah was determined not to give up and came back swinging. "You made out. Big deal! I was her first kiss."

"You probably didn't even please her one iota compared to me!"

Noah growled angrily, like a wild animal, and charged his cousin with his hands aimed firmly at Austin's chest. Austin was pushed back and retaliated with a snarl and clenched fist. I was prepared to run in and stop everything, but Austin grunted and calmed himself down.

"This is crazy!" Austin buried his face in his hands as he really thought about the things that were said and what he had almost done. I was surprised he showed so much restraint and rationality. "I'm not gonna fight you over a girl we barely know. It's insane! I love you too much, Noah."

He threw his hands up in the air, exasperated. "I'm done. You win. You can have her if it makes you feel better."

I didn't want to get in the way of their relationship, but I couldn't say I was unaffected by Austin's submission. I did truly care for him, and I wasn't sure if I was ready to let him go yet.

I think Austin believed Noah would be grateful, but he slowly simmered and stirred until he exploded with rage. "You don't get to decide that! I could win all on my own. I don't need your sympathy."

"You don't need sympathy?" Austin asked in disbelief. "She's only bothering with you because you're dying!"

I gasped. I couldn't believe he would say anything so terrible to Noah, and Austin couldn't believe it either. Noah put his head down, so his face was unreadable, but his shoulders were shaking. Austin, however, was completely horrified and reached out to touch his cousin's shoulder. "I'm sorry, Noah. I just—"

I covered my mouth as I gasped again at the quick jab to Austin's cheek. Austin staggered back and wiped the blood from his mouth. He seemed surprised. Noah was ferocious and waiting for his cousin's retaliation, with his hands guarding his face. He possessed some fear, but Noah believed he was fighting for his honor. I prepped myself to run after them. There was absolutely no way Noah was going to beat Austin in a fair fight.

"Stop." Austin stared at the blood on his hand. Maybe he was extremely disappointed in his little cousin, but it was no more than the disappointment he had in himself. "I'm not gonna fight you, Noah."

Noah's chest rose and fell from intense breaths. He still had his face guarded like he didn't believe Austin. I think he even wanted to fight. I don't know what it would prove. It was still my choice to make.

I watched long enough and emerged from behind my tree. "Boys?"

Austin took notice, and his eyes bucked at the revelation that I had been spying on them, but my voice never reached Noah's brain. No, he was still bound and gagged by his anger, and he had to do something rash to break free.

"Noah, don't!"

With all his might, he charged Austin and shoved him up against a tree that was several feet away from him. Austin was shocked and did nothing to retaliate, and I saw how the wind was knocked out of him when his back pressed up against a branch, and his head hit the very hard bark.

"Noah, stop!" I ran to grab the two of them, but Noah grabbed Austin's waist, and they wrestled until Noah lost his footing and took Austin down the side of the rocky hill behind them.

I rushed down after them. They had fallen about twenty feet down. Noah got up with a few cuts and bruises sure to quickly form. But Austin was lying still. The only movement coming from him was his fluttering eyes and the blood pouring onto the rock underneath his head. "Noah, what have you done?"

Noah hadn't even noticed yet. He was too busy whimpering from idiotic, self-inflicted wounds to realize what he had done. "What?"

His eyes followed mine as I ran to Austin and cradled his body in my arms. I hadn't cried since I was a child, but I was so frightened of losing him that I sobbed uncontrollably. Those boys were not cruel to each other before my arrival. I did that to them, just like I killed my mother.

Noah was still, but his eyes shook, and his lips quivered until he finally collapsed in a rush of tears. "I'm sorry! I didn't mean to. I was just so angry and…"

"Silence!" I was so furious with him! Just because I influenced Noah didn't give him an excuse. Austin might have succumbed to evil words, but he wouldn't let his violent urges get the best of him. That was Noah's decision.

"There's a lot of blood. He's losing consciousness." I felt myself beginning to collapse on top of Austin in grief, but I pulled myself together. A wound like that could have ended Austin's life, and I had to act quickly if I expected him to live. I needed to get him to a human hospital, but I didn't know if there would be any time. If Austin died, Noah would have been convicted of murder, and he'd have to live the rest of his short life in prison, for something he didn't mean to do. It was too much of a risk. Mortal means couldn't save him.

"I should call nine-one-one."

"No!" I leaped up with Austin in my arms. Noah was dumbfounded, but I didn't have time to be coy about my strength. "I'll handle this myself." I trod up the hill with enough speed to look like a football player carrying a doll. I was sure Noah would question me, but I couldn't let that hinder me. At least the other boys were too passed out with booze to be any concern.

I carried Austin inside my tent and set him down. He luckily hadn't lost consciousness yet, but he wasn't aware. As I reached for my cooler, I saw so much blood on my hands. It seemed silly to be disgusted by it, considering how many men I mercilessly killed, but I never made a mess.

"What is that?" Noah asked.

I cradled the glass jar of elixir to my chest. How Austin thought it was a protein shake was beyond me. It looked like ooze or slime. I couldn't blame Noah for being cautious. "It'll help...hopefully."

Noah took a breath to protest, but I snapped my head back and glared at him. He nearly killed Austin. I wasn't going to let him stop me from saving his life. Of course, there was always the chance that my elixir could kill him or change him into something fearsome. I had enough time to think about my choices, and I clearly decided it was worth the risk.

I gently lifted Austin's head onto my thighs. "Austin?"

He wouldn't even respond or look at me until I moved his chin to guide his eyes. I still don't think he really saw me.

"Austin, you have to try to drink this. It'll make you better." His eyes closed, but they opened right up as soon as I got the lid off, and the scent covered the tent. I heard him sniffing, and then I saw a light in his eyes again.

I hesitated for just another moment. If he weren't an addict, I was pretty certain I was setting him on his path. That was a problem for another day. I lightly pressed the glass to his lips and slowly poured the elixir. At first, it overflowed on his lips and spilled down his cheeks. Barely any passed through the small crack of his lips. But when that first drop hit his tongue, I saw the thirst in his eyes, and I jumped as his hand grabbed the glass and took control.

Poor Noah had no idea what was going on. He couldn't even breathe. He clutched his chest and gritted his teeth, hoping for his cousin to pull through.

Once the contents of the glass jar were empty, Austin's hand fell, and he huffed out a massive amount of air before completely losing consciousness. Noah grabbed his mouth and moaned with instant tears, but I could still feel his heart beating, and it was faster and stronger than anything I had ever felt. "It's okay." I tilted Austin's head. It was covered in blood, but I moved his hair about until I knew for sure that the gash was gone. "He'll be fine. His wound has closed."

Noah's emotions still exploded everywhere, and he cried in his hands. He sobbed over his shame of what he had done and what he was capable of. Then, in a quiet and glorious roar, he laughed in relief. I thought he would immediately jump into a thousand questions, but he didn't say anything for a while. He kept wiping his eyes until he was able to reconstruct his flailing pride.

I gave Noah some time to compose himself. It gave me some time to think about what I could say. How could I explain the healing properties of my elixir? Perhaps it didn't always act in that way. Clearly, Fate wanted Austin to survive, but I couldn't properly explain that to Noah. He was going to ask why I healed Austin, and why I was perfectly satisfied with watching him die a slow and miserable death.

"What did you give him?" Just as I thought, the question came with a million possibilities and hopes for himself.

"It's complicated."

"Are you a faith healer from a church out in your farm town? Are you some kind of runaway government scientist? Are you an alien?"

His last spat of nervous panic made me chuckle. "I'm Rose Queen. That's all you need to know."

"No! That's not all I need to know. I need the truth." He grabbed my wrist and looked straight into my eyes. I killed men for less, but I let him handle me for the moment. "I could have killed him, and you saved his life. I need to understand how. Please."

I did think he needed to understand, for Austin's sake, but I knew all of Noah's dying tour was just a lie. He wanted me to tell him how I could save his life.

I slightly glared at him, and he quickly released my wrist. "I'm not human."

His head perked up. "You mean you're from another planet or something?"

"No." I blinked hard. I imagined telling Noah my origin, once or twice, but I never suspected he would be so calm and accepting about it. It was quite a load off my shoulders.

"I was born here on earth, just like you. I'm just different." I didn't want his feelings for me to change, but I had to be honest. "I was born into a unique society. We look like humans. If you observed our DNA, your equipment wouldn't even be able to tell the difference between most of us.

"I'm different, though." My eyes shifted from him. I just wasn't ready to tell him that I could suck people dry. "This elixir made me different. I was fed it as a baby until I was ready."

"Ready for what?"

"Ready to be the queen."

His eyes widened once again, and they were so bright and vibrant. "You're literally a queen?" He was so amazed.

"'Rose Queen' is a name made up for when I came here to visit. We don't have names where I'm from. My people refer to me as 'Virgin Queen.'"

Noah cleared his throat, but his voice still cracked when he spoke. "They throw that in your face, huh?"

I began to laugh, but restrained myself to only a smile. "We don't use the term 'princess.' A 'virgin queen' is a term given to a queen that..." I lightly blushed. "Well, I believe it's self-explanatory."

I didn't know what was wrong with me. Sometimes when I was with Noah, I felt so young—as young as I really was—and the world felt bright and new. I had been fighting so long to be a mature powerhouse. Was it good to finally be a normal girl?

"So why did you come here? What's wrong with your kingdom?"

"I came here to find a suitable mate." I couldn't look Noah in the eye because I could feel him drilling holes into my skin. "My people are mindless followers, and I've read one too many books about knights, princes, and gentlemen. I wanted to find someone worthy enough to be my king."

I finally caught a glimpse of Noah. If he made an attempt to hold his composure, it was pathetic. His mouth was open so wide that his jaw could have been broken. "And you're going back and forth between Austin and me?" He was obviously flattered, but his pupils were shaky in a terribly afraid kind of way.

"Currently." I could find other prospects if I needed to. Love was my mission, but I really wanted to keep the boys from killing each other. I could only imagine how much more desirable I'd be to Noah with him knowing the potential of our union.

"Wow!" Noah laughed nervously and rubbed against his chest. "That's a real game-changer there. King? Me? That's really something..." He kept shifting from smiling uncontrollably to looking like he was about to puke.

"Is this too intimidating?"

"No!" his voice shrieked. "I'm completely okay with this. It's cool..."

I grinned. Yes, he was completely and totally overwhelmed, but I also knew he was in love with me and willing to bulldoze his way right through his concerns to go for my crown.

"It's alright if you're intimidated. I'm different than anyone you've ever met, Noah."

"I know. That's why I like you." Noah might have been devious about a few minor things that he misled me on, but his heart was bright. I could feel it radiating through me every time he smiled.

"The queen can have many children, dozens even."

"D-dozens?"

"But if I don't mate with someone before I turn twenty-one, I'm going to lose my reproductive capabilities. Then my colony will have no queen."

"What about a next of kin?" Why would he ask me that? Was he afraid of being a father? "Camellia seems like she'd want to start a family."

"She can't. No other woman in the colony can." Noah was so expressive with his face, and I was ashamed of my women's plight when his mouth dropped, and his eyes bulged. I had to turn away from him. "And even though it may be true that Camellia is my sister, we weren't even close prior to arriving here in California. She was only a servant who aided my mother. She was no one to me."

He sighed heavily. "It seems pretty tough where you live."

"My people don't realize that. They believe they're happy taking care of me, training to take care of me, or...whatever. I've always been unhappy, though." It was refreshing being able to complain about my world. No one else from within could see it for what it was. "There are elders there who try to rule my life and the colony. We have twisted traditions that I'd like to stop."

"Why do you have to go back? Why can't you stay here with us?"

It made me extraordinarily happy that Noah wanted me to stay with him and Austin, especially after learning what I was. He still had yet to learn what I was capable of, but I had a feeling he would love me still. It would have been a wonderful life if I could surf with Austin in the morning, talk about books with Noah in the afternoon, and enjoy one of their joint dinners. The three of us as friends forever would have been magic.

But that was just a dream, and dreams were for children. "I am a queen. I still have a duty to perform, regardless of the fact that I hate the elders. I want to be a mother and a true leader to my people. I think if I found a good man to be my king, we could be a family and show my people love."

I thought Noah would have jumped up and volunteered, but he turned to his cousin and ignored me. He brushed some of Austin's hair out of his face and watched him sleep. "What's gonna happen to Austin?"

"I don't know. He actually drank some of my elixir before. He thought it was a protein shake and swiped it right from underneath my nose."

Noah snickered, but he quickly ceased once I cut my eyes at him.

"Now, with the bigger dose, I don't know what will become of him."

"Did it give you your super strength?" He crossed his arms and tried to pretend he wasn't excited. "I noticed you carried Austin as if you were a big, burly man, and it suddenly makes sense how you trashed him in basketball."

"That's not how I became stronger..." He was intrigued, but I wasn't ready to let him know yet. He was too sensitive. I had to be delicate with him and my past.

"However, the elixir may be having an impact on Austin. When we were cliff diving today, I hit the bottom. If I were like one of you, I would have broken my spine. Austin probably hit the bottom as well."

Then I noticed that small glimmer of hope in his eye. I was breathless because I knew he was about to ask the absolutely impossible from me. "If you can heal him, could you heal me too?"

His eyes slowly approached mine, and I fell into them. I was suffocating from his hopes and desperation. "I don't know, Noah."

No matter what I said, he was going to be angry about the fact that I used it to heal Austin and wouldn't even try it on him. There was nothing I could say to make it better, but I certainly did have to try. "My elixir has some kind of life of its own that I don't understand. It could have killed Austin. It may still kill him!"

He couldn't even be concerned about Austin's life. His shoulders kept slumping as his head lowered from disappointment.

I touched his shoulder and pleaded with him. "It's just not safe until I know more about it! It made me capable of something dark."

He raised his head. "Like what?"

"Things you couldn't imagine."

I felt that he was unsatisfied with my answer, but he shook his head and smiled, amazed. "This is all so weird. Am I the only one who knows about this?"

"The only human, anyway."

"Wow..." He began to grin, and it was obvious as to why. We were bound together by my secret, and until I confessed the truth to Austin, Noah would be my number one confidant. "How many of you are on earth?"

"From my colony? Thousands."

"Are there other colonies?"

"I've only been to my own, but I know there are others." I wondered if it was fine to tell him that. Was it my place to really talk about other colonies? I wouldn't want anyone to endanger my people. "Queens are very territorial over their colonies, and let's just leave it at that."

I recognized the look on Noah's face. I always had the same look when I was in the middle of a very entertaining book. He was intrigued, mystified, and excited with me. I'd never be able to get rid of him until the end. He was a finisher, like me. "I'll keep your secret, Rose. You can trust me."

My eyes followed his hands as they came on top of mine. It was just a simple human hand, and yet it felt heavy like the shackle we figuratively placed around each other. "We should leave in the morning. You both should keep your distance from me and regain some clarity."

"I have clarity." He took a deep breath and exhaled jitterily. "I love you."

It's not like I had never heard the phrase before. This time, I could actually feel it. I expected that moment would be different. For example, I didn't think the man who said it would have a voice that cracked.

"Perhaps we're too different—"

"You think telling me that you're an inhuman queen was going to make me less invested in you?" he laughed. "That's kind of amazing, Rose."

While I was learning to accept reality, I was probably fulfilling every fantasy Noah ever had about a woman. It would be a lot harder to break up with him, but I had to try. "I release pheromones, Noah. You and Austin almost can't help that you're bickering over me. I can't even be sure if your feelings for me are real."

"I know that they're real!" he insisted. "Don't sell me short like you usually do, Rose."

I wanted to believe Noah more than anything. If he really could love what I was, then I wasn't a fool for thinking I could one day be happy, despite my curse. It's what my mother wanted for me. If I could fulfill her wishes, her death wouldn't still feel so painful.

But there was no way to know the truth. "You can sleep in here with your cousin. I'm going to your tent."

As I walked away, I heard Noah say, "Goodnight, my queen."

I turned around and saw him grinning, and he reminded me of all my other followers. Noah honestly cared for me, but that still didn't mean he truly loved me. "Please, just call me Rose."

Chapter Twelve

All night, I kept worrying about Austin. I didn't know if he'd be different. I was half expecting him to fall at my feet, worship me, and beg for more elixir. The other half of me didn't know what to expect, but I figured it would be worse. Then, in the afternoon, he poked his head inside his tent, looking bewildered.

I waited for him to say something. I didn't know what Noah told him, and I didn't want to ruin whatever cover story we had going on. I saw Noah standing behind him, but he didn't say anything either. It wasn't long before my heart raced. Maybe Noah told him everything, and he was wondering how he was supposed to interact with someone who wasn't human.

"Last night…"

"Yes?" my voice quivered. "What about it?"

"I…" He lowered his head and laughed to himself. "I asked you to breed?"

"You did…" I prepped myself to fight him off if I needed to. "What about it?"

"Geez!" He slapped his forehead and groaned. "I didn't mean to get that wasted. I don't even remember drinking."

"Drinking?" I laughed short. "You were drunk?"

"I know!" He was dissatisfied with himself. "I told you I didn't do that stuff, and then I wake up not being able to remember how I ended up in your tent with a migraine."

I was relieved. Considering that he could have died from his injury, I was grateful and gladly accepted his discomfort. "Only a migraine?"

"Yeah…" There was something more. I could just see it in his eyes, but he didn't know how to describe whatever was happening to him. "I said some pretty messed-up things to Noah."

"Oh, Noah isn't innocent!" I learned every day that he was a bit more scoundrel than I gave him credit for. I understood why he left out that he rammed his cousin off a ledge and nearly killed him, but I hoped he didn't make the fight entirely seem like Austin's fault.

"I'm sorry that you had to see me when I wasn't my best."

"Don't worry about it." Considering I killed everyone who pushed me too far, it was only fair to forgive him for saying awful things to Noah. "I hope you never have to see me when I'm not my best."

We left it at that. I returned to my tent to pack, and he returned to his. We made up a story about Noah feeling sick, and Austin insisted they went home. Pete, Dylan, and Skylar were disappointed. Austin was as well, but he kept making remarks about how he felt strange. I think he wanted to go home. Dylan didn't share any sympathy and disappeared for a good hike with Pete and Skylar, so we didn't even end up leaving until late in the afternoon.

Pete and Skylar rode in the front of the car, and Dylan spread out in the back, so I ended up sitting between Noah and Austin. I tried to keep my mouth shut to avoid any unnecessary tension.

"I'm sorry for getting sick," Noah said. "I didn't mean to cancel what was left of our trip."

"Don't apologize," Austin said. "It's my job to take care of you."

"It's not your fault he has an autoimmune disease," Dylan said. "It's just your fault that you let him tag along. You knew he couldn't hang."

Austin turned around quickly and seethed hatefully toward his buddy. "You say another word about Noah, and I'm going to snap your neck!"

Noah's eyes widened, but he didn't discourage his cousin's outburst. After the initial shock, I think he was a little proud.

"Fine, dude, I was just saying." Dylan sank back into his seat and closed his eyes. I didn't think Dylan could ever stop talking, but he didn't say another word for the entire trip. I couldn't blame him, though. Austin was quite feral.

Dylan was the first to get home, then Skylar, then Pete. I mentioned something about being hungry, and without discussion, Austin drove the three of us to a place that had a ton of pizza, and we ate as much as we liked. Noah ate a couple of slices and was done, but Austin and I took advantage of the opportunity. When we were full, we paused to talk to make room for our stomachs.

"Did you enjoy your camping trip?" Austin asked.

"I did." Despite being worried half to death over what would become of Austin, I did enjoy helping Noah overcome his fear of heights, and kissing Austin was nice until he severely freaked me out.

Noah began to smile and even chuckled a little. "Do you remember when we went camping when I was twelve?" he asked Austin.

"With your mom and dad? Yeah. I remember." Austin had a lost look on his face, like he wasn't sure how he was supposed to feel about Noah's parents. "Your mom was so paranoid about us getting hurt. She barely let us have any freedom."

"Well, you did get us infected with poison oak, so she was right!"

"Yeah," Austin banged on the table excitedly, "but we got to stay indoors, and she let us eat ice cream to make us feel better!"

Noah rolled his eyes. "No big deal. She always let me eat ice cream when I was sick."

I was intrigued. "Do you still eat ice cream when you're sick?"

"No." He grinned and looked at me with a little bit too much obviousness in his eyes. "It would be awesome if there were some magical food or drink that could cure me."

Austin nodded in agreement, and then Noah intensely eyeballed me. I had to find a better way to explain why the elixir wasn't a good option. I wanted Noah to live, but its powers were unpredictable.

"Well, there's always ice cream." I jumped out of my seat and pulled on the boy's shoulders. "Let's go get some right now."

"I'm stuffed!" Noah moaned. "I really can't eat another bite."

"You've got to." There was a shop a couple of doors down. I saw a blue-colored ice cream in a cone and took the liberty of ordering us all the same thing. When our order was complete, I handed the boys their cones and held up mine as a proclamation. "This is our hope that Noah will get better, and we'll be able to stay together—the three of us."

Austin was about to clank his cone against mine, but then he drew back. "In what capacity?"

That was actually the first time the two of them had outright confronted me about my intentions. I wondered how they would react if I told them what the elders wanted me to do. Would Noah just be happy to be accepted, one way or another, and would Austin have his fill of me once I had succumbed to his charms? He only asked me to breed with him. He didn't profess his love like Noah had.

But I didn't care what the elders wanted. I still wanted a husband, and in the end, I would need a friend as well. "In whatever capacity that allows us all to continue to love each other. I'm still working on it, but my main priority is keeping the peace between the two of you."

The two of them were ashamed. Austin was the first to raise his cone against my own. "Don't worry. Noah comes first. I'm not gonna fight against him for you. We'll figure this out."

I smiled happily and turned to Noah. "And what about you?" I was a lot more judgmental of him. If he wanted to prove to me that my pheromones weren't controlling his life, then he had to get a better handle on his emotions. He could never fight Austin again!

"He's my brother." He pressed his cone against ours, and his eyes shimmered. I'm glad he didn't shed any tears, but I hoped he recalled all the good times they had together and realized nothing was worth jeopardizing what they shared. Not even me. "I'll do better."

The ice cream was delicious, and after I finished my cone, I requested another and enjoyed it on the way home. When I pulled up, there was a tan van sitting in front of the house, but I knew it wasn't Camellia.

"Whose car is that?" Austin asked.

Her boyfriend was rich and drove a red sports car. He wouldn't be caught dead in something so old and beat up. There weren't any lights on in my house, but upon closer observation, it looked like the door was cracked open. "Stay here."

"Are you insane?" Austin grabbed my arm before I could get out of the car. "I'll take care of this. You wait and call the police."

"I can take care of myself, Austin. This is my house. I will see about its business."

He gritted his teeth. I don't know why he defied me. He should have known better. "Fine! Just stay behind me."

We all got out of the car and found things to arm ourselves with. Austin had a filet knife, Noah was armed with a tire iron, and I carried a large flashlight. We snuck to the front door, but Austin turned around and pushed Noah in his chest. "Not you. You stay in the car."

"Are you kidding me?" he yelled. "You wanna let a girl go in, but you don't want me to help?"

I pushed on Noah's chest and warned him with my eyes. "You know I'm not a normal girl!" He had yet to learn the depths of my strength, but I was obviously more equipped to handle the situation than either of them. I couldn't convince Austin of that, but he knew better. "Let me handle this."

He grunted and pointed at his cousin's chest. "I'm not staying behind, Austin."

Austin grumbled, but we were short on time. "Let me be in front."

I stayed very close as we eased to the front door. We were all quiet and listened to the noises coming from the inside. If the broken lock on my front door wasn't enough of a hint that I was certainly being robbed, the loud shattering certainly was. Fury rose in my face. I couldn't believe someone would dare to do something so bold against me. I was about to barge right in and destroy them all, but Austin pushed me back in my chest.

"Calm down!" he whispered harshly. "I don't want you getting hurt."

It was strange accepting his role as the dominant figure. Of course, I could take care of myself. I could take on him and our attackers, but if I wanted a husband to be a partner, then perhaps it was time I learned how to follow directions. "Lead the way."

The door creaked open, and I gasped as I saw my house run amok. My home was furnished with expensive art and trinkets. They were subtle pieces but still of great value. Those, along with every appliance, from my blender to my sixty-inch flat-screen television, were gathered in the foyer. Those were my things they touched. That was my home they raided, as if I were weak and helpless.

"Call the police," Austin ordered Noah, and he reached into his pocket for his phone.

"No." I snatched it from his hands and tossed it in a bush before he could dial the first number. "Don't call them."

"What's your problem?" Noah shrieked.

"What are you doing?" Austin tried to grab me, but I rolled my eyes and walked inside my home.

I spotted two burglars coming from the top step, carrying a large television that I recognized from my room. They noticed me coming in and panicked amongst themselves, and in the midst of their fear and anxiety, the idiots dropped it. I didn't mind that it was broken. I only turned it on once, but I cared that they violated my room. Every man who ever tried ended up dead, and I didn't have the heart to fight tradition.

"Rose? Don't!"

I couldn't pay heed to Noah's warning. I leaped through the air before he could stop me, and landed between the two of them. The one in front gasped while the one behind me shrilled in the most annoying scream I had ever heard. I reached behind me and tossed him off the balcony and into the glass fireplace down below. I didn't bother to look, but he was obviously down for a little while. That was good. It gave me enough time to do what I needed.

"Get out of there, Rose!" It was sweet that Austin cared so much, but there was no need to worry.

The burglar in front of me pulled back his arm and thrust forward with the hardest punch he could possibly manage. I was surprised, and my head did move. I heard Austin growl like a primal animal, and he charged the steps, so he could save me before the burglar could deliver another blow. He attempted another punch, but I caught it effortlessly and slowly faced him again with a smirk. "You dare strike me?"

Austin stopped rushing and watched to see what I would do.

The burglar dropped to his feet and moaned as he fell. He murmured in pain as I crushed his hand, begging for forgiveness, and pleaded for me to let him go. He must have only been a boy— no older than Noah—but older than the first man I killed.

My hands gripped tightly around his neck, and I raised him up above my head. Seeing another victim made my stomach feel quite ravenous. I threw my head back and breathed in their fear. I could taste his life-force, and it was even more delicious than my sweet elixir.

"Rose?" It was becoming clearer, and Austin was torn between what he should do. "Why don't you put him down?"

I glanced behind me. Austin approached me with his hands up as if I were an animal that needed to be tamed. It disgusted me, but I couldn't stop. I was starving, and that robber was a plague to society. I was certain he would not be missed. His purpose in life was nothing more than to be a tender morsel for me to devour. The hunger inside of me scratched in rhythm with the beat of my heart so hard that I felt it throbbing in my head. I had to stop it. I had to feed!

"Rose!"

I didn't regain myself until I tossed his lifeless body over the balcony. I looked back at Austin. He was just as afraid as everyone else. I didn't want to be a monster that he was afraid to touch. I didn't know that Austin could be afraid of anything. "Austin—"

He took a step back. "What are you?"

"I'm…" I didn't know what to say. I was the queen of a people I had done nothing for, most of whom feared me, and I even jeopardized our future by pursuing my conquest of love. What was I? "I'm still the same girl I was before."

"You just killed that man!"

"That man was a thief. I couldn't let him get away with what he did!" Why couldn't he understand that I was justified? Those humans offended me with their disrespect.

Austin pulled on his hair as he looked down at the bodies below. He had lost color in his sun-kissed skin from fright. "What about the law?"

While I could certainly understand his concerns, I very well couldn't relate. Even the rules of the elders escaped my care. "I'm not bound to humans' laws. I make my own."

His head snapped back at me, and his shaking finger pointed up at me. "You're not human?" Was it really so strange? Austin thought I was extraordinary. I didn't think such an open-minded, free, life-loving boy could be so puzzled by learning he was not alone in the universe.

"Guys!" Noah screeched.

We both hung over the balcony to get a good look below. Another burglar appeared. He must have come up from the basement, and the possibilities of what he could have discovered enraged me, but he shared a similar reaction when he came into the living room and saw one of his comrades with a busted skull, and another lying lifeless on the wooden floor. "What have you done?"

I narrowed my eyes as the voice registered in my mind. I heard it before, and I didn't have a very long list of suspects. "You!"

He growled and reached into his pants for something. My people only fought with blades, so it escaped my mind what sort of weapon he had, but Austin screamed and ran for Noah before we even got a glimpse of the gun. "Get down!"

I knew Noah. His heart was definitely racing. I suspected that he would be bound with fear and unable to protect himself. Austin was too far to save him, and my mind still wouldn't allow me to react. There was no one to save him.

But Noah was a surprising boy, and he took off running as fast as he could toward his attacker, screaming like a wild man. Austin and I thought that was a horrible idea, and we screamed for his dear life as the gun aimed at his chest.

I leaped from the balcony and onto the floor to save him before it was too late, but my ears were already ringing by the time my feet hit the ground. I didn't know if Noah had been hit or not. He dodged a little bit, and I think I heard him grunt in pain. He still rammed his attacker in the chest before slamming him to the ground. The burglar was still holding onto the gun and fired it two more times, accidentally, before I stomped on his wrist until he screamed in agony, and released it.

I growled and grabbed the vile scum from his neck, and Noah rolled off him, like water, and onto the ground, as I raised my next victim high. "You took my address, so you could rob us. Why?"

He was cool and sly while in the shop. Now, he was nothing more than a pitiful coward, murmuring and near the verge of tears. "I overheard that you had a lot of money."

Was it truly that simple for him to decide I was an easy target? Well, he needed to be taught a lesson. What if Camellia had been there alone and had gotten hurt because of his moronic behavior? "You tried to kill my friend, and you stole from me. You take from me, I take from you."

"Don't!" Austin came running up from behind, but he was too late to convince me and too powerless to actually do something about it. Within a matter of seconds, all the burglar had left was a husk of flesh, and I dropped him like a sack.

I wiped my lips as I turned to see the petrified faces of the boys. Noah's terrified expression changed within a few seconds after a hardy gulp. Then, he nervously laughed quietly with his eyes still wide and said, "Thank you for saving my life."

I crossed my arms. "Your life wouldn't be in jeopardy if you had listened and stayed in the car!" I didn't mean to snap, but I would have preferred it if neither of them had seen me consume.

"That's not fair—"

"The same goes for your cousin." I stepped closer to Austin until we were practically nose to nose. He didn't step back or run, but he certainly did flinch. I wanted to look into his eyes to see if there was ever a chance the two of us could be together. At the time, I was unsure. All I saw was fear. "You both should have let me handle this alone."

Austin's head perked up, and he scoffed quietly, but intensely offended. "Oh, you handled this, alright!"

"It's okay," Noah jumped to his feet and made room to stand between us. "She's still Rose."

"What is Rose?" He threw his hands up hysterically. "What have you been keeping from me?"

I didn't even have to say a word. Noah was ready to spout it all out like a children's fairytale. He at least had the respect to look to me for permission, and he did not begin until I gave my nod of approval. "She's the queen of her people. She came here looking for a mate to help her—"

"Breed?" He slapped his face and screamed into his hands, before throwing them up again, and practically growled at me. "What have you done to me?"

I cocked my brow. I hadn't noticed many effects, but he must have felt something himself. "You did it to yourself when you drank my elixir. You shouldn't have stolen from me."

He placed his hands on his hips and grumbled to himself. I bet he'd never steal a single thing again in his life. "So, am I gonna become a life-sucking parasite?"

My entire body tensed up. His jab mildly stung, but it annoyed me that he meant to intentionally hurt me. "I'm unaware. We'll have to wait and see what will become of you."

"Don't talk to Rose like that," Noah pleaded to his cousin. "When you get scared, you rush into doing something you can't undo and say something that can't be taken back."

Austin grabbed Noah by his shirt collar and pulled him until their chest bumped against each other. "You knew what she was, and you didn't tell me?"

"It's not my secret to tell." Noah pushed himself away from his cousin and stumbled back a few feet. He had such conviction in his eyes, though his whole world was spinning. He was so deeply rooted in truth that he could never completely fall off balance. "She's still the same person I fell in love with."

We all would have taken a moment to swoon if Austin didn't stomp his foot and shake his fists in a fit of disgusted rage. "She just killed three people!"

Noah turned his head and mumbled, "Maybe they deserved to die..."

"Please, don't sound like a crazy person right now!" Austin threw his head back and moaned. "We have to get away. Let's go home." He snatched Noah's hand and made his way to the door.

Noah looked back at me with big, wide, and desperate eyes. The thought of losing me was agonizing for him, and as he was torn away from me, I felt my chest ache. I had already lost Camellia. Was I truly meant to be alone? Was that one of the curses my mother prophesied on my life? No friends? No family? No love?

I always yearned for affection, but the only instance when I had it was with my mother in my garden, and when she held me right before she died. I often revisited those moments in my mind and took all I could to sustain myself. It didn't matter what the elders did to me, as long as I had the memory of love and the hope that I would be able to find it again. Camellia was my first bright spot after my mother's death. Then I met my precious boys. I didn't know how much of their feelings were generated on their own, but I knew every bit of happiness they brought to me was real.

I started to chase after them, but I stopped myself. I didn't want to frighten Austin more than I already had. I would never purposely hurt either of them, but I couldn't blame them if they thought otherwise.

Austin was absolute in his decision, but Noah finally exploded and broke free from Austin's grip before they got to the door. "She just saved your life!"

Austin glanced at me for only a second, but it was a piercing eternity on the receiving end. "What do you mean?"

"You weren't drunk the other night." I knew Noah never intended to tell Austin the truth. His voice trembled, and his hands were shaking. "We were fighting over Rose, and things got intense. You said some things that made me really mad, and I attacked you. I didn't mean to push you over the hill, but I was so angry!"

For a moment, he relived those painful words that Austin spouted out, and Noah was once again enraged. But it died down within a matter of seconds, once he recalled his own role in the avoided tragedy. "You hit your head, and there was so much blood. If Rose didn't carry you back to her tent and feed you her green juice stuff, then you'd be dead. I would have killed you."

Noah looked to me and smiled reverently. "I owe her everything."

I was glad Noah still adored me, but he probably always would, despite whatever I did. I should have chosen him right there and then for his loyalty, but I found myself wishing for Austin to share his cousin's unwavering devotion.

I wanted Austin to still want me. I wanted him to love me the same way Noah did. Completely. Noah would throw his life away for me, and maybe it was easier for him, considering how close he was to death, but Austin should have been inspired by his cousin's ability to dive into a relationship.

But to be honest, I could understand that he had a hard time grasping reality. I had demons I didn't want to face either. "Am I still human?"

I saw his eyes, and he looked so pathetic that I wanted to run into his arms and embrace him as a comfort, but I wasn't sure if he would accept that. "Yes, but there's not much of a difference between my people and humans. You could shift—change—I'm not sure. I'm still observing you."

"I need a doctor," he mumbled to himself.

"They can't do anything for you. They can't tell the difference between our species. There are hundreds of us hiding among your kind. We mix with your blood, and then your children become a part of my colony."

His eyes widened. "So, you're trying to seduce both of us to breed more like you?"

I hadn't truly realized how horrible it all sounded until I said it out loud. Even Noah's mouth was open in an expression that could only translate to awkward horror.

"I assure you both; I only wanted to pick one of you. I want to find true love and start a family. I want to change my people for the better and live in peace with the humans—"

"As opposed to what?" Austin became defensive. "What's the goal of your people?"

I very well didn't want to say, but I couldn't lie to them. Austin practically knew the truth anyway. "Either all of you assimilate, or our numbers will overrun yours. We'll destroy you."

Austin fumed up his face and turned to his cousin with a steady glare. Noah shrugged his shoulders and buried his eyes in the floor. "I didn't know that."

"What else do aliens want?"

"I'm not an alien!" I was not so unlike them, and I deserved a place on my planet just like they did. "My people have been here for hundreds of years. We're a race of ancient beings, and we're just as old as humans. We've been evolving and preparing."

"For a hostile takeover?"

I shut my mouth tight for a moment. Seeing how angry Austin was about my origin made it one hundred times worse to explain. "It would depend on the ruler of the moment. I have no intention of ruling this planet. I want a family!"

There had to be a way to make him understand I was innocent in the scheme to take over the world. My heart wasn't in conquering. All I ever wanted was a family to love. I wanted children to play with. I wanted to raise a daughter who didn't have to live as tragically as I did, and who wouldn't have to turn into a monster. I knew they could help me succeed if they could only look beyond what I was and see who I was.

"This can't be your first kill." Austin was so sure, and his assurance cut me into a million pieces. I hadn't been ashamed for a very long time, and yet he had me regretting every single face.

But I swear, I was justified! "My purpose as a queen is to make children. The elders of my colony tried to force men on me, and I killed them. It was better than being raped!"

Noah silently gasped, but Austin swallowed hard and remained silent. But he certainly didn't hold such contempt anymore.

I hated that he made me regret anything at all! I had to protect my heart by encasing it in stone, and being the strong and cruel queen that her people feared. I was born with a curse and not a choice. "I've had so much taken away from me. All I have left is what's in my heart, and I want to give it to the right man. Then, he will lead as my king and be a true partner."

Austin had to understand where I was coming from and what I was trying to accomplish. I could see it in his eyes. He was close to accepting me. "Let's go home, Noah."

That couldn't be the end of us. "That's all you have to say?" I couldn't ask him to stay or reconsider, because I could hear my voice break up and felt tears in the back of my eyes. I refused to cry. I absolutely wouldn't.

"Yes." He hid his eyes from me and grabbed Noah's arm. "Let's go."

Noah was clearly torn, but he dragged his feet through the door.

I waited a little while for them to turn around and come back in. Austin would apologize for being so judgmental, and Noah would tell me how much he still loved me. I didn't let go of my delusions and collapse on the floor until about ten minutes later.

Chapter Thirteen

"Do you see what's so wrong with the humans now?" After I was alone with the dead bodies for about fifteen minutes, Mr. Jones casually called to ask how I was doing—as if he didn't know! But since I was in a dire situation, I ordered him to come to my home. I knew he was a driver, but something told me he was equipped to handle it. After a phone call and ten more minutes, men dressed as carpet cleaners arrived with body bags and wiped down my home.

"We would never do this. Stealing." Jones sneered. "It's disgusting."

"It's not exactly on par with what my warriors tried to do to me."

"You know how our people in the colony are. They have no specific needs or desires. They were only following orders, like I'm doing for you now."

"You're saying my potential rapists were innocent?" I watched the men work from the bottom step, but I marched to Jones to properly scold him. "I refuse to look at them in such a way, but I do know the majority of the blame rests on the shoulders of the elders."

I don't know why Jones didn't fear me. He didn't move in the slightest. "The elders have reasons for everything they do."

"And so did the thieves! That doesn't give them the right or make them any less dead now."

Jones was incapable of agreeing with me. He was probably the type who believed I should call our people to action. "We'll take care of everything, your highness. You don't have to worry about anything."

"Good." I turned around and walked up the stairs to my bedroom. The mysterious cleaners were wrapping up anyway. "Now, leave me."

I plopped on my bed, stared up at the ceiling, and pondered the wretched human lives I had taken. I couldn't feel sorry for what had happened to them, but I did wonder if I had somehow taken things too far. I didn't like that Noah and Austin were so frightened by my actions. Did that mean, somewhere deep inside of me, I was ashamed?

I wished I didn't have my unique power. If I didn't, then things would have been different with my mother. She would probably still be dead, but at least I wouldn't be burdened by the role I played in her death. But without my dark power, I would have already fallen prey to my destiny, and I wouldn't have had my chance to search for true love.

"Love?" I chuckled to myself. Wasn't I foolish to believe a human could love a monster like me? My own sister abandoned me. If I didn't despise the elders so, I probably would have packed up everything and returned home.

The next few days of my life were quite lonely. Camellia had yet to return, and I was beginning to doubt if I'd ever see her again. I often held my cellphone, waiting for the boys to call, but the phone never rang, and I was too proud to reach out myself.

I wandered the beach to search out more potentials. I saw many attractive men, and they did gander upon me. I offered a flirtatious smile, and they came chasing after me. The truth was that I could fulfill my mission. There were so many humans, and they were physical creatures full of life and lust. But after I was finished with light conversation and bodily flirtations, I bid them adieu with an awkward, drawn-out goodbye. Everyone left disappointed.

It didn't matter how handsome a boy was. It didn't matter how physically fit they were. It didn't matter if they sounded intelligent and sweet. I was always reminded of something Austin did or something Noah said. I was even close to kissing a boy at the beach, but I remembered the scent of Austin's sun-kissed skin, and then I could practically taste his lips. I could have pushed through it all, but in my heart, I knew I didn't want anyone else.

An entire week went by without communication from my boys. I suspected Austin was keeping Noah from me. I hoped he was going mad without my company, as I yearned for his presence.

I even read the book he gave me about flowers over and over, because I relived his smile when he handed me the book.

At the start of week two, I was angry. I hated that they dared to ignore me and felt they could properly get away with it. I was angry at Camellia for abandoning me as well. I was in my room when I heard the doorbell, and I slammed my flower book shut and stomped down the stairs, determined to give my visitor a piece of my mind.

When I opened it, I was taken aback. "What are you doing here?" My anger slipped away as soon as I saw into Austin's eyes, but I held on to it as tightly as possible and crossed my arms. "You made it very clear that you didn't want to be burdened with my presence anymore."

He stubbornly turned his head from me. He certainly didn't seem like he was about to drop to his knees and beg for my forgiveness. "That stuff that you used to heal me...I've noticed that it's had effects."

My arms fell like wet noodles as my heart dropped. If he were somehow hurt because of my decision, then it would have destroyed me. "Like what?"

"I had this skateboarding competition that I..." He shrugged and chuckled happily. "I dominated! I have sponsorship offers up the wazoo, and my friends are all scratching their heads, wondering how I managed to pull it off."

I couldn't see how that would have been a problem, but once Austin came down from his high, he frowned and knitted his brows together. "Is it permanent?"

I sighed heavily. "I'm not giving you anymore if that's why you're here."

"I'm not here for me!" he snapped. "I'm here for Noah."

I didn't think it was possible for my heart to sink any further, but I think I felt it in my feet, and I wanted to run away to the quick beating rhythm. "Austin—"

"I don't like what you did, and I'm uncomfortable with your whole 'take over the earth' way of life, but if you can save my cousin from dying..."

I could see the breaking of Austin in his eyes. He had no idea how he was going to survive Noah's death. It was going to ruin him.

"Austin, I care about Noah, but—"

"He had a real bad night. He won't take his medicine. I think he just wants it all to end, but he's in such pain. I can't stand to see him like this, and I don't want to lose him. Can you please help him?"

I didn't even want to imagine what Noah was going through, but I didn't want Austin to hate me forever if Noah turned into a creature somehow worse than me. "Do you realize what you're asking me?"

"No, but he's like my brother. I've got to do something!"

I could barely look at Austin. He was like a little puppy that had been kicked around. I tried to avoid his eyes, but his own were searching for mine, and when they collided, it was all over. "Let me grab my elixir."

I grabbed a thermos and went down into the basement while Austin waited in the foyer. There were so many reasons why I should have turned him down and let Austin die at the campsite. No one but me was supposed to have the elixir, and I could see why. But besides tradition and rules, there was also the fact that I didn't know what was living inside of it, and how it could control us all.

As dangerous as it was, Austin stared at the thermos once I brought it up. His mouth began to water as if he were about to ask me for some, but then he forced it shut and walked with me to his car.

After a couple of minutes on the road, I was too curious not to ask. "Do you thirst after it?"

"Sometimes, but I can deal."

I should have grabbed the wheel and forced us to turn back around, but I didn't want to be the one who said no to saving Noah's life. "There's a life to it. The elders told me that it had a will of its own. They said it was Fate."

He exploded into quiet laughter, and while I appreciated how handsome a smile looked on him, it was no laughing matter. "Are you telling me that this weird juice has plans for me?"

"Perhaps." I thought it was pretty clear that Austin was tangled up in my mess. Noah might have been more willing, but I wanted to keep him from changing. "I don't know what will become of Noah. Hopefully, he'll be healed, and there will be no side effects."

Tension suddenly formed and exponentially grew between the two of us, and it wasn't anything in a romantic sense. Austin was angry, and he eventually beat on the steering wheel and snapped. "I can't believe you want to take over the world, and that you suck people dry like a succubus. You didn't think that was important information I needed to know before going into our relationship?"

I tried to keep calm and poised. "I don't have to feed off anyone to live. It's a taste I've acquired."

"So, you're a junkie?"

"I've only killed those who I felt deserved it. Those thieves were the only ones, outside of the warriors who tried to have their way with me."

I did not deserve to be burned at the stake for my actions. I was a product of my environment, and I was fighting with everything I had to make a difference! "Imagine watching your mother die, and her killer sending men to rape you. They considered me nothing but a tool for their master plans. Don't you dare judge me!"

I was steaming, and thank goodness, he had enough sense to shut up and stop provoking my wrath. But I think he also pitied me. I didn't want him to. I just wanted him to understand that I was a survivor.

"Would you ever hurt me?" he barely asked above the sound of his own breath.

"Never!" I was instantly wracked with guilt. "I did hurt my mother, though..."

His eyes judged me once more.

"When I was thirteen, the elders stabbed my mother, and as she was dying, my ability activated. I sucked out what was left of her life. I didn't realize what I was doing until it was too late." When I thought back to that moment, I could still taste her going down my throat. The light was warm and vibrant. I became stronger—greater—but inside, I was dead. "It was the most awful day of my life. As I cried in a pool of her blood, they hailed me as their new queen."

I could feel the apology in the air, but Austin was too proud to utter it. "And you want me to be a part of this sick world?"

"I want you to come with me and change it." I glanced at him, and we both blushed. We talked about commitment, but there were so many details to work out. He thought I was special enough to dedicate himself to before, but going away to a secluded island of extremists might have been too much for him. I couldn't blame him.

"It sounds like the elders are pulling the strings. We should take them out."

"We?" I was filled with such untamable joy. I thought I would explode out of my skin, and my heart would blast off like a rocket up to the moon. Austin and I destroying the elders and avenging my mother was probably the most romantic thing I could think of.

"*You,*" he quickly corrected. "I care about you so much, Rose. I do, but this whole new persona of you is too much. I can't breed with you and continue growing your race of…whatever you are."

My shoulders slumped. I didn't realize how badly I wanted him to come home with me until I fantasized a thousand lifetimes into one second of real-time. "This opportunity could be the only one to save your world from us."

"Or I could change and be a threat to the world." He shook his head. "In your world, you have creepy elders who believe a daughter should kill her mother and men who wanna rape little girls. It doesn't sound like your world should be saved. It sounds like it should be burned to the ground."

He was wrong. We weren't all evil. The servants were good people. Even the warriors trained to protect me were good. It was the elders who corrupted everything. "We're not so much different than your people; we're just not malicious and petty."

"Killing humans because they steal a TV—that's probably insured—is as petty as it gets. So, I guess there's not much difference between us after all."

I turned to the window in defeat, but I would not admit to it. I didn't think I was acting out of pettiness, but maybe I was. It all happened so fast. I decided their fates faster than I could think. I wasn't sure what was in my heart.

I didn't speak another word to him while we rode together. I didn't want to give him my self-righteous speech that would only make him more uncomfortable, and perhaps even angry. He needed silence to properly think.

When we pulled into the garage, I noticed one of their cars was gone. They usually had two, but the white Cadillac was nowhere to be found. "Where's Noah?"

Austin took the key out of the ignition, but he kept staring at the wheel. Perhaps he regretted what we were about to do, but he eventually grunted and forced himself to persist. "He locked himself in his room. He wouldn't come out."

I gulped. I was also trying to convince myself to turn back. I just didn't know if I should go on with feeding Noah my royal nectar. It changed Austin, and I was an extreme example. If Noah turned out to be an entirely different creature, would he still be my potential for love?

The house was incredibly quiet, but I noticed a couple of wrapped boxes on a kitchen counter that had yet to be touched. "Is it his birthday?"

"No. My parents brought us some souvenirs from their trip. They felt bad for ditching us, so they went all out. When Noah wouldn't come down, they got really freaked out, and that didn't help. Noah threw out his medication, so they went to pick up some more. I wouldn't be surprised if they came back with a whole hospital wing full of doctors."

I gripped the thermos. Despite all my reservations and valiant plans to convince Noah not to use my elixir, I knew I was going to be the one to buckle. "I need to see him."

I rushed up the stairs and picked the door that was locked. "Noah?" I paused for two seconds before I anxiously knocked. I could break the door down effortlessly, but I didn't want to escalate the situation. Besides, he loved me. He would want to see me. "It's me, Rose."

"Go away." His voice was broken up by the tears in the back of his throat. He sounded so pitiful—broken even.

I turned around to Austin, and he shrank in his shoulders. He didn't know what was happening to his cousin, and I knew if he would utter a word of speculation, he would ruin his cool persona and break into tears himself. That truly worried me, and I was concerned Noah was nearing his end.

"Please, let me in!" I banged on the door again. I often wondered if I could respect his decision to let him die, and now I ached with everything I had. I didn't want him to let me go. He was honestly all I had, and I prayed he would be all I needed. "Noah, I beg of you!"

There were some heavy breaths behind the door, and then it cracked open a few seconds later. I heard Austin rush behind me, but I shook my head at him, and he paused. I needed to go in by myself. I didn't want anyone else to be a part of what I was about to do to Noah.

I slipped inside the crack and immediately felt the air on my back when the last molecule of me came in. Noah's room wasn't exactly what I imagined. I thought he'd be a complete neat freak, but he had clothes and junk food wrappers all over the floor, and pop cans around the desk where his computer sat.

Noah noticed I stared at his pile of dirty underwear. "What do you want?" His eyes fell to what I was carrying in my hands, and his voice began to brighten as he held off a smile born of hope.

"What's the matter, Noah? Why have you gone insane and locked yourself in your room? Why won't you take your medicine? Austin is going out of his mind with worry!"

"Austin's going out of his mind?" he laughed sarcastically, but his twisted smile couldn't hold as his lips quivered into a furious bout of tears. Noah angrily tossed a clump of hair on the ground, and he meant to shout at me all of the things wrong in his world, but all he could do was point and collapse against the door.

I was disgusted—not with Noah—that such a good person could have such a condition to suffer through. There was only one person, in particular, I would wish such a thing on, not my dear Noah.

I sat beside him and placed the elixir behind me. I hoped my presence was enough to soothe him, whether it was my pheromones or his genuine feelings. "You have to be strong, Noah."

He buried his head in my chest, shook, and sobbed. "I'm so sick of this, Rose! I'm so sick, and I'm afraid."

I kept my head above his to hide my tears. I had to demonstrate strength if I expected him to be strong. It was a wonder how I managed with such an ache in my soul. I hadn't known him for very long, yet I couldn't imagine what my life was going to be like after he died. All I could imagine was emptiness.

I gasped quietly. Could it be that I was in love with Noah and not Austin, or were my circumstances clouding my judgment? Austin hardly wanted anything to do with me, and Noah made it clear that he would never abandon my side. But relationships have to be tried, and hearts have to be proved.

"Don't be afraid, Noah." I reached behind me and placed the elixir in his hands. "It's alright."

He gawked at the thermos. Brave Noah wanted everyone to believe he could handle dying. But I always doubted his resolve, though I understood the façade. Inside, he was just a boy who desperately wanted to matter, and he was scared of time and the truth, that though it was infinite, there was never enough of it. "You really mean it?"

There would be no going back once I established myself as his savior. Honestly, I didn't want him to. "I care about you too much not to do everything within my power to save you."

"You do?" he seemed surprised.

"Of course, I do." I swallowed the nervous lump in the back of my throat. I wanted to tell him that I thought I loved him, but I didn't want to go back on my word if it were a mistake. "Don't leave me yet, Noah."

One final nod of approval was all he needed before he devoured the elixir. He made an odd expression as soon as he had his first taste, but he didn't stop to take a breath until he consumed everything. He even licked the rim. I hoped that was his desperation to be healed and not his new status as a junkie showing.

He collapsed on my chest and breathed in and out, slowly and deeply, for a few minutes. I think he was waiting to feel better, and I was afraid to ask him too early. I didn't want to disrupt his faith. I hoped, with everything I had, that he would become well enough. I had glorious plans for him.

"Do you still love me, Noah?"

He smiled. "Yes."

I wanted to tell him I felt the same way, but I truly didn't know. I couldn't change my mind about something that important. "How do I know if what you feel is real?"

His lips quickly made an impact on mine. It wasn't the same immature and unsteady kiss that we had before. He tasted sweet, and I felt his pure intentions on his lips, and then on his tongue. He really wasn't afraid anymore. He was confident that he would be enough. "Doesn't it feel real?"

I touched my lips. They were still tingling. Something had changed between us, and I don't think the elixir had much to do with it. I think the two of us were just…ready for each other now.

Noah gently took my hands and gazed into my eyes. "Only the love I have for you and Austin is real or worth anything. I don't have anything else to hold onto."

My heart beat a little bit faster. Noah was willing to give me everything. He was willing to accept me for what I was. He always did everything in his power to treat me like a queen, even before he knew I was one. I believed that he deserved me just a little bit more.

"Would you be comfortable if I asked you to be my king?" I saw his eyes widen, and I had to look away. I felt so wrong for even asking. He didn't know what that meant. "What if I wanted to take this world?"

"Would anyone get hurt?"

"Maybe. Maybe not." I wasn't wrong about him being naïve, but I couldn't let him believe his childish fantasies. "We've probably assimilated more humans than we can possibly know."

Noah bobbed his head from side-to-side before he admitted the truth with dodgy eyes. "I don't want to sound like some kind of psycho, but people talk about ruling the world. They joke about it, but I think most people—who aren't too lazy—would like to. I at least know I certainly wouldn't mind."

To say I was stunned would be an understatement. He wasn't joking when he told me that he could always surprise me. "What about democracy?"

He chuckled shortly, but then bigger. "I only believe in democracy because I'm not in charge."

My eyes widened, and I waited for him to correct himself, but all he did was laugh again. "Just when I think I have you figured out, you show me a new side of you."

He quickly kissed my lips. Despite admitting to wanting to take over the world, he was still incredibly kind. "I wanna take you somewhere and show you some things. Meet me downstairs. I wanna get dressed."

"Alright." I figured he must have been feeling better. I didn't want to pester him about his illness and jinx his miracle. I gave him his much-needed space and made my way downstairs.

Austin wasn't waiting by the steps as I thought. I found him in the dining room with an older man and a woman who both bore a resemblance to Austin. They all appeared worried, and then the three of them all looked at me with wide eyes. Austin nearly jumped out of his seat. "What happened?"

I couldn't explain the truth with his parents there. If Austin couldn't take the truth of my origin, I highly doubted that he would try to tell his parents about it. "He'll come down. He wants to take me out somewhere."

"So, he's feeling better?" Austin fought to keep his smile from coming to the surface.

"From what I can tell…" I couldn't say Noah looked any healthier, but he was certainly more positive. Besides, I couldn't let Austin down after he had some hope.

Austin's mother carefully watched both of us as we interacted. I could see the wheels in her head turning. She politely smiled and asked, "I thought you were Austin's girlfriend?"

I blinked hard, and I was at a complete loss for words. I had no idea that Austin had been talking about me with his parents at all, but he apparently had his own spin on it. Should I have outed him in front of his parents? It would have only been right to claim Noah as my own, seeing that I had just implied to Noah that I was proposing. I had to talk to Austin first. "I'm not with anyone at the moment. We're all dear friends."

Then, I felt a fast whirl of questions whiz by us like a vicious firing squad with poor aim. I got the sense that they were nosy. Austin's mother looked as if she were going to explode if she didn't bother me with one million questions. It was his father who stepped forward. "Well, we'll leave you alone."

His father grabbed his wife's arm, and the two of them reluctantly left our side. Austin waited awkwardly with shrugged shoulders. "Thank you."

"What? For revealing your single status to your parents?" I chuckled. "If you told your parents we were together, I'm sorry to blow your cover, but you did overstep your bounds."

"I did mention to my parents that I was seeing someone, but I didn't give them the impression we were serious, if that's what you're implying." Austin grinned, and I dare say he seemed so charming. "That's not what I was referring to, though. I'm thanking you for being there for Noah and saving him."

I just couldn't look at him with that smile on his face. I was trying to get over him and move on with Noah. "You don't have to thank me."

"Yes, I do!" He jumped out of his seat, grabbed my hands, and maneuvered his way until he found my eyes. I loved his stupid green eyes, and it infuriated me how helpless someone as powerful as me could be.

"You really don't." I managed to pull away from his grasp, and I crossed my arms. I needed clarity on whether I was going to succeed in my goal. "Noah wants to be my king. I'm deeply considering letting him."

Austin was so angry with me when I killed those burglars. He couldn't accept me, so I assumed the two of us were finished. He breathed deeply, and his eyes danced. I didn't know if he was more furious or hurt. "You can't take him away from me!"

I understood he felt abandoned, but he abandoned me first! He was pushing me away. I wasn't sure if he wanted to hold onto his cousin or sabotage our relationship. "You wanted me to give Noah his life back. Don't keep him from living it."

"You said you didn't want to come in between the two of us, and now you want to take him away from me forever, so he can be king of your little cult?"

I covered his mouth to silence his testy attitude. I didn't want his parents to hear about my origin and forbid me from ever being with the boys. I wouldn't remove my hand until his burning eyes simmered down.

"Noah loves me, Austin. He can save my people. He can change them for the better. He wants to do something great. He wants to matter."

"He matters to me!" Perhaps he was more afraid of losing Noah than he was of losing me. But Noah wanted more than being loved. He wanted to be honored, and I didn't know if that would be possible while living in the shadow of his cousin.

"How can I convince you that this is for the best?"

I think I saw Austin's eyes glisten, but he turned his head to the side and smiled from...deliriousness? I'm not sure. I just knew he was trying to hide whatever he still felt about me. "Tell me that you love him more than me, and he's not your last option because I can't accept what you are."

I became enraged because Austin thought of me as a "thing." I was a creature, and it didn't matter what we felt when we kissed or touched. We could never go back. "Noah was always the better man, Austin."

His nostrils flared, but he kept his jaw tight and his lips shut.

"My people need his kindness, not your arrogance and brashness." I only hoped Austin didn't know that I never confessed my love for Noah. I loved him, but I just couldn't admit to it yet. "It's better this way."

"What's going on?" Noah asked from the top step. He had certainly cleaned himself up nicely in a white dress shirt, a sweater vest, and a pair of khakis. His hair was very polished and brushed back. He was completely handsome.

Austin's mother emerged from across the house and came to the bottom step, full of concern. "Are you up to going out, Noah?"

"I'm fine," he insisted. He even ran down the stairs quickly to help prove his case. "I'm going out with Rose."

Austin crossed his arms and carefully analyzed every single bit of Noah. "Are you really feeling better?" I'm not sure what Austin thought he discovered. Noah looked perfect to me.

"Yeah. I feel great."

"I don't know," Austin's mother said. "You were just locked up in your room—"

"You can't keep me here," Noah said firmly. He probably didn't take that sort of tone often with his adopted parents, because she certainly looked surprised.

"I just worry about you."

"I feel wonderful, Aunt Karen!" There was a brightness in his eyes that I don't think could have existed if he expected to die. I was beginning to accept he had been healed, and I wasn't the only one.

"Let him go," Austin said. "I'm sure he'll be back early." Austin's eyes locked with mine, and he made me promise with my eyes that I wouldn't do anything rash with his cousin. I solidified our agreement with a nod. I wasn't going to lose my virginity to anyone except for my husband. It might have very well been Noah, but I wasn't consummating anything that night!

"Come on, Rose." Noah grabbed my hand and kissed it gently. "Let's get out of here."

My face bubbled with smiles, and I giggled. I was so proud of the gentleman before me, and it also excited me that I could feel Austin's jealousy rising higher and higher from behind. "Where are we going?"

"To a place where I can show you something you don't understand."

I would have been a tiny bit insulted if I weren't intrigued. I decided not to rack my brain, and I let him lead me out of the house and to Austin's car. I was curious what sort of questions Austin would have to answer about the dynamic of our relationships, but I could wonder about that another day. My attention was better focused on celebrating Noah's new life.

I continuously observed Noah while we were in the car together. He didn't look to be in any discomfort, but that didn't mean anything. "Do you feel any side effects?"

"I just feel lighter than I have in a really long time."

"What do you mean?"

"The heaviness from the burden of my illness is gone," he grinned, "and it's all thanks to you."

I was genuinely happy. Now that Noah was better, I could look to the future of our relationship. I could see that I did want to be with him, beyond feeling pity for his condition, and I didn't have to automatically choose Austin because I needed a long-term mate. They were on even ground now.

I looked outside of my window, and the lovely homes began to decay around me. Unique symbols were splatted alongside buildings in particularly urban flair, and the type of pedestrians walking by had mean faces like they were going to war with the world. "What's this?"

"This is a rougher neighborhood. It's nice that we got to spend all of our time on the beach relaxing and having fun, but there's a whole world out there that doesn't get to live like us."

Noah drove down a few alleys and ended up where a couple of teenagers were fishing in the dumpster, outside of a restaurant. Most of the food was wrapped or boxed up, but I was still disgusted by their way of survival. How could they stomach living in such a way? I read about such poverty, but I had never seen it with my own eyes before.

Noah observed the children, and he saw something inside of them that I could not. I tried my best to find what his eyes were gripping onto, but I only saw children.

After a while, he smiled very sadly. "If it weren't for my aunt and uncle, I'd be in the Foster Care system. No one would have wanted me—a sick kid."

"But you're wonderful!"

"Most kids are. We look at the world differently from adults. Then we get older...we see the reality of the world around us. It changes us..." Noah often appeared so boyish and innocent that I hadn't noticed how aged his eyes were. He had been through something so much deeper and darker than most people, and he was only a boy. I had the same eyes, but mine weren't only tarnished with reality. They were infected with darkness, from the inhumanity I forced my enemies to suffer, in order to keep what little bit of light I had left.

"You know, I would have been in Foster Care until I turned eighteen. I would have either had crappy living accommodations or I would have been with this group of teens over here."

It was difficult imagining Noah making a home with those kids. He was so gentle and polished. I couldn't see him roaming the streets to find food in the dead of night. However, he was a survivor. Perhaps he was the toughest out of all of us.

"I'm not grateful to have this disease, but I have a good life." He smiled sadly. "It's just too bad that it's destined to be a little short."

"But that's all changed now." I took his hand and squeezed it tight. "You're gonna live a long and full life with me now."

Noah's cheeks began to redden. "And I'm looking forward to it."

I leaned on Noah's shoulder and tried to imagine our lives together. With him being the king, I could fire the elders. They would most likely try to resist or cause a rebellion, so I'd have no choice but to order their execution. How could anyone turn against my word if I were impregnated with the future of our race? It was going to be a brave new world for my people, and I would lead them into greatness and happiness. After so much misery, we all deserved that chance.

"You wanted to show me the reality of the world? I've read about wars and poverty, Noah. I'm not completely naïve."

"But what about the little people caught in the crossfire? They're not fighting for good or working for evil. They're just existing and doing the best they can. Who cares about the mundane? Who makes sure their lives are protected? Who makes sure their lives are worth living?"

"Things are different in my colony. Everyone fulfills their duties. Everyone believes they're serving me, so they believe they're happy."

"It's not your people I'm worried about. We need to fix our world first. These people should have homes and families. They shouldn't have to worry about where their next meal is coming from. They need a chance to make something of themselves. They need a chance to matter."

"They matter to me, and when I return to being queen, I'll do my best. That's all I can offer you, though, Noah." I took Noah's hand and held it. I remembered how desperate he was to make a difference in the world. Well, I was going to make him my king, and we would join our worlds together and free them both.

Noah wanted to go home after that. He seemed to be bursting with joy, but I still got the feeling something was wrong. I hypothesized it could have been the thought of leaving his family.

When Noah parked in front of my house, I didn't make a move to get out. I wanted to know why he was so quiet. "What is it, Noah?"

He blushed and sank his head down. "You really don't mind marrying me?"

"Noah!" I chuckled and kissed his cheek. "I more than mind. I mind it very much, but in a very good way!"

He grinned adorably before slowly nodding his head. "Okay. I just have to go home and talk to my family about this."

"Then I should come with you. Just give me a moment to drink my elixir, and I'll—"

He pecked my lips, and my conversation came to a positive end. "I'll handle my family. I'll call you after I work everything out."

"And you don't mind being the king of an inhuman species that could potentially be hostile to your people?"

"Not if the right person is leading." Noah made me feel like I was reading one of my fairytales again. I forgot about all the awful things I had done to preserve myself. His love cleansed me of my evil.

"I'll see you later then, fiancé." I could barely keep myself from being a giddy fool as I proclaimed his title. I was actually doing it. I ran away to find love, and I was going to return with a king to change my world. Everything was exactly as it should have been.

Chapter Fourteen

With my goal of having a king by my side complete, I only had one wish for myself left. I wanted to reunite with my sister. If she wanted to stay behind with her lover, I wouldn't stand in the way of that, but it was only right to inform her that I'd soon be returning home to our colony. Besides, she'd want to know I chose the cousin who wasn't rude.

I hadn't inquired about Camellia because I didn't want to look weak. She should have come back to me, and certainly never the other way around. But the truth was that I deeply missed my sister.

I needed to find her before the elders received word that she was beyond our control. They would probably send spies to kill her, or at least drag her back home.

I stared at the rain streaming down the window glass in its unique pattern as I thought about us. No matter how unpredictable and independent we tried to be, it always seemed like our paths were predestined. No matter which way the rain fell, it was all going down.

"Where would you go, Camellia?" I asked aloud. "Where would you feel safe?"

I took an umbrella and retraced the steps we took together. I walked by the store where the thieves worked. I peeked through the window to see if I could spot her. The girl, who was once polite and helpful, stared at me like I was a vengeful ghost she feared and loathed. She must have known the thieves had last attacked my house, but how could she question me? It must have been a terrible position to be in, but if she ever tried to come after me, she wouldn't have a happy ending.

I combed the beach next. It was the first place she met her human friend, Thomas. If they were nostalgic, they probably came back to the beach often. After all, it was difficult for me to walk on the sand and not think of Austin standing above me with a smug smile. When I looked out into the water, I remembered how fearless and reckless he was when he surfed for the first time, and I recalled how much I wanted to be like him.

I then realized that I was making an egregious mistake and forced the memories away. I couldn't be with Austin. He hated me and what I was. Noah would be more than my husband. He would become a part of me. We would rule together, my people would be free, and my children would know love.

There wasn't the usual crowd at the beach. It was cold, growing darker, and the rain was coming down harder with each passing second. Even still, I pressed forward and peeked in on shops and restaurants to see if she was near, but I never saw her radiant face.

I didn't even know what I was looking for. I suppose I thought through our bond, I could somehow latch onto her. I hoped she truly was never far from me at all, but I was nothing but a fool living off my dreams again. We were only blood bound. She would never love the woman who killed her mother.

Completely and utterly defeated, I started on my journey home. My socks were already squishy after two minutes of walking. I was miserable and cold. To add to my total discouragement, I still had no idea where my dear sister was.

I was about to surrender to grief and feel sorry for myself. Perhaps even have a light cry, but I could not. About a block away from my house, I saw something I didn't expect to see and, suddenly, everything changed forever.

"Rose..." My sweet boy approached me with a white rose in his hand. He was either shaking from his nerves or shivering from the cold. He was soaked to the bone. The poor thing should have driven, but it was incredibly sweet what lengths he was willing to go to please me.

"Noah..." I was going to reach out to grab his hand, but I drew back. The white rose in his hand signified so much to him, and I was aware of its deeper meaning. It wasn't just another romantic gesture to get the leg up on his cousin. He planned on never turning back. "Are you insane? You could catch a cold in this weather!"

"I didn't see you at home. I tried to drive, but I got a flat tire, so I decided I had to find you." He grinned like a beautiful fool. "Rose, I don't want to wait."

I blinked hard and opened my eyes wide. My cheeks were burning. "Wait for what?"

He cupped my face and abruptly pulled me in for a kiss. It wasn't like our first kiss or even the second. He poured himself into me, and I felt every bit of love and passion. I could still taste desperation, but it didn't feel so wrong to want to soak up the moment when I believed he was the one.

"Noah, what are you doing?"

"I am worthy of you." His voice cracked from his proclamation, but he gulped to gather his courage and stated it, once again, with more resolve. "I am, and I'd be a good king. I know that I would. I could make you happy for an eternity if I could have the chance, Rose. I swear I could."

"I know you could." I took his rose and smiled fully. It had been through hell. The petals were beaten apart by the rain. What was left on the stem was hanging on limply, but that defiant beauty continued to look lovely to me. "But I want to have my husband's child, and no one else's. We can wait."

He continued to smile, but I could tell in his eyes there was something wrong. "I want to marry you, Rose."

"Then let's wait!" I pecked his lips in excitement. "You have to properly explain things to your aunt and uncle. I'd like for Austin not to hate us both when we leave. I want Camellia to be there and—"

"I don't have time, Rose!" He was still smiling, but he was growing more uncomfortable.

"We have time—"

"I don't!" he snapped quietly, but with enough ferociousness to startle me.

"What's wrong?" I was in denial. I knew when I saw him after drinking my elixir that he didn't look any better. He was only chipper because he accepted his fate.

Even so, I still needed to hear him speak it. "I'm still sick. I think I'm even worse." And yet he kept smiling as he pretended he hadn't ruined everything we were planning.

I was furious! How dare he let me believe we were going to have a life together when he knew there wasn't any hope? He should have told me the truth. I failed Noah, and I hated whatever majestic being flowed through the elixir and decided Noah wasn't worth saving.

"We have to get you inside." I grabbed his hand and led him home quickly. He was stumbling behind me, but I wouldn't let up. His body was extremely sensitive. That storm was no place for him, especially not for some silly flower. Was he trying to get himself killed?

When we got to my home, he started coughing. I was beginning to feel motherly toward him, but I pushed myself to keep my anger. "Are you insane?" I led him to the electric fireplace and turned it on. "What if you catch pneumonia?"

"It wouldn't matter."

My hand ran against his face so fast; I hadn't realized I slapped him until I heard the smack of my hand against his skin. He looked so pathetic that it was extremely difficult not to take pity on him, but I had to hold onto my anger, or else the only thing left would be the pain. "How dare you?"

I meant to scream, but my voice was overcome by the tears I had been fighting off. "Everything matters! You matter to me, Noah."

"Some people are meant to live long, full lives. Some people are meant to have legacies." He chuckled. "Then there are people like me."

"No, Noah. That's not true." I shook my head. He just couldn't give up! "You are meant for greatness. You're gonna be my king." I stroked the very red spot on his face. I didn't mean to hurt him, but I cared far too much to let him slip right through my fingers.

"You said your elixir was Fate. Well, Fate doesn't want me to go on. Austin is still better than fine—physically anyway—and I'm dying faster than I was before." He took my hands and stroked them with his thumbs. "I can feel everything breaking down. My life is fading. The only part of me that feels whole is the part that wants you."

I didn't know what to do. I was supposed to be in complete control, and yet I felt like I was falling and had nothing to hold on to, besides the poor grip he had on my hands. For a little while, I focused on his touch. It felt good, and I knew how much he wanted me, but everything shifted. "I don't know what you're asking of me. If you think you're dying, how can I be your wife?"

He swallowed hard and kept his nervous eyes focused on our hands joined together. "I know a little bit about how your world works. If all I can leave behind in this world is a child, then…"

If he could barely ask it of me, then how was he ready? I think I was ready. I had been anticipating it my whole life. My heart was racing, and my stomach was all in knots, but it didn't feel like the romantic way. I felt like I was going to puke.

"We've gotta get you out of those wet clothes. I'm gonna find some blankets." I pecked his lips and rushed upstairs. I knew I wouldn't have any clothes that fit him, so I grabbed two fluffy blankets from my room and brought them downstairs to Noah. He was so cold that his lips were blue. "Take your clothes off."

He looked at me oddly. I didn't understand why. How did he think the two of us were supposed to have sex? "Okay." He took his shirt off, and I swear he flexed his chest, so I could see his abs on his little body. Then, he took off his socks and pants. He reached for his boxers, but I grabbed his hands.

"That's enough." I grabbed two ends of the blanket and wrapped him up. I tried to avoid his eyes, but he was so focused on me that the moment I slipped up, he was there to trap me inside his. I felt my heartbeat, and I swear I felt his as well. He let the blanket slip, and he grabbed a hold of my shoulders and pulled me in for a kiss.

I was so wrong. He was ready. I could feel it in his fingertips as he traced them down my arm and moved to my back, so he could press my body into his. I felt his heart pumping through his ribcage, and I tried to get carried away. I tried to lose myself, like when I went out surfing. I wanted to be one with the rhythm—one with nature and instinct—but there was still too much of me, and I couldn't let go of my control. I knew that if I didn't stop, I was bound to crash and drown.

I tore myself away from Noah. I couldn't pretend like I didn't enjoy it. I was breathing deeply, and my skin was still tingling, but my mind was somewhere else. I could block out my feelings, but it wasn't fair to him.

I had never been fair to him. "I'll call Mr. Jones to come and fix your tire for you. You focus on getting better."

As I tried to walk away, he grabbed my wrist. "I don't have much time."

"Don't say things like that!" I didn't mean to explode on him, but I was so overwhelmed. I felt like I was back in the ocean, being pounded by the waves that I once thought were gentle and abundantly graceful. "You want me to have your children. It's my duty, but I want more than that. I was not put on this planet to be an incubator! We have to find a way to fix you."

He slightly glared. "Are you stalling?"

My mouth dropped, but as offended as I was, I felt like he had caught me. "I'm not stalling. I just want to do this the right way."

"Or you're stalling." He laughed hysterically and threw his arms up in exasperation. "I know you don't wanna do this alone, but you'll find someone else."

"Maybe, but my babies will have your eyes, and then I'll remember you're not here for them." I touched my stomach instinctively, but my imagination took me far away from that point of contact. When I held my very first baby in my arms, I wanted to be able to look up at their hovering father with pride in his heart and a smile as glorious as the sun itself. I didn't want the elders to be the ones to take them, so they could start listing my children as slaves.

"The elders will grow impatient. I have spies watching me. If they find out I've consummated and haven't married, they'll try to rush me back home. I'll never have the time to find a husband, and they'll never let me leave home again!"

I researched many things about human mothers. There were many women without husbands and many children. It might not have been difficult to find more lovers, but it would be nearly impossible to find a good man willing to settle down with, who I could trust to love my children as much as I would. Considering my life was already complicated enough, I didn't expect to ever find someone else to genuinely love me again.

"Noah, you're the only person left in this world who cares about me. I can't lose you."

I thought Noah would be a ball full of blushing smiles, but he scrunched up his face as he began to look sicker. "That's not true. Austin still loves you."

"He can't. I remember the way he looked at me." I never felt like the terrible things I had done were unjustified until I saw how disgusted and afraid Austin was of me. I couldn't afford to feel that with my life and the lives of my children at risk. "He'll never understand."

Noah shook his head and dug his foot into the floor like a child in trouble. "He tried to convince me not to marry you. He said he didn't want me to leave. He told me you were a monster. He tried everything he could possibly think of to convince me to stay.

"Things got heated. I accused him of still having feelings for you. I thought he'd say something smart or maybe even punch me in the face," he laughed, "but he just stood there in awe."

Noah smirked, and he looked so much like Austin. "I don't think he realized it before I mentioned it to him, but he's still crazy about you."

"I see…" I couldn't breathe. I took a step back and stumbled. Noah had to catch me to keep me still, but my head was still spinning.

"I just thought you deserved to know the truth." He pulled me close and kissed my forehead. "Can we just be together? I know you're not going to hurt us, Rose. If you have a piece of me, maybe my child can help you save your world, and my own."

I was overtaken by the waves, but I could feel myself beginning to come up for air. I envisioned being lifted out of the darkness, and when I could breathe again, I saw my savior. "I do love you, Noah. I always will, no matter what happens. I just don't think I can do this with you."

His lips slightly trembled, and he wasn't going to cry, but I felt as broken as he was when I saw his eyes. "Because I'm dying?"

"No. It's because I'm still very much in love with Austin."

I was beyond baffled by my actions. All I did was argue with Austin. He constantly challenged me! He acted like a scoundrel. He made my blood boil! But as angry as he made me, there was just something deep inside of me that let me know the passion between us was a profound connection.

"I wish I could choose you, Noah. I thought finding love would be simple, and yet I've made a mess of things. You have the kindest soul I've ever felt, but my heart is connected with his, even when he broke it into a million pieces."

I felt completely horrible for what I had put Noah through, but there was a burden lifted off my chest. I had been searching for that clarity, and to finally have it was such a relief. I didn't know if he'd ever accept us, but at least I knew who I was fighting for. "I want him to be my first. I want my children to be his."

Noah pressed his forehead to mine. I can't say he was surprised. I knew he wanted to go out in a blaze of glory, but he was tired. "I don't want to die alone. I need to leave something behind. I don't want to fade away and have the world forget I was ever here, to begin with."

I wanted to do it for Noah, but I couldn't oblige his request out of pity. Even if he believed his entire self-worth was trapped within his loins, I couldn't be the one to give him a legacy. Besides, he was terribly mistaken.

"Noah, not all men can leave behind lavish buildings or glorious empires. You don't need to solve a world crisis or bring about world peace. No matter how great men become, someone will always be hungry, and a new disease will take someone's life. Sometimes, living our lives is the best we can do. But putting love in someone's heart is the greatest monument anyone can ever build."

I took his hands and kissed them. I had nothing but respect for him. People met my needs my entire life, but he was the first person to ever want to know who I was, and he didn't mind the "what" either. I naively believed in true love, but I had forgotten that kindness was real. The humans were worth saving if there were more men like him in the world.

"I swear to you, Noah, for as long as I live, I will never forget you. And as for dying alone, I'll be with you until the bitter end."

My hands fell on his chest, and I felt his heart pulse through my fingers. He was still freezing, but I was beginning to make a difference. He leaned in closer, and I feared he would try to kiss me again. I was going to push him away, but he quickly pulled me in for an embrace. "Thank you, Rose."

I stayed with Noah by the fire to warm him. I told Noah everything about my life. I told him about the riches and the loneliness. I told him about the precious time I spent with my mother, in the garden, and the shame of when I took what was left of her fading life. I even confided in him about all the lives I had taken to protect my heart. He listened carefully and didn't judge.

When I finished my story, he told me about his life growing up. Austin would spend the summer with Noah and his family when his parents went away on long trips. They would play in their backyard for hours. They would create their own world where the two of them were brave rulers. One day, they got overly ambitious during their adventure and explored the forest. They were lost for hours until Noah suggested they use the North Star to guide them home. Since they didn't live north, and since they had no idea which star really burned the brightest, they were lucky they ended up back home, safe and sound, with blind luck alone.

My tales were grim, but Noah's were full of laughter and joy. I asked him to tell me more stories, so I could live vicariously through them. I imagined many worlds, roles, and special abilities while reading my books, but nothing was as wonderful as the beauty of an ordinary life.

We talked until we couldn't keep our eyes open. While I slept, I dreamed that I was with them in the woods, running and laughing as a young child. I was still in one of my elegant dresses, so I had to hold it up as I ran, but I kept up with the boys just fine. Noah tripped on the train when he got close to me. Austin and I were quick to come to his aid, but he got up on his own. Noah dusted himself off and gave us a goofy grin. Then, Austin and I knew he would be alright.

"Rose…"

I awakened at the sound of his coughs. I could hear the pain in his voice, along with the sickness. His body was moist from sweat, and he was burning up. "Noah?" I rose off him and held his face. "Are you awake?"

His eyes were glossed over. I'm not even sure if he could see me. I gently moved his face, but he still responded. I could feel slipping.

"Just hold on a little bit longer. I'm gonna call an ambulance and…"

He coughed again, and I knew I wouldn't be fast enough to send for help. With each breath he took, I felt his life escaping. I had felt this a dozen times before, starting with my mother, and continuing with every other life I had taken.

"Noah…" Tears slipped from my eyes and onto his face. I was losing him, and Austin wasn't there to say goodbye. "I love you."

I closed my eyes and touched my lips to his. I breathed in through my nostrils to inhale his scent, and with it, I could feel his warmth. I wanted to remember the love he had for me and keep it always.

Then, I realized I could do more than feel his warmth. I could taste it. "No!" I jumped and backed away from him. I had to make it stop! I couldn't take his life away. I covered my mouth and nose, but the warm and wispy light continued to pull out of him and circle me. I cried and tried to shut it out. My hunger came upon me like a ravenous beast that clawed from my stomach and up to my throat. My mouth began to open on its own, but I kept my hands tightly pressed on my face. I would not take Noah's life!

I could feel his life slipping through the cracks between my fingers. I accidentally breathed in his sweet innocence, and I wanted more. I squeezed my fingers together and completely stopped breathing. I told myself that if I didn't take his life, then he could have it back. He was too young to die, and he was too good to be stripped away from us all. Even if he had to leave, I couldn't take him. Austin would never forgive me.

I held out as long as I could, until my head ached. I felt dizzy, and I dropped to my knees. I gasped for air, and his life force found its way inside of me. I had never felt so wretched in all of my life, but there was no way to escape what was coming. I released my hands and sobbed as all that Noah ever was, and would have been, came inside of me.

Chapter Fifteen

"Here we are again." If I weren't so distraught over the loss of Noah, I would have snapped Mr. Jones in half and sucked him dry. "I thought you were sent here to breed with the humans, and yet you keep killing them."

"I didn't kill him. He was sick. I thought I could make him better, but..." I sat on the bottom step while his team came inside to take Noah's body away. I leaned against the banister, and tears lazily slipped from my eyes when they zipped the black body bag. "I guess it just wasn't meant to be."

"So, if you're innocent, why would you need me to clean this up?"

"I don't want Austin to suspect I had anything to do with it. I could tell him Noah died from his lupus or pneumonia, but in the back of his mind, he'd suspect me."

"And you never want to tell him the truth?"

"I didn't kill him!" I yelled desperately. "I didn't mean to take what was left of his life." I needed someone to believe that. I loved Noah. I probably should have sent him home or to a hospital, but I knew he wanted to be by my side. It was all I could offer him.

I stood up and pointed at Mr. Jones's face, and he finally looked petrified. Good. If he didn't keep his mouth shut, I was going to destroy him and anyone else who stood in my way. "I have a very slim chance of finding love. Austin is afraid of my life and what it means. He doesn't understand how we fit. I have to convince Austin that I can work with him to change our world, and I can't do that if this gets out!"

I shoved Mr. Jones in his chest, and he flew across the foyer and into a giant mirror. He shattered it into pieces and fell to the ground bleeding. It did cross my mind that I should end his life right there and then. People like him were only a threat to my revolution. Besides, devouring Noah left me feeling empty emotionally. Taking Mr. Jones would have given me some satisfaction.

He saw it coming, and he began to tremble. "My queen—"

"Silence!" I was so angry that I could hardly take it. The men who followed the elders' orders were the reason I had to defend myself. They turned me into a monster. They were the reason I had a hunger that consumed everything. They had to pay for changing me!

I stepped forward to take his life, but I stepped on a piece of glass, and it sliced my foot. I hissed and stepped back to see the bloodied reflection. Is that all I had to offer? Was that the legacy I would leave behind for myself and my children? There had to be more to me than the hurt. I needed to be more than the witch.

"Just follow my orders. Do not question me. Take care of Noah's body, and never utter his name again."

He gulped but then nodded his head. I knew he could be an obedient servant once he learned his place. "Yes, my queen."

I didn't know what they were going to do with my beloved Noah, and I didn't ask. I trusted they wouldn't allow his death to be traced back to me. I thought I wanted to see his face one last time, but it was too painful.

I waited for hours for some sort of word on Noah. I expected a call from Austin, but time dragged on and on. I had to get my mind off everything, so I decided to drown my horrible world in the fantasy of a book.

I wished I had found a copy of the tale of the witch, the princess, and the knight's son. I searched every inch of that bookstore where I met Noah, but they didn't have a copy. I even tried other local stores, but I guess it wasn't meant to be.

I don't remember what book I read or what it was even about. I just remember that about halfway through it, the pages began to wrinkle from tears. How could I ever pick up another book and not remember how charming Noah attempted to be at the bookstore when we first met? His eyes would haunt me forever.

"I'm so sorry, Noah!"

"Rose…?"

I gasped and hopped on my feet. Could it really be possible? Was I imagining her? I was hesitant to turn around and see, but I needed to know. "Camellia!"

She looked so different. Her hair was cut right above her shoulders, and she had a delightful glow about her. She no longer wore her clothes with uncertainty. Camellia had grown into a confident woman. She smiled slightly, but I'd like to think that she was happy to see me. "How are you, sister?"

I thought I would be too full of pride to properly make up with Camellia, but I ran into her arms and poured my life into her. When her arms came around me, I understood why she was the big sister. I instantly felt better. "I thought I'd never see you again!"

"I could feel you."

"Feel me?" I loosened my embrace so I could take a step back and see her face. "How is that possible?"

She gently rubbed her thumb across my cheeks to wipe away the tears. "It was like you were reaching out to me. I knew you were in pain, and I knew you needed me. It felt like you were calling me."

"The Call?" I laughed, and I'm not exactly sure why. I suppose I knew I was capable of performing it now, but I guarantee the elders never thought it would be for a hug. "Thank you for answering."

She looked a little hurt that I would say such a thing. "It's my duty."

"As one of my subjects?"

"No!" she chuckled and kissed my forehead. "I'm your sister—your big sister—and I will always love you."

I smiled and attacked her with another hug. I wondered if I would have made so many mistakes if she were by my side. It was too late for regrets, though. We could do things right now.

I sat with her on the couch and got her caught up on everything that happened. She was appalled that I gave the boys my elixir and slightly scolded me. She understood, given the circumstances. She looked frightened when I explained how I killed the burglars, but she was also angry and felt violated. She didn't speak out to judge me. She was happy I asked Noah to be my king. Camellia was glad I didn't choose the rude one, and that's when I cried all over again. When I told her why I was so full of grief, she shared my pain.

I was terrified to tell her what I had done to Noah because I took away two people she cared about. "I feared you would despise me forever, Camellia. I would understand if you did."

Camellia took my hand and set it in her lap. She held onto me with a firm grip as if she would never let me go. "I was upset about our mother. She was the only thing in this world that I ever truly loved. Now that I've gotten to know you and Thomas...I understand what it's like to have something to lose."

Her eyes glistened, but she smiled. "I understand that you were trying to protect your heart, Rose. I can't fault you for it, because I think I'd fight the entire world to protect you." Then, I saw her stern, protective look, which I had seen many times, only it was more menacing than before. "If the elders are behind all of your suffering, then we should make them suffer!

"You are not a villain. You have the ability to be a mother. You have taken life, but you were put on this earth to give it. That's your power. It's only right if you can create it with someone you love."

My mother told me my life was a burden. That's what it seemed like on most days, but all our lives would have been much different if she had even bothered to know my father's name. "I love Austin, but I'll never have him."

"He may understand."

"He won't," I said quickly. Perhaps he would if my life were a fairytale where forgiveness was simple, but love was much more complicated in the real world, and Austin was as real as it got. "He can never know."

I could tell Camellia was not pleased by the way she pouted, but she nodded in respect. "I will keep your secret, Rose."

Camellia offered to make me something to eat to cheer me up, but I insisted on helping her. I needed to do something to keep busy, or else I was going to go mad. We decided to fill the house with sweet things. We started making cakes and cookies—all from scratch. Camellia didn't need any recipes. She told me what to do, and I did it.

While Camellia mixed the batter, my curiosity grew bold enough to finally inquire about her time away. "What happened between you and Thomas? Did you consummate your relationship?"

She became bright red instantly, sank her head, and stared into the chocolate batter. "We did…"

My eyes widened. I told Camellia she would drive men mad. She was certainly a gorgeous girl. "And how was it?"

She left the mixer alone and approached me with her shoulders still slumped. "It was pleasing. I enjoyed it very much, but I almost wished that we hadn't."

"Why?"

She shrugged like an adorable child. "We're connected now in a way that I'm not connected to anyone else. He wasn't a virgin, so it was more special to me than to him. It was the most magical moment of my life, and for him, it was casual." She wrinkled her nose. "He didn't love me at the time, yet I felt obligated to give myself to him. Now, we're going to break up, and I'll have all of these memories and ties to someone I have to move on from…"

I could see in her eyes that she truly did not want to leave him. She was right about being connected. There was a glow in her skin and a brightness in her voice. "Why are you breaking up?"

"He is a musician." She smirked, impressed. "He's going on tour, and I can't exactly run away and join him. My place is here by your side." She touched my arm and rubbed against it. "Besides, I can't give Thomas a family."

I felt a pang of guilt for the part I played in that predicament. "Does he talk about wanting one?"

"Not right away, but I can't lead him on like some people would," she mumbled.

She turned around and resumed her baking, but I was unsettled. "And what's that supposed to mean?"

She gasped and spun around, as frightened of me as when I first met her. "I didn't mean to imply you, Rose!"

"Oh, really?" I was more amused than angry, but I had never toyed with anyone besides the elders, and I wanted to have some fun. "Well, you must be punished for your actions." I kept a stern look on my face and approached Camellia with a bag of flour. She wasn't as scared as I thought, but that might have been because my trick was breaking from a smile.

I reached inside the bag of flour and quickly splashed a handful in her face. Camellia screamed and closed her eyes in fear, but once she realized her face was covered in white powder, her mouth opened wide from shock, and she shook her arms from a quiet rage.

I didn't mean to laugh at Camellia so loud and obnoxiously, but it was hysterical! She was the most uptight person I knew—outside of the elders—so it was kind of amazing to see her so caught off guard.

I hunched over and laughed until I felt slime explode across my face. I gasped and looked down at the ground to see what was left of the eggshell. I could not believe she would do such a thing to me!

My eyes slowly came up to Camellia. Her eyes were wide and terrified. She covered her mouth and snickered into her hand to mask the sound, but I could tell she was laughing at me from the way her shoulders shook. Once the snicker erupted into a full-blown laugh, I was done!

I grabbed a fistful of flour and threw it at Camellia, but she expected it and leaped out of the way. I grunted and reached back inside for another fistful, but she was quick and catapulted a spoonful of chocolate cake batter. That genuinely angered me, but some of it did land in my mouth. It was delicious, and I took a moment to lick the splatter from the side of my mouth. "Throw anything but that."

Camellia was still defensive and clutched onto the batter as if it were a bomb she meant to unleash upon me.

I cautiously stretched my arms toward her and eased in her direction. "I'm serious, Camellia. It's delicious. Don't sacrifice your hard work."

I don't know if it was because I looked ridiculous or because I was pleading with her to save cake batter, but she burst out into laughter and set the mixing bowl down. "Okay, my queen."

"I told you to call me your 'sister!'" I reached for one of the eggs and smashed it on top of her forehead. She gasped, but she also laughed. I also initiated a full-out war. I don't know why we decided to bond in such a childish way, but I needed it. For a few moments, while I was with Camellia, I forgot about the pain inflicted by the elders and myself. I felt like how I believed Noah and Austin were when I saw them playing in those family pictures.

Camellia ended her assault when she tried to tackle me. My superior strength made it impossible to knock me over, so I wrestled with her a bit and picked her up off the ground. She screamed, which made me laugh. I was going to walk with her around the kitchen as a display of my greatness, but my heel slipped on some egg yolk, and my butt made an abrupt impact with the wooden floor, and Camellia landed on my chest.

"Do you give up?" She beamed from ear to ear.

I snickered and rested my head against the floor. It was such a silly moment, and yet I wanted it to last forever. I often looked outside my window as a child and stared at the children running around. I was curious about them, but I never truly understood what I missed until now.

"Are you alright, Rose?" Camellia asked with a hint of worry.

I grinned. "I'm perfect."

The doorbell began to sound off, and the two of us looked at each other, frightened. It was either Austin or Mr. Jones, and neither one would lead me into a conversation I wanted to be a part of. I hoped it was Mr. Jones, though. At least I terrified him now. With Austin, it was the other way around.

We wiped ourselves down as fast as we could. I wasn't going to get all the egg yolk off without a good shower, but we put in a good effort before I headed to the door.

I saw through the side glass panels that it was Austin shifting from side-to-side. He didn't look to be his cool self at all. I stopped about three feet from the door. I just didn't know if I could face him. He deserved to know the truth, but he would hate me. I couldn't lose both of them, especially not after realizing I wanted to spend my life with Austin.

"You have to face him," Camellia encouraged from far behind. I didn't turn around to see her, but I imagined she was pushing her hands forward to give me an air nudge. "You are strong enough to do this."

I didn't know if what she said was true, but I took a deep breath and opened the door anyway.

Austin came out of his funk and stepped back, startled. "What on earth happened to you?"

My face felt sticky, but I knew we had gotten all the globs off. My hair and clothes were still a mess. "Camellia and I were baking, and it got a little out of hand."

A small smirk curved in the corner of his mouth. My heart could hardly take it when he looked that sexy. "The food must taste really good or really bad."

I blushed, laughed, and clasped my hands together. "I can assure you that it tastes excellent. Camellia is masterful, and I am a good apprentice." Austin was uncomfortable, and I felt the heaviness, but I wasn't sure if he knew about Noah yet. "Would you like to come in? We just have to put the cake in the oven and—"

"I can't stay." Austin's lip quivered, but he kept himself from crying.

"It's Noah, isn't it?"

He nodded, and his lips quivered more. His whole body trembled for a second, but he composed himself as much as possible, and only a single tear slipped from his eye. "The police found him this morning. He was on the side of the road in his car, dead. The doctors say it was pneumonia."

He wiped his tears away and cleared his throat. "Did you see him last night? I know he was going to see you."

"He did." I felt the truth fighting to blurt right out of me. My convictions were powerful, but my fear was also strong. "He found me in the rain and gave me a white rose. Noah said he wanted to be with me, and he didn't have time to wait until we got married. He told me the elixir didn't work, and that he was dying faster."

"Why didn't you tell me?"

"He was supposed to go home!" How could I tell him the truth when he was so furious with me already?

What was wrong with me? I knew he would rather have died by my side than in a hospital bed, but Austin would have forced him to fight for a little while longer. I practically delivered him to my slaughter!

Austin's rage twisted his face, and I panicked. "I told him that I did love him. I always will, but you see, Austin…"

I took Austin's hand. It was probably the wrong time, but I needed him to know how I felt. "I'm in love with you. I know you may despise me, but I couldn't be with Noah, because I want to marry you."

His eyes stayed focused on my hand holding his, but he wouldn't even hold it back. All I needed was one good squeeze to know that my love wasn't completely one-sided. "And then he left?"

Tears were forming more rapidly. My chest ached, and I couldn't breathe. My hand was still holding onto his, but it felt cold. Still, I couldn't give up! I smiled and took a step closer toward him. I knew he was hurting because of Noah's death, and he was angry with me for various reasons, but surely, he could respect Noah's final act of nobility. "He told me that you were still in love with me first. He thought I deserved to know you hadn't given up on us."

His hand pulled away from me. "He lied to you." There was such contempt in his beautiful eyes. "I don't love you, Rose."

I clutched onto my chest. I couldn't catch my breath. I couldn't think. All I could do was ache.

He must have seen how he crushed me, and yet he continued like a tyrant. "Ever since I had the elixir, I don't feel that haze you put over me. I can think clearly now and..." He chuckled cruelly. "...I know that I never did. Noah probably didn't either."

"Austin—"

"Just go home to your cult, Rose!" He bent down to my face and seethed. "You and I will never happen. I could never love something like you."

Mr. Jones's words rang in my ears, and I collapsed on my knees. He warned me that humans wouldn't accept me, and I didn't believe him. Noah and Austin were supposed to be different. Austin wasn't supposed to judge. I was an extreme case, but to be so harsh to me...

Austin stood over me for a little while. I think I saw him beginning to reach out to me, but then he rushed away and left me to sob and grieve for Noah alone. Camellia came and held me in her arms. She kissed my cheeks and apologized on behalf of Austin a dozen times, but she was always on the fence. I was such a fool. Where was my haze? No illusion led me to believe I loved him. What I felt was extremely real, and it was the greatest pain I ever suffered.

Chapter Sixteen

Humans were so fragile, just like the white rose I held in my hands. It had begun to wilt. It was strange that Noah's sign of affection hardened as my heart had. It appeared to be stronger, but it broke into pieces at the touch.

I set it down on my desk and watched my reflection. Wasn't I a queen? Wasn't I a witch? I should have had better control of my emotions. Besides, I pulled myself together when I murdered my mother. I should have been able to manage once more.

There was a light knock on my doorframe. "Noah's funeral is today. Are you going to get dressed?" Camellia asked.

I had never been to a funeral before. My mother's death turned into my coronation. I understood that it was a chance to say goodbye and to give tribute, but Noah wasn't exactly gone. How could I sit and listen to everyone say such sad and beautiful things while his life was trapped inside of me? "I'll be downstairs soon."

She left me to get ready. I lost track of time and stayed in the shower for a long while. I just didn't see the point in rushing. Every time I thought about seeing Austin hover over Noah's body, my stomach started to twist up.

Camellia set out a black dress for me to wear, and I did my hair and makeup, but I still felt naked when I looked at my reflection. Nothing that I did to my body, to make it look beautiful, would rid me of the knowledge of what I kept inside. I was a creature, and I would never find anyone to genuinely love me, despite what I was. Perhaps the elders were right to force the heart out of the equation. I was chasing a destiny that didn't exist.

Eventually, I stopped sulking and made my way downstairs, so I wouldn't prolong Camellia. I caught her and Thomas pulling away from a kiss, and I could have turned green from jealousy.

Camellia was beaming when she reintroduced us. "Rose, you remember Thomas." How could I forget? He was all hunk! Thomas was built like a seasoned gladiator. He had very broad shoulders, a chiseled chest, and a slim waist. He also had very powerful thighs and calves. If he were standing among a crowd of my warriors, he would have caught my eye.

I forced myself to smile and reached out my hand. "Pleasure. Thank you for making my sister happy."

As our hands collided, I could see something in his eyes change. When I first saw him at the beach, he was captivated by Camellia. He admired her from afar, and he was enchanted. Now, he caught a big whiff of my scent, and my pheromones were beginning to work their charm.

I pulled away and took a step back before I corrupted him. Camellia didn't notice. Thomas didn't exactly understand. He was dazed and tried to brush it off. "It's been an amazing time. I only wish I had more to spend with her."

Thomas deeply cared for her. Maybe he loved her, but it was apparent, by the way she looked at him with such longing, that she did. I didn't understand why she didn't want to take the leap of faith and see where he stood. "You should go on tour with him."

The two of them looked at me as if I were insane, but they smiled a little bit. Thomas was stuck in a fantasy future, but Camellia refused and grabbed my arm. "Excuse us." She led me to the kitchen. "Rose, you know I can't. It would be forbidden."

I grabbed her arms and gently shook her. "I allow it! I am your queen."

She threw her head back and moaned. "If it works out between the two of us, I can't have a family. Thomas deserves to be happy."

I suddenly thought of those children Noah showed me. Camellia and I were orphaned as well, but we had people take us in. "Not all families are born of blood. You could adopt a wonderful child and make them feel loved. Taking care of people and making them feel safe is your power. You deserve to do that with someone you love."

Camellia pouted, but it was obvious she wanted to run away with him. "He's leaving tonight."

"Then go with him…" I didn't want my sadness to mask our marvelously romantic plans, so I had to push through my rising pain. "You need to leave before the spies figure out that you're planning on defecting. Just go! Leave right after the funeral."

She knitted her brows together and began to protest, but she instead rushed into my arms and held me. I really did care for my sister, and I wanted her by my side, but the greatest gift I could offer was to set her free. How tragic was that?

"What about you?"

I should have gone to the funeral, but I found a worthy excuse, and I was going to let it be my salvation. "I can't be around Thomas. I don't want my pheromones to tear you two apart. Besides, Austin hates me. If I told him what I did to Noah, he'd probably wish me dead."

"I don't believe that Austin never loved you!"

"My pheromones clouded his judgment—"

"His fear is clouding his judgment!" She took my hands and gave me her stern big sister look. I was being threatened to believe whatever she was going to tell me. "Not everyone has mystical abilities to protect their heart, Rose. He's scared, so he pushed you away."

I read stories like that, but none of it felt as evil as when he spoke those words to me. I didn't see fear. I saw disgust. Besides, I wasn't going to debase myself long enough to run after him. "I'm not going to beg him for his love, Camellia. I am a queen."

She perked her head up and blinked in surprise, but then she accepted it with a little smirk. "You certainly are."

Camellia already had some of her things in Thomas's car, but she quickly gathered a bag together. I wanted to interrogate Thomas for the short time allotted, but I couldn't risk being around him. I aided Camellia instead. She would be late for the funeral if we didn't hurry.

Then, it was finally time to let go. I didn't think I'd ever see her again after she learned of my mother's death. I was grateful she returned to me. It wasn't fair that I was about to lose her once again, but it was better if I delivered her from the evils of my world. My life was a burden, and now she could be free.

"Thank you for understanding." Camellia gave me one final hug. I took in everything about her. I named her after my mother's scent, but she was her own woman with her own identity. "I hope you find your happiness."

"I know I will." I lied, but it was only to protect her. If she didn't think I'd be alright, Camellia would have never left.

Thomas prepped his arms for a hug. "Thank you, Rose—"

I took a step back and raised my hand to motion him to stop. "Do you love her?" I had to be point-blank about it. I didn't have time for games or second guesses. I was putting Camellia's future in his hands, and if he ever mistreated her, his life would be in mine.

He glanced at his side to her, and I could feel it in that subtle moment. Even if he never said a word, I'd know forever. "I do."

I offered him a quick hug that happened so fast, he didn't have time to wrap his arms around me. He would probably think that I was strange, and hopefully, he'd never think anything better of me. "You're welcome, Thomas."

I had to kiss and hug Camellia one last time in the doorway, and then I let her go. They were so happy together that I couldn't believe they were on their way to a funeral. They'd probably be thinking about their new lives together throughout the entire program.

But wasn't it a good thing they were happy? Noah never made me feel sad about anything. I would miss him, and I would carry guilt with me for the remainder of my life, but he wouldn't want me to be unhappy. He asked me to have his children, but he hinted that he would have liked for Austin to be with me and raise them in his stead.

Everyone lives, and they die. That was the tragic truth about life. Noah would never be forgotten, and that's what he wanted more than anything. Now that I had built a monument to him in my very soul, it was time to honor him. I would embrace my life because my death was inevitable.

I thought long and hard about what it all meant to live. I tried love, and I failed miserably. One thing that wasn't going to change was my responsibility as a queen. I couldn't bring a human into my world. Mr. Jones was right about most of them, and I doubted I'd ever find another soul like Noah. Either way, I wouldn't want to corrupt him.

The elders were wrong to force men on me, and I'd never forgive them. If at all possible, I was going to destroy them. However, it was probably best if I kept to my kind. I was going to contact my people in the morning and return home, where I belonged. Love was no longer a dream I could afford to engage in.

It was a human commodity that could be bought, fought for, and won. My sister lucked out, but only because I granted her permission.

I would perform my duties, but I did plan on changing things. As soon as I returned home, I was going to find a way to destroy every elder. I'd slit their throats in their sleep if I had to. Then, the colony would be mine alone to control.

I couldn't stand to be alone in my house and began to walk. I didn't have any particular destination in mind. I just wanted to watch the humans and really see them with my newfound clarity. The swimsuit shop was closed when I walked by. That was strange for a Friday night. I hoped they were having some misfortune. I trusted them with our business and our information, and they took advantage of our relationship. That was a fine example of how manipulative humans could be.

I walked by a parking lot where a young woman, decked out in diamonds and fur, was getting into a gorgeous black sports car with an older man. I was not unfamiliar with the term "gold digger," and her love interest probably didn't care because she was beautiful. It was another example of how shallow and materialistic humans were.

I thought I figured out everything, but there was one mystery that boggled my mind and destroyed my authority with each passing minute. When I walked by the beach, I saw defiant waves that would not bend to my will. No matter how much I attacked the problem, I still hadn't mastered surfing. That had to change before I went home.

I rose, just before the sun did, and took my new board out to the water. There wasn't really anyone on the beach, which excited me. I didn't have to suffer any humiliation as I plowed through accomplishing my goals.

I did everything I knew to do. I paddled far out in the water and waited for something worthy—a completely massive wave—to make me feel like I had overcome my failures. When I saw the waves rise, I paddled toward them as fast as I could.

My mind was focused on the singular mission of being the best surfer possible. Waves came at me, but I paddled over them to get to the larger one further up. I was hurled backward by other waves that came against me, and I became tired after a while, but I couldn't turn around.

A sizable wave came upon me, and I decided to at least compromise a little bit. As soon as I found my footing on the board and stood up, I had already been knocked over by the mountain of water.

I lost grip of my board and tumbled in the rush. I didn't understand how I could be made to feel so weak and meaningless. There had to be a way to gain control! I didn't understand how I could be at anyone's mercy besides my own. My entire universe twirled around like a spinning top, yet the world was as still as it always was.

I eventually found my way to the surface. I only found my board because it was attached to my foot, and I think I only knew that my foot was still attached because I did find the board. I leaned on it while I recovered. My pride had been brutally beaten, but I was going to find a way to push through.

I tried the process again and again, but I couldn't get to the larger waves I wanted to ride, and the smaller ones easily overcame me. There were a few that I began to ride, but I never lasted long, and it never gave me the satisfaction I craved.

Eventually, I decided to give myself a break and made my way toward the shore. In the distance, I saw someone sitting on the beach. Through pure instinct, I knew it was Austin. I had finally gotten some closure, and yet he arrived to haunt my new state of mind and to mock my failures.

Austin looked quite sheepish with his chest pressed against his knees. He looked like a child in trouble. He made me think of Noah, and it made me want to sink deeper into the sand until it consumed me whole.

But I could not let my guilt make me weak. I would not let Austin know how much he scarred me. I crossed my arms and stood in front of him, with defiance in my heart. "What are you doing here? I thought you didn't get up early."

"I couldn't sleep."

I waited for him to say something else to me. I suppose I was waiting for an apology, or maybe I was waiting until I was ready to give one. Neither happened, and we were left with incredibly awkward silence until I rolled my eyes and moaned. "Well, I'll leave you alone. I'd hate to put another haze upon you."

"Don't!"

His arm quickly pulled on mine to keep me there. He really didn't look like an angry or bitter person. He almost seemed a little desperate. "It's fine. I'm thinking clearly. You don't have to leave because of me."

I didn't care, though. I pulled my arm away and peered into his eyes with as much ferociousness as I could muster.

His head darted away from me. "I see you still can't surf."

My mouth dropped until I recalled I had fallen for the notoriously rude cousin. "If you're here to criticize me—"

"The reason why you can't ride the waves properly is that you're too forceful!" He took my arms and flipped them over, so we could both see the palms of my hands. They were just my hands to me, but deadly weapons to someone as fragile as a human. "You attack everything and always try to remain in control. Maybe you can do that in real life, but that's nature out there, and you can't fight against it. You have to bend to its will. Once you accept that, you can work with it."

I grunted and ripped my arms away from him. "I've had to be strong and push back. It's the only way I could have endured for this long!"

"I'm not disagreeing with you!" He rubbed the temples of his forehead, but then his eyes shone as he smiled. "Sometimes, you're so bright like Noah. But other times—like when you killed those kids—you were dark and ruthless."

Austin grabbed my shoulders and looked so deeply into my eyes that I thought he was hexing me, as I had accidentally done to him. "You don't have to be so cold, Rose. I know you're incredibly strong, but you can't protect yourself from everything. Even if you loved someone, and they loved you in return, could you let them be the one to protect you?"

I laughed. I couldn't pretend to need him just to accommodate his ego. "Protect me from what exactly?"

"From yourself."

I was torn. I screwed up so much, especially when it came to Austin and Noah, but I could justify most of my actions. Didn't that absolve me of my sins? "Maybe darkness is in my nature. Maybe it's something I can't fight against."

"Children are born innocent. This darkness is a product of your world."

"I don't have a choice but to live in it!"

"Why?" He furrowed his brows and shook his head at me. "You could have stayed with Noah and me. You didn't have to plan to take him away and leave me behind..." His voice trailed off, but I had already heard the pain in every syllable.

I never meant to tear Noah and Austin apart, but what did they expect of me? I couldn't be like Camellia and run away with the first cute boy interested in me. Austin was a child incapable of understanding the tremendous burden placed on my shoulders.

"I can't leave my people to the elders. I'm a queen, Austin. Besides, how do I know they won't cause an uprising until I return, or because I didn't?" There would be more bloodshed than they ever thought possible. If we tried to hide, everyone Austin ever loved would be murdered until we came forward. Besides, my people belonged to me—not them.

"You may have to return home, and maybe you have to do some questionable things, but you don't have to be a stone."

"Stone?" I tried to be like a stone, but I could never harden my heart enough to keep him from piercing straight through it. "You don't think my heart aches? You don't think it bled when you said you never loved me?"

He was completely silent and looked like he was tensing his face in preparation for a good slap from me. I could have knocked his head clear off his shoulders. Pain for pain seemed appropriate, but my power was useless against him.

Instead of ending him, all I could do was poke him hard in his chest as I attempted to scream, but I lost my voice in a raspy cry. "I am not heartless! I felt every single piece when you made it shatter..."

Then he looked upon me with...pity? That's not what I wanted. I only needed him to understand and to want to help me save my world. I didn't need him to see me as something broken that needed to be fixed.

"Hearts have compassion," he said. "You showed it to me when you saved my life, and when you tried to save Noah—I'm extremely grateful—but not to those kids. There's more to ruling than strength, Rose. It may be wise to fear a ruler, but your people need hope and a future. If you rule them with an iron fist, don't be surprised when they're fashioned into weapons of war. At this rate, they will attack us, and you'll probably let them."

I was stunned and angry. I wasn't sure if what he said was right, but he did make some valid points. I would never debate destroying the elders. They deserved exquisitely bloody deaths, but my reputation among my people only made them fear me. Perhaps my children would genuinely love me, but everyone else was terrified that I would kill them if they disobeyed. Could I possibly go to war with humans? I was so angry when those humans stole from me. I was angry now that I had no one. Not even I knew the extent of the darkness that raged within my heart. I felt like if I dwelled upon it, I would be sucked into a void.

"Excuse me, but I'm going surfing now." I grabbed my board and headed for the water. I only had one more task before I could return home and take over my world. I'd then find out who I truly was, and so would everyone else.

"Just try what I said, Rose." Austin ran in front of me, with his board in hand, and ran out to the water. "Let go."

Let go? It was easier said than done. I thought I was working with the waves. I didn't literally expect to bend them to my will...I think.

Anyway, despite my stubbornness, I decided to listen to Austin. I felt like he was trying to show me up, so I was a little perturbed with him. That would all change when I finally defeated him at his own game.

There was a wave in the distance that we both spotted and paddled toward. He might have been like a fish, but I was much stronger than him. It was nothing to take the lead. I turned around and smirked, but he still had a confident grin on his face, like it didn't matter. I rolled my eyes and continued. There was a smaller, but troublesome wave coming our way, and I needed to paddle through it to the bigger wave. Miraculously, Austin started to catch up. I was curious about how he planned on handling such a delay. I expected him to go over his obstacle as I intended, but when I looked back at him again, he sank his body and board.

I was so confused that I hesitated long enough to let the oncoming waves overtake me. I was swallowed once again, but I rose out of it as quickly as possible, so I could watch Austin. When another opposing wave came against him, he did the same thing. He should have taught me that technique when he instructed me! But I suppose I did want to surf every single wave I came against. I'm not sure I would have listened back then.

Then, when he got to the worthy wave, he stood up on his board, as quickly and easily as if he would on land, and he rode it with ease. He didn't force anything, and he was as calm as the dawning sky. It was easy for him because he let it be.

As a woman, I wanted to be that graceful and serene. To be at peace with the world would have been a great legacy to leave behind for myself and the humans. But letting go was difficult. I was only eighteen, but I was tired.

Austin was right about me. I did want to be a stone. Love was hard. Forgiveness was a vice, not a strength, and compassion was a sign of weakness. I should have never bothered to love Austin because not being loved in return was the epicenter of hell itself. I had given up, or I at least gave it an effort to try. I thought giving love to Camellia would be enough to appease my heart before I bled it dry.

Now, things were different. I was floating in the middle of the ocean—literally and figuratively—and I had never faced such a fearsome challenge. "Let go," I told myself. "All I have to do is let go…"

I closed my eyes and let myself be rocked by the waves. I was treating the water like an obstacle or an enemy, but the truth was that it was gentle when I let it be. It was only formidable when I treated it like it was. It was natural. It was raw. It was pure. As long as I respected it, I could use its power for my gain.

I opened my eyes and realized I had fallen back closer to the shore. Austin had already retired and started paddling back toward the beach, but I couldn't stop until I could properly surf.

Again, I paddled. I was going to try to surf smarter—not harder. I wasn't afraid of being cast into the depths, so I didn't have to work up my nerve. I only had to prepare my mind when the first wave approached. I paced myself and dug deep, right before it overcame me, and dove in. I felt myself fighting to stay under the wave, so I pushed down my weight against the board. I could see how it could be difficult for a human of my size, but it wasn't difficult with my strength. When I felt like I had submerged far enough, I pressed my body back to my board and aimed the front up.

I gasped for air as I came out of the wave and immediately laughed with joy. I accomplished a great task in my eyes. I could even hear Austin cheering from a distance. I felt enough assurance to continue going forward.

The wave I had been waiting for was upon me. I finally had my chance to prove myself. I could either attack it like I had been doing, or I could trust my teacher, and the man I once believed to be my friend.

I stood up and kept my balance easily enough. Balance was never my problem. I caught onto that quickly. Patience wasn't my problem. I had been dealing with the elders for a very long time. It was submission. The only safety I had was in the fact that I was powerful enough to destroy anyone who ever tried to hurt me.

But once I had the revelation of the raw and pure power of nature, I could respect it. After all, nature was a mother too.

I couldn't even believe I was in my body as I glided on the board. I could feel my body completely in tune with the rhythm. I didn't push. I just let go, and it was marvelous. My heart was doing backflips as the top of the waves funneled over me, but I concentrated on the sun peering over the horizon in a gorgeous array of reds and oranges. The light shimmered off the drops of water on the edge of the waves, and they resembled beaded pearls. In something so stunningly simple, I found the reemerging hope that I needed in my life again. In my heart, I knew it was never too late.

I didn't care when I lost control and wiped out. It didn't wash away the feeling of ecstasy I had. I couldn't stop smiling or giggling like a silly fool. I was fearless, and I felt like I could do anything.

"I did it!"

Austin grinned hard and clapped for me. I was afraid that when Noah died, he'd never be happy about anything again.

"I did it! I did it!" I wasn't thinking and jumped into his arms. He was caught up in the moment and spun me around, but he got a little too carried away and tripped on the board I dropped, and we both collided on the wet sand. Poor Austin took the brunt of the fall, but he didn't appear to be injured. I got a pretty good look when I landed right on top of him. Our eyes collided into one another, and my lips were only a breath apart from his own. "I…"

My heart thumped against his chest, and I felt the spark of our natural and wild passion. He told me there were just some things I couldn't fight against. My desire for him was natural. It was raw. Powerful. Pure. Perhaps all would be forgiven if I just let go…

If I'm not mistaken, his neck reached out just a little further to reach my lips, but I was the one who truly kissed him back. I could taste the salt from the ocean on his delectable lips, and I quite enjoyed the flavor of him. My fingers explored his shoulders and rested on his biceps. He pressed me closer against his chest as he kissed my cheeks and neck. I did my best not to laugh, but I was ticklish and scrunched up my neck on instinct. He backed off and began to sit up.

I didn't mean to ruin the mood, but after seeing his somber expression, I knew I was in trouble. "Why didn't you come to Noah's funeral?"

An elephant could have been sitting on my chest from the heaviness that suddenly fell upon me. "I felt responsible for his death." That was true. It wasn't the whole truth, but it was enough for the time being. "Besides, you made it quite clear that you never wanted to see me again."

He grinned quickly. I guess he remembered I wasn't the only disappointing jerk in the relationship. "I was angry that Noah planned on leaving with you. I didn't want you to take him from me, and I didn't want to lose you. When I found out that he died alone and rejected, it was a little too much for me."

I thought my lie would be better than the truth, but now I wasn't so sure. He might have been angry for what I accidentally did to Noah, but at least Austin would have known that he died with someone he cared about. I couldn't grant him closure unless I granted him the truth.

"Do you know what the last words I ever said to him were?" He had such utter disgust in his voice, and then he turned to face me. "I told him you were incapable of loving him."

A furious pang of anger pounded against my chest, and I had to seriously resist the urge to slap him. After the intense anger took a second to pass, I was instantly saddened. "Do you really believe that?"

"No, of course not." He ran his fingers through his magnificent hair. "I would have said anything to make him stay."

There was still something I didn't understand, and I assumed it was because I'm not a human. "But why would you push me away if you still wanted to be with me?"

He threw up his hands, confounded at himself, but I gave Austin a good enough glare for him to realize that wasn't an acceptable answer. "Your elixir is some kind of higher power?"

I didn't understand it all myself, but I nodded.

"It enraged me that 'Fate' believed I deserved to be saved, but Noah had to die. Your world sounds…insane! I just don't know if I can be a part of it."

He wasn't wrong. Sometimes, when I closed my eyes, I saw my mother's bloodied body as the elders hailed me as their queen. My worst fear was that I would be unable to stop the cycle, and my own daughter would do the same thing. I believed in my capabilities, but I was just so certain that I could properly protect my daughters if they had a father in their lives. That's what they were supposed to do.

"If you accept my proposal, you will be my king. The elders won't stand idly by, so I will do what I must, but I will create a true partnership." I took Austin's hand and gave it a good squeeze. "I promise that I will let you protect me."

He raised his brows. "I really don't want this. I've taken care of Noah, but this sort of responsibility is just too much. I've never even been in a relationship for more than two months."

It didn't surprise me that he was afraid of commitment, but I was in no position to be picky anyway. I snickered and mumbled under my breath without thinking, "I've never been in one that didn't result in someone's death."

I turned to Austin, and I swear he lost all color in his face. His brows rose even higher, and his eyes were the size of half-dollars. "I'm sorry!" I leaned against him and rubbed his back. "That doesn't exactly make you want to be in a committed relationship."

"Well, it is supposed to be 'til death, right?"

I perked up. I was confused, and I figured it was our cultural barrier getting in the way again. "Are you saying you want to be with me?"

Austin looked out at the rising sun as he stroked my hand with his thumb. It was a gentle and small gesture, but it brought such pleasure to me that I could hardly imagine what he could do after we were wedded. I needed him to have a change of heart. He spoke to me in a way that no one else would. The elders challenged me all the time, but it wasn't out of love. I liked to believe that Austin was my greatest critic because he was my greatest fan.

"At Noah's funeral, I had all of my friends and family there in my time of need. I appreciated every face that I saw, but I kept waiting for you to show up."

I breathed heavily—practically wheezing—and resisted the urge to cry miserably for feeling like the most horrible girlfriend in the universe. I honestly didn't think he would want me there. Austin was kind, though, and kissed my hand. He wasn't blaming me in any way, and I calmed down.

"I realized that I needed you there, and if you leave and go back to your colony, I'll always wonder what we could have had. I don't like lingering questions or regrets. I can't let that be a part of my life." He lazily rested his forehead against mine. "I believe in going with the flow of nature, and for some reason, my heart keeps leading me back to you."

I believed that he was going to kiss my lips, but he kept me lingering in suspense as he tenderly stroked my face. No one else could make me feel the way he did. It's like I could feel all of him, every time he touched a single part of me, and there wasn't a single speck of me that didn't want him. "I'm ready," he said.

My stomach began to explode with tickles. It was too much joy for me to contain, so I had to ask. "Ready for what?"

Chapter Seventeen

Hours had gone by, and I still felt the same butterflies in my stomach that were present when Austin first asked me to be his bride. After I accepted, we both became extremely excited and rushed around the shops. I bought the first white dress I could find, he rented a tuxedo, and he bought a ring. It wasn't a very sizable diamond, because he didn't have time to move more money into his checking account. But that was one thing I didn't particularly care about. I was already a queen. The only treasure I wanted him to give to me was his heart.

We quickly gathered some clothes from my home, and we ran away. Austin had a change of street clothes in his car, but nothing else. I couldn't convince him to slow down or stop by his house. He said we had to be completely spontaneous. At the time, I was only thinking about getting married, but I grew concerned. "Are you sure your parents will be alright with this?"

He laughed! "They'll be furious, but they would try to stop our union if I tried to explain everything. Even if I left out the complicated inhuman stuff, they would say I was just acting out because of Noah's death."

I pouted and sank deep into my seat. "Are you?"

"Partially," he shrugged, "but I can't wait any longer."

"But you're such a carefree spirit, and you don't like rules and commitment—"

"I'm also spontaneous, brash, and I leap before I look…sometimes, literally."

I didn't want Austin to turn the car around, but I wanted him to be sure. I didn't want him screaming at me ten years down the road and blaming my pheromones, or my elixir, for clouding his judgment. "I know that I don't want to wait, but you have other obligations and aspirations. What about your dreams of being a professional surfer or skateboarder?"

"It wouldn't be fair." He gripped tightly onto the steering wheel and tightened his jaw. He wasn't exactly happy, but he was stubborn. "I'm different now. I'd always win my competitions, and it would be like stealing. I don't want to be a fraud."

Austin said many things that attracted me to him, but he didn't make me swoon much. That was a notable moment. "You are profoundly ethical, Austin. I'm deeply impressed."

He grinned. "Besides, it'll be kind of awesome to be a king." If Noah had a fantasy about ruling the world, I had to believe Austin at least had a daydream.

"We live on an island, so you can still go surfing every day if you want to. You can teach our children." I didn't throw out any random numbers yet. I wanted Austin to be comfortable. If I had to have children one at a time or stop at fifteen, I could do that. As long as they all had the love of their father, I was perfectly happy. "I'm sure they'd love it."

"I can't believe you did a duck dive with a longboard. It's nearly impossible and incredibly dangerous. That's why I never showed you how to do it. I was waiting until you advanced a little bit more, so I could get you a shortboard."

I was puzzled. "It didn't seem that hard."

He laughed and shook his head. "That's because you're super strong, Rose. No one else can do the things you can." He looked at me with a smile on his face. I liked it when he admired me. I felt like royalty again.

"Is there anything we should get for you?" he asked. "Is there anything you'd like to experience?"

I began to blush wildly. "You mean besides tonight?"

"Yeah." Even he began to look a little flustered, but I knew he was excited. "Is there a food you didn't get to try or a movie you didn't get to see?"

"There's a book I wanted to read. The elders burned all of mine, and I didn't find it locally." I should have inquired about it from Noah. He was the intellectual cousin. He probably could have found me any book I ever wanted to read. "It's a tale about a princess and a knight who grow to love each other. The knight's father loved the queen, but they both died when the witch attacked the kingdom. The princess—"

"Was raised by the trusted knight, and she fell in love with the son."

"Yes!" I slapped his leg in excitement. "You have read *The Knights of Ember Island?*"

"I read it for a school book report. I thought it was pretty good for a girly book."

I resented the fact that he called it "girly," but I let it slide. "Do you still have a copy?"

"I think it's somewhere at my house."

"I need you to find it for me!" That story had been eating away at me for years. I was rooting for the princess and the knight to find true love, but I didn't feel like I could claim to be her. I was too powerful. I was too dark. "I left off at the part when the princess was taken by the witch."

"I can tell you what happened—"

"No! You can't spoil the ending for me." I have already waited for so long. I could contain my suspense for a day or two. "I will read it myself."

"Fine. When we return home, I'll look for it right after my parents finish chewing me out for eloping with you."

I couldn't imagine what it was like to answer to anyone. The elders opposed me, but they very well couldn't stop me from doing what I wanted. "Do they at least know you love me?"

"I told them you made me feel different than I've ever felt with anyone else. They know I admire your tenacity, and they definitely know I think you're the most gorgeous woman I've ever met." He looked at me, out of the corner of his eye, and smirked. "If all those things gave them that impression, then yes, they know."

I felt lucky to have him by my side. He was such a unique individual, like Noah. I could never really guess what he was going to do. I trusted he would always do what he felt was right, though. He broke my heart, but it required a lot of courage to come back to me and admit fault. I was proving to be the lesser of the two of us.

"I think my mother would have liked you." I imagined her smiling with pride at our union. "She would appreciate that I found such a free spirit with integrity, but I think she'd be appalled at how rude you are."

He chuckled. "How is Camellia by the way?"

"She ran away with someone she loves. I hope she can marry him and live a long and happy life." It was still painful to think about, but I did the right thing. "Away from the colony and me is the only way she can do that."

Austin nodded and even seemed impressed. "It's nice that you let her go. I couldn't do that with Noah."

"I'm so sorry that he's gone." That was the only apology I could manage to give him. I didn't want Noah to be a dark cloud that hung around our heads forever, but I didn't know how else to keep Austin by my side.

"I have some peace knowing that he's no longer suffering. There's no more pain."

"Yes. There's no pain…" At least I could find solace in that fact. He wanted it to be over. Noah got his wish.

"He's in a better place."

"A better place?" I wasn't sure about that. Could his soul have moved on to another and better realm? Did I keep him from passing on? Did I steal his life, or did I steal his soul? Was he aware of it? If he were, I hoped he knew how much I truly loved him, and that I never meant to take what was left of him. "Yes. I hope so…"

Austin took us somewhere we could be joined together forever. Apparently, most humans who wanted to get married in a hurry went to Las Vegas. I had read up on it. It was a city of sin. Secrets were left buried until one returned to bury more on top. I suppose it was the perfect place to marry Austin, considering that I was keeping such a secret from him about Noah.

We arrived in the afternoon, but it was a magical place. There were bright lights, giant billboards, and unique scenery everywhere. Where else in the world, besides in the imagination of a book, could I find pyramids, the Eiffel Tower, and people dressed like cartoon characters roaming the streets as if it were nothing?

"Have you been here before?"

Austin had quite the mischievous grin on his face. "Once or twice."

I slightly glared at him. I was playing with him, but I was a bit concerned. After all, there were billboards of topless men and women. Some men roamed the streets passing out flyers to strip clubs. I was concerned if Austin had given in to darker temptations and lost himself in a wild weekend with harlots.

Camellia told me that when she lost her virginity to Thomas, it was casual for him. I didn't want it to be casual for Austin. I wanted it to be the best night of our lives. I didn't want him to pass me off as nothing, but I also didn't want him to compare me to anyone he might have indulged in.

Austin drove us just outside of the Strip to a white building that literally had "Wedding Chapel" studded in gold lights for all the world to see. I thought it was a bit tacky and gaudy, but Austin was beaming when he parked the car. "Are you ready to be my bride?"

I didn't have many reservations—besides the secret about Noah—but I couldn't let anything stop me from marrying Austin. We could have been stranded in the middle of the ocean on a life raft, and I would have still wanted to marry him. "Of course."

The inside looked a lot nicer than I anticipated. The chapel was in a white room with tiled flooring. The room was decorated with greenery, and the aisle was lit by candles, raised up by holders, and some that sat on the floor. It was simple and quite lovely, but I wished there were more flowers. Even still, I was reminded of my garden where my mother hummed her lullaby.

"Here you are." Austin handed me my dress, which was protected in a plastic bag. I thought I would wear something that flowed on for days, but the train of my dress was minimal. We were rushing everything so fast, I didn't have time to find exactly what I daydreamed of.

Austin must have read my somber expression because he raised my chin with his finger. "I know it's not as enchanting as it could be, but at least you get to wear white."

That did cheer me up. I was aware that human women no longer valued the symbolism of a white dress, but it meant the world to me. It meant I had defeated the elders and found love. It meant Austin was more than a tool for pleasure. He was someone I could value as my partner. It meant I could have a family and a future, and I didn't have to live the rest of my life fighting alone. I had won. "Anything is perfect while I'm with you."

I lit up like a beacon and took my dress to the bathroom to change. It was a silk, Grecian-style dress with a V-neck line that hung against my back. The dress cinched into my waist and draped down to the floor just right, and it gave me the perfect hourglass figure. I felt like a woman ever since my mother was murdered. Now, I certainly looked the part.

I took the lessons from my dear sister and curled my hair to perfection. My makeup was very light and natural. To top off my look, I took a white jasmine from the fake bowl of flowers and placed it in my hair, as I did as a girl.

Austin waited outside the bathroom door with his hand behind his back. He had a particular grin on his face that was somewhere between mischievous and gorgeous. When he saw me completely prepped to marry him, his eyes lit up.

"Did you get me something?"

"Oh, yeah!" He laughed nervously and revealed the bouquet of white roses. "I know what these mean, too, and I thought it would be a good way to honor Noah."

I lost my breath, and I was afraid to even touch the bouquet. I couldn't tell him the truth. It would ruin everything. He'd probably abandon me in Las Vegas and never speak to me again.

"Did I do something wrong?"

I shook my head and took the bouquet with my trembling fingers. I needed to take a moment to calm down before I spoke to him, or else I was going to start wailing out all my secrets in a blubbering cry.

"I miss him too." Austin embraced me and kissed my forehead. "Noah and I had our disagreements about you, but he would want the two of us to be happy."

"I know…" That was all I could manage to say without completely losing my composure. I was so close to being married and replenishing my race. I could not let one accident doom everything I had worked for.

"Then let's go get married."

I smiled at his face and caught one tear that quickly managed to escape. My mascara was waterproof, so I took the tear out before it caused too much damage.

I locked arms with my fiancé, and we made our way into the chapel. Our witnesses were other brash couples about to wed. Some of them were young, some of them were probably drunk, but a few of them looked to be as in love as Austin and me.

The priest was in a strange white jumpsuit, studded with fake gold diamonds. He also had on a very bad black wig. I cocked my brow and looked to Austin, but he was amused. "I never thought

I'd get married by an Elvis impersonator, but I'm sadly not too surprised about it."

Then I was even more confused. "Why can't we get a real Elvis?"

He cut his eyes at me, but I was doe-eyed and clueless. "I'm going to try to pretend like I just didn't hear you say that."

I shrugged and added it to the pile of things I didn't understand. "As long as he can marry us, I don't really care."

He shook his head and laughed at me! "I love you, Rose."

My heart skipped a beat. "I love you, too."

The priest made a few strange and yet prominent gestures with his hands and pelvis that amused everyone else, but confounded me, before he began the ceremony. "Dearly beloved, we are gathered together to celebrate the union of this man and this woman, Austin Smith and Rose Queen."

The priest turned to Austin. "Austin, do you—?"

"I have a confession to make, Rose."

I couldn't breathe. He took one of my hands, and I nervously squeezed it too tightly. He hissed, so I loosened my grip, but I couldn't let go. I didn't want to lose him.

"I knew it was wrong of me to flirt with you on the beach when you were on that date with Noah. I played it off like it was innocent and that I tried to resist you—I did sometimes—but the truth is I wanted you from the moment I bumped into you on the street."

He grinned. "I am rude. I'm selfish. I'm brash, and I may even be trouble. I don't know if this will end up being the worst mistake of our lives, but I am in love with you, Rose."

I grinned as he gently pressed his forehead against mine and locked our eyes. "If you're scared that *Fate* has intertwined us here by circumstances we couldn't control, screw that. I loved you from the moment I first saw you."

I was frightened that my pheromones had brought him to me, and my elixir did have influence over him at least once. But if what he said was true, then I didn't have anything to fear. "Are you telling me that you believe in true love at first sight, like in a fairytale?"

"No, of course not," he said quickly. "That would be ridiculous."

Before my shoulders could slump, he smirked. "But considering my personal experience, I'm beginning to like the odds."

I giggled uncontrollably. The world rushed around me, and my buildup of adrenaline was making me so excited that I wrapped my arm around his neck and pulled him close. "I confess to you that I do love Noah, just in an incredibly special and different way. I couldn't bring myself to end things quickly, but I always knew that you were exactly what I wanted."

He gave me an extremely complicated and small grin. "Rose—"

I couldn't take it anymore and collided my lips with his. He hesitated out of surprise, but his fingers eventually pressed against my back as he pulled me in. I sort of forgot about the world around us. There were cheers in the distant background from our witnesses, but that was the only thing getting through the taste of his luscious lips.

Eventually, Elvis cleared his throat and said, "I now pronounce you man and wife."

Our lips parted, but my eyes never left his. "We're married?" I squealed.

"We're married."

"I'm married!" I pecked him on his lips before I clutched onto his hand and dragged him down the aisle, through the chapel, and to the outside world. He thankfully kept up with me, but our hands slipped apart when we got outside, and I spun with arms outstretched and the bouquet still in my hand. "I did it!"

The elders probably never expected I'd be able to pull it off. I didn't care that it wasn't a royal wedding or that it was rushed. I didn't care that I wasn't married by a real Elvis. Of course, I had regrets that would haunt me, and loved ones that should have been with me, but at least I could have a real family. "I'm married! I'm married! We're married!"

"We are." Austin grabbed me by my waist and lifted me as high as his arms would stretch. He was going to set me down, but I grabbed hold of him for another kiss. I got a little too excited and squeezed his shoulders. "Ow!" He laughed, but his pride was a little wounded. "Be careful. You're a lot stronger than I am."

"Sorry." I smiled naughtily. "I promise I'll be gentle."

He raised his brows, but then he smirked ever so sexily. "Not too gentle, I hope."

We booked ourselves two nights in the hotel shaped like a pyramid. There were columns and hieroglyphics like in the books I studied as a child. It was odd, though, seeing frozen yogurt stores and slot machines mixed in with the old world, but I was highly amused.

Austin pointed to a restaurant that was currently populated by a bunch of people. "Do you want to eat anything?"

I shook my head. Not even my stomach could think about food when I was no longer ethically bound to hold myself off. "We can eat if you want to, but I'd like to visit our room..." My cheeks reddened. "I mean...you get what I'm trying to say?"

He crossed his arms and just grinned and nodded over and over, but he didn't say anything.

I felt embarrassed and punched him in the arm. "Say something! Do you want to be with me right now or not?"

He raised his brows a few more times before busting out in laughter. "Come on."

I closed my eyes as we rode on the elevator and felt my racing heart. Very soon, I would be impregnated with my first batch of children. I could hold off my pregnancy if I wanted. I probably should have. There were things the two of us needed to work out. We didn't really know each other too well. Children would have complicated things, but I wanted to love a child and give them everything I never had.

"Come on." Austin reached for my hand when the elevator came to a stop and led me down the hall. I was fascinated with how far up we were. It was like I was standing at the window of my home, overlooking a village. The humans certainly were special for creating such magnificent structures. I wondered if Noah could have designed such an impressive place if he had the chance.

When we got to our room, Austin opened the door by sliding in an electric key. He grinned when the lock clicked, and the little light turned green. He pushed the door open, and I saw that our things were already inside waiting for us. I was about to walk in, but Austin pushed me back. "I have to carry you over the threshold."

"I've read about this!" I jumped into his arms so fast, he almost dropped me. "Do you have me? I can carry you instead if you need me to."

"I'm fine." He grew an evil glimmer in his eye. "You're just a lot heavier than you look."

"Oh, haha!"

Austin turned sideways to get us both in. I can't say I felt anything different once he passed the threshold, but everything took a sudden turn when I laid eyes on the bed the Virgin Queen would die upon. "I'm going to need a new name..."

He sat me down. "Rose isn't fine enough?"

"That wasn't my name until I came here." I walked by it and pressed my hand into the mattress. It was firm, but it had enough bounce to it. I would sleep like a log. The entire room was spacious and warm with rich colors and wood. It was odd because it was slanted, but I suppose that's because I was inside a pyramid.

I walked to the window and looked outside at the world. I hadn't been with humans long, but I was really beginning to like their world. The thieves might have enraged me, but not everyone was petty and dishonest. I found a knight to believe in. "I was classified as a 'virgin queen' in my world. I will simply be their 'queen' now."

"I like Rose."

"I do too." I placed my hand on the glass. The sun was beginning to set, but it was still hot outside. I felt a chill go down my back, though, from Austin's breath tickling my neck. I recalled my book and how happy the princess was when she discovered she loved her knight. It wasn't long before the witch stole their happiness away. "That book about the princess and the knight...I see myself as the witch."

"Why? She killed thousands of people for no reason." He seemed offended, but I don't know how he could be. He was afraid of my power.

"I'm not innocent, Austin. Besides, this power I possess is wicked. What if I hurt you?"

His hands snaked around my waist from behind, and his lips tickled my neck. I kept myself from pushing him away, but that was mostly because each touch we made now electrified my senses. It was like flicking on every switch in a circuit breaker.

"You're a lot like the princess, Rose. You're strong, competitive, smart, and rapturously beautiful. By no means do you need to be rescued, but you're not afraid to let yourself need someone."

"What if letting you in costs you everything?"

He laughed off my valid question and stroked my arms ever so gently, and my back melted into his chest. I took a deep breath and felt hot and flustered. I couldn't think straight. "You finish your book, and you'll see that you're the princess."

"No," I smirked. "I'm actually a queen."

"Then that makes me a king." My dress began to loosen, and I panicked at the sound of the quiet zipper being pulled down my back. His fingers tugged on my dress until he pulled it up.

"Yes. Yes, it does." I was bashful, but I raised my arms and helped to free myself of my wedding dress. I turned around and slid my hands onto his chest until I slipped under his suit jacket. I nudged it off his shoulders and pulled it off him. When I got to his buttons, my fingers were too twitchy! I was easily frustrated and ended up ripping it open, popping off a couple of them.

"I thought you said you would be gentle."

I hid my hot face into his chest.

"Don't blush on my account." He raised my head by tapping my chin with his fist. "I've never been in love before, Rose. This is a big deal for me, too."

I took a final gulp of my fears and wrapped my arms around his neck, and I kissed him with everything I had. I had my entire life to live with that man, so I had to make a commitment to start sometime. He must have approved because his charming foreplay was gone, and the two of us became instruments intertwined in our unique melody. The rhythm of our bodies was so harmonic, it was as if we had been singing the same song our entire lives.

But somewhere, in the middle of the symphony, I realized that the voice performing was not my own. I struggled to reach out and stop the imposter, but I was completely blocked. I saw everything, but I was a captive audience member with absolutely no control over the outcome. I prayed that Austin would somehow realize I had lost control of my body, but the imposter lip-synced perfectly, and Austin never knew that, somehow, I was screaming hoarsely as I watched someone else sing to my king.

Chapter Eighteen

I felt her love for me like warmth resting on top of my chest, before I physically felt her arms around me. I leaned back into her bosoms and didn't question our time together for a while. I felt like I did when I was a little girl. I was safe in a world where I wasn't horrible.

"Is this a dream?" I finally asked.

"Yes," she said sadly.

I sighed deeply. I knew that it had to be, but delusions were more tempting than truth. I looked up into the tree limbs. The sky was so bright that it didn't even look blue. The sun shone through the pink leaves and coated our skin in pale pastels. "I only dream of the night you were taken from me. Why are we here again after all these years?"

She stroked her fingers through my hair in a gentle and adoring way. I wished I had memories of sitting on her bed while she brushed it carefully. "The worst is upon you, my daughter. I did not love your father. I did not know him, but it ruined me when I saw what I had done."

My eyes bucked, and I lost my breath. I did not mean to judge as others judged me, but I thought I was the only monster in our family. I carefully eased beside her, so I could see her face as I asked, "What did you do to my father?"

I could see in her glistening eyes that she did not lack compassion or grief. "I told you this life is a burden—"

"I've changed everything!"

"Or maybe you've made it worse."

I was silenced by my anger. I was not a bigger tyrant than the men who killed her! "When I return home, I will free our people from the elders. I will destroy them with my bare hands."

"The elders are the least of your problems."

I looked beyond her and saw other women with faces as lovely as hers. Some differed in looks, but I knew that the women in my garden belonged to my bloodline. My mother took my hand, and we both stood to see them all. "This curse has connected many of us together. Within you are all the lives that she's taken in order to make herself strong. When she's ready, she will take this world as she's taken others."

It was the elders I had fought against my entire life. There was no one else that I hated. "Who are you talking about?"

She looked surprised that I didn't know. "The Queen."

"I am the queen!"

She shook her head and grinned out of pity. "It's only a title, my daughter. As long as we have this curse upon our lives, we can never be anything. Every time you drink her elixir, you connect to her will. She may let you live your life unbound by her rules and agenda, but she may decide to call upon you. After all, there's never been a queen as strong as you before."

I clutched onto my chest as I felt the ache of her words. Was my entire life completely in vain? Was I truly just a puppet for another queen to rule through? I knew of the other colonies, but I never knew that I was being conditioned as a vessel. Now that I had been impregnated, I would soon become useless.

"She's wrong, Rose!"

"Noah?" I silently said his name like a prayer. Everything inside of me began to break as I turned to see him grinning goofily. "I'm so sorry." I abandoned my mother's side for his embrace. I didn't understand what realm I had slipped into, but I didn't care. "Is it even possible for you to forgive me?"

"I know that you didn't mean to do what you did." He touched the sides of my face and held me in his eyes. "I just need you to promise to take care of my cousin, Rose. Please, don't let him be a casualty in this war."

"I won't!" I was naively optimistic about his chance of survival, but I needed to believe that something good would happen after Noah's death. The universe owed me something.

"And you've got to promise to actually win this thing." He clenched his fingers and made tight fists. "I know you, Rose. There's no way you could ever be a puppet. You live your life as best you can, and I admire you for it."

"You are a queen like the rest of us," my mother interjected. *"As long as you bear that burden, there is nothing else. Do not challenge the elders or our High Queen. You will lose what's left of you, my daughter. I would hate for them to snuff out the light that I saw within you."*

"My name is Rose!" I snapped. *"I am a person, despite what you or anyone else believes."* I knew she wanted me to escape the life that was given to me, but I had to simply deal with it. Just because my burden was heavy didn't mean I'd be unable to carry it on my shoulders and run. *"I have fought to have an identity, and I have created it. I will never lose it."* Good or evil—I was who I was.

I defiantly stood against the other queens with my head raised. One by one, they began to fade into smoke until only my mother remained. She still looked terribly sad for me, but she did smile. *"Keep your heart, my daughter. Your heart is why you were chosen. My first instincts told me that you would endure. Prove my young and naïve self correct."*

I nodded and kept calm as she faded away from me, but I truly wanted to embrace her one more time. *"Goodbye, Mother."*

Noah pouted. *"Austin is in danger. You have to go back and save him."*

His words pressed on my insides and crushed them. If a queen were controlling the elders, I would kill her as well. I would not let them take Austin from me. I would die first. *"Goodbye, Noah."*

I closed my eyes, and when I opened them, I was lying in the bed I had made love to Austin in, but I was alone. Fear rushed over me like a cold front. My eyes welled up with tears, and I couldn't breathe. I took a second to regain my nerves. He had to be somewhere.

"Austin?" I jumped out of the bed and ran around the hotel room, but he was nowhere in sight. I ran my fingers through my hair as I felt my head beginning to explode. I did a quick turnaround and then noticed the light on underneath the bathroom door. I nearly broke it down to get through. "Austin—?"

"Geez, Noah!" He turned to the side as he finished up his "business." He was shocked to see it was me and slumped his shoulders in embarrassment.

I turned around and stared at the ceiling. We saw each other naked, so I don't know why I thought it was so strange to see him relieve himself. "Why did you call me Noah?"

"He…" He sniffed and then chuckled. "Noah always, *always*, waited until the very last second to use the bathroom. He barged in on me all the time, and I guess it was just reflex."

I wondered how long we would both feel the sting of his loss. "I dreamed about him last night."

"Oh, yeah?"

I was still uncomfortable with our current arrangement and walked out of the bathroom. "I'll tell you about it when you're done."

It didn't take Austin long to finish up, but he took his time coming out and washing up. I waited anxiously for him on our bed, and yet he lazily leaned up against the wall. "I don't know if I can hear about Noah right now. It's still really hard to deal with, and I want to enjoy my night with you."

I looked out of the window and saw that the sky was still blanketed with darkness. It didn't exactly help my disposition. "I dreamed that we were in danger, Austin. I dreamed that you were in danger from me."

"I know I gave you a hard time—I'm not apologizing because I feel it was warranted—but I don't believe you would hurt me."

I was glad he believed that—and I wanted to, more than anything—but it was hard to tell, now that I knew the truth. "I didn't do anything strange to you last night while we were together?"

He cocked his brow, but he paused and really thought about it. "There was kind of one moment when you gave me this look that I've seen before, and I freaked out inside. It reminded me of when you killed those burglars."

"You thought I was going to eat you?"

"I'm sorry." He shrugged and laughed. "It was only for a moment. I didn't think you noticed." He sat beside me and kissed my lips as a way to ask for forgiveness. That only made things worse.

"You okay?"

I shook my head. Even if we were married, I feared he wouldn't be able to get past what I discovered. But it was more dangerous than the secret I kept about Noah. If I loved him, I had to let him know. "My mother's life-force is inside of me, and last night, she connected with me. She told me the elders were the least of our worries. They're controlled by a higher power."

"The 'Fate' in your goop?" he mocked.

I slowly nodded as I braced myself for the end of us. "There's another queen, and she somehow controls through it. I lost control last night while we were together. You made love to something that wasn't me."

I could see in his eyes how much his mind was swirling with questions about our encounter. He touched his lips, and we both recalled colliding into one another. His hands were soft and warm, and he was tender as he held me in his arms. I thought I would have wanted to stay trapped in his embrace for eternity, but then I was literally frozen inside of myself. "Which time?"

"I was there for the beginning, but I lost myself after the first time…"

His mouth dropped, and he paced the room while he breathed heavily. "If you can be controlled, then can I?"

"I think she did once. Remember when we were in the tent, and you asked me to breed?" His distant eyes still frightened me.

"This is too freaking weird!" He grunted while muttering inaudible things.

"I'm sorry." I buried my hands into my face and shook my head, over and over again. I was such a fool. "We shouldn't have gotten married. I should have never come to America."

Austin came to a halt as he was hit with some kind of revelation or a new sense of confirmation. "I have another confession, Rose." Austin rushed to his knees in front of me and grabbed my hands. "I love you. I really do, and I need you to understand that, but I sort of have ulterior motives for marrying you."

"Such as?"

"I don't trust your crazy world. I think this power of yours is dangerous, and I don't want to be your enemy. I don't believe you want to destroy humans, but I think you can possibly be persuaded. Noah wanted to fix your world and save our own. That's what I'm going to do."

"What exactly do you plan on doing?"

"These elders of yours…they need to die."

I smiled widely. My eyes were probably beaming out stars. "I wholeheartedly agree, but—"

"They die, and we take over." He was very stern about it. I always thought of Austin as a man, but it was like he aged another ten years before my eyes. "You said we would be partners. I expect you to honor that promise."

I had already dangled the carrot in front of his nose. That's what I wanted. I wanted a king to help me lead my people, but there was still a little foulness left in my mouth. "I will."

"I wanted to figure out the mystery of this elixir that you drink. I need to confront this High Queen. Seeing that she tried to kill me last night, she may need to die too."

I was baffled by the man before me. I remembered how appalled he was when I destroyed the men who violated my home. "You're not a killer, Austin."

He smiled smugly. "Good thing I'm married to a mass murderer then."

My heart felt like it had been struck with a blunt object. "This isn't a joke."

"I'm not joking. I am totally serious, Rose. I really am." But he couldn't wipe the smile off his face. I think it was from hysteria. "Noah wanted to play ruler, but he never had the stomach to do what was necessary. He probably thought he could, and maybe he tried to convince you, but he couldn't. I'm straddling the fence myself, but I'm going to suck it up. It's the price I've chosen to pay for…"

"Being in love with me?" I was always selfish, wasn't I? To ever dream of trying to bring someone into my world was damning them to a nightmare. I should never have tried to curse someone with my blessing.

Austin sat beside me, and he kept holding my hands. "Rose, we've gotta get you off that elixir. We have no idea what it's doing to you."

"I need it to survive."

"Maybe that's what the elders tell you, so you won't stop. Maybe it's another tool to control you."

Austin might have been right about the elders lying. He was very correct about how I needed to break my connection to the High Queen, but he didn't understand how I felt. My eyes teared up from pure embarrassment. "But I get hungry and…" How was I supposed to explain that I didn't know if I could stop killing people without it? "Austin, I…"

Austin offered me a kind smile and gently cupped my face with his hands. "I can't imagine how addicted you must be to that stuff, because I thirst for it too. I was never addicted to anything before, but I know it's hard to completely kick old, bad habits. Let me help you."

I started to feel another person trapped inside of me who was unlike me. She was desperate and afraid. It took a lot of strength to keep her from screaming at Austin, but I restrained our voices to a whisper. "I'll try."

"Hey, we're still gonna be together, Rose." I didn't understand how he could smile and be so optimistic. "I still love you, and we're gonna raise a family when it's the right time. We just gotta be smart about this."

I knew Austin was telling me what I wanted and needed to hear, so I would continue trusting him. He was plotting to make my world very different, but that was what I thought I wanted. I only hoped my people could benefit from his vendetta against the High Queen.

"Let's go walk the Strip."

"Right now?" he asked a bit whiney.

I placed my hand on his chest and kissed his cheek as some incentive. "Right now, it's cool, and I wanna eat some yummy street food." I was hungry, and I needed to replenish my energy. I didn't want to outright tell him that, because I didn't want him to be afraid for my health or his safety.

"Okay. I'll get dressed."

I took a few minutes to change and mentally prepare myself for a world without my elixir. I didn't know how many calories I would have to consume to even match what the elixir did for me, but the satisfaction might have been all in my mind. Perhaps the fatigue was something I could ignore as well.

I hoped once I ate, I could fully understand how I had changed. My mother had abilities I never manifested as a virgin queen, and I certainly felt more connected with my body. I knew I had the power to will my children into conception, but there had to be more. I just needed some time.

Austin urged me to wear something comfortable, but I wanted to look glamorous for my big debut as his wife. I grabbed a couple of cute things during my mad rush at the stores. I had a short black dress with long lace sleeves that I put on. I completed the outfit with a pair of black heels. Austin shook his head when he saw me.

I posed for him in what I thought would be a sexy manner. "Do you not think I look attractive?"

I must have done something wrong because he laughed at me. "You do, babe, but your feet may very well divorce you."

"I can crush a man's skull with my bare hands. I can leap off tall cliffs into shallow waters without any pain at all. I think I can survive a shoe."

He rolled his eyes and spoke to himself. "I don't know why I'm arguing with a queen about doing anything practical."

I grew excited and grabbed his arm. "You are my king, Austin. I am glad you are here to ground me into being practical." I pecked his lips. "But these shoes are staying on my feet."

"Okay, your highness, let's go explore Las Vegas."

Even though it was so late in the night or early in the morning, the streets were busy. There was such incredible rhythm, and it didn't feel like it was ever going to end. I think most people were curious wanderers like me, but there were a ton of strange people dressed very flashy and tacky, passing out flyers to various strip clubs. I was very uncomfortable with the people and their sins, but Austin was amused by each character.

I couldn't believe how many lights were on. I couldn't see too many stars in the sky in Vegas, but there was no need to look up at the sky unless you caught a glimpse of it while staring up at tall buildings. They were all so bright and shiny that I couldn't possibly decide which one to go into first.

I took a step toward a theater, but my legs started to give out on me. Austin caught me before I fell flat on my face.

"You shouldn't have worn the shoes," he teased.

"Yeah, ok…" I knew it wasn't the shoes, but I didn't have the time to argue. My feet didn't hurt. I was tired, but it wasn't in a way that could be solved by sleep. I just had no energy.

"Let's get you something to eat." He kept his arm around my waist, and I was grateful. I didn't want to fall over and bust my face open. I was practically tripping over my own feet. "You do know how to walk, don't you?"

"Of course, I do." We hobbled over to a little bar that had chairs inside and outside. I opted to be outside, so I could get some fresh air. On top of weakness, my head was spinning, and I felt nauseous. I couldn't have been pregnant. I had complete control over pregnancies, and I hadn't willed anyone into existence yet. My life was too complicated for a litter of babies.

Austin ordered twenty barbecue wings and a chicken quesadilla. He grabbed a couple of wings and a slice of my food before I devoured the rest of it. Austin looked a little amazed, and perhaps impressed, with my appetite. "Do you want more?"

I was going to nod. I was still hungry, but I even had less energy than before. I didn't know if I'd be able to eat. My arms were like wet noodles, and my head felt like it was as heavy as a truck. "Something is wrong."

Austin was alarmed and stared at me for a while, becoming more and more concerned. His look eventually became one of true horror, and he reached across the table and stroked my face. "What's wrong?"

"What do you mean?" I felt something warm and wet coming from my nose and oozing down my mouth. "This is strange. I don't think I've ever really bled…"

The world turned into a massive and powerful flash of light. I couldn't explain what happened, but the next thing I knew, I was on the floor with Austin hovering over me.

"Is it her?" he asked, almost threatening.

I held my head and tried to concentrate. I didn't feel like something was poking at my mind. I didn't feel myself slipping. I was just weaker than I ever had been in my entire life. "No, but I don't feel my strength."

I began to whimper from what that could possibly mean, but he was just glad I was alive. He helped me rise off my back and held me in his chest. "We'll figure this out," he promised.

I didn't understand. Was the High Queen trying to kill me because we were plotting against her? Was it because I didn't have any elixir? I had gone longer without it. I got hungry, but I had never lost my strength. Something else was happening.

"Hey," a taxi driver called from the street, "is she alright?"

"We're fine," Austin assured. "I'll take her back to our hotel. We'll be fine."

"I can give you a lift."

My head was pounding so hard that my brain felt like it was being throttled. My vision doubled, so I could see the man twice as much as Austin. He was Caucasian with sandy brown hair and brown eyes. He was a little scrappy and scruffy, so he looked like he sort of belonged to the city, but there was something about him that I could sense. There was a connection there. "He's one of mine."

"What?" Austin asked.

"He's from my island." I had so many fears overtake me. I had slept with Austin. I had his seeds within me. The elders were going back on our deal, and if I didn't do something soon, I would never see Austin again. "We need to run. Now."

Austin still didn't seem like he all the way trusted me, but he did want to protect me, and he certainly didn't trust my people. He scooped me up into his arms and ran down the Las Vegas Strip with me. There were still swarms of people pushing all around us like walls closing in. The lights were suddenly too bright, and they buzzed as the world around me whirled out of control.

I had to close my eyes because I thought I was going to vomit. I didn't need to see anything, though. I could feel more of them coming from all sides. They were trained warriors. There was no way Austin was going to be able to defeat or even outrun them.

"You have to leave me behind, Austin." He and his friends liked to free run. If I had given him an opportunity to survive on his own, he might have had a chance.

"If they catch me alone, they may kill me. They need to know that it's both of us or neither, Rose. I'm not abandoning you."

I held on tighter to him. I had to find a way to make my people respect him. I could only do that through a display of strength, but it took everything I had just to hold onto him. "I'll do whatever it takes to protect you."

"I'm supposed to protect you, remember?"

I smiled. "I—"

I felt us being pulled roughly, and we both ended up on the ground. I opened my eyes just in time to see a man closing a gate. We were trapped inside a movie theater, and there were at least three men behind us, armed with black blades.

I clutched onto Austin. I didn't want him to even attempt to fight them. I had seen warriors train my entire life, and they were raised to be without fear or mercy. They were to do anything necessary, and human blood was nothing to them.

I was so weak that I couldn't stop him. Austin jumped to his feet and attacked the man in front of him. The warrior was so much faster than Austin that it looked like a child fighting a grown man.

"Stop!" I begged. I couldn't stand by while they slaughtered him. "He's my husband. He's your king."

The warrior slightly glared and then moved into attack mode. He struck Austin three times quickly with two jabs and a hook. Then, for his finish, he performed a roundhouse kick that brought Austin to his knees and filled his mouth with blood.

"No!" I found the strength to jump up. I wouldn't cower in front of Austin and beg for his life anymore. I was going to take my vengeance. I practically tripped all over myself, but I stumbled right into the warrior's chest and clutched onto his shirt for support.

"You brought this on yourself." I may have been exhausted, but the hunger hadn't left me. I opened my mouth and prepared to devour his life. I saw the magnificent glimmer of fear in his eyes just as I began sucking everything he ever was away, but there was a sharp blow to my head before I could finish, and the world turned dark.

I thought when I dreamed once again, I would be able to see my mother or Noah, but there was literally nothing but an ache. When I awakened, I felt desperate and stressed. Even in my dreams, I worried about Austin's life. "Austin?"

I rose and looked around the room. It was as luxurious and spacious as I remembered, but it wasn't steady. I was on the yacht that brought me to America, and we had already set sail. "Austin!"

The door opened, and a warrior came through. He was probably only a few years older than me, but he was stoic and cold like he had lived through an eternity. "I hope you are feeling more comfortable."

The bed was comfortable, but I didn't feel any better. "What is happening to me?"

"I'm afraid that you're dying."

"Dying?" I laughed at first. He offered me no remorse, so I assumed he was being sarcastic and playing with my emotions. The longer I waited, the more apparent it became that he was just cruel in nature. "How?"

"The elders wouldn't disclose all the information, but it appears your children are malnourished, so they are taking the life inside of you."

I instinctively touched my stomach. I didn't care that my children were turning against me. The only fact that mattered was that if I did die, then they would also be dead. "I don't understand. What have I done wrong compared to my mother, or her mother before her?"

"I'm not sure. We need to bring you to the elders. They believe they can cure you."

It took everything I had not to cry in front of my warrior. I did not need him thinking I was weaker than what I already felt. "Where is Austin?"

"He's locked up tight."

"He's the king." I was disgusted with the little smirk I saw on his face. They would learn their place soon enough. "Austin should be treated with respect."

"The elders want him locked up and brought home."

"I don't care what the elders want," I lied. I cared because I was terrified of what they wanted to do with his body.

"They're the reason why Austin is still alive. Do you truly want to spit in their face now?"

I narrowed my eyes on him and found the strength to stand on my feet. I would never ever be grateful for anything the elders had done, and everyone who sided with them was against me. "Bring me to him, or I will kill you."

He appeared brave, but I saw the lump in his throat as he gulped. "Very well."

I didn't want to need any help, but I could barely stand, let alone walk. The warrior grabbed my arm and led me down to the brig. I wasn't sure why such a nice yacht had chains and a dungeon. It made me curious to know how much the elders foresaw.

Austin was alone, sitting in the far corner of the cell. When he saw me, he ran and grabbed the bars. "Rose!"

"Hi, Austin." I smiled. I was so grateful to see him alive. "Are you hurt?"

"No." He reached through the bars and stroked my face as a demonstration of compassion for me. I didn't understand why he didn't hate me when all I brought him was trouble. "Are you feeling any better?"

I considered lying to keep him from worrying, but there was no way for me to fake it. "No." I immediately began to tear up. I wasn't comfortable with how I had lived my life. Every action I ever took was about self-preservation. The only time I actually spent living my life was in my pursuit of love. Now that I had obtained it, the short amount of time I experienced wasn't enough. "Austin, I'm dying. Our children are dying."

I collapsed on the ground and held my stomach. I was such a terrible mother, and none of my children had even been born yet. My very existence was all amounting to a giant failure.

"Children?" Austin took a deep breath and pressed his head against the bars. "Are you pregnant?"

"I'm technically always pregnant. I choose to give birth whenever I want." Whether it was twenty years down the line or two days, it didn't matter. "They're not healthy, and they're taking from me to sustain their lives." I could barely breathe from the agony. I could gladly give my life to save them, but what would become of them once I was gone? How could I protect them? "I'm a terrible mother."

Austin slid down on the floor to be level with me, but we didn't make eye contact or speak to each other for a while. I could feel his heaviness suffocating me. I knew that he wanted to take charge and make it all better, but there was nothing either of us could have done. Eventually, Austin sighed heavily and exhaustedly. "What's going to happen to us?"

"I don't know. The elders think they can fix me, but they want to see you—"

"I don't trust them—"

"I don't either, but I would do anything to save our children." I wiped my eyes. I wanted to rip the elders to pieces, but I had no doubt they would find a way to give themselves the advantage.

"Everything will be okay, Rose. I swear I will figure this out. I'll save us." He had an assuring grin that was adorable, and it made me want to trust that smiling fool.

"Can you please tell me what happens at the end of my book?"

He looked surprised. I did want to read it myself, but things were beginning to look grim. I just wanted to finally put the mystery to rest, and I wanted to hear the sound of his voice.

"The knight leads a group of men to go save the princess, but when he arrives at their old palace, she's been overtaken by the witch's darkness. The princess fights her knight, and she intends to kill him, but he can't bring himself to truly defend himself against her. He loves her too much, and he remembers the good inside of her. He tries to break through the spell with a confession of love, but it doesn't work. He tries to kiss her, but she stabs him when he gets too close.

"He ends up kissing her, and she remembers how much she loved him. She vows to save his life and goes to confront the evil witch. The witch tries to use the evil she placed in the princess's heart against her, but she's strong enough to fight against it. The princess overpowers the witch and plans to take the revenge she's dreamed about her entire life."

"And does she get her revenge?"

"No."

"No?" My heart sank. "She doesn't avenge her parents?"

"She offers the witch a chance to save her life if she saves her love. The witch does it to save her own life, so the princess makes good on her deal and lets her go."

"I guess that's not a terrible ending, but..." Even though I identified with the witch, I still wanted to see her dead. The princess needed a happy ending. "What about her parents? She deserves justice."

"She deserves a chance to be happy, Rose."

I pouted. She and her true love were together. That's what was important. I should have been grateful that her knight didn't die, and she survived the darkness, but I was so bothered. "People like the witch don't change. She still needed to die."

"You're right," he said with a smile. "The day the princess was to be wed, the witch returned to kill her. It was her knight that finally ended the witch's life. It had nothing to do with revenge. It was to protect his future." Austin put a certain emphasis on his last sentence.

"I see what you're saying." But if he expected me to give the elders a second chance, then he was mistaken.

"The elders will be removed, Rose. I don't want you to kill them because they hurt you. I want you to do it because it's the only way to move forward and save our worlds."

I didn't care for the reasons. I just wanted them dead, and I wanted to kill them myself. "How are we going to win?"

Austin reached through the bars and grabbed my hand. He didn't even lose faith for an instant. He kissed my hand with a devious and charming smirk, like how the knight in the story would kiss his princess. "Through the power of love."

I listened to his brilliant plan and began to get excited. He was clever and cunning, like a true king should be. If his plan did succeed, I was going to enjoy celebrating with him.

When I was ready, I called for a warrior to help me back up to my room. I had never attempted what I was about to do, but I knew what I was capable of. I imagined each warrior around me, and I thought about the way I had made Austin and Noah pine for me. I thought about the way Austin made me feel when the two of us were together. There was so much passion between the two of us. I could taste it in the air. There was certainly enough to go around.

As a mature queen, I felt mystical and sexier than ever. Perhaps it was a gift the High Queen left activated in my body, or it could have been a natural progression of my powers. It could have simply been due to how successful Austin was in pleasuring me and awakening my sexual nature. It was difficult to tell. Whatever the explanation, I knew I had an advantage.

A few minutes later, I sensed someone coming by. I waited longer, and then I sensed more. There must have been about twenty men on my boat, besides Austin, and they all came to my door and waited outside anxiously for me. Eventually, one of them came up with enough nerve to knock.

"Come in."

They spilled inside my cabin, but they didn't pounce on me. They were sweaty, and their eyes were glossed over. They were certainly enchanted, but they were all aware of what would happen to anyone who forced themselves on me.

Inside, I was intimidated by my task. I was weak, and I didn't know how well I could defend myself if I had overdone my pheromones. But I couldn't show fear. I had to be supremely seductive. "Hello, my young warriors."

Each one perked their head up as if I were addressing them individually. I had to be careful, or else they would turn on each other.

"That overwhelming feeling you suddenly have is your love and lust for me, manifesting into its purest form. I have mated, but Austin doesn't have to be the only man to feel my touch."

I could see their eyes wandering around the room. They were brothers banded together to "protect" me and follow the will of the elders. Now, they were looking at each other with visceral eyes. Some of them were armed with their black blades, and they gripped them tightly. There would be blood spilled everywhere until one of them could have me. I couldn't let that happen!

"When we arrive home, I want the elders killed."

I gained all their attention. They were appalled, but still too entranced to truly speak out and stop my desires. I pushed harder. I could make them all my willing slaves.

"For now, you will act normally as if you were following their orders, but once I give the command, you will strike. Every one of you that brings me a head, gets to know my touch."

They were men bound by their truest instincts. Yes, I loved tales about romantic gestures like all the ones Noah prescribed to. However, men were protectors at their core. They liked their feats of strength. I was giving them a chance to prove their worthiness to me in exchange for my affection. It was a contract they all gladly accepted.

"Good, now let's hurry on home."

Chapter Nineteen

After years of fantasizing, the day had finally arrived. I was still weak, but the fresh air and the smell of the ocean were doing me good. I took everything in, including the glorious sunrise. By the time the sun set once more, my mother would be avenged.

"Are you ready?" Austin had been released by my orders. The other men were jealous of him, but I made my rules clear. They were willing to play my game.

"Of course, I am." I placed my hand on my stomach. I was in such incredible pain, and it was difficult to press through it. I tried to eat enough, but I knew there was something else I needed. I'm ashamed to say that I thought about feasting on my warriors, but I needed them to fight the elders. My death seemed inevitable if I wanted my revenge.

I believe Austin knew how stressed out I was. "Have you thought about any names?"

"Names?"

"Yeah, for our kids." He leaned against the rails and stared up at the sky. He had a small smile on his face, but I could hear how uncomfortable he was by the way his voice uncharacteristically quivered. "I was thinking they could all have themes, but if there's like thirty of them, then it may just be too hard, and—"

"You are incredible..." I was in complete awe of him.

"Excuse me?"

I shrugged. "Sometimes, I wonder if all of this was worth it. I wonder if I should have bit my tongue and done what everyone expected of me. I've ruined lives, Austin, and I've even ended them, all in pursuit of love. How can it be worth all this pain? How can I be so selfish when I have an entire kingdom to look after?"

I smiled as tears flowed from my eyes. "But then you do something like that—you make me feel like there isn't anything else in this world, and only you and I exist—and I know I would probably do it all again, just to know you. Maybe I'd do everything different with Noah…"

"He touched your life, too, Rose." I knew Austin had regrets. I could see them clearly in his eyes, but there was a lot of love in them as well. "You made him feel special, and I'm grateful he experienced what it was like to fall in love before he died. That's more than most people can get nowadays."

I was so honored to have Austin by my side. I knew now that my pheromones truly weren't affecting him, because he hadn't changed at all since I took control of my warriors. Still, circumstances didn't exactly let him come aboard with me willingly. He probably would have wanted to date for three years and not have to think about kids and responsibility. "I know you probably wouldn't choose this life with me—"

"Not exactly how it happened, Rose, but I would choose you. I did choose you." He shrugged and grinned. "We are married. For better or worse, until death do us part, we're in this together."

I grinned and looked to my island. Very soon, I'd either be dead or victorious. Either way, it would be over. "I want you to name them. I wouldn't know what to call them. Maybe I'll come up with some names later, but you can name the first batch."

"Batch?" his voice quivered again, but he recovered with a smile. "Okay. I've got some ideas. Maybe we'll make an alphabet book or something. We'll start with A and go from there."

"That sounds wonderful." I felt blood pour from my nose, and it dripped onto the deck. I tried to rush away before Austin noticed, but his arms were already around me before I could move my legs.

"Be careful," he urged. "You're almost home."

We waited together in my room until we were informed we had arrived. The plan was simple. We would both be marched to the elders. I would listen to what they had to say about my condition. I would give a command, and then the warriors would kill them. I hadn't worked out what I was going to do with them once they had served their purpose, but I was working on it. I had no intention of cheating on Austin.

Austin's arms and legs were shackled together, and he was marched by my side off the yacht. There was a crowd of my people there to greet me, but they were only mere servants there, in case I had any needs. They weren't there because they loved or missed me. Those would be foolish reasons, according to the elders, and the workers and warriors had much more important things to do.

They all gossiped as soon as they saw Austin, though. He was the biggest news since my succession.

Austin looked at everyone around us and shuddered after a while. "It's kind of creepy how you all sort of look alike."

"There are other colonies all over the world to accommodate other races of humans. There's an African colony, one in Asia, and so on. We're everywhere. We are everyone."

"That's not great at all..." His voice faded as we walked into a carriage to take us to the palace. Austin had to remain chained up as a part of our plan, but he sat beside me and placed his hands on my knee. It made me think of how intimate we were on our wedding night.

"Do you think things will be safe for us soon? Do you think we can...?" I blushed.

"I hope so." He grinned. "I think if this High Queen could control you whenever she wanted, we wouldn't be in this position right now."

I wasn't very afraid of her taking me over. I believed I was strong enough to overpower her if she tried to take me again. Besides, I hadn't had any elixir in days, and I never would again if it would endanger Austin and keep the two of us from being together again.

Austin peeked outside of the carriage as we approached my home, and his eyes widened. "Is this where you live?"

I rolled my eyes. "I know it's not as glorious as other mansions, but—"

"No, it's pretty amazing..."

It was a beautiful home with white columns, large windows that were blocked inside with large curtains, and it was made from limestone. It was large in stature, but nothing was as breathtaking as the greenery that surrounded it. The bushes, the trees, and the array of flowers were what welcomed me. It reminded me of my mother.

We came in through the front gate, and Austin squeezed my hand tight. "This is it, Rose."

I nodded. Finally, my mother would be avenged.

As I stepped out of the carriage, I lost my strength and fell into the arms of one of my warriors. He inhaled the scent of me as my neck hung over his shoulder. He squeezed me a little too tightly, and I caught a glimmer of light in his eyes. He was going to be my finest killer. "I've got you."

"Thank you." I let him aid me inside the mansion. I didn't want to burden Austin with my weakness as he gawked around.

"I feel poor," he muttered.

"Why?" I chuckled. "This is your home now."

He gave me a little grin. "I suppose it is."

I hadn't roamed much around the mansion, but I knew good and well where we were being taken when we were led to a far corner of the house and down a winding staircase. It was the same place where I was born, and it was the same place where my mother died.

I tried not to make eye contact with the giant pit of my elixir, but I could still smell it. I knew it was there. My mouth watered, and my stomach ached. I tried to hold it together, but I moaned aloud from the pain.

"It's okay," Austin said. "It's okay. You don't need it."

The elders were all gathered together before me. My mother's murderer was holding the same knife in his hand that he used to kill her. I became enraged and set my sights on him. I would not allow him to harm Austin.

"How are you, my queen?"

It was strange not to be addressed by my former title. It took half a second to realize he was talking to me. "I'm not feeling well, but you must have gathered that."

"Of course." He circled Austin as he observed him in close detail. His eyes especially zoomed in on his wedding ring. "I see that you two have gotten married and consummated."

"That was always my plan, and you agreed to it."

"Oh, I did." He laughed and walked in front of me. "I just don't understand why he's still alive."

My eyes widened, and I was breathless for a brief moment. I couldn't wrap my mind around such a question. "I love him. Why wouldn't he be alive?"

He laughed again so cruelly. I didn't know if he pitied me or thought me a fool—probably both. He was so vicious and sly as he bent down, so we would be completely eye level as he spoke in my face. "All queens—even your mother before you—take the lives of their mates during coitus."

I shook my head as my entire body trembled. "I don't understand."

"I mean, you aren't the only murderer in your family. Your mother killed your father."

I looked at the other elders. I expected them to expose the lie, but they all nodded along with him. If my mother were truly a monster, it couldn't have been her fault. "Only because the High Queen took her over."

"No," he yelled hysterically, "it was because her nature took her over. You're all beasts. We just give you a pretty title for politics. It doesn't mean anything." He always despised me. If he could have killed me a long time ago, he would have. But suddenly, he had a glimmer of adoration in his eyes for me. "If the High Queen contacted you, then you must be different. Well, we both know you're different."

He gripped the knife tighter and made a step toward Austin, but I threw myself in front of him. "Austin is my mate. He is my king!"

"You have to take his life. It's the only way to protect the future of our colony. He's providing the proper nutrients for your children." How dare he try to plead with me after all the hell he put me through? There was nothing in my colony that gave me even the slightest impression that Austin's life was worth surrendering for.

"No."

They all narrowed their eyes in on me. "Your title requires sacrifice."

Fury fumed up in my face. I never knew love as a child, except for very brief moments, and he stole it all away from me. They sent men to rape me. I sent my sister away because she could never be happy while I was near. I stole the life of my very best friend, who I would cherish for all of eternity. They asked me to murder my husband. Everything in my world was twisted and rotten. I could not give up the only light in my life for people who gave me a meaningless title. "You know nothing of sacrifice!"

"I know everything about sacrifice, girl!" He grabbed my face and squeezed my jaw tight. If I still had my strength, he wouldn't dare be so bold. Austin tried to fight to free me, but the warriors holding his chains pulled him back. They were nowhere near my strength at my peak, but they were stronger than him. The warriors were still itching to kill for me, though, but it wasn't time to give the order. I had to bear my elder's unjust rage.

"I understand the allure of the human world. I was born there. My father was born there. My son was born there. Then, we were called home. I was chosen to be an elder. I was transformed by the very same elixir that you drink." He squeezed a little bit tighter, and I screamed through my teeth. He received a sick pleasure from it. "Your mother thought my son was special, too. He was her first victim."

He tossed me to the ground as I reflected on each word he had spoken to me. I didn't know if that made everything we had been through better or worse. I wanted to know where I came from, but he was the devil who plagued my life. "You're my grandfather?"

"Yes, I am." Our blood meant nothing to him. He was usually so cold, and I thought he had no feelings besides when he slipped and showed his rage. But there was love in his heart for someone. It just wasn't for me. "Do you want to know what your father was like before we answered the Call? He was sweet, kind, and full of dreams. When we came to the colony, he was loyal and obedient. He thought your mother was lovely, and I—like a good elder— sent my son to her, so he could die." He reverenced the memory of his son. No wonder why he thought my mother was selfish.

I lowered my head in shame. Like a child, I imagined a perfect and happy family. My mother told me that wasn't so, but I still wanted to pretend sometimes. She took his life, and I took hers. Some part of me was a part of both of them.

Austin sneered at my elder. "You're sick."

"It's what is required of me."

I gasped and raised my head as a revelation hit me. "You knew I was leaving to find a husband. You knew this entire time that I was probably going to kill him?"

He raised his head and smirked. "It seemed cruel to tell you."

I exploded in rage and prepared to claw off his face. If it weren't for the warriors holding me back, I would have ripped his throat out with my teeth. "I'll kill you!"

"That's a little impossible, my dear. I assume your 'husband' had a little bit of your elixir. This makes him immune to your unique power. That's why you haven't been able to kill me."

"So, what?" Austin snapped. "You've brought me here, so she can kill me? You just established that she can't."

I recalled when Noah died. He very recently had my elixir. It didn't seem to have any effect on him at all, but he should have been protected from my power. But when he died, his life found a way inside of me, even when I wildly fought against it. "I can take their life if they're dying, right?"

My mother should have been as powerful as I was, or even more so, at the time of her death. She had to be weakened. "That's why you stabbed my mother, and that's what you're planning on doing to Austin right now."

Elder shook his head and pouted as if he were upset. "It's really too bad. Humans convert to make great elders. We understand what it truly takes to make something great. We can appreciate the sacrifices."

Austin appeared horrified, and I was as well. A transformation into an elder was the very last thing in the world I could stand. I would rather have killed him myself than let him become anything like my grandfather, and I think Austin would have agreed.

Elder raised his knife into the air and prepared to slash Austin's throat, but he was moving so slow to my eyes. It wasn't too late to change things. I would not let them take anyone else from me. "Attack!"

The warrior holding onto Austin pulled him back far enough to miss being slashed by my grandfather. Then, he raised his own blade to block my grandfather. The rest of the elders charged, but the warriors made their move as well. Each one was bound by their desire for me, and it fueled them to fight ferociously. They wielded their blades swiftly and with great precision. I was certain they would be able to give us all victory until a minute into their battle. I realized that every punch thrown was all in vain. I was unaware that the elders possessed great speed and strength, and their superiority was showing.

I was weak, but I rushed to Austin and struggled to get his chains off. I pulled the key out of my bra and freed him. We had to make a run for it before the battle was over. They couldn't make me kill Austin if they couldn't find him, and Austin wouldn't have to worry about his life if they found and killed me.

The chains fell off Austin, and he lunged forward to attack my grandfather, but I pulled him back. They were far too strong for both of us. Austin hesitated and watched the gruesome battle for a second. My grandfather took someone by the head and snapped his neck effortlessly, and he fell like a sack of bricks. We jumped back when his ruthless eyes set sights on us again.

I could feel Austin resisting me as I pulled on his arms. I remember begging him to run, but I don't know what I said. I only remember being incredibly frightened for his life. "Please."

He finally gave up and started to run with me, but I overestimated my body and stumbled. Austin wrapped his arms around me to hold me up, but that lapse in speed was enough for my grandfather to rush in front of him and bust Austin's nose. I fell to the ground with him, and the warriors who were supposed to murder the elders fell in sync with us. Their throats were slit, their bones were broken, and it hadn't even been two minutes. They died so quickly, I didn't even have time to take their life force. They weren't like Noah. Their lives didn't linger. They were gone in a flash.

My grandfather pulled on his robe sleeves to look a little bit more presentable before killing the love of my life. "That was amusing but pitiful."

Austin grunted and rose, determined to make a difference. My grandfather let himself be punched in the face the first, second, and third times. Maybe Austin would have been decent in an average human brawl, but he was not trained to fight anyone. He was fast and had the stamina, but he was simply no match. Eventually, my grandfather got sick of dodging and taking his ineffective hits, and he head-butted Austin to make him fall to the ground with a bruised forehead.

Another elder swept up behind Austin and kept him restrained, while the rest of the elders circled us.

"No, please!" I reached out to stop him, but another elder grabbed me. I looked around the room at all the savagery my warriors had to suffer. I couldn't let Austin die like that. "Please, don't kill him. I love him."

My grandfather turned around and stared at me, confounded. He used to love someone. I hoped he could see how important it was to me. I needed him to understand that I needed Austin. Life wasn't worth living without love.

Maybe things could be different. I could find another way to survive. I could keep the colony alive by having my children. I could spare the elders if I had to! I just wanted Austin to be by my side, always. I wanted my children to have a father who loved them more than they could ever imagine. I wanted a family.

But he couldn't understand. His confusion drew to a close, and I clearly saw the disdain he held for me. "You are our queen. You have no right to love."

"No!" The black blade shone in the light before it pierced Austin's flesh. He didn't scream or beg. He gritted his teeth and dealt with the pain so well that the only sound that could be heard was the squish of his organs and the smack of my grandfather's lips as his face curled into a smirk.

The blade was removed, and I screamed as blood poured from his wound and dripped onto the marble floor. The elders released us, and I rushed to meet my lover as he fell to his knees. I could already feel him slipping away when I touched him. I could smell his life-force. I could practically taste it on my tongue. "Austin, don't leave me. Please, don't leave me..."

I don't know what had him so calm. Perhaps it was the fact that he had to deal with Noah's condition for so long or that he lived so recklessly anyway. He really didn't have any fear, and he didn't show any signs of resentment toward me as he held my face and locked himself into my eyes. "Don't let them win, Rose. You can still change things. You don't have to let them change you."

How could he say such words to me? Each breath I took tasted foul. It was poisoned with hatred that was too intense to survive in. I was going to kill the elders as soon as I was well enough. I was going to kill everyone who stood in my way. The entire world would burn if it eased my aching heart.

"Austin, I don't know what to do." I could see myself as a tyrant. I literally could. It wasn't because I thought my people deserved to rule. I despised them for forcing me into such a position. They would become nothing more than disposable tools. If I wanted to send out the Call for war, I could. I was losing my faith in the entire world. It would die with my love. No matter how much I tried to reflect on how good and decent Noah was, and the truth that there had to be more men like him out there, I couldn't stop feeling the rage within me. "I need you to protect me from myself. I need you to look after my people."

I closed my eyes and felt the pain. There had to be more to my life. I was destined to be a mother. I was supposed to give life, and yet all I did was take it. Well, no more. I would not die a failure. I had to give life to someone.

"Goodbye." I granted Austin a final kiss. I could feel his life beginning to transfer over to me, but I wouldn't allow it. I recalled how it felt to snatch the lives of each one of my warriors. If I could pull from them, then I knew I was also powerful enough to push back. So, that's what I did. I pushed back everything I had taken from everyone else, and I gave it to the only love left in my life.

Austin gasped for air when I released him. I collapsed on my back and breathed in heavily. I could feel my own life being pulled simultaneously. There wasn't enough of me to accommodate myself and the future of the colony. It was becoming difficult to breathe, and my body was growing colder. It wouldn't be long at all before I and the future of my colony all died to save the life of one good man.

I caught Austin staring at his hands in amazement. He flexed his muscles. He wasn't physically different, but he felt a sudden change in his body. Once he knew for sure what it was, he growled like a beast before howling out a battle cry.

I couldn't see much because my vision began to leave me. I heard bones crunching like glass, cries of men, and the furious roars of my grandfather. Streams of blood danced across the room like graceful ribbons before splattering on my face. Seconds passed by, and one elder flew across my body and landed next to me.

My head fell to its side. Mostly everything had turned to darkness, but his body was highlighted to my eyes. I could smell his life-force.

It wasn't over yet.

I couldn't move. I closed my eyes and inhaled through my nostrils. I felt a warmth inside my chest, and then my stomach expanded. I still didn't have the strength to move, so I waited for another elder to fall, and then another. It wasn't very long before I found the strength to stand on my feet.

Austin had changed. It was as if I could see my warriors fighting alongside him. Perhaps they were aiding him. They all died because they offended me, but it was their duty to protect me.

They were misguided fools perverted by the elders. That didn't mean they didn't care about me at all.

There were only two elders left. My grandfather hadn't made his move yet. He watched Austin, completely appalled by his strength and power. Then, his eyes found me, and I realized just how little he knew me. He was genuinely baffled that I was willing to die for love.

Austin locked hands with an elder, and the two engaged in a test of strength. They pressed their feet into the ground as they struggled to move the other. This elder was the oldest and the strongest, next to my grandfather.

I cracked my neck by moving my head from side to side. If Austin weren't able to kill him, I knew that I had the strength to do so. The elders were very different from my warriors. I had never felt stronger, and the ache in my body was leaving.

Austin grunted as the elder appeared to be gaining the upper hand. The elder smirked in Austin's face, but he couldn't allow himself to lose. Austin bent down under the elder, and he pressed his forehead hard against the elder's chin. The elder released Austin's hand after his jaw cracked into pieces. Then, Austin yelled in fury as he rammed his fist straight into the elder's ribcage. I heard something crack, and the elder's mouth filled with blood. He stumbled around a little bit until I grew impatient and throttled him by his neck.

"When you all murdered my mother, I swore I would have my revenge." I opened my mouth wide and devoured what was left of his life. Once I was finished feasting, I knew that I could kill my grandfather. I had all the power in the world.

Austin picked up a blade from one of the elder's bodies and gripped it. He had taken many lives, but he hadn't grown cold. He was only trying to protect me and do what any good knight would, but he wasn't a murderer.

"Don't," I asked. "You've done enough, Austin."

He didn't want me to take my grandfather's life, despite what he had just done to Austin. I think he understood my grandfather needed to die, but he didn't want me to be burdened by it. That's what I assumed from the look on his face.

"Austin is my king. He will rule with me. We will change our lands, and I won't fight against the humans."

"The High Queen will change your mind," he said. "She may not be able to completely control you, but she can control your children. She can reach out to other queens and elders in other colonies. You can't change our world. You are a pawn—"

"I'm a queen." I rushed to his face until we were practically nose to nose. "I am the one with real power. You think you have control, but you're already off the board." If Austin stabbed him, I could take his life. The struggle would be over. I could live my life in peace.

But I wasn't sure if I would be at peace. He was my family, after all. He was my only real connection to my father, and he knew more than I did. He raised me blind for a reason, but I didn't want to lead blind. "If I spare your life, will you accept this new order?"

He burst into instantaneous laughter. "Are you serious?"

"Yeah, are you serious?" Austin asked, surprised.

"I am." I had no idea why the princess in my story decided to spare the witch. It was foolish, just as I chose to be foolish. "I will allow you to keep your life and your title, but only if you agree to bow down and respect our titles and the authority behind them."

His eyes softened. I'd like to think he saw the same kindness that lived in my father's heart, inside of my own. I'd like to think that he saw my mother and me as something more than monsters.

But that was only for a very brief moment. "Never."

Austin flew across the room and landed in the pit of elixir. I gasped and bolted toward it. I couldn't let the High Queen corrupt him like she tried to corrupt me. But as I began to run, I was yanked by my hair and forced to confront my grandfather. His hands launched for my face, but I blocked them. He was going to try to snap my neck if he got the chance.

"You can't kill me."

"I can. The High Queen will just have to send another queen. You're too much trouble, girl."

I growled and narrowed my eyes at him. "My name is Rose!" I had no formal combat training, but I think my form was excellent as I kicked him in the stomach. He doubled over in pain, and I became disgusted by how absolutely pathetic he was. My tormentor was finally groveling at my feet, and it was a lot more bittersweet than I imagined. "Now would be the time to end your life, wouldn't it?"

"Allow me." Austin was soaking wet and covered in green slime. He brushed his hair back to keep the clumpy mess out of his eyes. Thankfully, he appeared normal.

"Be my guest." I spotted the same jewel-encrusted black blade that was used to take my mother's life on the ground. It was only fitting that Austin used it to end the cycle of violence. I picked it up and didn't even think of using it myself. I didn't necessarily want the revenge anymore. I wanted to be free.

I placed the blade in Austin's hands, and with a very fluid motion, the dagger was stuck inside of my grandfather's stomach and twisted. I didn't even have time to reconsider, and neither did Austin.

My king removed the blade, and my grandfather held his wound and stuck his head up defiantly. He was too proud of nothing. Why did he have such dignity? He was a monster that hid behind a mask of duty. How could he not believe that separating a mother and daughter was an injustice? How could he think it was appropriate to send men to take advantage of me? He wasn't evil. He was sick.

"What now?" Austin asked in my ear.

I felt fine. I knew that I wouldn't need to feed on Austin to survive. I even felt better about trying to live my life without my elixir. I could let him die, but it just didn't seem very poetic to me. Every good story ended with some flair and a happy ending. "I feed one last time."

I wrapped my fingers around his thick neck and raised him above my head. He wouldn't be able to escape me, but he wasn't going to try. He was going to face his well-deserved death with dignity.

I breathed in his life, and one more power boost surged throughout my body. I could hardly believe that such a dark chapter of my life was coming to a close, but I felt the heaviness lifting when I finished swallowing the last bit of his life.

"Is it over?"

I blinked, and tears fell from my eyes. I dropped my grandfather and looked around at all the destruction, but I didn't see any lives lost. I saw a new beginning. I wanted to build a new world full of wonderful possibilities. I was so happy that I didn't know what I was supposed to do with myself. "It's over."

Austin rushed to my lips, but I took a step back as soon as I got a good whiff of him. "I'm not kissing you as long as you've got that green goop all over you."

"Sorry." He chuckled and wrapped his arms around me. "I guess this means that we're in charge now."

I hugged him tightly. He moaned a little bit, but I knew he could finally take it. He wasn't as strong as I was, but he could probably play a decent game of basketball now. "We are, my king."

I wasn't afraid of our future. The elders were gone. The High Queen may have been out there somewhere, but we would thrive together. I didn't see how any queen could fight against a king and queen with true power and love by their side.

Chapter Twenty

"So, the princess and her knight lived happily ever after, Momma?"

I smiled at the high-pitched sound of my daughter's excited voice. Every time she spoke, she brought such great joy into my life. "They certainly did, Annabelle."

Annabelle resembled her father. She had such an innocent and chubby face, like in the pictures I saw hanging on Austin's walls. She also had his eyes and his spirit. She tried her best to be a perfect princess, but she liked to wear sneakers under her gowns, so she could run with her brother. "I think this is a great story."

"It was one of my favorites as a young girl." I gently took the book out of her hands and sat beside her on my bed. It seemed like ages ago when the elders burned my book into ashes. Annabelle was too young to explain the significant meaning the story had to my life, but she'd appreciate it one day. "It's very violent, though. I'm not sure I should have let you read it."

She threw her head back and moaned. "I'm fine, Momma. I'm very mature."

"Yes, you are." I kissed her forehead. I smothered her with affection because I never wanted her to feel as I did as a child, not even for a second. "Are you all packed for when we go visit your grandparents in America?"

"I am." She slumped her shoulders. "I just don't understand why I can't bring one of my sisters with me. I get lonely when it's just my brother and me."

"It's hard to explain all of your siblings and what your father has been up to. It's easier if they believe it's just you, me, your brother, and your father." That was a decision Austin came to. He knew his parents a lot better than I did, so I trusted his judgment.

"They can never know what I am and what's become of your father. The truth would be more than they could take."

It was a terrible lesson to teach a child, but I had to make sure Austin's family didn't dig any deeper. They had money and resources to figure things out. There was no way they'd ever find out about the colony, but they could prove my cover story, about being a farmer's daughter, was a lie. "Okay, Momma."

I couldn't wait to go back to America. Hopefully, I would finally see my sister again. She learned to hide very well, and not even my spies received any word on her whereabouts. If only she knew that it was safe for her to have a family. I needed her to be a part of mine. I just wanted to know that Camellia was safe. Hopefully, she was a mother.

"You make sure you're finished packing. I'm gonna go spy on your father."

Annabelle went to her room and finished gathering her things with one of my servants, while I journeyed to the shore. My people weren't as they used to be. It took some time for them to get used to the fact that Austin had authority, but no one opposed it with the elders gone. I didn't break any legs or suck out any more lives. We changed things. We gave people choices. Men could work in the fields if they wanted, and women could challenge themselves with training. We opened schools that had nothing to do with infiltrating human society. My people learned about math, science, and literature because I wanted them to be well-educated and have imaginations. I wanted us to thrive. It was hard for some to soak in, but I noticed everyone's smile was legitimate when I walked by, and they bowed.

I often went out to the beach to see Austin teach our children how to surf. He liked it when we did activities together, but he always felt like I was checking on him. I didn't say anything for a while. I watched them from afar.

The twelve of them paddled around on their boards and swam like a school of fish. They were naturals like their father. Our son even rode a little wave before wiping out. Austin threw his hands up in the air and cheered him on.

As their lessons drew to a close, they all came out of the water. Brian grew a devious look in his eyes, though, and he wrapped his arms around one of his sisters. She screamed for him to let her go, but he dunked her in the water. Austin quickly broke it up by holding Elizabeth in his arms and scolding our boy. "Brian, come on. Be nice to your sisters."

"There are too many of them to be completely nice to all of them. I have to pick with a few."

I couldn't help myself and rushed to the shore when I saw the roughhousing, but I didn't reveal the slight panic I had. "I read in the bible once that a brother is born for adversity."

"It would sure seem that way sometimes." He sat Elizabeth down on the sand and nudged her forward. "All of you, go on. Surfing lessons are over. You've gotta get back to your studies, and some of you have chores."

They all moaned but ran along to their nannies. We were raising quite the little beach bums, but Austin was stern when it came to schoolwork. He truly did impress me. "You're so good with them."

"Fun is great, but discipline goes a long way."

I cocked my brow. "Did it with you?"

He hesitated for half a second. "No, not at all."

I chuckled and clasped my hands together in excitement. "Do you think we could handle a couple more?"

Austin rubbed the back of his head. He wanted to wait several years to have children, but we had our first batch to reaffirm to the people that I was a proper queen. I knew the first six freaked him out when they came at once, but we handled them just fine. We got a little overwhelmed when the next four were born, but we knew what we were doing when the last three showed up. What did he have to worry about? "We've already gone through half of the alphabet, and none of them are even six yet."

"I know, but I love having your children." I wasn't crazy about the actual birthing process, but I did enjoy rubbing my stomach and imagining the new life within it. "I love seeing you take care of them. I know they're going to grow up to be great people."

"You don't mind that they'll be more like humans or...whatever your normal colony folk is?" Annabelle was our first, and we decided together that we wouldn't give her any elixir. The High Queen wasn't going to get her hands on any of our children. Whatever the consequences were, we would deal with them.

"We don't know what they'll become at all. I'm hoping I've mastered my pheromones." I spent months alone meditating. If my mother could force out her powers to take away my ability to be a queen, then I was certain I could find a way to keep myself from making other women barren. I just wasn't sure if I had mastered that part of myself yet, but I was trying for my girls. "Hopefully, I won't have to be the only woman to produce children. We can't expose our children to the elixir."

"No, we can't."

I hugged Austin and kissed his neck as an incentive. I really wanted to make more children. "Your mother is going to be glad to see you, Brian, and Annabelle."

"They still miss having boys around." I could see in Austin's eyes, when he played with our children, that his mind went farther back to when he and his cousin were young. "They don't get why I left after Noah died. I guess they think I freaked and flaked out."

I smiled sadly. "To be truthful, I don't get why you left either."

He jerked his head back and held my face. "Noah knew you were messed up, but he loved you. He understood that you needed someone to trust. I knew how much he wanted to be that person for you, but I know he'd want me to take things up in his stead."

I felt the nag in my heart go on again. I thought that after keeping the secret for years, it would get easier, but Noah never completely faded away from me. "So, you loved me because Noah loved me?"

"I love you because I love you, but that doesn't mean I can't honor my cousin by honoring you."

I stopped. I stopped walking, I stopped him, and more importantly, I stopped the deception. I was sick of pretending that Noah died alone. I believed that was more painful to Austin than the actual truth. I was just too afraid to face it and try to relieve him of his burden. Now, the time had finally come. "I have a confession to make—"

"I know that you were with Noah when he died."

I lost my breath. It was my worst nightmare, and yet he wasn't screaming or plotting to leave me. "How?"

He placed his hand on his chest and closed his eyes. He was quiet and still as he sought out a light inside of him. "Because when you gave all that energy to save my life when I was dying, I felt Noah's pass on through to me. I feel him with me every day."

He opened his eyes and gave me a little smile. There was a lot of sadness, but it wasn't true grief like when he came to my beach house, all those years ago. He was even a little bit content. "I'd like to think that he's at peace somewhere, but a piece of him is with me. My brother is making sure I can make it without him. I wasn't sure how I would before, but I know he's watching over us both."

"I'm sorry!" I collapsed into my hands and prepared to lightly sob. "I wanted to tell you, but I never knew how. It was an accident. He was still sick and—"

"You don't have to say anything." He was clearly hurt, but he shrugged his shoulders like it wasn't a big deal. "I've known for years, Rose. I stuck things out with you, so I could see if you genuinely wanted to rule your people with love, or if you were too far gone."

"And what have you concluded?" I needed to know what he honestly thought. People were beginning to trust me, but some of them would never be able to forget their fear. I would always be capable of being the witch if pushed too far. It was in my nature.

"I see that you're a good mother and a kind queen." He chuckled and looked at his waterproof watch. It wouldn't be too long before the yacht was ready to take us to America. He liked visiting home when he could, but we couldn't go too often.

"And you're okay with how life turned out?"

He sort of smirked as he picked up a stone. With a slight flick of his wrist, the stone skidded down the surface of the water for miles. He didn't display his strength in the outside world, but he did show up his old friends when they played sports. "Six years and thirteen children later, and I'm still amazed by how happy I am with you."

Considering how horrible things could have turned out, I was lucky. No, I was more than lucky. I was blessed. "I'm amazed by how happy I am as well."

Austin's eyes followed the stone as far as he could, but it became lost to his sight as he caught a glimpse of something else approaching. "Does anyone else know about this island?"

"Why?" I followed his line of sight. Far, far away, I saw a yacht that seemed to be on a course for our island. "I don't think so. Only those who have been here before know how to get here and other queens…"

It was unprecedented for other queens to intrude on each other. I dug up some of the archives from the elders. I read awful stories about queens attacking one another. There was a reason why one queen ruled a single colony. When two were in the same location, one of them was bound to be killed. "Do you think it's a queen's ship? Do you think the High Queen is coming to wage war against us? What should we do?"

He grabbed my hand and kissed it like a gentleman. "Whoever they are, we'll take care of it."

Austin did it again. He made me feel like there was only our family. I had no worries—at least none that mattered—to stop me from having a wonderful life. If it were a friendly crew, we would greet them and let them move on. If we needed to fight, I swear we would do whatever was necessary to protect our children. We'd leave a mountain of corpses in our wake if need be.

But until they arrived on our shore, we looked out into the distance and watched the yacht draw close, together.

Continue the journey.